"You're right. The teacher is always right."

With that, Willis turned and headed out the door.

"Willis, wait. I'm sorry," Eva called after him.

"You're forgiven. If the boy has trouble in school, let me know and I'll speak to him about it."

"Fair enough." She arched one eyebrow. "I don't have many friends in this new place. I'd hate to lose the first one I made here."

"You haven't lost me. I live just across the road." He nodded in that direction.

A sliver of a smile curved her lips. "I should be able to find my way over if I try hard enough."

"I suspect you can be a very determined woman."

"I have occasionally heard my name associated with that adjective."

"Occasionally?"

"*Frequently* might be closer to the truth." Her grin widened.

After thirty-five years as a nurse, **Patricia Davids** hung up her stethoscope to become a full-time writer. She enjoys spending her free time visiting her grandchildren, doing some long-overdue yard work and traveling to research her story locations. She resides in Wichita, Kansas. Pat always enjoys hearing from her readers. You can visit her online at patriciadavids.com.

Leigh Bale is a *Publishers Weekly* bestselling author. She is a winner of the prestigious Golden Heart® Award and was a finalist for the Gayle Wilson Award of Excellence and the Booksellers' Best Award. The daughter of a retired US forest ranger, she holds a BA in history. Married in 1981 to the love of her life, Leigh and her professor husband have two children and two grandkids. You can reach her at leighbale.com.

USA TODAY Bestselling Author

PATRICIA DAVIDS

The Amish Teacher's Dilemma

&

LEIGH BALE

Healing Their Amish Hearts

LOVE INSPIRED
INSPIRATIONAL ROMANCE

LOVE INSPIRED®
INSPIRATIONAL ROMANCE

Recycling programs
for this product may
not exist in your area.

ISBN-13: 978-1-335-40246-2

The Amish Teacher's Dilemma and Healing Their Amish Hearts

Copyright © 2021 by Harlequin Books S.A.

The Amish Teacher's Dilemma
First published in 2020. This edition published in 2021.
Copyright © 2020 by Patricia MacDonald

Healing Their Amish Hearts
First published in 2020. This edition published in 2021.
Copyright © 2020 by Lora Lee Bale

All rights reserved. No part of this book may be used or reproduced in any manner whatsoever without written permission except in the case of brief quotations embodied in critical articles and reviews.

This is a work of fiction. Names, characters, places and incidents are either the product of the author's imagination or are used fictitiously. Any resemblance to actual persons, living or dead, businesses, companies, events or locales is entirely coincidental.

This edition published by arrangement with Harlequin Books S.A.

For questions and comments about the quality of this book,
please contact us at CustomerService@Harlequin.com.

Harlequin Enterprises ULC
22 Adelaide St. West, 40th Floor
Toronto, Ontario M5H 4E3, Canada
www.Harlequin.com

Printed in U.S.A.

CONTENTS

THE AMISH TEACHER'S DILEMMA 7
Patricia Davids

HEALING THEIR AMISH HEARTS 227
Leigh Bale

THE AMISH TEACHER'S DILEMMA

Patricia Davids

This book is dedicated to my wonderful critique partners and friends, Theresa, Deb and Melissa. Your help is deeply appreciated, but your friendship is beyond price.

Let the word of Christ dwell in you richly in all wisdom; teaching and admonishing one another in psalms and hymns and spiritual songs, singing with grace in your hearts to the Lord.

—*Colossians* 3:16

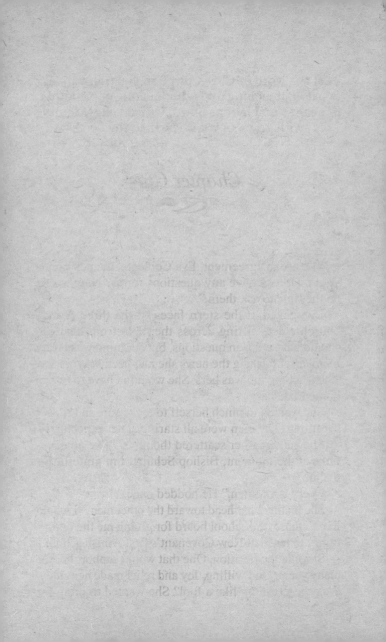

Chapter One

"We are in agreement. Eva Coblentz, the position is yours. Do you have any questions for us? Now would be the time to ask them."

Eva gazed at the stern faces of the three Amish church elders sitting across the table from her. She should have a dozen questions, but her mind was oddly blank after hearing the news she had been praying for. The teaching job was hers. She wouldn't have to return home in defeat.

She wanted to pinch herself to make sure she wasn't dreaming. The men were all staring at her expectantly.

She gathered her scattered thoughts. "I've no questions at the moment, Bishop Schultz. I'm grateful for the job."

"Very *goot*, then." He nodded once.

She inclined her head toward the other men. "I would like to thank the school board for giving me the opportunity to teach at New Covenant's first Amish school."

She had the position. One that would support her for many years, God willing. Joy and relief made her giddy. Was she grinning like a fool? She wanted to jump for joy. She lowered her eyes and schooled her features to look modest and professional.

But a tiny grin crept out. She had the job! She could do this.

She glanced up. The bishop gave her a little smile then cleared his throat. "The house and furnishing will be yours to use as you wish."

"Danki." A job and a home. A huge weight lifted from her chest. Her brother Gene was going to be shocked. He had discouraged her wild plan to travel to Maine alone as a foolish whim. Only her younger brother Danny understood her need to go. Gene said she would be back begging for a place to live in a matter of weeks, but she wouldn't.

The bishop gathered his papers together. "I think we can adjourn, brothers."

The meeting was being held in her future classroom. The building itself was so new it still smelled of cut pine boards, varnish and drying paint. Dust motes drifted lazily in the beams of light streaming through the south-facing windows that lined the room. The wide plank floor didn't show a single scuff mark, and the blackboard's pristine condition begged her to scrawl her name across it with chalk. It was a wonderful place to begin her teaching career.

"You do understand that this is a trial assignment," the man seated to the left of the bishop said. She struggled to recall his name. Was he Samuel Yoder or Leroy Lapp? The two had been introduced to her as ministers who shared the duties of overseeing the Amish congregation along with the bishop, but she had been so nervous their names didn't stick with their faces. They were men in their fifties or sixties with long gray beards, salt-and-pepper hair and weathered faces.

"I do understand that my contract will be on a month-by-month basis until I complete a full school year." She had the job, but could she keep it? She had never taught before. She wasn't sure what would be expected of her. Her school days were far behind her. What if she wasn't any good at teaching? What if the children didn't like her?

The man beside the bishop sat back and crossed his arms over his chest. "I have taken the liberty of writing out a curriculum." He pushed a thick folder across the table to her. "We expect modest behavior at all times. You must be an example to our *kinder*."

"Of course." So no jumping for joy. She had the feeling her actions would be watched closely by this man.

"Not everyone is suited to life in northern Maine. Our winters are harsh," the same man said, giving her a stern look.

She decided he was Samuel Yoder, the newly elected school board president. Well, it got mighty cold in Arthur, Illinois, too, and that had never kept her from her duties.

She lifted her chin slightly, not wanting to appear overly bold or prideful as she had been accused of being in the past. "I plan to remain in New Covenant for many years. I'm not one who gives in to adversity easily. I rely on *Gott* for strength and He has not forsaken me."

"That is as it should be. Isn't that so, Brother Samuel?" Bishop Schultz tried again not to grin, but a corner of his mouth tipped up. She liked him a lot.

Samuel Yoder's frown deepened. The man to his right grinned widely. He had to be Leroy Lapp. "You may count on my wife and me for any assistance getting settled in here."

"*Danki*." Eva started to relax for the first time during her interview. A loud banging started outside the windows. It sounded like someone hammering on metal.

"*Das haus* is acceptable?" Leroy raised his voice to be heard over the racket.

"*Ja*, it's a fine house." It was the perfect size for her. A small kitchen, a sitting room with wide windows, a bathroom with modern plumbing and two bedrooms. In the backyard was space for a garden and a large blackberry bush loaded with fruit. She would have a home all to herself. Would it feel lonely? She could always get a cat.

Samuel Yoder leaned toward her. "Our children have attended the local public school up until now. Some will find the change to a one-room schoolhouse difficult. I hope you can handle the situation."

Was he trying to scare her away? She looked down. "I will pray for guidance."

"We'll leave you to inspect your new school." The bishop rose and the other men did likewise.

Eva realized she had forgotten one important thing. "Bishop Schultz, could some bookshelves be added to this classroom?"

"I don't see why not. How big and where do you want them?"

She looked around the room and settled on the perfect place behind her desk. She crossed the room. "Here. About six feet long and three shelves high. I want the smallest child to be able to reach them all."

"It will take a lot of books to fill that much space."

Samuel's dour expression showed his disapproval. "We don't have the budget to buy so many."

She grinned at him. "Oh, you don't have to buy them. I already have them. My brother will ship them here for me." A job, a house and with the arrival of her beloved books she would have everything she needed to make her happy.

The men exchanged glances, shrugged and filed out after lifting their black hats from a row of pegs near the door. The clanging outside continued.

Her new school.

Eva savored the words. She had spent the last of her savings to get here, and here she would stay no matter what her brother or Samuel Yoder thought. She got to her feet and turned in a slow circle with her arms held wide. This was her new life. Her new career. Her way to serve the Lord in the newly formed Amish settlement of New Covenant, Maine.

At thirty years of age she would no longer be dependent on her older brother to provide for her. She could make her own decisions now. From the time she was fifteen she had been living off the charity of her brother Gene. Charity he gave grudgingly. She'd kept house and cared for their elderly grandparents who lived in the *daadihaus*, or grandfather's house, next to the main home, tasks Gene's wife, Corrine, claimed she couldn't do because of her poor health. She had all she could manage taking care of her three boys.

It wasn't that Eva had been treated badly. She hadn't been. Mostly she had been ignored. Like the extra cots Gene and Corrine kept for guests. Never thought about until they were needed. She hadn't minded. It gave her more time to read. Books took her everywhere and anywhere. Each evening she would read to her grandparents who had both suffered from failing eyesight. Mostly she read the Bible and the newspaper to them but after her grandfather took himself off to bed Eva would get out one of the novels her grandmother enjoyed as much as she did. Eva treasured the memory of those evenings.

Rather than risk losing Eva to marriage, her brother Gene had steered away every would-be suitor except one persistent fellow. Eva had quickly learned she couldn't talk to a man who didn't love books as she did. She wasn't disappointed when he stopped seeing her.

"Marriage isn't for everyone," her grandmother had told her. "*Gott* must have other plans for you. He will show you in due time."

When her grandparents had gone to their rest within a month of each other, Eva had been at a loss to fill the void in her life until she saw a newspaper ad for an Amish schoolteacher in Maine. Somehow, she knew it was meant for her. God was showing her a new path. She'd never taught school, but Amish schoolteachers received no formal training. She would learn right along with her students. It had taken all the courage she could muster to answer that ad and to tell her family she was leaving.

Clang, clang, clang.

The hammering outside grew louder. She scowled at the open door. Hopefully, she wouldn't have to compete with this much noise when she was trying to teach. She moved to the window to locate the source of the clatter. Across the road she saw a man pounding on an ancient-looking piece of machinery with steel wheels and a scoop-like nose on the front end.

The man was Amish by his dress, not one of the *Eng-*

lisch neighbors that vastly outnumbered the Amish in their new community. He wore a straw hat and a collarless blue shirt with the sleeves rolled up, revealing muscular, tan forearms. He wielded the heavy hammer like it weighed next to nothing. His broad shoulder strained the fabric of his shirt.

She saw the school board members get into their buggies and drive off. They waved but didn't stop to speak to the young man.

When he had the sheet of metal shaped to fit the front of the machine, he stood back to assess his work. Eva couldn't see any imperfections, but he clearly did. He knelt and hammered on the shovel-like nose three more times. Satisfied, he gathered up his tools and started in her direction.

She stepped back from the window. Was he coming to the school? Why? Had he noticed her gawking? Perhaps he only wanted to welcome the new teacher although his lack of a beard said he wasn't married.

Maybe that was it. Amish teachers were single women. Perhaps he wanted to meet the new unmarried woman in the community. The sooner everyone understood she wasn't husband-shopping, the happier she would be.

She glanced around the room. Should she meet him by the door? That seemed too eager. Her eyes settled on the large desk at the front of the classroom. She should look as if she was ready for the school year to start. A professional attitude would put off any suggestion that she was interested in meeting single men.

Eva hurried to the desk, pulled out the chair and sat down as the outside door opened. The chair tipped over backward, sending her flailing. Her head hit the wall with a painful thud as she slid to the floor. Stunned, she slowly opened her eyes to see the man leaning over the desk. "I'm fine. I'm okay," she said, wondering if she spoke the truth.

He had the most beautiful gray eyes she'd ever beheld. They were rimmed with thick, dark lashes in stark contrast to the mop of curly, dark red hair springing out from beneath his straw hat. Tiny sparks of light whirled around him. "You need a haircut."

Had she said that out loud? She squeezed her eyes shut. She couldn't see him, but the stars were still floating behind her closed eyelids.

"I've been meaning to fix that chair. Just haven't gotten around to it yet. A haircut is at the bottom of my list of stuff to get done." His voice was smooth, husky, low and attractive. She kept her eyes shut, hoping he would speak again.

"Are you all right? You can't be comfortable like that."

At the hint of amusement in his voice Eva's eyes popped open. She was lying on her back with her feet still hanging over the front of the chair. "I'm not comfortable. Would you kindly help me up?" Unless she ignobly rolled one way or the other out of the chair, she wasn't going anywhere. The wooden arms had her boxed in.

He grabbed the back of the chair, dragged her out from behind the desk and sat her upright with one arm as if she weighed nothing at all. She looked at the long scratches the process left on the floor. It wasn't pristine anymore.

"I'm Willis Gingrich. Local blacksmith." He squatted beside her and grasped her wrist with one hand while easily holding her chair upright. "Can you tell me your name?" It took her a few seconds to realize he was checking her pulse.

The warmth and strength of his hand on her skin sent a sizzle of awareness along her nerve endings. "I'm Eva Coblentz. I am the new teacher and I'm fine now." She pulled away from him.

Willis let go of her arm. Her pulse was strong if a bit fast. She didn't seem to have suffered any serious damage.

The new teacher was a slender woman wearing a gray dress with a white apron over it. She had eyes the color of green willow leaves in the early spring. They regarded him steadily as if she saw more than his grubby face or his soot-and sweat-stained clothes. Her direct gaze was oddly discomfiting. "I suggest we find you a more stable place to sit, Eva Coblentz. Can you walk?"

"Since I was eight months old. Of course I can walk."

The color was coming back into her face. Her snippy remark proved her wits weren't addled even if there was a slight tremor in her voice. She stood, took a deep breath and headed to a nearby bench along the wall, rubbing the side of her head as she walked. "Is this one safe or are there other surprises in store for me?"

She had some spunk. He liked that. "Want me to try it first?" He sat, bounced up and down a couple of times and stood. "Feels okay to me."

She sank onto the bench with a sigh and pressed one hand to the side of her head. "I have collected quite a goose egg."

He frowned. "Seriously? I thought your hair would

have cushioned the blow." Amish women her age had hip-length hair folded up inside their *kapps*.

"I must have turned my head to the side. It's behind my ear."

He had been too quick to laugh off her fall as a minor incident. He needed to assess her injury. He held out his hand. "May I?"

She nodded and began pulling out the hairpins that held her heavily starched white *kapp* in place. Her neatly pinned honey-brown hair remained in a large, tight bun.

He gently felt the area she indicated. She did have a good-size goose egg behind her ear. "Is your vision blurry? Do you feel dizzy?"

"*Nee*. I feel foolish. Does that mean anything?"

He grinned at her. "Only that you're human. Sit still. I'll get some ice to put on that knot. I just live across the road."

"I don't think that will be necessary."

He had spent weeks learning first-aid skills before moving his brothers and sister from Maryland to the far north of Maine where medical help might be long in coming. This was the first chance he'd had to use the knowledge he'd learned from a retired fireman turned potato farmer who lived in the next town.

"Ordinarily, I take a woman at her word, but this time I have to disagree. Sit still. I'll be back in a few minutes and you will stay right here. Understood?"

"I will stay," she repeated, closed her eyes and leaned her head back against the wall. Her color was a little pale. Was she really okay?

Something about her prompt agreement troubled him. He was torn between the need to get the ice and a reluctance to leave her alone.

She opened one eye to peek at him. "I thought you were going to get ice?"

"I'm waiting to see if you plan to obey my orders or if you'll take off as soon as I'm out of sight."

Both her eyes opened wide and then narrowed in speculation. "You must have sisters."

"Just one. She doesn't like to do as she is told, either."

"Very well. I promise to stay here until you return."

"That is exactly what I wanted to hear."

Willis hurried out the door and down the school steps. His house was only about fifty yards across the way. He barged into his own kitchen, startling his little six-year-old sister Maddie, who was coloring at the kitchen table.

"Willis, you scared us."

Maddie was the only one in the kitchen. He figured the *us* referred to her imaginary friend. "I'm sorry. I didn't mean to frighten you."

"Bubble says that's okay. She wasn't really scared. Do you like her picture?" Maddie held up a sheet of white paper.

"It's a blank page, Maddie."

His half sister and her two brothers had only been with Willis for a few weeks. He still wasn't used to sharing a home with them, let alone with Maddie's imaginary friend who required a place at the table and was always being stepped on or sat on by someone. Had he made a mistake by moving the children so far from everything they had known? He thought living with a family member would be best after losing their parents, but what if he was wrong?

It wouldn't be the first time. Normally, his mistakes didn't affect anyone but himself. Now there were others who might be hurt by his failures. The lingering fear that he couldn't properly care for his siblings often kept him awake at night. He tried to put his trust in the Lord, but he wasn't good at giving up control.

He grabbed a plastic bag from the box in a drawer beside the propane-powered refrigerator and then pulled the ice tray out of the freezer. He began emptying the cubes into the bag.

"Willis, you hurt Bubble's feelings. Tell her you like her picture."

A knock at the door stopped him before he got into another discussion with his sister about the existence of Bubble. He opened the door and saw Craig Johnson, the farmer he had promised the potato digger would be ready for today. The man's red pickup truck and a black metal trailer were sitting on the road.

"*Goot* morning, Mr. Johnson. I'm sorry but I'm not quite done with it."

"I need it now. My farm auction starts at two o'clock and I won't get any money for a broken digger that's still at your shop. You're new here and I took a chance on you instead of using a machine shop in Presque Isle. I won't pay for something that's not fixed."

"I understand." Willis couldn't afford to lose business if an unsatisfied customer started telling his friends how unreliable the new Amish blacksmith was. He could only put out one fire at a time. He turned to his sister. "Maddie, where are Otto and Harley?"

"I don't know." She held her hand to the side of her mouth and whispered into the empty air. She turned back to him and shrugged. "Bubble says she doesn't know."

Neither of his brothers were turning out to be much

help. He held out the bag of ice. "Take this and a kitchen towel up to the school and give it to the new teacher."

Maddie's face brightened. "My teacher is here?"

"*Ja*, and she got a bump on her head so hurry. I'll be there soon."

Maddie got down from the chair, pulled out the one next to hers and helped her invisible friend out of it. "Let's go meet our teacher."

She took the towel and ice bag and rushed out the door. Willis led Mr. Johnson to the potato digger he had been working on. "Once I get the bolts in and check that it is level, I will help you load it."

"Okay, but make it snappy. I don't have all day."

Willis watched his sister long enough to make sure Maddie crossed the road safely and went into the school. He would have to see about the new teacher once he was done here. He hoped Maddie wouldn't tell Eva Coblentz about her imaginary friend or what a poor job her brother was doing at raising her. He prayed his little sister would be too shy to say a single word, but he knew he was going to regret sending her alone.

Chapter Two

Eva opened her eyes when she heard someone enter the schoolhouse. It wasn't the man she had been expecting. It was a little Amish girl about six or seven years old wearing a purple dress with a black apron and a black *kapp* on her bright blond hair. The child stopped inside the door and stared at her.

Eva smiled. "Hello."

"Are you the new teacher?"

"I am. Who are you?"

"I'm Maddie. This is my friend Bubble." The child gestured to one side.

Eva didn't see anyone. "Bubble is very thin."

Maddie looked up and down. "That's because my brother Willis is a terrible cook. Mostly he makes dry scrambled eggs and oatmeal. Bubble hates oatmeal."

"I'm sorry to hear that," Eva said, smothering a laugh. What a charming child she was.

Maddie walked forward with a bag of ice cubes and a white kitchen towel. "Willis said to bring this to you."

Eva took the plastic bag, wrapped the kitchen towel

around it and applied it to the side of her head. "*Danki*. What happened to your brother?"

"Grumpy old Mr. Johnson came and said he wouldn't pay Willis because his potato digger wasn't fixed so my brother had to finish the job. He's always working. He's sorry he couldn't come back and take care of you."

"It's only a minor bump. He shouldn't worry about me."

"Can I ask you about school?"

Eva nodded and winced at the pain in the side of her head. It dawned on her that her students weren't some vague group of well-behaved children. They were going to be real kids like Maddie with questions Eva might not have the answers for; then what? Here was her first test. "Ask me anything you want."

"Can my friend Bubble sit beside me?"

Eva pondered the question. What would the school board say if she asked for a desk for an imaginary child? She smiled at the thought. "What grade will you be in?"

"The first grade. We've never been to school before, but my brothers Otto and Harley went to school back home before *Mamm* and *Daed* went to heaven."

A wave of pity for the little girl swept through Eva. "I'm sorry. That must have been a very sad time for you and your brothers."

Maddie sat beside Eva on the bench and stared at the floor. "It was. Bubble cried a lot, but she was happier when Willis said we could come and live with him."

"I'm glad she is happier. And did you cry a lot?"

"Not too much. Our old bishop said it was *Gott*'s plan for them and not to be sad."

"It's okay to be sad. *Gott* understands that we miss the ones we love."

"He does?"

Eva nodded. "The Lord knows everything in our heart and he understand our grief."

Maddie put her arm around her imaginary friend. "Did you hear that, Bubble? It's okay if we cry. Not right now. Maybe later."

Eva slipped her arm around Maddie. "If we have enough desks for all the students Bubble can sit beside you. Otherwise, she can stay here on this bench during school hours. Does that sound acceptable?"

"She says it is."

What an adorable child. "How long have you lived with Willis?"

"I don't know. A lot of days."

Days, not months or years so her grief was recent. "Were you here in the winter when it snowed?"

"Nope. The snow was mostly gone when we came. Willis says we will see a lot of snow before Christmas. Maybe even before Thanksgiving. It can snow up to the roof sometimes. I like the snow, don't you? I like to catch snowflakes on my tongue."

"I do like the snow." Eva wasn't so sure about snow that was roof high. She would have to invest in a good snow shovel.

"Otto says he hates school. I won't hate school. I think it will be wonderful."

"Maybe Otto won't hate it if I'm his teacher." Or maybe he would. How would she know if she was doing an adequate job or not?

"Will you tell Otto he's stupid if he gets something wrong?"

"Oh, *nee*. That wouldn't be nice."

"Otto's last teacher told him he was stupid. *Daed* and *Mamm* were mighty upset."

Eva filed that piece of information away. It sounded as if Otto's former teacher wasn't patient or kind, but it was possible Maddie had misunderstood. "What does Harley think of school?"

"He says it's okay as long as he gets to play baseball."

"I'm sure we will play lots of ball." That was something she hadn't done since she was fourteen. Even then she wasn't good at it. She'd spent most of her recesses reading.

"My brothers don't help Willis much. He works and works all the time. He never has time to put shoes on my pony so I can go riding. Otto is always mad that he had to leave his friends in Ohio, and Harley disappears into the woods for hours without telling me where he is going. Bubble gets mighty put out with them sometimes." Maddie gave a long-suffering sigh.

"I can see why." Eva was tempted to laugh but managed to keep a straight face.

"You do?" Maddie smiled brightly.

"Absolutely. Bubble is very perceptive for someone so young."

"I don't know what that means. Bubble says Willis needs a wife to help him."

Eva laughed. "Bubble may be right. Especially if Willis is a bad cook."

The outside door opened and Willis came in. Maddie jumped off the bench. "I have to go." She darted past her brother and ran outside.

He shook his head and crossed the room to where Eva was sitting. "How's the bump?"

"Much better. *Danki* for the ice." She handed the bag and towel to him. "Your little sister is delightful."

His expression grew wary. "She is an unusual kid."

Eva chuckled as she got to her feet. "She is that. I met Bubble and I enjoyed talking to her. She's a fountain of information."

His eyes narrowed. "About what?"

"Oh, everything. I really must be going. I have a lot to do before school starts next month. Goodbye." She pinned her *kapp* to her hair as she headed for the door.

"I'll get that chair fixed for you," he called after her.

Eva went down the steps and chuckled all the way to her new house a few hundred feet south of the school. Poor Willis Gingrich had his hands full with his siblings if Maddie was to be believed. She glanced over her shoulder and saw Willis standing on the steps of the school, watching her. An odd little rush of happiness made her smile. She raised a hand and waved but he was already striding toward his workshop and didn't wave back.

She went into her new house that had been sparsely furnished by the school board and church members. Eva had arrived in New Covenant by bus two days ago. Bishop Schultz and his wife had graciously allowed Eva to stay in the teacher's home until after her interview. Now she wouldn't have to repack her things. She was home.

At a small cherrywood desk she pulled out a sheet of paper and sat down to write to her brother. She tapped the pen against her teeth as she decided what to say.

Giggling, she dictated to herself as she wrote. "Dearest Gene. I got the job. Send my books. Your loving sister, Eva."

* * *

Willis thought he had enough time to fix the new teacher's chair, put four shoes on Jesse Crump's buggy horse and get supper on the table by six o'clock. It was seven-thirty by the time he came in to find his family gathered around the kitchen table with a scowl on every face. Thankfully, he couldn't see Bubble but he was sure she was scowling, too.

"I know I'm late. One of Jesse's horses had a problem hoof and I had to make special shoes for him. I'll fix us something to eat right away."

He went to the refrigerator and opened the door. There wasn't much to see. "I meant to set some hamburger out of the freezer to thaw this morning but forgot to do it."

"You should leave yourself a note," Harley said. He was paging through a magazine about horses. He was always reading. Willis fought down the stab of envy.

If Willis could write a note, then he'd be able to read one. He couldn't do either. The most he could manage was to write his name. No one in New Covenant knew his shameful secret. Children as young as Maddie learned to read every day but he couldn't. No matter how hard he'd tried. There was something wrong with him.

He hid his deficiency from everyone although it wasn't easy. He'd been made a laughingstock by the one person he'd confided in years ago. He'd never been able to trust another person with his secret. The bitter memory wormed its way to the front of his mind.

He'd been twenty at the time and hopelessly in love with a non-Amish girl. She was the only person he had told that he couldn't read. He hadn't wanted to keep secrets from her. She claimed to love him, too. He had trusted her.

Later, when they were out with a bunch of her friends, she told everyone. They all laughed. He laughed, too, and pretended it didn't matter but the hurt and shame had gone bone deep. He didn't think anything could hurt worse than Dalene's betrayal, but he'd been wrong. She and her friends had much more humiliation in store for him.

He pushed those memories back into the dark corner of his mind where they belonged. He had to find something to feed the children gathered at his table. "I guess I can scramble us some eggs."

"Again?" Otto wrinkled his nose.

"Bubble says to be thankful we have chickens." Maddie beamed a bright smile at Otto.

"Bubble can't say anything because she isn't real, stupid." Otto pushed his plate away.

Willis rounded on him. "Never call your sister or anyone else *stupid*, Otto. You know better than that. Apologize or go to bed without supper."

"Sorry," Otto murmured. He didn't sound apologetic.

A knock at the door stopped Willis from continuing the conversation. Who needed a blacksmith at this hour? He pulled open the door and took a step back. Eva Coblentz stood on his porch with a large basket over her arm.

She flashed a nervous grin. "I'm used to cooking for more than just myself and I made too much tonight. I thought perhaps you could make use of it for lunch tomorrow. It's only chicken and dumplings."

Willis was speechless. Maddie came to stand beside him. "Teacher, how nice to see you."

Eva smiled at Maddie. "It's nice to see you again, too. How is Bubble?"

Maddie stuck her tongue out at Otto. "She's fine but kinda hungry. We haven't had our supper yet. Willis had to give Jesse Crump special shoes so he was going to make scrambled eggs again, but Otto isn't thankful for our chickens."

Eva blinked her lovely green eyes. "I see."

"Do you?" Willis couldn't help smiling at her perplexed expression. "Then you're ahead of me most of the time."

Harley came to the door. "Let me help you with that." He took the basket from her and carried it to the table. He began setting out the contents.

Otto pulled his plate back in front of him. "That smells great."

Harley dished up his own and then passed the plastic bowls along. Willis thought his siblings were acting like starving animals. He could hardly blame them. He was going to have to learn to cook for more than himself. Normally, he didn't care what he ate or when he ate it. That had changed when the children arrived, and change was something he didn't handle well.

Eva folded her arms across her middle. "I will be going so you can enjoy your meal in peace. Have a wonderful night, everyone."

He didn't want her to go. He stepped out onto the porch and closed the door from the prying eyes of his family. "How's your head?"

She touched it gingerly. "Better."

"I fixed the chair. You won't have to worry about tipping over again."

"I appreciate that." She turned to go.

"The school board hired me to supply and install the hardware in the new building. I'll get the rest of the coat hooks, cabinets and drawer pulls installed tomorrow. Have you had your supper? You are welcome to join us."

"I have eaten. *Danki.* Don't forget to feed Bubble. She's much too thin."

Willis raked a hand through his hair. "I don't know why Maddie makes things up."

She gave him a soft, kind smile. "Don't worry about it. A lot of children have imaginary friends."

"Really?" He wanted to believe her. When she smiled he forgot his worries and his ignorance.

"Absolutely. She will outgrow her invisible friend someday soon. Until then, enjoy her imagination."

"I reckon you have seen a lot of things like this in your teaching career." It made him feel better to know Maddie wasn't the only child who had a pretend companion.

"This will be my first year as a teacher. I was actually surprised that the position didn't go to someone with more experience. Perhaps my enthusiasm won the school board over."

"I think you were the only applicant."

She laughed and clasped a hand over her heart. "You have returned my ego to its normal size. How can I ever thank you?"

He smiled along with her. "We are blessed to have you."

She leaned toward him slightly. "We will have to wait until we have Bubble's assessment of my teaching skills before jumping to any conclusions. *Guten nacht*, Willis Gingrich."

"Good night, Teacher."

She walked away into the darkness. He watched until he saw her enter her house across the way. There was something attractive about Eva Coblentz that had nothing to do with her face or her figure. She was the first woman in a long time who made him want to smile.

He went back inside the house. The children were still eating. He took his place at the head of the table, bowed his head for a silent prayer, then reached for a bread roll. It was still warm. He looked at Maddie. "What did you say to your teacher that made her bring food here tonight?"

Maddie shrugged her shoulders. "I don't know."

"You must have said something." He took a bite of his roll.

Maddie had a whispered conversation with the empty chair next to her. She looked up and grinned at him. "Bubble says that she told teacher you need a wife who is a good cook."

He started coughing. Otto pounded on his back while Harley rushed to give him a glass of water. When he could catch his breath, Willis stared at Maddie in shock. "Eva thinks I'm looking for a wife?"

Maddie nodded.

Willis hung his head. Nothing could be further from the truth. There was no way he could keep his secret from a wife. Even if he found the courage to reveal his handicap to a woman again, there was still one pressing reason he had to remain single.

Amish ministers and bishops were chosen by lot from the married men of the congregation. At baptism every Amish fellow vowed to accept the responsibility of becoming a minister of the faith if he should be chosen. What kind of preacher would he make if he couldn't read the Word of God? The humiliation didn't bear thinking about. He would remain a single fellow his entire life. That was God's plan for him.

He turned his attention back to Maddie. "You were wrong to tell your teacher that I'm looking for a wife. I'm not. Now what am I supposed to do?"

Maddie lifted both hands. "Just tell her you don't want a wife. How hard can that be?"

Chapter Three

Early the next morning Willis hurried to get the cabinet pulls installed on Eva's desk and on the cupboards in the school. He glanced constantly toward the door, hoping she wouldn't show up until after he was gone. He had no idea how he was going to face her. He tried to convince himself that it had simply been kindness that brought her over with a delicious supper last night and not because Maddie had said he was looking for a wife.

Maybe he shouldn't even mention it except to thank her for the food. If he kept quiet, was he encouraging her or discouraging her? How could a six-year-old get him into hot water with her teacher in less than twenty-four hours?

He needed to make Eva understand that he wasn't interested in marrying without hurting her feelings or embarrassing her. She wasn't a giddy teenage girl. She seemed to be a mature and sensible woman. He would remember that and not beat around the bush with her. Maybe. Unless his courage failed him. These days it seemed in short supply.

He was fastening the final coat hooks in the cloakroom when he heard the outside door open. Maybe if he waited quietly she would go away without realizing he was in the building. So much for his courage.

He closed his eyes and listened for her footsteps. He heard her cross the room and open the drawers of her desk one by one. After a few minutes he heard her crossing the room again. Was she leaving? He held his breath.

"There you are. *Goot* morning, Willis. I didn't think you were about."

He opened his eyes. She was smiling at him from the doorway of the cloakroom. His heart sank. His courage had deserted him for certain. He couldn't meet her gaze. "I'm almost finished here. I'll get out of your way as soon as I can."

"You're not in my way."

He concentrated on installing the next hook. Only three more to go. "I know you must have work to do. Don't let me keep you from it." How did a man broach the subject of not looking for a wife like a rational adult?

"Is something wrong?"

"Nee." He pulled another screw from the large front pocket of his leather apron but fumbled the thing. It dropped and rolled across the floor to her feet.

She picked it up and held it out in her hand. "Maybe it's just my imagination but you seem upset."

"Nope." He snatched the screw from her palm. *"Danki."*

"Well, then, I'll let you finish so you can get home to your family. Please tell Maddie that I said hello."

He turned to face Eva. "I'm not looking for a wife."

Her eyebrows rose. She tipped her head slightly. "Okay."

"I know Maddie led you to believe that I am, but I'm not." His neck felt as hot as his forge.

"What makes you think Maddie gave me that impression?"

"You know. The supper you brought over." He rubbed his damp palms on the sides of his apron.

Her eyebrows drew together, creating a tiny crease between them. "I'm sorry, I still don't understand."

"Maddie told you I was looking for a wife who was a good cook."

Her eyes widened. "Oh, and you think I brought you supper to prove I had the culinary skills you are looking for? Sort of an audition for the position?" She covered her face with both hands and burst out laughing.

It dawned on Willis that he had made a huge mistake. He waited until she got a hold of herself. "This is the part where you tell me Maddie never mentioned I was looking for a wife who was a good cook, right?"

She broke into peals of laughter again but managed to shake her head. It wasn't the first time in his life that he felt like a fool, but it was the first time he felt like laughing about it. He chuckled. "You are a pretty good cook."

That set her off again and he was soon laughing with her. She wiped tears from her eyes. "I can see how it must have looked but I'm not angling for a husband with chicken and dumplings as bait," she choked out.

"Your rolls were fine, but the dumplings were gummy."

"They were not. I dare you to make better ones." Her mirth subsided. "You poor fellow. Has this been on your mind all night?"

"You have no idea. I barely got any sleep trying to

figure out how to let you down easily. I'm going to have to have a serious talk with Maddie."

"She did tell me that you were a terrible cook and that Bubble believes you need a wife. I honestly made a batch of dumplings that was too large. I thought you and the *kinder* might enjoy them."

"The children all but licked their plates."

"I'm glad. Willis, I don't intend to marry so rest easy. I may be an old maid all my days, but I intend to put the years *Gott* grants me to good use."

He had a hard time believing she considered herself an old maid. He saw a mature, attractive woman who wasn't afraid to speak her mind or laugh at herself. He admired that about her. Any man would.

She folded her hands primly in front of her white apron. "In the future please don't hesitate to tell me if Maddie has shared something you aren't sure about. I shall do the same. That way we won't need to tiptoe around each other. Agreed?" She held out her hand.

He was more relieved than he could express. He took her hand. It fit as if it had been made for him to hold. "Agreed."

"One more thing. If you can quietly spread the word that I'm not interested in marriage I would appreciate it."

"If anyone asks, I'll let you know before I send them on their way. You might change your mind if the right fellow comes along."

Eva's fingers were swallowed inside Willis's large, calloused hand. She didn't mind the roughness of his skin. It was proof that he worked hard. She drew away reluctantly. "I appreciate the sentiment, but there is no need to check with me. I am excited to begin my career as a teacher and as you know, Amish teachers cannot be married women."

His nearness was doing funny things to her insides. He smelled of smoke and leather and something more that was uniquely him. She inhaled deeply and took a step back. "I do have work I need to get done. I've been going over the curriculum Samuel Yoder gave me. I have to say, seeing my duties laid out in black-and-white is daunting."

"Any new job is."

"You're right. I remember how much I enjoyed school. I want all my students to have the same feeling of happiness at gaining knowledge that I had. Maddie said Otto hates school. I hope that isn't the case."

Willis looked down. "Not everyone enjoys school."

His dry comment told her he was one of those. "You didn't? Why not?"

He still didn't look at her. "It doesn't matter. It was years ago. I've got work to do and so do you."

"You're right. I won't keep you from it any longer." Eva left the coatroom wondering why a man as bright as Willis hadn't enjoyed his school years. Maybe one day he would tell her but for now she had her own students to worry about. Willis left a short time later. The building felt oddly empty without him.

She sat at her desk and pored over her notes and lesson plans for each grade. The school board was thorough. She opened the enrollment forms and began to memorize the names of the students in each grade. If she knew the name, she wouldn't have trouble putting a face to it when school started. Looking through them she noticed she didn't have enrollment forms for Maddie, Otto or Harley. She would remind Willis the next time she saw him. She considered dropping by his home again that evening but decided against it. She had to draw a line between friendly and too friendly. Evening visits to his home were definitely out. Samuel Yoder would frown on that for sure and certain, but there was no reason why she couldn't stop by the smithy while he was working.

A loud grumble from her stomach reminded her it was long past lunch. She slipped her paperwork into the desk drawer, stood, stretched with her hands pressed to the small of her back and then walked to the window. A middle-aged Amish matron and several younger women were all getting out of a buggy in front of Eva's new house. Each of the young women had a baby in her arms. Eva rushed outside to meet them.

The women began unloading boxes from the backseat of the buggy. "Can I give you a hand?" Eva called out as she approached.

"Are you the new teacher?" the older woman asked.

"I am. I'm Eva Coblentz.

"*Wunderbar.* I'm Dinah Lapp. This is my daughter, Gemma Crump, and our neighbor, Bethany Shetler. Give her the *kinder*, girls, and let's get this stuff inside."

Gemma Crump deposited her baby in Eva's arms. "This is Hope."

The tiny girl with red hair gazed solemnly at Eva. "Hello, Hope."

Gemma turned away to pull a large box from the back of the buggy and carry it inside.

Bethany stepped up to Eva. "This is my *sohn*, Eli." She laid the babe in Eva's free arm and began helping the other two women unpack the buggy and carry boxes inside.

Eva smiled at the babies in her arms and chuckled. "Clearly, we are supposed to stay out of the way." She began to sway back and forth to keep her new charges happy. For the first time in years she was struck by the notion that she had missed out on something special when marriage passed her by. Perhaps that was why God had chosen her to be a teacher—so she could have dozens of youngsters to enjoy and look after. It was a humbling thought.

The sounds of running footsteps made her turn around. Maddie came rushing up to her. "What's going on?"

Eva nodded toward the house. "Some women have brought me gifts."

Maddie stared at the babies with wide eyes. "Do you get to keep them?"

Eva laughed at her expression. "*Nee*, I'm holding Hope and Eli while their mothers are busy."

Maddie took a step closer. "Can I hold one? Bubble has always wanted a baby sister."

Dinah came out of the house and motioned to Eva with little sweeps of her hand. "Come on in. You need to tell us where everything goes. Hello, Maddie."

Eva mounted the step and handed Hope to her grandmother. Bethany was waiting inside to take Eli from her. Maddie came inside, too. With both hands free, Eva parked them on her hips and surveyed the room. More than a dozen boxes took up much of the small sitting room. "What is all this?"

"When my husband, Leroy, told me you had accepted

the job of becoming our teacher, we got together a few little things we thought you might need."

"A few little things?" The ad had mentioned a home would be provided. When she first opened the door and saw the kitchen appliances and a table with two chairs, she thought she would have to provide the rest. There was a bed and a rocking chair for the bedroom and a desk in the sitting room but nothing for the second bedroom.

"The men are bringing over the larger furnishings on our wagon tomorrow," Gemma said.

Dinah handed the baby to Gemma and opened the first box. "Kitchen towels and dishcloths."

"This is very kind." Eva was overwhelmed.

"We are thrilled to be able to start our own school," Dinah said. "The public school has been very accommodating to our students but as the bishop says, 'Raise up a child in the way that they should go and they will not vary from it,' and that means educating our *kinder* without undue influence from the outside. Okay, next box. Flatware, knives, canning jars and cooking utensils." Dinah looked at her expectantly.

"In the kitchen." Eva led the way.

Soon they were all unpacking boxes. The two infants were nestled together inside one of the larger boxes so their mothers would have free hands. Maddie knelt on the floor beside them, talking to Bubble and the babies nonstop. In less than an hour's time Eva had sheets and towels stored in her linen closet, a full set of dishes, a teapot and a coffeepot along with a pantry full of preserved fruits and vegetables and three new *kapps* in the style the New Covenant women wore. She would wear her old congregation's style *kapp* until she had been accepted into Bishop Schultz's church, but it was heartening to see they believed she would remain among them.

When everything was put away, Eva used her new kettle to heat water for tea.

The box she was most excited about was the one containing school supplies. "Maddie, come see this."

Eva lifted out pencils and rulers, colored chalk, paints and plenty of wide-ruled notebooks for the children to write in.

"Is this for me?" Maddie asked.

"For you and all the school children," Dinah said.

Maddie picked up a box of crayons. "Bubble is really glad she gets to go to school. It's going to be so much fun." She put the box on the table and patted it. "I'm going to go tell Otto that this school is a lot better than his old one." She charged out the door.

Eva glanced at all the women. "*Danki.* I'm very grateful and so will my students be when class starts."

"We weren't sure what you would need," Bethany said, picking up her baby who was beginning to fuss.

"Sadly, I'm not sure what I need. I've never taught school before. From my own school days I remember the teacher wrote out the date and the arithmetic assignments for each of the classes on the blackboard first thing in the morning. After that she chose a passage to read from the Old or the New Testament. Following the reading, we stood up, clasped our hands together and repeated the Lord's Prayer in unison."

Formal religion was not taught in school. That was the responsibility of the parents and the church community.

Gemma chuckled. "That's what we did, too. After

the prayer we scholars filed to the front of the room and lined up in our assigned places to sing."

Singing was an important part of the school day. It was all a cappella. No musical instruments were used in Amish schools or church services. "It was the same for me," Bethany added.

"I have a copy of *Unpartheyisches Gesang-Buch.*" The German songbook had been used in Amish schools for decades. "Will the bishop find that acceptable?"

"It's the school board that decides which books will be used. Hymns that are in common use will be fine. I used to allow the *kinder* to take turns choosing the hymns. Sometimes they would sing English songs and hymns. They sure enjoyed their time singing." Dinah smiled at the memory.

"You were a teacher?" Eva clasped her hands together. How wonderful to know there was someone she could turn to with her questions.

Dinah nodded. "Only for five years and that was a very long time ago."

"That's better than never. Where do I start?"

"Find out what they know." Dinah took a sip of tea from a white mug. "Parents in this community have made certain that their little ones understand a *goot* amount of English before the first grade because they were going to attend an *Englisch* school. That may not be the case for some of our new arrivals."

Amish children spoke Pennsylvania Dutch at home but school was where they learned English to communicate with non-Amish neighbors, merchants and customers. English and German reading and writing were both taught in school but only English was spoken there.

"You will need a teacher's helper," Bethany said. "My little sister Jenny will be happy to take on the task."

Eva had often been a teacher's helper. It had been her job to hand out readers to the three lowest grades and help any of the younger children with their schoolwork. Having such a position was the only preparation a young Amish woman normally had before becoming a teacher. It was the responsibility of the teacher to show her replacement what she needed to know for several months before letting her take over.

Eva remembered the oldest students working on their math or science assignments during the morning hours while the teacher listened to the small ones read. When the older students were finished with their work, they helped the younger children who needed assistance. In the Amish school she had attended, each scholar knew what was expected of them, and they did it without instructions. For many of the children it would be a big change from learning in a public school. They would all have to become accustomed to new routines. As would their teacher.

"You can expect mothers to sit in on classes to see what their children are learning for the first few weeks," Dinah said. "I'm sure you remember school outings."

She did but she hadn't considered that she would have to plan them. There would be picnics and special trips to be arranged. Eva sighed heavily. She wasn't sure she was up to the task. Becoming a teacher had seemed so easy when she was reading the want ad in her brother's home.

Dinah refilled everyone's cup. "This year will be our first Amish school Christmas program. I know the children and the parents are excited about that."

The Christmas program! How could she have forgotten about planning a Christmas program? There would be songs and poems to be practiced. Somehow, she would have to come up with a play for the children to perform. She grasped Dinah's arm. "How do I find Christmas plays and poems for the *kinder*?"

Dinah patted her hand. "Not to worry. I will give you the address for *The Bulletin Board*. It's a newsletter put out by Amish teachers. You can ask any question and get a dozen sound answers from teachers with years of experience and some who have new ideas."

Gemma frowned slightly. "I wonder where my husband is. Jesse was going to pick me up this afternoon. Hope has a doctor's appointment and Dale Kaufman was going to drive us into Caribou."

"Has she been sick?" Eva asked in concern.

Gemma shook her head. "Nothing like that. She was born prematurely, and she is at risk for developmental delays. Our midwife insists that Hope's pediatrician keep close tabs on her. So far she is hitting all her milestones, *Gott* be praised."

"*Gott* be praised indeed," came a man's deep voice from the sitting room. He stepped into the kitchen and dwarfed the little room. Eva had heard the expression a mountain of a man but she had never met one until now.

Gemma got up from the table with Hope in her arms. "I thought you forgot us."

"Never. I was sidetracked for a few minutes by a little girl who wanted me to push her on the swings because her brothers were all busy and Bubble said I could do it."

Eva grinned. "Maddie is adorable. I wish I could be like her."

Bethany laughed. "Because she gets to say anything

and blame it on her imaginary friend? I can see the appeal in that."

"Are you going to take a meal to the Gingrich clan again tonight?" Jesse asked with a rumble of humor in his deep voice.

Eva shook her head, not the least bit surprised that Maddie had mentioned her gesture. "I may do some baking for them tomorrow. I was going to spread the word at the next prayer meeting that they need some ready-made meals."

The three women exchanged puzzled glances. Dinah drummed her fingers on the table. "We took the family meals for the first week after they arrived, but Willis insisted he didn't need more help."

Eva could see him letting his pride get in the way of accepting help. "According to Maddie and Bubble he is a poor cook. Speaking of Bubble, what am I going to do with Maddie's imaginary friend in the first grade?"

"That you will have to decide for yourself," Dinah said. "I've known of a few Amish children with imaginary friends but never one that brought his or her friend to school."

Outside a car horn honked. Jesse took the baby from his wife's arms. The look in his eyes and his tender smile told Eva how much he loved his little girl. "We should get going. Dale hates to be kept waiting."

Dinah rose to her feet. "I should get going, too. My husband says my work would take half as long if I stopped talking. I hate to tell him it's never going to happen."

Eva follow her guests outside. She waved as Jesse and Gemma were driven away in a yellow pickup by a middle-aged *Englisch* fellow wearing a red ball cap.

Dinah helped Bethany into the buggy on the passenger side and closed the door then turned back to Eva. "As a teacher you will be in a unique position to judge the welfare of your scholars. Our bishop is a kind man. If you feel a child's family may be in need, don't hesitate to mention it to him."

It was another aspect of being a teacher that Eva hadn't considered. She would be responsible for more than teaching the children to read and write and umpiring their softball games at recess. Could she do it all well enough or would Samuel send her packing?

She hadn't been in New Covenant for more than a few days, but she would be sad to leave the friends she had made if she failed to please the school board. She gazed across the road and saw Willis shoeing a small black-and-white horse. It looked like Maddie would finally get to ride her pony. Willis looked up, smiled and gave a brief nod of acknowledgment in her direction before turning his attention to his task once more.

Of all the people she had met in New Covenant she suspected that Willis and his family would be the ones she would miss the most.

Eva went back inside the house. Her footsteps echoed on the hardwood floors as she crossed to her desk and picked up her favorite story. She sat down to read. Halfway through the first chapter she closed the book and laid it aside. The house was too quiet.

She crossed to the window that overlooked the street and opened it. She heard Willis calling his siblings in for supper. Harley and Otto were in a good-natured shoving match on the way to the door. Maddie walked behind, scolding them loudly as they ignored her. Willis admonished them to hurry. When they were all inside he shut the door, cutting off the sounds of his active family.

Eva slowly closed the window. She wouldn't get a cat to keep her company. Cats were much too quiet.

Chapter Four

The following morning was cool with a drizzling rain that dampened Eva's spirits. A restless night had weakened her resolve and left her wondering if she had made the right decision coming to Maine. Would she be able to provide the guidance and education the community expected her to deliver to their children? What if she wasn't suited to the job? What then? As Samuel had pointed out, her employment was only guaranteed for one month at a time.

Would that be enough time to learn all she needed to know?

If she lost the position, she would have to ask her brother Gene for the funds to return. She didn't want to go home with her tail tucked between her legs and admit her new adventure had turned out to be a folly just as her brother had predicted.

She had finished her second cup of coffee when a two-wheeled cart piled high with her promised furniture arrived. The driver hopped down with ease. His passenger, a large yellow lab-mixed-breed dog remained seated but watched her master's every move. A gangly youth sat on the tailgate.

The driver tipped his head toward Eva. "Good morning. I'm Michael Shetler. You met my wife, Bethany, yesterday."

"I did. And your new baby."

Michael's grin almost split his face. "Eli! He's a mighty fine little fellow except for his insistence on getting fed at any hour of the day or night." He gestured toward the back of the cart. "This is Bethany's brother Ivan, and the dog is our Sadie. She'll be at school most days because Bethany's little sister Jenny will be one of your scholars. The two are seldom apart."

"It's nice to meet you, Ivan. And you, Sadie." The dog barked once.

"That means hello," Ivan said, hopping off the wagon bed. "Where do you want this stuff?"

"I'll show you." She held open the door as they carried in a sideboard and had them place it in the sitting room against the wall across from the windows.

The door opened and Willis came in carrying a trunk on his shoulder. "Where?"

Her spirits rose at the sight of his smiling, soot-smudged face. She didn't stop to consider why he had such an effect on her. "At the foot of the bed. *Danki*, Willis."

She heard barking outside and saw Maddie playing tag with Sadie on the lawn. Willis stopped beside Eva. She grinned at him over her shoulder. "It appears Maddie has a new friend. Bubble may be jealous."

Willis stepped up beside her. "Nope, Sadie is an old friend. The dog was the first to visit us when we arrived."

Michael walked past them. "She likes to keep an

eye on her flock. She might look like a lab, but she has shepherd in her somewhere. She visits all the children in the area at least once a day. Where do you want the bookcase?"

"A bookcase, how wonderful! Now I can get my books out of my suitcase. In the sitting room, please." Eva rushed into her bedroom and pulled a suitcase out from beneath her bed. Willis saw her struggling with it and came to help.

His eyes widened when he picked it up. "What's in here? Rocks?"

"A few of my books. The ones I didn't want to be without."

"Books about what?" He set it on the floor in front of the bookcase.

Eva unzipped the case, opened the lid and sank to the floor beside it. "About everything. My favorite books of poetry." She clutched several thin volumes to her chest. "The devotionals I enjoy, some adventure stories, even a cookbook. You're welcome to look through them if you want. You and the boys might enjoy reading some of them."

Willis held up one hand. "Another time."

"Where do you want the end table?" Ivan asked.

"Beside my rocker. This is very *goot* furniture. I assume it stays with the house for the next teacher?"

"I reckon so," Michael said. "The horse and cart are yours to use for as long as you need. You will want to invest in a closed buggy before winter or make sure you have someone who can transport you to church and such when the weather gets bad. One of our newly arrived families, the Fishers, are wheelwrights and buggy makers. I'm sure they can fix you up with a small buggy at a reasonable price."

"You're welcome to use my closed buggy if the weather turns bad before you can get your own," Willis said.

She was touched by his kindness and the generosity of all the people she had met in New Covenant. "I will take you up on that offer if I'm still here when winter arrives."

Willis frowned as he helped her to her feet. "I thought you were staying for the entire school year."

"I hope I will be but Samuel Yoder made certain I understand I am working on a month-to-month basis. You should see the amount of paperwork he left me." They all walked out onto the porch.

"Don't let old sour face fool you," Ivan said. "He's happy to have an Amish teacher here. He has two grandsons who will be attending your school."

"I pray that sentiment continues. I appreciate the loan of the horse and cart."

Michael walked to the horse's head and rubbed the white blaze on his brown nose. "I brought hay and grain for him. His name is Dodger. Where shall I put him?"

"Stable him at my place for now," Willis said.

"The church plans to hold a frolic next month and put up a barn and corral for you," Michael added.

It was news to Eva but it made sense. Most of her students would walk to school but some would need to come by buggy or ride horseback. In the winter those in outlying areas would arrive in horse-drawn sleighs. The school would need a place to stable those horses.

She had been involved in many of the working parties the Amish called *frolics*. When work needed to be done, the entire community would set aside a day to raise a barn, repair a home or harvest a crop for someone in the hospital. Everyone from the youngest to the oldest looked forward to the event and everyone helped.

After the men left Eva put out her books and then returned to her paperwork and lesson plans. She had a lot to learn before school started.

After two hours she decided against spending the day inside even with the drizzle. She took a cup of tea out on the porch and saw Maddie with Willis through the open door of his smithy. Without considering why, she grabbed a gray shawl and swung it over her shoulders then crossed the road to see what the pair was up to. The little girl was sitting on a stool, watching Willis pump the bellows to heat his forge.

"Maddie, you look so glum. What's the matter?" Eva asked.

"I can't tell you anything that Bubble says anymore."

"And," Willis prompted.

"I can't make up things for Bubble to say."

"That severely limits your conversation, doesn't it?" Eva winked at Willis. He shook his head as if wondering which side she was on.

Maddie leaned closer to Eva. "Bubble isn't happy."

Eva fought back a smile.

Willis kept his focus on his forge but glanced up at her briefly. "Did you get settled in?"

"For the most part. I should be working but I have decided to play hooky for the rest of the day. I can't look at one more lesson plan. May I try working the bellows?"

"By all means." He stepped aside.

She took over pumping a large wooden arm that

worked the bellows. A few ashes floated onto her face and she brushed them away.

He glanced her way. "You'll have to pump faster. I'm losing the heat."

She picked up the pace. It wasn't as easy or as much fun as it had looked. The heat from the forge soon had her sweating. She cast aside her shawl. Willis turned a block of iron in the coals with a pair of long tongs. "When do you know you have it hot enough?" she asked.

"By the color. Iron glows red, then orange, yellow, and finally white when it's heated hot enough. A bright yellow-orange color indicates the best forging heat."

"Isn't it yellow-orange enough yet?" Her arms were getting tired.

"Almost."

She kept pumping until her arms were burning. "That's enough," he said.

Grateful to step aside, she let him take over. No wonder he had such muscular arms. "Now what?"

"Now I beat on the iron until I make something."

"What are you making?"

"A brake pedal for a buggy." He lifted the hot metal from the forge and placed it on an anvil. She watched him mold the metal into the shape he wanted by pounding on it. When it grew too cool it went back into the coals. In a surprisingly short amount of time, he had a new brake pedal ready to be attached.

"That is amazing. How did you learn to be a blacksmith? Was your father one?"

"Papa made furniture," Maddie said.

"Our *onkel* had a smithy near our farm in Maryland. He taught me the trade."

She tipped her head, glad for the chance to learn more about Willis and his family. "What made you move all the way up here?"

"The same reasons a lot of Amish folks are here. Farmland is cheaper than back home. Plus, I got tired of the *Englisch* tourists that came to gawk at us Amish. I wanted to practice my faith and my trade without feeling like I was a circus act."

"I know what you mean. I have this wonderful book that talks about how we strive to live apart from the world but by simply being Amish we are being drawn into that world more every year. Have you read it? I can loan you my copy."

He started pumping the bellows again. "I don't have time to read."

Eva swallowed her disappointment. "I understand. I reckon I've played hooky long enough. Thanks for letting me help in my limited way."

His mouth lifted in a brief grin. "You did okay. If you get tired of teaching, come look me up. I could use an apprentice."

She rubbed her aching forearms. "I don't think this is the trade for me."

"Can I help you at the school, Teacher?" Maddie asked.

"I would like that if your brother doesn't object."

"She is all yours. Remember what we talked about, Maddie." He leveled a stern glance at her.

"I remember." Maddie hopped off her chair and took hold of Eva's hand.

Willis met Eva's gaze and grinned. She marveled again at what beautiful eyes he had. She knew dozens of men but none intrigued her the way Willis Gingrich did. He was easy to talk to. She wasn't sure why she felt so comfortable around him. Maybe it was because she'd never had a friend who was a man before. "Maddie and I will be in the school if you need us."

He gestured toward several iron bars waiting to be made into something else. "I'll come get her when I'm done here."

"Don't hurry. Maddie and I will have fun. Oh, and before I forget, you need to fill out enrollment forms for the children. I'll need them before the end of the week."

His easy smile vanished. "Can't you take care of it?"

"I don't know their history or where they went to school before they came here. I'll need those records, too."

His frown deepened. He began pumping the bellows again. "I'll send Harley over to get the papers as soon as he gets back."

"Danki."

He didn't respond so she left and crossed the road with Maddie beside her, wondering if she had somehow upset Willis.

At the steps of the school Maddie looked back. "Whew. Bubble sure had a hard time keeping her mouth shut today."

Eva tried not to laugh but couldn't help it. "Why don't I read a story to you. That way Bubble doesn't have to talk and neither do you."

"Okay. I like stories. Do you have one about ponies? I sure wish Willis would put shoes on my pony."

"I thought I saw him shoeing a pony last evening."

"It wasn't mine. Harley brought it over from his *Englisch* farmer friend. Would you ask Willis to shoe my pony? He likes you."

Eva hoped that was true. "I'll remind him."

She saw he was watching them. She waved. He hesitated and then waved back. She entered the school with a light and carefree step.

For the next hour she read to Maddie and occasionally to Bubble when she couldn't be silent. Eva sighed when Willis came through the door to get his sister. She had enjoyed spending time with Maddie even more than she thought she would. The child had quickly wormed her way into Eva's heart.

"I was just about to teach your sister to write her name on the blackboard. Do you want to show her how it's done?"

He held up both hands. They were black with soot. "You don't want me handling your clean chalk and erasers."

"Okay, Maddie is spelled with a capital M, lower case a, d, d, i, e." She glanced at Willis. "Unless you spell it with a y or a single i?" She waited for him to clarify the spelling for her.

He shrugged. "Spell it however you like."

His comment puzzled Eva. "I want to teach her the correct way."

There was a thump against the side of the building. She glanced toward the windows. "What was that?"

Willis shook his head. "I don't know. Maybe a bird flew into the side of the school."

She frowned. "Do they do that?"

"Sometimes a bird will fly into a window by mistake. The first way you said. That's the right way to spell Maddie's name."

"Okay." She wrote the letters out and handed a piece

of chalk to the child. "Your turn. All you have to do is copy what I've written."

Shattering glass caused Eva to jump and Maddie to shriek. They all turned to look at the broken window. A fist-size rock lay on the floor amid the shards of glass. Eva and Willis stepped to the opening. She saw at once who was responsible. Otto stood a few dozen yards away with a bat in his hands. His eyes were wide with fear or shock. He dropped the bat and ran up the road.

"I can't believe he just did that." Willis scowled.

"It must've been an accident," Eva reassured him.

"Who did it?" Maddie came over to look out the broken window, avoiding the glass on the floor.

"Your brother, Otto. I'll bring him back to clean up this mess." Willis left the school and headed down the road with purposeful strides. Eva followed him as far as the front porch.

Out on the road a woman had stopped her buggy. She leaned out the door. "I saw the Gingrich boy break the window. He was deliberately hitting rocks toward the school," she called out loudly.

Eva's heart sank. She had assumed it was an accident. "Are you sure you aren't mistaken?"

The woman scowled, apparently offended by Eva's suggestion. "I am not. The bishop and the school board will hear what has happened."

"They will be informed, of course, but it would be best if the confession comes from Otto. He needs to face the consequence of his actions."

"Then he shouldn't have run off." She slapped the reins against her horse's rump and drove away.

Maddie came out to stand beside Eva. The child planted her hands on her hips. "Otto makes Willis want to tear his hair out every day. He's not sure what he's going to do with him."

"I'm sorry Otto and Willis aren't getting along. Otto shouldn't have run away, but I can imagine he was frightened."

Maddie looked up. "He could have said Bubble did it."

"That would be a lie, wouldn't it? You don't blame something on Bubble if she didn't do it."

"I did when she knocked over my glass of milk last week."

"Were her feelings hurt? If you said I did something but I didn't do it, my feelings would be hurt."

Maddie scrunched her face and then beckoned Eva to lean down. She cupped her hands around her mouth near Eva's ear. "She's not real so she doesn't have feelings," she whispered.

"Willis will be delighted to hear that." Eva walked down to the lawn. "I think it would be best if you went home now, Maddie."

"Okay, see you tomorrow, Teacher. I'll practice writing my name tonight."

"That's an excellent idea. Have your brother help you."

"I'll have Harley do it. He's a right helpful fellow. Even Bubble says so."

As the child crossed the road, Eva turned her attention back to the broken window. It would need to be boarded up until it could be replaced. Poor Otto was off to a rough start at his new school.

Chapter Five

Willis found his brother sitting behind his smithy on a small, rickety bench that came with the property when Willis purchased it. He stopped beside Otto. The boy wouldn't look up. Willis gently kicked the bench leg with the toe of his boot. "I always meant to burn this in the forge. I just never got around to pulling the nails out. Besides, I like having a place to sit where no one can see what I'm doing. Do you know what I mean?"

Otto looked up. "Sure."

Willis shoved his hands in his pockets, leaned back against the wall and crossed one boot over the other. He stared up into the bright blue sky. "Do you ever feel like hiding out?"

"If you mean like right after I break someone's window?"

"I'm going to assume that today was an accident. Accidents happen when we are knocking rocks into the air with a baseball bat. Want to tell me why you were hitting rocks toward the school?"

"Because I hate school, but I wasn't trying to break a window. Honest. I just hit one too hard."

"I see."

Otto cast a sidelong glance at Willis. "How come you aren't mad?"

"What makes you assume I'm not?"

"Because when *Daed* was angry he yelled, a lot."

Willis shared a wry smile with his little brother who was still so much a stranger. "I remember that about him. It seemed he was always upset about something. Maybe I should say it seemed that he was always upset with me."

"After you left I became his headache. Harley could do no wrong and Maddie was always with our *mamm*."

Willis raised one fist to the sky. "'If I had a nickel for every mistake you made, boy, I would be the richest man in the county,'" he quoted in his best imitation of his father's deep, disgusted voice.

Otto chuckled softly. "He changed it to 'the richest man in the state' for me."

Willis slipped his hand back in his pocket. "I miss him. I should've come to visit more often. A week every Christmas wasn't enough to get to know you *kinder.*"

"He talked about you a lot."

"Did he? That surprises me."

"He said you didn't have book smarts but you knew metal inside and out the way his brother did and you could make anything you wanted."

"He never told me that. It would've been nice to hear him say something good about me."

"Yeah, it would've been nice," Otto muttered softly as if he was lost in his own thoughts. He took a deep breath and sat up straighter. "*Mamm* said that he loved us. He just didn't know how to show it. Did you move away because he married her? Because she took your mother's place? That's what some people said."

"*Nee*, my mother died when I was a baby. I have no memory of her. I was happy my father found someone new. A few folks thought it was strange that he married someone so much younger but I didn't see that it made any difference. She loved him. I could see that. I moved away for other reasons that don't matter anymore."

"I reckon I gave the new teacher a reason not to like me today. Teachers always think the worst of a fellow."

"I don't believe Eva Coblentz is that kind of teacher."

"We'll see." Otto didn't bother to disguise his doubt.

"If you start at a new school with that kind of attitude, she may be forced to think unkindly of you. You need to give her the benefit of the doubt. She strikes me as a fair woman. I get it that you don't like school. I heard your *mamm* mention it often enough when I visited. I sure didn't like school."

That seemed to catch Otto's attention. "You didn't?"

"*Nee*. Like *Daed* said, I wasn't book smart." It was the closest Willis could get to admitting he couldn't read or write. He didn't want Otto to be ashamed of his big brother. He was the one the boys should look up to even if he was a poor substitute for their father. "I reckon you should board up the window and clean up the floor before going to tell the bishop what happened. I'll help you cover the window."

"Is the teacher going to punish me?"

"For what? For breaking the window or for running away instead of facing what you did?"

"Both, I guess." Otto rose to his feet. "Teachers can be mean. Do you think she'll believe that Bubble broke it?"

"She might, but I won't. Maddie may not be old

enough to know the difference between truth and imagination, but you are."

"I was just kidding. I know I shouldn't have taken off without saying I was sorry. I guess I got scared. I'll have to pay for the new window, won't I?"

"That is only right."

"Okay, I'm ready to apologize."

"You will feel better after you do."

The sidelong glance Otto shot Willis showed he didn't believe his brother.

The two of them selected several pieces of plywood that Willis had stored in the horse barn. They carried the pieces to the school along with the ladder and were almost finished nailing the boards in place when Samuel drove up in his buggy. Eva came out of her house and crossed the lawn.

Otto glanced at Willis up on the ladder and then walked over to speak to Eva. "I'm sorry that I broke the window, Teacher. I didn't mean to knock that rock so hard."

"I thought as much." Her smile seemed to ease Otto's fear of her.

"Were you deliberately hitting stones toward the school?" Samuel demanded as he approached the boy. "Why would you do that?"

Otto shrugged but couldn't look the man in the face. "I don't know." He glanced at Willis as he descended the ladder and then straightened his small shoulders. "I guess I was mad because I don't want to go to school here and I miss my friends back home. I didn't mean to break the window. I am sorry. I'll clean up the broken glass. Don't worry about that."

Samuel's stern face relaxed. "I appreciate your honesty and I accept your apology, but you chose to do a foolish thing without thinking of others. Agnes Martin told me both your sister and your teacher were inside the building. What if that rock had struck your teacher or the broken glass had fallen on your sister? I know the loss of your parents must weigh heavily on your mind, Otto. Your move to our community was not your choice but one made for you by your brother. In all things joyful and sorrowful we must accept the will of *Gott* without question."

Otto stared at the ground and didn't reply.

"I spoke with the bishop and Leroy Lapp," Samuel said. "We will meet with you tomorrow morning at eight o'clock to decide your punishment."

A worried frown drew Otto's eyebrows together as he looked up. "Is that necessary? I said I was sorry."

"Our actions have consequences. It is important you learn that." Samuel nodded toward Eva and Willis and then returned to his buggy and drove off.

Eva laid a hand on Otto's shoulder. "Don't worry. Devouring wayward children is against the law. I'll be there to make sure they remember that."

Otto didn't smile. Neither did Willis. It had been years since Willis had been called before the school board to explain his actions, but he still remembered the sick feeling in his stomach. As much as he wanted to spare Otto the humiliation, he knew he couldn't.

Eva entered the school the next morning and found the broken glass had been picked up and the floor swept clean as Otto had promised. It wasn't long before Bishop Schultz, Leroy Lapp and Samuel Yoder came in. They examined the window without speaking to her, muttering amongst themselves. She hadn't been invited to sit in on the meeting but none of them objected to her presence. Finally, they moved a table to the front of the room, lined their chairs up behind it and sat down to wait. It was very reminiscent of her interview only days before. She wondered if poor Otto was as nervous as she had been that day.

She clasped her hands together. "I have a suggestion to make regarding Otto's punishment if you are willing to hear it."

"We're listening," the bishop said.

Eva explained her plan. The men listened in silence. When she was finished she sat on the bench under the unbroken window and waited.

Willis and Otto walked in at eight o'clock. Willis took a seat beside her. Otto walked over to stand in front of the school board with his straw hat in his hands. The men spoke to him in low voices. Willis leaned toward Eva. "Any idea what this outcome will be?"

"I did make a suggestion, but I don't know if they will follow it. I don't believe Otto meant any harm but destruction of school property is a serious matter."

"He already dislikes school. This isn't going to make it any easier on him. The families in this area are excited to have their own school. They're not going to like that a newcomer broke out a window before the first day of class."

"People will understand that such things happen," she whispered.

"I hope so."

The bishop gestured to Eva and Willis. They came and stood on either side of the boy. Willis laid his arm across Otto's shoulders.

Samuel Yoder put his elbows on the table and steepled his fingers together. "The window must be paid for. We don't feel it is right to penalize you, Willis, for something your brother did."

Willis gave a half smile. "I'll be happy to provide the labor to put a new one in."

"That is acceptable. The school board has enough funds in the treasury to replace the window, but that money should've gone toward schoolbooks and supplies for everyone, Otto. Some children may go without because of your carelessness."

"I can get a job and pay you back."

"Where? There are not many jobs around here for a boy your age. Your teacher has come up with a plan we agree with."

Eva smiled at Otto. "When school starts you will stay after each day for two months to sweep up, clean the blackboards, dust the erasers and take out the trash. At the end of two months we will consider the debt paid as long as you do a good job."

She glanced at Willis. He nodded his approval.

"Are we settled, then?" Willis asked. "I'm behind in my work and I must get back to it."

"Eva has an additional task for Otto today, but you may go, Willis." The bishop stood up. "We all have to get back to our work. Let this be the last time we meet this way, Otto Gingrich."

Otto nodded without speaking. The men filed out, leaving Eva alone with the boy. She squeezed his shoulder. "That wasn't so bad."

"I guess not. The bishop said you had something else for me to do."

"When my teacher wanted to make sure I remembered something important she made me write it on the blackboard one hundred times. I want you to write, 'I will respect school property' one hundred times."

"Now? Willis needs me to help in the forge today. I have to get going."

He started to turn away but she clapped a hand on his shoulder. "I want it today. The sooner you get started, the sooner you will finish and then you may go help Willis."

Otto shuffled toward the blackboard. She returned the chairs to their places and sat down at her desk and began to read through the first grade primer to see what she would be teaching.

"There's no chalk. Guess I'll have to do this later." Otto headed toward the door.

"I have some chalk here." She opened the top drawer and pulled out a box of chalk sticks. She held it toward him.

He took one from the box as gingerly as if it were a snake.

She didn't know why he was stalling. "Hurry up so you can help your brother."

He faced the board and wrote a lowercase i. He hesitated and pulled at his lower lip with one hand.

"Is something wrong? Is there a word you don't know how to spell? That should be a capitalized I."

"This is stupid." He threw the chalk into the corner and ran out of the room.

"Otto, come back here!" She sat stunned for a moment then rose and followed him out the door but he had already gone out of sight.

She crossed the street to the smithy. The sound of hammering told her Willis was hard at work. She stepped through the door but didn't see Otto. "Willis, did you see where Otto went?"

He held a red-hot horseshoe in a pair of tongs. He plunged it into a barrel of liquid. Steam hissed and splattered his leather apron. "I thought he was with you."

"He became upset and ran out of the schoolroom."

Willis pulled the shoe out of the liquid and examined it before looking at her. "Upset about what?"

Eva shook her head. "I'm not sure. I asked him to write that he would respect school property on the blackboard one hundred times."

"He refused?"

"He just ran out of the room without doing it. Do you know where he is?"

Willis carried another horseshoe to the forge and plunged it into the glowing coals. "I don't. Try looking behind this shop. He goes back there sometimes. Why would he run off? Did he say anything?"

"He said it was stupid." Eva wished Willis would show more concern but perhaps she was overreacting. Willis was Otto's parent for all practical purposes. She wasn't sure where her duty as a teacher lay. "I'm not going to let him get by with this kind of behavior. He will have to finish this assignment sooner rather than later."

"He will. I'll see to it as soon as he comes home. I know the boy. He won't miss lunch." Willis began pumping the bellows.

She took a step back, feeling dismissed. She certainly couldn't make Willis leave his work and go searching for his errant brother. She walked out of the forge and saw Maddie sitting on a swing in the school playground. Maddie spied her at the same time and gave a halfhearted wave.

Eva walked over to the playground and took a seat

beside Maddie in one of the swings. "I'm not sitting on Bubble, am I?"

Maddie shook her head but kept her eyes downcast. "She's not here. She had to go home for a while. She was missing her mother."

"I see." So was one lonely little girl unless Eva missed her guess. "You seem sad today. Is something wrong?"

Maddie slanted a glance at her. "Do you think the other kids will laugh at me because I talk to Bubble? Otto says they will."

"It isn't right to poke fun at another person. I will make sure everyone knows that. The Lord wants us to be kind to each other."

"That's what I thought."

"Did you see your brother Otto leave the school a short time ago?"

Maddie nodded and pointed toward the woods behind the building. "He went to see Harley."

"Can you tell me where I can find Harley?"

"Harley likes to visit his friend, Mrs. Arnett. She has a farm beyond the woods. You can follow the path through the trees, but Harley says I can't go that way because I'm too little and I might get lost in the woods."

Eva tried to think of a way to cheer the child. "You can come with me. Would you like to do that?"

Maddie shook her head. "I'm going to wait here for Bubble."

"I understand." Eva stepped out of the swing and headed into the woods. The trees grew close together and the underbrush was thick and leafy. Within a few steps she couldn't see the school building behind her.

Several game trails crossed the footpath, and once she took the wrong trail but quickly realized her mistake and returned to the correct one. Harley was right not to let Maddie take the path alone. She stopped when she thought she heard her name being called, but when it wasn't repeated she decided she had been mistaken.

After nearly half a mile she came to a neat farmstead with a big red barn and white painted fences. There was a young woman on her knees in a garden plot. Eva approached her. "Excuse me, is this the Arnett farm?"

The woman sat up and brushed her shoulder-length dark hair out of her eyes with the back of her wrist. "It is. I'm Lilly Arnett. How can I help you?"

"I'm Eva Coblentz. I'm looking for Harley Gingrich. Is he here?"

"He was but he left with his brother Otto a short time ago."

"I didn't meet them in the woods. Is there another way back to New Covenant?"

Lilly smiled and pointed toward the nearby highway. "I let them take one of my horses. You will find the county road is easier walking, but it is a little longer. Harley said he would be back later to finish mowing the lawn. I can give him a message."

Eva smiled. "Tell him his new teacher needs to speak to Otto."

"I'll let him know."

"Danki." Eva chose to walk back to the school on the roadway rather than tramping through the woods again. She could only hope that Otto had returned to finish his task.

When she reached the school, Maddie was gone. A black-and-white pony stood patiently at the hitching rail in front of the school. The door of the schoolhouse stood open. Eva stepped inside. Harley was sitting at a student desk in the first row. Otto was at the blackboard writing out his assignment. Eva gave a deep sigh of relief. She had been prepared for a battle of wills with him. It seemed that wasn't going to be necessary.

She watched and waited quietly until Otto turned to his brother. "That's all, right?"

Harley walked up to the board and began counting the lines. "Yep. I count one hundred. Now I got to get back to the Arnett place."

"Danki, brudder."

The boys grabbed their hats from the pegs on the wall and walked past her. "I'm glad you finished, Otto." She wanted to ask him why he had been so upset earlier but decided it could wait.

She walked to the blackboard, picked up an eraser and was about to rub out Otto's work when she noticed something was wrong. She looked at the first sentence on the board. It was clearly a different hand than the rest of the work. First sentence was neat with the words well spaced. The next sentence, while correct, wasn't neat. Some of the words were smooshed together while there were extra spaces between some of the letters. The more she looked the more she saw errors. Some of the letters were actually backward. A few words had missing letters. She put the eraser down. Otto's writing skills were far below his grade level. She decided to get Dinah's opinion and ask her what she thought.

She left the school and was walking toward her house when she heard Willis call her name. She stopped and saw him jogging toward her. He came to a halt a few feet away and rubbed the palms of his hands on his pant legs. "I wanted to apologize for being abrupt with you earlier. Please forgive me. I have so much work to catch up on. Otto is at home if you are still looking for him."

"He returned a short time ago and finished his work. I'm sorry I bothered you earlier. I'm new at teaching and I feel the need to panic at least once a day."

He gave a halfhearted smile. "I'm new at parenting, and I feel the need to panic all day, every day. I'm sorry Otto was rude to you."

"Come with me. There's something you should see." She led the way back inside the school and walked up to the blackboard. "This is Otto's work."

He looked at the board. "Okay?"

"Look at his writing."

"I am. He finished the assignment, right? If that's all I should get back to work."

"He finished by copying the sentences his brother wrote out for him. I don't think Otto could do it by himself."

"So he had a little help. I don't know what you want me to say."

"He has turned some of the letters around. He has copied all the letters but he hasn't divided them into the proper words. Right here he wrote, I will respect school property."

"Okay, so his writing needs work. You will have the next nine months to help him improve. That's what a good teacher does, right?"

"Among other things. I don't think you are taking this seriously."

"Maybe I'm not. A few scrawls on the blackboard don't put food in the mouths of hungry kids. That takes hard work. Not busywork."

Willis needed to get out of the building. It felt like the walls were closing in on him. He didn't see what was wrong with Otto's work and he didn't want Eva to know he possessed fewer writing skills than his little brother.

Her gaze was piercing, and he flinched from it. "Reading and writing are not simply busywork, Willis. They are the foundation by which we learn everything from God's Word to the latest baseball scores."

"You're right. You're the teacher and the teacher is always right. Even I learned that in school."

"This isn't about who is right and who is wrong."

"I don't know why you are getting angry," he finished lamely.

"Because I get the feeling that you don't care about Otto's education or his future."

"I care that the boys will be able to put food on the table for their families. That will take farmland, which I don't have much of yet, or it will take a skilled trade. That is something I have and can teach them." He turned and headed out the door, wondering if he had revealed his own shortcomings. Eva wasn't a woman who could be easily fooled.

"Willis, wait."

He stopped at the bottom of the school steps. She was a tenacious woman, too. "I thought we were finished."

She stopped, framed in the doorway. Her green eyes brimmed with some deep emotion. "I don't mean to criticize how you are raising your brothers and sister. I know it can't be easy for you. I'm sorry for saying that you don't care about their education. It's no excuse but I find myself in uncharted territory. I may have crossed the line just now but I have no idea where the line should be drawn or how to change it. And that rambling explanation is my way of saying I'm sorry. I will limit my lectures to my scholars and try not to offend their parents or guardians."

"You're forgiven. If the boy has trouble in school let me know and I will speak to him about it."

"Fair enough." She arched one eyebrow. "I don't have many friends in this new place. I'd hate to lose the first one I made here."

"You haven't lost me. I live just across the road." He nodded in that direction.

A sliver of a smile curved her lips. "I should be able to find my way over if I try hard enough."

"I suspect you can be a very determined woman when you put your mind to something."

"I have occasionally heard my name associated with that adjective."

"Occasionally?"

"Perhaps *frequently* might be closer to the truth." Her grin widened.

"I'm not sure I've ever met someone like you," he said in amazement.

She crossed her arms over her chest and looked down. "A bossy old maid who speaks her mind isn't that rare of a creature."

"Perhaps not but I think you are one of a kind, Eva Coblentz."

Chapter Six

Eva watched from the doorway as Willis returned to his workshop. He might consider her unique, but she placed him squarely in the same category. In a society that valued the community above the individual and encouraged conformity, finding someone who wasn't offended by her outspokenness was rare.

She looked back at the writing on the blackboard. Her instincts said Otto's angry attitude was more than a simple dislike of school. Dinah was the person she hoped could help her solve the riddle of the troubled child.

Two hours later Dinah and Mrs. Kenworthy, a schoolteacher from the local public school, studied the blackboard carefully. Eva was grateful Dinah had been free on such short notice and had wholeheartedly agreed with her suggestion to call one of the local teachers to render another opinion. "What do you think?"

"Otto is eleven so he must be in the fifth grade?" Dinah looked over her shoulder for confirmation.

"That is my understanding. Harley is thirteen and

will be a seventh-grader. Maddie is seven and will start the first grade."

Mrs. Kenworthy shook her head. "This is not the work of a boy in the fifth grade. It could be he has a learning disability."

"Could it be simple bad penmanship?" Eva asked. Was she making a mountain out of a molehill?

Mrs. Kenworthy's mouth twisted to the side. "I see more than that. For the most part he has the letters in the right order but he doesn't seem to realize that they aren't grouped into the correct words."

"For one boy in my former community, the problem was as simple as needing glasses," Dinah said.

"Aren't all Amish children given hearing and vision exams when they start school?" Eva asked.

"They are in Maine," Mrs. Kenworthy said.

Dinah turned away from the blackboard. "The vast majority of Amish students are tested by public health officials in their area, but not all. I'm sure it will be in his records from his previous school."

Eva held her hands wide. "I don't have them yet. The children haven't even been officially enrolled. I have reminded Willis that he needs to get it done but he seems overwhelmed with his new responsibilities. I hate to bother him with one more thing."

Dinah scowled. "Shall I have my husband talk to him about it?"

Eva shook her head. "We have a few more weeks before classes begin. If he hasn't turned in the forms by Friday I will speak to him again."

Mrs. Kenworthy tapped the writing on the blackboard with one finger. "The sooner you can address what is wrong with young Otto, the better off he will be. It appears someone is willing to help. The first line is in an entirely different hand. You think it was his older brother?"

"That was my assumption," Eva said. "I think he wrote out the sentence for Otto to copy and stayed with him until the assignment was finished."

"Speak to Harley," Dinah suggested. "Perhaps he can give you some insight. That way you won't have to bother Willis again."

"All right I will."

The three women walked outside. Dinah tipped her head toward Willis's home. "Is Maddie still conversing with her imaginary friend?"

Eva looked around for the child. "I'm not sure. I saw her earlier and she said that Bubble had gone home to visit her mother."

Mrs. Kenworthy laughed heartily. "Children do say the most amazing things. That is one thing we should warn you about. As a teacher you will hear many things parents never expected would be repeated in school. Do not be fooled into repeating it as gossip because most times the children have it all wrong."

"Thank you for the advice. I will take it to heart and seal my lips."

Mrs. Kenworthy walked down to her car. Dinah turned to Eva. "I had best get home. The bishop and his wife are coming over for supper this evening along with Gemma, Jesse and Hope. I can't get enough of my grandbaby. I praise *Gott* he let me live long enough to see and enjoy her."

"How did her doctor visit turn out?" Eva asked.

"Healthy and happy was the diagnosis the doctor

gave Jesse and Gemma. Hope is still small for her age, but she is catching up."

Eva smiled with relief. "I'm glad to hear that."

Dinah started to walk away but stopped and turned back to Eva. "You are welcome to join us for supper. I made plenty of fried chicken, Gemma is bringing a casserole and Constance Schultz made some fresh apple pies for dessert."

"*Danki*, but I have more homework. I never knew there was so much paperwork involved in teaching."

"Oh, I remember those days. And the long nights getting everything ready for the first day of class. Being a wife and a mother was the fulfillment of a dream for me, but I do miss teaching at times. All those bright faces so eager to see me in the mornings. It is a satisfying profession and one that isn't always valued as it should be. Don't forget that other teachers, Amish and *Englisch*, are willing to help you get off to a good start. Several of the teachers at our public school have stopped in to tell me they will miss having Amish children in their classes."

"Thank you again for your help and tell Gemma and Jesse that I said hello."

"This coming Sunday is the off Sunday in our community so no prayer meeting. We will expect you to come visit us, and homework will not get you out of it." Dinah smiled as she issued her invitation.

Eva inclined her head. "I wouldn't dream of missing an afternoon in the company of you and your family."

Harley came strolling past the school, headed for home. "Good evening, Teacher. Good evening, Mrs. Lapp."

"Harley, can I speak to you for a moment?" Eva said.

"Sure."

"I have to get going. Let me know what you find out," Dinah said.

Eva turned her attention to Harley. She sat down on the steps of the school and motioned for him to do the same. "I noticed that you helped your brother with his writing assignment today."

"All I did was write it once. He did the rest."

"Maddie tells me Otto doesn't like school."

"Maddie talks to an imaginary kid named Bubble. I'm not sure you can believe much of what she says."

"Good point. Still, Otto has given me the same impression. Can you tell me why?"

"School is hard for him. Our last teacher never wanted to help him, so I do. He's smart. He's not stupid and people shouldn't say that he is."

"I would never call someone *stupid*. I'm sorry that your brother has been hurt by careless people. I will do everything I can to make Otto feel he is a valuable member of my class. At your last school did the children have their eyes checked?"

"Sure. And they checked our hearing, too. Why?"

"I haven't received those records, so I wanted to make sure the tests had been done." That was one reason she could eliminate for Otto's problem. "Has Otto always had trouble in school?"

"I think so. *Mamm* used to spend a lot of time helping him with his reading. *Daed* used to say he was just being lazy. Can I go now?"

"Of course."

He hopped up and jogged toward home. Eva remained on the steps. Mrs. Kenworthy had confirmed what Eva had thought. It seemed Otto would need additional help from her.

Harley stepped out the door of the Gingrich house and cupped his hand around his mouth. "Send Maddie home for supper."

"She's not with me," Eva shouted back. The playground was empty and the child hadn't been with them in the school.

Harley waved and went back inside. Eva rose and walked the short distance to her house. She turned on the oven and pulled a turkey potpie from the freezer. She heard footsteps on her porch and looked at the screen door.

Willis pulled the door open and came inside. "Have you seen Maddie today?"

She tensed at the concern in his voice. "Not since this morning. She was on the swing set and said she was sad because Bubble had gone home to see her mother."

"We can't find her."

"Perhaps she's gone to play with some other friends. Where might she be?"

"She doesn't know many of the children her age yet."

Eva turned off her oven. "We should ask the neighbors if they have seen her."

"I don't mean to scare you. It's just not like her to wander off."

"I'm not scared, Willis. Concerned, yes, but Maddie is with God wherever she goes. He is her protection. Let me make sure she isn't here in the house."

"I will double-check the school." He went out.

Eva made a quick room-by-room search of her house and came up empty. She stepped outside and saw Otto and Harley near the trees. Harley had something black in his hands. They both came running up to Willis. Harley handed him a small black *kapp*. "I found it snagged on a tree branch a few yards into the woods. We yelled for her but she didn't answer."

Willis wadded the fabric into a tight ball in his hands. "She isn't supposed to go into the woods. She knows that."

Eva pressed a hand to her lips. "I asked her if she wanted to go with me when I went looking for Otto. She said no but she might have changed her mind after I was gone. I thought I heard someone calling my name once, but it wasn't repeated so I went on. What if she was trying to follow me?"

It was growing late. Eva's heart started racing. Maddie could have followed her into the woods. Why had she invited the child to go with her? "She wouldn't leave the path, would she?"

"She could easily lose her way," Harley said. "There is a second path that cuts across it and leads down to the river where some people go fishing."

Eva remembered the spot. "I almost went that way myself. What should we do?"

Willis handed the *kapp* to Eva and faced his brothers. "Harley, you and Otto take the path to the farm and keep calling for her but remember to stop and listen, too. Take it slow. Eva, you and I will drive over to the farm and see if she is there and check with our neighbors along the way to find out if anyone has seen her. I'll hitch up your cart."

"I have two flashlights in my kitchen. The batteries are brand-new. The boys should take them. It will be dark before long."

"Get them. I'll get your horse." Willis ran back to his property.

Eva fetched the flashlights and handed one to each of the boys. Their eyes were wide with fear. She tried to reassure them. "I'm sure she is fine. Stick together. If you get off the path in the dark stay where you are. We will find you."

They took off and she hurried down to Willis's barn. He was backing Dodger between the shafts of the cart. Eva went around the horse and quickly attached her side of the harness. She climbed up to the seat.

Willis handed her the lines. "If she is there we will wait for the boys."

"If she isn't?"

"I will follow the path to the river while you bring the boys home. I pray one of us finds her along the way and she will spin us a story about how Bubble led her into the woods." He tried to smile.

Eva saw the effort it took and her heart ached for him. "Have faith."

"I'm trying." He climbed up beside her, lifted the reins and urged Dodger to a quick trot out onto the roadway.

Willis was grateful for Eva's calm presence beside him. He should have kept a better eye on his sister. He had no one to blame but himself. Maddie was too little to run wild the way he had allowed the boys to. Something would have to change.

When he reached the first house along the road, Eva hopped down and hurried to the door. She spoke to the man who answered her knock and then hurried back to the cart.

"They haven't seen her. They are going to call the warden service to get a search started. If we find her they'll let the warden know. They are going to head over to the farm in case more people are needed for the search."

"I don't even know them. They aren't Amish."

"There are *goot* people everywhere who are willing to help. Not all of them wear plain clothing, bonnets and straw hats."

"Sometimes it's easy to forget that."

A small smile curved her lips. "From time to time, I will remind you."

He looked at the remarkable woman beside him and thanked God she had chosen to come to Maine. He realized just how much he had grown to like Eva and how much her friendship meant to him. There wasn't anyone else he wanted with him during this crisis.

The car from the previous house went around them on the narrow road. Willis saw their taillights disappear over the hill. For the first time since he was a teenager he wished he had a car instead of a horse to get him where he needed to be quickly.

The next farm along the road belonged to a new Amish family in the community. The husband, wife and four grown sons were sitting down to supper when Willis pulled up. Ezekiel Fisher came out. "Good evening, Willis Gingrich. What brings you here?"

"My Maddie's missing. Have you seen her today?"

"*Nee*, I have not." He spoke to his wife and sons who had come to stand behind him. He turned back to Willis. "None have seen the child. We will help look."

"*Danki*. She was headed to the Arnett farm."

"We will search the woods between here and there in case she came this way."

Willis set the horse in motion. The sound of the animal's rapid hoofbeats on the pavement and the jingle of the harness were the only sounds as he urged Dodger to a faster pace.

Eva sat silently beside him. At last the Arnett farm lane came into view. The English couple from the first house and Mrs. Arnett were out on the stoop waiting for him. There was no sign of Maddie.

Mrs. Arnett stepped up beside the cart. "I've already called the sheriff department and the warden service. I also called a friend who is a neighbor to your bishop. He has gone to let the Schultz family know what has happened. The sheriff wants everyone to meet at the school and set up a search from there. Jacques Dubois and his wife will drive you back. You can leave the cart and the horse here."

"Otto and Harley are coming this way on the path."

Mrs. Arnett nodded. "I will get word to you if they show up with her."

"I thought I would search the path that leads to the river." Willis was reluctant to go back without Maddie. Somewhere she was lost, maybe hurt, frightened and depending on him to come and find her.

Eva laid a hand on his arm. "Maddie may already be home and wondering why no one is about."

She was right. He got down and helped Eva out of the cart.

Eva got in the car and scooted over, making room for Willis. In a matter of minutes they were back at the school. Willis called for Maddie and went to check in the school. Eva made a quick search of her own home, calling for Maddie as she went from room to room. There was no trace of the child. When she stepped out onto her porch she saw Willis coming out of his house. The look on his face told her what she already suspected. Maddie hadn't come home.

The sound of an approaching siren caused them to look toward the road. The siren stopped when the white pickup turned into the school driveway but the lights on top continued flashing. A tall man in a dark green uniform got out. "Are you the ones with a missing child?"

Willis stepped forward. "We are. Her name is Maddie and she is seven years old."

"I'm Sergeant O'Connor of the warden service. I will be in charge of the search at this end. We have more local law enforcement on the way to help. It will be full dark soon. Is there somewhere we can set up a command center?"

"In the school," Eva said, eager to help.

"I see that you folks are Amish. Is there electricity?"

"Nee." She shook her head. "But we do have propane lighting in the building."

"I have a generator," Willis said. "Will that work?"

"Perfect." Sgt. O'Connor looked toward the woods. "How much of the area has been searched?"

Willis gestured toward the trees. "My brothers are working their way through the woods on a path they often take to Mrs. Arnett's farm. Mr. Fisher and his four sons are searching between their place and her farm in case Maddie wandered north."

"And how far is this farm?"

"About half a mile as the crow flies," Eva said.

Sgt. O'Connor turned to face her. "What makes you

certain that she went into the woods and not to some-one else's house?"

Willis pulled Maddie's *kapp* from his pocket. "The boys found this a little way into the woods along the path."

"Do you think there could be someone with her?"

Willis shook his head slowly. "I don't think so but I can't be sure. Maddie has been told not to go into the woods alone."

"Kids don't always do what we tell them. Don't worry. We're going to find her." Sgt O'Connor's sense of confidence buoyed Eva's spirits.

The clatter of galloping hooves on the road filled the evening air. A team of draft horses pulling a large wagon came charging into view from the valley below. The wagon was packed with Amish men, women and boys. Jesse Crump was driving. Bishop Schultz sat beside him, holding on to his hat. Jesse pulled the team to a halt. The passengers piled out.

The bishop walked up to the warden. "We are here to assist in any way we can."

Sgt. O'Connor looked over the crowd of volunteers. "Every warm body is appreciated. We're going to set up a command center in the school and plan out a grid search of the area. We have a K-9 search and rescue unit on the way, but it will be several hours before they can get here."

Michael Shetler and a young Amish girl pushed their way through the crowd to stand beside the bishop. The dog Sadie stood at the little girl's side with her tail wagging. The young girl gestured toward the dog. "This is Sadie. She can find Maddie."

The warden looked skeptical. "And who are you?"

"I'm Jenny Martin."

"Is your dog trained in search and rescue?"

"We didn't train her. I think *Gott* did. She rescued me when I was buried in the snow the winter before last."

Sgt. O'Connor smiled at her. "I appreciate the offer, but I'm not about to send another child into the woods even if she has a wonder dog with her."

"I understand your skepticism," Michael said. "But I think it's worth a try. The dog has proven tracking skills. I'll go with them. Willis, do you have something that belongs to Maddie? Something she wore recently?"

Eva handed over the *kapp*. Michael looked at the sergeant. "Can we go?"

The officer sighed. "I may be making it harder for our own dog with more scent trails in the woods but okay. Come with me. I'll get you a radio so you can keep in contact."

Another car pulled in behind the officer's truck. Lilly Arnett got out. Eva's hopes rose but sank when she saw Lilly give a slight shake of her head. Otto and Harley got out of the car and raced to Willis. "Did you find her?" Harley asked.

"*Nee.* I want you to stay with Eva," Willis said before joining Michael and Jenny at the officer's pickup where they were being outfitted with a two-way radio. Otto and Harley moved to stand beside Eva in front of the school.

She took one look at their tear-stained faces. "Don't worry. We're going to find her."

Neither of them spoke. She didn't doubt Willis's affection for his brothers, but they needed his comfort now, too. She wished she could hug them all. She walked over and touched his arm. When he looked at her she tipped her head toward the boys. "Your brothers are worried and scared."

Willis had been so wrapped up in his need to find Maddie that he hadn't given a thought to what his brothers were going through. It took Eva to point it out to him. She was better at looking after his family than he was. He touched her cheek briefly. "I'll speak to them. *Danki*."

Harley and Otto stood off to the side of the school, looking as dejected and as tearful as he felt. They needed him. He wasn't used to being needed. He walked over to them, struggling to find the right thing to say. "This is not your fault."

"You should be yelling at us." Harley sniffled and his arms clasped tightly across his chest.

"Why?" Willis asked softly.

"*Mamm* always said we had to watch out for Maddie and keep a close eye on her. We didn't." Harley wiped his face on his sleeve.

Otto laid a hand on Harley's shoulder. "Willis doesn't yell. Haven't you noticed that? Maddie is going to say that Bubble got her lost."

Willis managed a wry smile. "I thought the same thing."

He pulled the boys into a tight hug in spite of his desire to start searching. Eva was right. They needed comforting, too. "I don't blame either of you. I'm the one who should have been keeping an eye on her. You are all my responsibility."

He glanced up and saw Eva watching him with a look of approval. He drew away from the boys. "I know you want to come with us but I need to know you are both safe so I can focus on finding Maddie. Do you understand?"

They nodded. He smiled at them. "Bring the generator over for the *Englisch* officer to use and help however you can but stay here."

Sgt. O'Connor, Michael and Jenny took Sadie to the place where the path came out of the woods. The dog cast about sniffing for a scent. Within a few seconds she gave a loud bark and strained at her leash. Willis joined them. Eva appeared at his side and handed him a flashlight.

She turned on the one she carried. "I'm coming with you. The bishop and his wife will look after the boys."

He took hold of her hand and tried to share how much her presence meant to him with a gentle squeeze as they listened to Sgt. O'Connor.

"Let the dog go first. Try not to get ahead of her. She may not be on the right scent so I'm going to set up a grid and have other searchers comb through these woods systematically. Be careful. Stay within sight of each other if you can but spread out and look for any sign of her. I'll stay in radio contact." He headed back to the school.

Willis reluctantly released Eva's hand, and their group began walking into the forest.

Chapter Seven

Eva missed the comfort of Willis's touch as soon as he let go. She curled her fingers into her palm to hold on to the warmth he'd left behind. In spite of the short time Eva had known him, she was starting to care for him on a level deeper than that of friendship. Her practical side put it down to the unusual circumstances they had encountered together.

Ordinarily, it would have taken her weeks to get to know Willis and the children so well, but they had been together frequently since she had arrived. She didn't dream that Willis returned her warmer feelings. She was standing by him as a friend because that was what he needed now.

She was happy if Willis found her presence comforting but to read anything else into his lingering touch just now was foolish on her part. She knew that. He wasn't interested in more than friendship. She suspected his reliance on her had as much to do with his insecurity regarding the children as anything else. She'd never had to worry about keeping her emotions in check in the past, but she would have to in the future where Willis was concerned.

Praying that Maddie would be found soon, Eva plunged into the woods behind Willis. The dark shadows of the pine trees swallowed the searchers' silhouettes within a few yards. All Eva could see were the bobbing flashlights of the people with her. The underbrush clawed at her clothes, and branches scratched at her face and hands as she trudged forward. Willis shouted for Maddie every few minutes, and Eva strained her ears to hear a reply.

They had been moving forward slowly for about thirty minutes when the light Jenny was holding danced wildly. "I found something," she called out.

Eva and Willis moved to join Michael and Jenny in a small clearing. Sadie whined, clearly eager to forge on.

Jenny held a scrap of fabric in her hand. She looked at Willis. "What color dress was Maddie wearing?"

He shook his head. "I'm not sure."

Eva shut her eyes and thought back to that morning. She remembered seeing the girl's black *kapp* and apron as she sat on the swing. She opened her eyes. "Blue, her dress was royal blue with a black apron over it."

It was hard to tell the color by flashlight, but Eva was sure it was the same material. "That's from her dress."

Willis grasped her hand and squeezed gently. "It means we're on the right trail."

The radio Michael carried crackled to life. "This is Sgt. O'Connor. Do you copy?"

"We hear you. Sadie is leading us away from the Arnett farm and down toward the river," Michael said. "Over."

"Do you think she is still on the trail of the child?" O'Connor asked.

"We do. Jenny found some torn material on a thornbush. Eva says it's the same color Maddie was wearing. We seem to be following a game trail. It's narrow and twisting. Between the darkness and the terrain, we are holding Sadie back. She could cover the distance much faster without us. Over."

"She's your dog. Will she stay with Maddie if she finds her?"

"She will," Jenny said with confidence.

"Willis, what do you think?" Michael asked.

Willis rubbed a hand across his chin and turned to Eva. "What's your opinion?"

"I think having Sadie with her will give Maddie comfort until we can reach her, but it's your decision."

Willis looked at Michael. "Let's do it."

Michael spoke into the radio. "We are going to send Sadie ahead. Over."

"Understood. The radio you have is equipped with GPS. That means we can track it from here. Can you attach it to the dog?"

"I can use my *kapp* and tie it around her neck," Eva said.

There was silence on the other end. Finally, Sgt. O'Connor came on again. "I'm sending two deputies on ATVs down to the river. They'll work their way toward you. The four of you follow the dog if you can. Your GPS says you are a quarter of a mile west of the river. Keep moving east. Do you have a compass? Over."

"We don't but I see the Lord has provided a big yellow moon rising now. We'll be able to keep it in sight through the trees."

Eva knelt and tied her *kapp* tightly to Sadie's collar with the radio inside it. She prayed it wouldn't be pulled loose by the dense underbrush.

"Find her, Sadie," Eva whispered into the dog's ear. Sadie lifted her head and growled deep in her chest. Michael unsnapped her leash and she bolted away, barking loudly.

Willis helped Eva to her feet. Sadie's barking rapidly grew faint, but Eva could still hear her. Willis kept a hold on Eva's hand as they pushed forward. He shouted Maddie's name when Sadie stopped barking.

There was only silence. The rising moon gave Eva enough light to see Willis's worried face. Had it been a mistake to let the dog loose? If she had gone home, how would they know?

He pulled Eva to the top of a small rise. He cupped his hands around his mouth and yelled Maddie's name again.

"Hello? Sadie, stop licking my face. Hello?"

Eva threw her arms around Willis at the sound of that welcome reply. He hugged her tight as relief sucked the strength from her bones. "That's her. She's okay. Thanks be to *Gott* for His mercy," she whispered against his chest.

He let her go and they all hurried down the hill, shouting that they were coming. A snarl erupted in the dark ahead of them followed by Sadie's fierce barking and Maddie's scream.

Fear gripped Willis. "Maddie! Answer me." He tried to rush forward but the thick brush held him back. He finally forced his way through into another clearing. His flashlight showed Sadie standing on her back legs with her front paws on a dead pine. She began jumping and barking again. Ten feet over her head a black bear clung to the tree, glaring at them.

Willis heard a whimper behind him. He spun around. Behind a fallen log, Maddie was crouched with her eyes closed and her hands over her ears. Relief sent a surge of joy to his heart. He dropped to his knees beside her. "Maddie, it's Willis."

He didn't see any blood. Was she okay? He wanted to grab her up but knew that would frighten her even more. He reached out and gently touched her shoulder. She flinched, her eyes popped open and she launched herself into his arms.

"I knew you would come," she sobbed.

He held her tight as he struggled to his feet. "It's okay. I've got you. Are you hurt?"

"Bubble got us lost."

Willis caught sight of Eva standing a few feet away with her arms around Jenny. They were both smiling although he saw tears on Eva's cheeks. "Shame on Bubble. You should stop listening to her."

He carried Maddie to Eva. She cupped Maddie's cheek. "You scared us. Are you okay?"

Maddie nodded but didn't release her grip on his neck. "I got scared, too," she said in a small voice.

Michael had snapped the leash on Sadie's collar and pulled Sadie away from the tree. Jenny dropped to her knees and hugged the dog. "You are such a *goot hund*. I love you, Sadie Sue."

Willis knelt beside the dog and used his free arm to rub her head. "I think Sgt. O'Connor was right. You are a wonder dog."

Jenny beamed a smile at him. "I told you Sadie could do it."

The rumble of engines preceded the lights of a pair of ATVs as they made their way through the trees toward Willis and his group. Eva untied her *kapp* from Sadie's collar and put it on.

The two officers drove into the clearing and turned off their engines. The one in front pulled off her helmet and smiled brightly. "This looks like we've come to the right place."

Thirty minutes later Willis carried his tired and disheveled sister into the schoolroom. He was immediately surrounded by people of the community offering congratulations, patting his back and giving thanks. Sadie stood at his side, wagging her tail as if the excitement was all for her.

Harley and Otto pushed their way through the crowd to his side and locked their arms around him. "She's fine. *Gott* was *goot* to us this day."

Willis caught sight of Eva coming in. The smile she sent him made his heart leap. He didn't know how he could have made it through the day without her.

Maddie reached for Harley. Willis handed her over to him. She cupped his face with both hands. "Are you mad at me, Harley?"

"You know you weren't supposed to go into the woods alone and don't tell me Bubble was with you. She doesn't count."

"I won't tell you she was there, but she was," she finished with a whisper. "Willis is kinda mad at her, too."

He leaned toward her. "Only because you frightened

me half to death. You're never to pull such a stunt again. Is that understood?"

Maddie lifted her shoulders in a big shrug. "I didn't know I was pulling a stunt. I thought I was following Eva to the Arnett farm."

Inside the school, he found the women of his congregation setting out food along with napkins and coffee cups on a long table. He heard the hum of his generator outside the back door of the building. Sgt. O'Connor worked his way to Willis's side. He patted Maddie's head. "Best possible outcome. Once all the searchers are in, we will get out of your hair."

Willis gripped the man's hand. "I can't thank you enough for coming."

"The way I hear it you didn't really need us." He petted Sadie's head. "My deputy says Sadie found Maddie and treed a bear all by herself."

Maddie made Harley put her down. She walked over to Jenny. "Can Bubble and I come over and play with Sadie sometimes?"

"Sure, as long as that's okay with Willis. I don't think you should go anywhere without telling him first."

"Okay. *Danki*. I'm hungry. I missed my supper."

"We all missed our supper because of you, little girl." Willis patted her head. He looked at Eva. "Maybe your teacher can find you something to eat."

"As a matter of fact, I can. Dinah Lapp brought over a chicken and rice casserole. I think there's enough left to feed you both. But first a very grubby little girl needs to wash her hands and face. Come into the bathroom and I'll take care of that." She took Maddie's hand and led her to the back of the building. Willis hated to let

Maddie out of his sight, but he knew she was safe with Eva. She always would be.

Fortunately, someone had stocked washcloths and towels on the shelves in the washroom. Eva turned on the faucet. There wasn't hot water, but cold water would work just as well. She wiped Maddie's face and then her hands. She checked the child's arms and legs, finding a few scrapes and bruises but nothing serious. It could've turned out so much worse. She hugged Maddie and kissed the top of her head. "*Gott* was looking after you, little one. I will be forever grateful."

Maddie reached up to touch Eva's cheek. "Are you crying?"

"They are tears of joy." She brushed them away and straightened.

Dinah and the bishop's wife came in as Eva was drying Maddie's hands. Constance Schultz smiled at the child. "You had quite an adventure today, didn't you?"

"It wasn't much fun. I don't think I'll do it again."

Dinah and Constance laughed. Constance pulled a black *kapp* from the pocket of her apron. "I believe this belongs to you."

Maddie tipped her head to the side. "How did you get my *kapp*?"

"Michael Shetler gave it to my husband to keep for you. I'm afraid it has a tear in it."

Maddie poked her finger through the hole in the top of the bonnet. "Aw, this is my last one. Now what do I do? Willis doesn't know how to sew."

"Don't worry about it. I can make you another one," Eva said.

Constance folded her arms over her chest. "That's very nice of your teacher, isn't it?"

Maddie nodded solemnly.

Constance looked at Dinah. "What Willis Gingrich needs is a wife to take care of the *kinder*. One who can cook and sew for all of them. We may have to find him one."

Dinah chuckled. "It's been a while since I've done any matchmaking, but I don't think I've forgotten how."

Maddie gave her a puzzled look. "What is matchmaking?"

"A matchmaker is a person who helps a single fellow, or a single woman, find someone to marry," Eva said.

"Oh." Maddie cocked her head to the side.

Eva was amused by the concentration on Maddie's face. "I think your hands are clean enough. I'll fix you something to eat now."

Eva held Maddie's hand as they walked across the schoolroom. Maddie stopped and looked up at Eva. "Can anyone be a matchmaker?"

"I suppose."

"Could you be a matchmaker?"

"I could but I think I would make a much better teacher."

"Couldn't you do both?"

"I guess but I've never had the opportunity to try."

Maddie darted away from Eva and ran straight to her brothers. "Guess what?"

Willis held a plate of food in one hand and a cup of coffee in the other. Harley and Otto were both eating chicken drumsticks.

"What?" Otto asked.

"The bishop's wife, Dinah Lapp and Eva are going

to help Willis find a wife. Someone who can cook and sew and look after us."

Eva closed her eyes for a second. "That's not exactly what was said." When she opened them she met Willis's thunderous expression.

"What exactly was said about finding me a wife?" Willis ground out each word as if he were chewing glass.

Chapter Eight

Willis glared at Eva. He had just endured the worst five hours of his life and now she was plotting to find him a wife. "I thought we had this conversation once."

"Dinah and Constance mentioned matchmaking in passing. They only want to help."

"And you didn't set them straight?"

"Lower your voice, Willis. People are staring. It's nothing to get upset about."

"Come outside with me." He started to walk away. He glanced back. She had her arms crossed over her chest and a stubborn expression on her face. He was almost too tired to argue with her, but he couldn't let this pass.

He walked back and leaned close to her ear. "Please step outside with me, Eva. I would like to continue this discussion."

"I'm not sure I want to."

"You started it."

"Very well." She stomped out the door. He glanced around the room. Everyone was looking their way, but he didn't care. He caught Harley's gaze. "I'll be back in a few minutes. All of you stay right here. Understood?"

The children nodded, their eyes wide at his harsh tone. He managed a reassuring half smile. "Finish your meal. We'll go home soon."

Outside he waited until his eyes adjusted to the dark. He spied Eva waiting for him on the swing set. He took a deep breath and forced himself to calm down. He walked over to her and sat in the swing beside her. Neither of them spoke for several minutes as he gathered his thoughts. He saw the searchers leaving in small groups, some in buggies and some in cars. Gratitude for the kindness of friends and strangers alike slipped across his mind, blowing away his anger.

He tried to read Eva's face, but the moon had slipped behind a passing cloud and it was too dark for him to read her expression. "I think I have already mentioned that I'm not looking for a wife. I'm certainly not going to marry just to provide my siblings with a cook, a babysitter and a housekeeper."

"I understand that. Constance and Dinah reached the conclusion that you needed a wife without a word from me. I wasn't sure how to respond so I kept quiet. Maddie was intrigued and excited by the idea. You know how she is."

He blew out a deep breath. "*Ja*, I know how she can be. So how do I stop Constance and Dinah from matchmaking on my behalf?"

"I have no idea. Meet some nice women but don't marry any of them," she snapped.

He chuckled at her prickly attitude. He leaned his head back and stared at the stars twinkling between the clouds drifting overhead. How had his life become so complicated so quickly? "I wish school started to-morrow instead of in two weeks. I'm never going to get caught up on my work at this rate."

"I can offer a suggestion but only if you promise not to bite my head off."

"I'm listening."

"I will look after Maddie and the boys for you during the day."

"I appreciate the offer but you have your own work to get done." He backed up, lifted his feet off the ground and swung forward.

"You will be helping me out in a way. I can ease into teaching gradually. I'll have three students instead of fifteen. I can give Otto some extra attention before school starts so he isn't as far behind, as well."

Willis braked to a stop. "What do you mean? How is Otto behind?"

She twisted sideways to look at him. "So much has happened today that I forgot to speak to you about Otto's poor writing. I had Dinah and Mrs. Kenworthy, one of the *Englisch* schoolteachers, come to look at the sentences he had done on the blackboard."

"Why would you do that?"

"Because I was troubled by what I saw but I wasn't sure there was a problem. They agreed that his ability to write is not at a fifth grade level. Harley says their mother helped Otto with his reading a lot but he hasn't mastered it. I was going to offer to tutor him."

Willis surged to his feet and walked a few steps away. "So he doesn't read well. So what? A lot of fellows have trouble reading. Once he's out of school it won't matter."

"Willis, reading does matter!"

Her shock made him see how far apart they really were. She was a woman who clutched a book of poetry to her chest the way a mother might cuddle a babe and spoke of it in loving terms. To her, someone who couldn't read was behind. Slower. A problem. She was too kind to call someone *stupid* but she thought it just the same. The whole time they had been searching for Maddie he thought of Eva as an equal, working as hard as he had to find his sister. He'd been comforted by her steadfast faith. He had forgotten just how unequal he would be in her eyes if she learned his secret.

He scuffed the dirt with his boot. "It's important to you, maybe. You like books and poems and writing letters. I don't have time for that stuff."

"Surely you have time for reading the Bible to the children at night? Seeing you seek the wisdom and comfort of God's Word teaches them to find it for themselves."

"Teaching our faith is the duty of the bishop and his ministers. I appreciate all you did today, Eva. Maddie and the boys have learned their lesson and so have I. I won't need your help or anyone else's to look after them. We'll take care of each other. It's been a long day. I'm taking the children home."

He half expected her to continue the argument, but she rose from the swing. "I'll go in with you to tell Maddie good-night," she said quietly. He glanced her way. The clouds parted, allowing the moonlight to bathe her in a soft glow. She was studying him with a curious expression on her face.

He wished he could read her mind. Which was a good joke. Even if she wrote out what she was thinking he wouldn't be able to understand it.

* * *

The following day was the off Sunday, and Eva was glad to stay in. She was too tired and sore from dozens of scratches on her arms and legs to visit with the Lapp family. She didn't see Willis except at a distance for the next three days. The children she saw playing together outside the smithy but they didn't come over to the school. Maddie waved once, but Otto pulled her hand down and shook his head. Maddie stuck her tongue out at him and ran into the house. Later Eva heard Harley shouting, "It's your turn to watch her, Otto. I'm leaving."

It seemed things weren't running smoothly at the Gingrich house.

Eva was only mildly surprised to find Willis on her front porch late Wednesday morning. She opened the screen door, unable to believe how happy she was to see him. She tried not to show it. "Hello, Willis. What brings you here today?"

"I have to pick up some iron bars in town. I thought you might like to ride along with the children and me and see some different parts of the North Country."

She sensed there was more to his sudden invitation than he was letting on. Her curiosity got the better of her. "I would like that."

"*Goot.* I'll bring up the wagon." His look of relief almost made her laugh.

Maddie was sitting on the wagon seat when he pulled up in front of Eva's house. The boys were sitting on the floor of the wagon behind the bench seat. Maddie grinned from ear to ear. "Hi, Teacher. We're going to town. I'm so glad you can come with us. Bubble has been asking to see you for days."

"That's no lie," Otto said drily from his place behind her.

Maddie nodded. "Yep, Bubble has been asking day and night if we could visit you. Willis is tired of her talking about it."

Willis leaned across Maddie and held out his hand to help Eva up. She cocked an eyebrow as she gazed at his embarrassed expression. "Is that so?"

"Yep, it's so," Maddie continued as she scooted over to make room for Eva. "He's going to buy some material so I can have a new dress and a new *kapp*, too."

"Has your brother learned to sew?" Eva had trouble keeping a straight face.

"I don't know." Maddie turned to look at Willis. "Can you?"

"*Nee*, but I thought I might be able to bribe someone I know into doing it with a nice lunch in town."

"That's rather presumptuous of you, isn't it?" Eva wasn't about to let him off the hook so easily.

"Desperate times call for desperate measures," he muttered.

Maddie lifted the front of her apron. "Harley sewed this patch on my dress." The stitches were uneven, and the fabric was puckered.

"I told you not to tell anyone." Harley's annoyed voice caused Eva to look back at him.

"It's nothing to be ashamed of, Harley," she said softly. "Your sister is blessed to have such a caring brother."

"Willis made me do it." Clearly, Harley hadn't enjoyed the task.

"Otto fixed supper last night," Maddie said with a

wide smile. "He made grilled cheese sandwiches. Bubble doesn't like burnt cheese and bread."

"Bubble can cook her own supper from now on," Otto shouted.

"You made her cry." Maddie's lower lip trembled as she cuddled her imaginary friend.

"She's not real," Harley snapped.

"Enough!" Willis's commanding tone silenced everyone.

Eva cleared her throat. "It sounds like you have had a trying few days, Mr. Gingrich."

Maddie leaned closer to Eva. "He broke his best hammer, too," she whispered. "Did you matchmake him a wife yet?"

"Nee," Eva whispered back. "Willis doesn't want a wife."

"He needs one," Harley muttered.

"I can turn this wagon around and take you all home," Willis threatened, proving he had heard Harley.

Maddie looked appalled. "But then Bubble won't get to eat ice cream."

Willis fixed his gaze on Eva. "Is the offer to watch these darling children during the day still open?"

Maddie pressed her hands together as she looked at Eva. "Please, please, please."

"Ja, my offer is still open."

"Does that include lunches?" Otto asked hopefully.

"I think I can manage to feed you, as well."

"Wunderbar!" The relief in Otto's tone made Eva laugh.

Willis gave her a wry smile. "I think I may owe you my life. Their joy at finding their lost sister has worn off."

"Because she is back to being an annoying pest," Otto said.

Maddie rounded on him. "I'm not a pest. You just don't like playing with Bubble. You wanted her to stay lost."

Eva slipped her arms around Maddie. "We are all glad you didn't stay lost. Right, boys? They cried when they couldn't find you."

"They did?" Maddie wasn't sure she believed that.

"They did," Willis assured her. "Your brothers love you. You should try being nicer to them. They don't have to play with you all day. They have things they like to do."

Maddie pressed her head against Eva's side. "But I don't like being alone. What if the bear comes to get me?" Her voice broke on a sob.

Eva met Willis's astonished gaze. She could see this was the first time he had heard about Maddie's new fear.

Harley stood up and tugged on the ribbon of Maddie's *kapp*. "No bear will come within a mile of our place."

"That's right," Willis said. "They don't like fire, and I always have a fire going in the smithy."

Maddie looked up at Eva. "Is that true?"

Eva nodded. "That is true. I read it in a book once. Bears won't come near a fire."

It took them a while to restore Maddie's good humor, but she was happily talking about starting school in a new dress by the time they reached the nearby town of Fort Craig. The foundry was located on the north end beside the river.

Eva and the children waited in the wagon while Willis purchased his iron bars. He spent the next twenty minutes loading them with Harley and Otto's help.

Willis climbed up to the wagon seat when they were done. The boys sat on the sideboards of the back. Willis looked at Eva. "Are you hungry? There's a nice restaurant in town if you'd like to try it? It's buffet style."

"I'm always happy to sample someone else's cooking."

They drove the wagon to an empty lot and left the horses there while they walked to the restaurant. It was busy inside, but the waitress was able to seat them at a small table in the back corner. The room was cozy with red-and-white-checked tablecloths and lace curtains on the windows.

Most of the patrons were *Englisch* families enjoying an afternoon out. Some of them gawked at Eva and Willis in their plain clothing.

Willis followed Eva as she filled her plate and helped Maddie make her choices. After Eva sat down, Willis and the boys returned with two heaping plates of food each.

Eva looked at them in amazement. "Can you really eat all that?"

"This will be a good start," Harley declared.

Otto licked his lips. "Did you see the dessert bar? I'm hankering for a big piece of that lemon cake."

"The owner of this place is going to lose money on us," Eva said.

Willis gestured toward Eva's plate. "You and Maddie eat like birds. We balance each other."

Eva treasured the warmth spilling through her veins as he smiled at her. They did balance each other in many ways. She dropped her gaze to her hands folded on the table. She had to be careful or she would find herself in trouble. Sitting with his family didn't make her a part of his family. She already liked Willis and the children way too much. He wasn't interested in finding a wife, and she had a job to do. That was what she needed to focus on.

Willis bowed his head and began silently reciting the *Gebet Nach Dem Essen*, the Prayer Before Meals.

O Lord God, heavenly Father, bless us and these Thy gifts, which we accept from Thy tender goodness. Give us food and drink also for our souls unto life eternal, that we may share at Thy heavenly table, through Jesus Christ. Amen.

He followed it with the Lord's Prayer, also prayed silently, knowing he had much to be thankful for.

He raised his head to signal the end of the prayer for Eva and the kids. The boys began eating like they would never see food again.

Eva pressed a hand to her lips to stifle a smile.

Willis cleared his throat. "You'll founder if you don't slow down."

Otto shot him a questioning look. "I thought only horses could founder from eating too much grain?"

Willis rolled his eyes. "Don't put it to the test. Slow down and enjoy your food."

"It smells like our house used to before *Mamm* died," Harley said. Otto and Maddie nodded.

The aroma of warm bread and pot roast filled the air. Willis thought back to the food his stepmother used to make. Roast beef, roast pork, fried chicken and potatoes, schnitzel with sauerkraut, all served piping hot from her stove, with fresh bread smeared with butter and bowls of vegetables from her garden. He never gave a thought to how much work she had done in making those meals until he had tried to feed his siblings three times a day. A few evenings he had caught the same delicious aromas drifting from Eva's place. Her house smelled like a home should. The children were going to enjoy eating at her place.

The thought brought him back to why she was here with him. "I can't pay you much for watching the children. You'll have to wait until after the potato harvest for any kind of payment, I'm afraid."

She waved aside his suggestion. "I refuse to take money. I have already told you having the children will benefit me."

"All right. When shall I bring them over?"

"First thing in the morning?"

"Agreed."

The rest of the meal passed pleasantly. When they finished, they crossed the street to the fabric store where Eva picked out a soft green cotton for Maddie's new dress and a yard of white material to make her new *kapps*. Willis didn't mind the expense. Seeing Eva's enjoyment while shopping with his sister and Maddie's bright smile was worth the cost.

Back at the wagon he climbed aboard and stowed the packages before reaching down to help Eva up. A sizzle of awareness spread through him as his hand engulfed her slender fingers. The desire to pull her closer shocked him. Her gaze flashed to his. Her green eyes widened. Was she feeling the same sensation? Her fingers were so delicate. Her skin was soft and smooth, not calloused like his. It was a pointed reminder of just how different they were.

It was something he shouldn't forget. Her world was filled with books, poetry and beautiful words to describe the world and the people in it. His world was hot glowing charcoal, heat, smoke and the deafening ring of a hammer striking iron. There was nothing soft or gentle about it.

She stepped up quickly and sat down, pulling her hand away from him. There was something about Eva that left him constantly off balance. He rubbed his palm on his pant leg, determined to erase the feelings from his mind, too. The sooner he got back to his smoldering pit, the sooner he could forget about the quiet magnetism that seemed to draw him toward her.

The children were quiet for a change on the way home. He glanced toward Eva a few times, but she seemed more interested in the scenery than having a conversation. It was just as well. He had no idea what to say to her. He dropped her off at her house and guided the horses to the back of his smithy. Harley stayed to help him unload while Otto and Maddie headed to the house.

Otto came back a few moments later with a piece of paper in his hand. He held it out to Willis. "Someone left this on our door."

Willis pulled another length of iron from the wagon bed to hide his shaking hands as his heart began racing. "Read it."

"It's for you." Otto waved it as if Willis couldn't see he held it.

"I've got to get this unloaded. Is it important?"

"I don't want to read your stuff. You take it."

Harley tossed his length of pipe on the pile, snatched the message from Otto and scanned it. "It's from Bishop

Schultz. He says he'll be back to talk to you tomorrow at noon."

Willis let out the breath he'd been holding. "Does he say what about?"

"Nope."

"Danki." He began unloading his iron with renewed vigor. His secret was safe for now. He glanced up and found Harley watching him with an odd expression on his face. Willis swallowed hard. How much longer would it be before one of his brothers learned the truth? He cringed at the thought. What would they think of him then? What would Eva think of him?

The following morning Otto and Maddie tried to hurry out of the house before breakfast, but Willis stopped them at the door. He glanced at the empty wire egg basket on the counter. "Maddie, did you do your chores this morning?"

She looked up at him with wide, innocent eyes. "Not yet."

He frowned at Otto. "Have you fed the chickens and geese?"

"I thought I'd do it after breakfast."

"No one is going to Eva's house until their chores are finished. I will have breakfast ready for you by then."

Maddie frowned. "But Eva might have something better than you make."

"What's wrong with my oatmeal?"

"Nothing," Otto said. "If you like oatmeal."

Willis stifled a grin. He was getting tired of oatmeal, too, but it was a good, hot meal that would last a fella until noon or later. Eva was willing to make their lunches. He wasn't going to test her patience by sending the kids over for breakfast, too. He sent them on their way a short time later. Harley was the only one who finished his bowl of cereal.

Willis managed to catch up on some of his back-logged orders for potato-digging parts and cultivator shovels before the bishop showed up in his buggy. He wiped his hands on a rag. "Welcome, Bishop. What can I do for you today?"

Bishop Schultz glanced around. "Where are your brothers and sister?"

"Eva is keeping an eye on them today. Why?"

"The children are why I'm here. After Maddie went missing, several of the women in the church have expressed concerns about your ability to care for them."

Harley was reading in Eva's sitting room while Maddie and Otto were decorating sugar cookies in the kitchen when she heard someone at her door. She opened it and saw Willis with both arms braced on either side of the door and a fierce scowl on his face. "Were you in on this?"

She leaned back. "In on what?"

"On the bishop's visit to my home today."

She could see he was angry. She stepped out on the porch, forcing him to let her pass, and closed the door. "Willis, I don't know what you are talking about."

"The bishop wanted me to know that some of the women in the community are worried that I'm not raising my siblings right."

She slapped a hand to her chest. "I never said anything of the sort to the bishop or anyone else. I think you're trying hard to replace their mother and father. It can't be easy for you, but you're doing okay."

He raked a hand through his hair. "You're wrong

there. I know I'm doing a lousy job. I never expected to have the children living with me."

"What exactly did the bishop say?"

Willis shot a sour glance her way. "He suggested I find a wife."

"Oh. I'm well aware of your aversion to matrimony."

"My what?"

She waved one hand. "Aversion. It means you can't stand the idea."

"Why didn't you just say that? Why do you have to use big words?"

She folded her arms across her middle. "Because I like the sound of them. Words are the decorations of life. Good words are like frosting on a cake. Exemplify. Emancipate. Enlighten. They sound magnificent because they are magnificent."

"Do you even know what they mean?"

"Of course I do, but I digress, which means I got off the subject."

"I'm not completely ignorant."

She took a step closer and gazed intently into his eyes. "I never thought that for a minute. This will blow over when school starts and the children are occupied all day. The good ladies of the church will find a new mission."

"Maybe they are right. Maybe the kids would be better off with someone else."

"You can't mean that."

"Maybe I do." He turned and walked away. Eva longed to call him back, but she knew he had to decide what was best for his family by himself.

She went back into the kitchen and saw Harley had joined the younger children there. He was writing on a piece of paper while the other two looked on. "Is this all?" he asked them.

Maddie and Otto nodded. Harley handed them the paper. "I think it's a dumb idea but here it is."

Maddie grinned as Eva walked in. "Teacher, we have a list for you."

Eva put aside her concern for Willis. "A list for what?"

"To help you matchmake a nice wife for Willis."

Eva narrowed her eyes and hooked her thumb toward the door. "Did you hear us talking outside?"

They all shook their heads. Eva took a seat at the table. "What's on the list?"

"She has to be pretty," Harley said. "That's my only suggestion."

"And not old," Otto added.

Eva tipped her head to the side. "What do you consider old?"

The kids exchanged looks. "A hundred," Maddie offered.

"That's really old," Harley said. "Maybe fifty. Like you."

Eva bit down on her upper lip. "Under fifty. What else, Harley?"

"That was my only suggestion. Ask them."

"Well?" She looked at Maddie and Otto.

Maddie held the list out like she was reading it. "She has to be a good cook. She has to smell nice. She has to have a dog. What else did we say, Harley?"

"She needs to sew and not make us take too many baths," Otto finished.

Eva took the list from Maddie. "This is a tall order. It may take me a while to matchmake someone with all these qualifications. What happens if Willis doesn't like the woman I find?"

Maddie scrunched her face in deep thought. She brightened suddenly. "We could get our own dog."

Eva folded the list and put it in her apron pocket. "Let's not tell Willis about this. He has a lot on his mind today." Someday she would share the note with him and they would both laugh about it. Now wasn't that time.

Harley came into the barn as Willis was finishing feeding and grooming the horses that evening. He let himself out of Dodger's stall. "Where have you been?"

"The Arnett place."

Willis hung up his brush and currycomb. "What are you doing over there every day?"

"Chores mostly. Lilly always has a list of things for me to do."

"You've been gone so much I was beginning to think you had a girlfriend."

Harley blushed bright red. "I don't and I don't want one."

Willis snatched off his brother's hat and ruffled his hair. "*Goot.* You're growing up too fast as it is."

"I didn't get much choice in the matter."

"No, you didn't." Willis slipped his arm around his brother's shoulders. Otto and Maddie came out of the house. Willis gestured for them to come over. They gathered in front of him. Maybe the children would be better off with someone else. He had to at least consider the possibility.

He could give them the choice. "The bishop came to see me today."

"What did he want?" Otto asked.

"He's concerned that I'm not raising the three of you properly. What do you think?"

Harley hooked his thumbs in his suspenders and stared at the ground. "You're doing okay."

"All that praise will go to my head." Willis bent sideways to see his brother's face. "How about the truth?"

Harley shrugged. "There are things you could improve."

"Enlighten me," Willis said, choosing one of Eva's words. He sat down on a bale of hay beside the barn door.

"I guess we want to feel like a family again. We can take on more chores. We aren't babies." Harley's voice trailed away.

Willis looked around at three unhappy faces. "The bishop could find you another family to live with if that's what you want." He barely got the words out of his tight throat.

Otto glared at him. "Is that what you want?"

Willis wanted his old life back, didn't he? Where he didn't have to be concerned about anyone but himself. Where he was never a disappointment to anyone else. He cleared his throat. "I love you. I want what's best for you."

Maddie climbed onto the bale beside him and rested her head against his arm. "Bubble doesn't want to live anywhere else."

Harley glanced at Otto. "Neither do we."

"I miss the things *Mamm* and *Daed* used to do with us," Maddie said.

"What things?" Willis asked.

"*Mamm* used to read us Bible stories at night. And

she used to tuck me in real tight. You don't tuck very well."

"I can learn to do better. Why haven't you said anything before?"

They looked at each other. Maddie sighed deeply. "I was scared you wouldn't like me and you might send me away."

He put his arm around her. "Nope. Not going to happen. I'm not sending Otto away. I'm not sending Harley away and I'm not sending Bubble or you away. You are my family and you can stay with me until you have families of your own. Okay?"

They all nodded and smiled. Willis swallowed the lump in his throat. "Otto, you're in charge of Dodger, my buggy horse and the draft horses. Feed them and make sure they have water. Keep them groomed, keep their stalls clean and make sure Dodger gets plenty of exercise. We don't want him to act up when the teacher is driving him."

"Can I drive him?" Otto asked hopefully.

"Okay. You're old enough to handle the reins. Maddie, you will feed the chickens and geese every morning and gather the eggs. Plus, you will sweep the kitchen every day after breakfast. Got it?"

She nodded. "Got it."

Willis looked at Harley. Maybe this was the time he should confess how dimwitted he was but his insecurity ran deep down into his bones. "Harley, I'm putting you in charge of bringing in the mail, reading it and letting me know what things are important."

"Eva needs our enrollment forms filled out," Harley said. "I can do that."

"I almost forgot about those forms. It would be great if you could do that for me." He wanted to hug the boy.

"It will be up to you to find stories and prayers to read to us in the evening. Eva has lots of books. She's offered to loan us some and I think we should take her up on that."

Maddie's eyes lit up. "Oh, do you think she has *Rebecca of Sunnybrook Farm*?"

"I'm not sure. You should ask her. Eva also needs some help learning to be a teacher. She's never done it before. She would like you, Maddie, and you, Otto, to be her first students."

Otto scowled. "I don't want to go to school. School is stupid."

"I felt that way about school when I was your age and my opinion has never changed, but I didn't have a teacher as nice as Eva. I think you should give her a chance, Otto."

The boy stared at his bare feet and drew a circle with his big toe in the dirt. "I'll go but I won't like it."

Maddie got off the bale and took Otto's hand. "She can make it fun. You'll see."

Willis stood up. "All right, this family meeting is officially over. I think we should have a family meeting every week to make sure we're on the right track. Bishop Schultz is worried that I can't take care of you. So I think we're going to have to take care of each other. We're going to be a family team."

Harley grinned and held out his fist. "This is how the team does it. Everybody put your hand in." Maddie had to stand on the bale, but they all stacked their hands on top of each other's.

"Go, Gingrich team," Harley declared. The boys

cheered as they tossed their hands in the air. Maddie jumped up and down, clapping her hands.

Willis was struck by the notion that there was one set of hands missing. Eva should've been in on this. She wasn't a member of the family but she was becoming important to him and to the children. And that scared him. He'd never felt this way about any woman, not even the one who hurt him the most.

Chapter Nine

Eva was disappointed when Willis didn't accompany the children to her home the next morning. Harley came in and handed her the enrollment forms she had been asking Willis to provide. She took them happily. Harley sat with them for a while, but he soon excused himself. He stopped before he went out the door. "I will be over at the Arnett farm today if you need me."

"*Danki*, Harley. Has your brother written to your old school asking them to send your records here?"

"I don't think so. Can't you do it?"

"I reckon I had better if I'm to get them before the start of classes." It was a simple thing she could do to help Willis.

"I will need your former teacher's name and the school address. Do you know it?"

"Sure." He supplied the information and she wrote it down.

"Where is Willis today?" She tried not to sound too curious about him.

"He's gone to a farm sale hoping to pick up some

scrap metal and another anvil. He said he would be home by five o'clock."

So she wouldn't see him until later. Hiding her disappointment Eva stared at the two children watching her. Maddie was all smiles. The dour look on Otto's face didn't bode well for the day. "Otto, I will have you start by sweeping out the classroom and making sure all the desks are clean and lined up. Maddie, I'm going to need you to help me make cookies."

"Will they be snickerdoodles?"

"I think I have the ingredients for some. Otto, what kind of cookie do you like?" She needed to engage with the boy on some level. If she couldn't break through his barrier of resistance the school year was going to be difficult.

"Oatmeal chocolate chip," he muttered.

"Two of my favorites mixed together. Good choice. The broom and dust rags are in the coat closet at the school. I'll be over later if you need any help."

His eyes snapped with anger. "I'm not so dumb that I need help sweeping the floor."

"Of course, you aren't. That isn't what I said and certainly not what I meant."

He stomped out of the house without looking back, letting the screen door slam behind him.

Maddie shook her head. "He hates it when people treat him like he's slow."

"I wasn't trying to hurt his feelings. I was only offering to help."

"I know. *Daed* used to say Otto had a chip on his shoulder and that's why he gets mad but I never see one."

Why was the boy so prickly? She didn't know and

she wasn't sure how to find out. She could only hope things improved before he started school.

Eva was finishing up in her kitchen after making a batch of blackberry jam from the bush out back when she saw a white car turn into her drive. Two women got out. They turned out to be the county social worker and a public health nurse. They left Eva papers showing what they suggested should be taught regarding health and science and gave her a schedule for vision and hearing tests in October. Working with local health and welfare people was another part of her teaching position she hadn't given much thought about. She would have to visit with the school board and learn how much of what the outsiders offered the community would accept.

They left after a brief visit and Eva was about to go across to the school when a second car pulled into her drive. This time an Amish fellow got out. She couldn't see his face but there was something familiar about him. He pulled a suitcase out of the trunk. When he turned to look at her she gave a squeal of delight and raced out the door and flew to hug him. "Danny. What are you doing here? Oh, it's so good to see you."

"It's good to see you, too, Eva." He turned to inspect the school. "So this is where you'll be spending your days."

"*Ja*, isn't it lovely? It's brand-new and so is the house. In a few days the community is holding a frolic to add a barn and corrals. I can hardly believe how fortunate I am to have landed here. How long are you staying?"

"A week or so, I think. Gene wanted to make sure you were getting along up here since the only thing you have written us about is the need for your books."

She laughed "If I wrote about everything that has

happened since I arrived in New Covenant, I would have my own book to be published."

His eyebrows shot up. "I like a good story. Maybe you should fill me in."

She took his arm and led him toward the house. "Come into my lovely little house and I will make us both some *kaffi*. I must warn you I have company. The children from across the street are staying with me during the day. Harley is thirteen, Otto is eleven and Maddie is six. I should warn you that Maddie has an imaginary friend named Bubble so please be kind to her."

"When have you known me to be anything else?"

"Never. That makes me wonder how you inherited all the kindness in the family and Gene inherited all the sour. How is he? I never thought I would say this but I have missed him and his grumpy looks. I even miss Corinne and her litany of aches and pains."

"Gene is fine, but some things have changed. I'll tell you about it over that coffee."

Eva held open the screen door. A single bark alerted her to the fact that Sadie was on her way to make a visit. She glanced inside the house and saw Maddie coloring at the kitchen table. "Maddie, Sadie is coming."

Maddie's eyes grew wide with joy. "She is? Can I go outside and play with her?"

"You may go outside and play with her but don't stray from the yard."

Maddie stopped in the doorway when she saw Danny standing behind Eva. "Who are you?"

Eva held a hand toward her brother. "Maddie, this is my brother Danny who has come for a visit."

"I'm Maddie Gingrich and this is my friend Bubble."

Maddie put an arm over the shoulder of her imaginary friend.

Eva waited eagerly for Danny's reaction. He glanced at her and then took his hat off. "Pleased to meet you, Maddie and Bubble."

Maddie grinned. "We're going to go play with Sadie. She kept the bear from eating us."

His eyebrows shot up. "Did you say a bear?"

"*Ja.* Come on, Bubble." Maddie raced down the steps of Eva's porch and out to see Sadie. The dog held a thick stick in her mouth. She gave it to Maddie who promptly threw it for the happy retriever.

"The bear was imaginary, too, right?" Danny asked.

Eva covered her mouth with her hand and giggled as she shook her head. "*Nee*, it was quite real. Come in and sit down. I'll tell you the whole tale while I brew you some stout *kaffi*."

After she had a pot fixed for the two of them and while it perked she recounted her adventures in New Covenant.

"All this took place in a week?" He shook his head in disbelief.

"I dread to think what the next month will bring."

"I hope you don't find yourself with a bear in the classroom."

"Fortunately, Sadie comes to the school with the children so I don't think we'll have a problem."

Eva poured them both coffee when it was finished and spread her fresh jam on several pieces of homemade bread. She sat across from her brother, took a sip from her mug and then put it down. "So. Why are you really here, Danny? It's only a little over a week since I left."

"Gene thought perhaps you would be ready to return by now."

"Oh, he did? He has very little confidence in me. So I assume he sent you to escort me home, is that it?"

Danny leaned back in his chair and ran his fingers through his thick black hair. "In a manner of speaking, but that's not why I came."

She leaned back with her arms crossed over her chest. "Do tell."

"I wanted to see for myself if you were happy here. Are you?"

Eva heard footsteps on her porch. She looked out and saw Willis in the doorway. A jolt of happiness sent her pulse racing. She smiled at Willis. "*Ja*, Danny, I am happy here. Come in, Willis. I have fresh coffee and some jam to send home with you. This is my brother Danny who surprised me with an unannounced visit."

Willis stepped inside, and the two men nodded to each other. "We are blessed to have your sister as our new teacher. I won't interrupt your reunion. I'm home from my errand. I'll take the *kinder* off your hands. Thanks for watching them. I see Maddie playing with Sadie. Where is Otto?"

"He's doing some cleaning for me inside the school."

"Has he been trouble for you?"

"Not a bit." She grabbed an unopened jar of jam and pressed it into his hands. "For you and the *kinder* to enjoy."

Willis shot a glance at her brother and mumbled his thanks. He walked to the edge of the porch and shouted for Maddie and Otto. Maddie came running with Sadie beside her. A few moments later Otto appeared at the schoolhouse door. Willis gestured for him to come on.

Otto sauntered down the steps, crossed the lawn and paused in front of his brother.

Willis smiled at the boy. "I brought pizza from town for our lunch. How does that sound?"

Maddie jumped up and down. "Yea, I love pizza. Let's go."

Willis tipped his hat toward Eva. "Thanks again."

Otto shifted his weight from one foot to the other and folded his arms tightly over his chest. "I think Teacher will want to check my work before I leave."

She shook her head. "Nope. If you did your best, then I can't ask for anything more."

He seemed surprised by her answer but didn't say anything. He took off running to catch up with Willis and Maddie. Eva waited hoping Willis would look back. He did. She waved and called out, "See you tomorrow."

He lifted his hand in a brief salute. She was still grinning as she turned back to Danny. "Where were we?"

"You were telling me that you're happy here. I can see that for myself. It didn't take you long to meet the neighbor. Seems like a nice guy."

"He is. The children are his half brothers and sister. He took them in after their parents died. It hasn't been an easy adjustment for him or for the children. I've been doing what I can to help him. As a good neighbor."

"As a neighbor. I see." Danny's grin widened with the hint of humor in his voice.

She wasn't sure what he thought was funny. "Not to change the subject but why are you here?"

"I hate to be the bearer of bad news but Corinne's mother suffered a stroke two days after you left."

"I'm sorry to hear that." Unlike Corinne, her mother was a kind and hardworking woman.

"She's still in the hospital and very weak. The doctors say she'll need a lot rehabilitation, but she should be able to come home at some point. Unfortunately, she has lost the use of her right side. Her husband isn't going to be able to take care of her alone. Corinne wants them to move into the *daadihaus* on our farm."

"That should make it much easier for Corinne to help."

"Well, that's the rub. Corinne doesn't feel she can do it by herself. Gene agrees."

Comprehension dawned and Eva's heart sank. "He wants me to come home and take care of her parents. That's why he sent you."

Eva turned away and walked to the end of the porch. She wanted to pound her hands on the railing. Her family needed her again, but she had already accepted the teaching job. She didn't want to leave New Covenant. She was making friends here even if one of them was imaginary. She bit down on her thumbnail as she wrestled with her conscience. What should she do?

"You don't have to make a decision today."

"Gene knows I want to do this. Why can't he get help from someone else in our family or from Corrine's?"

"Eva, you are under no obligation to return home. I think it's time Corinne stepped up and took care of them. They are her parents."

"But I'm the one with the most experience caring for the elderly." It was true. She'd had many years of practice. She could already visualize the things that would be needed.

"I don't know what to say. I know I should return but I don't feel that I can. I have made a commitment to this community. I have a house and it has been filled with furniture donated for my use. I have the loan of a horse and cart. I've even received three new *kapps* in this congregation's style. The people here have welcomed me with open arms. How can I walk out on them after everything they have done for me?"

"If you feel that strongly you should stay."

She spun around to face Danny. "Do you really think so? Is Gene adamant that I come home?" What was the right thing to do?

Danny shook his head. "He didn't insist that I bring you back."

"Yet." She supplied the missing word.

"It would be easy for me to tell you what to do, but you are going to have to decide for yourself. Either way, the woman is still in the hospital. There's no rush to make a decision. She may recover better than expected."

"But there is a rush. If I decide to leave, the school board will have to start searching for a teacher all over again. The more advance notice I can give them, the better."

She didn't want to leave. She knew exactly the kind of life that would be waiting for her at home. She would return to working in the background, caring for someone who could no longer care for themselves, reading about adventures rather than having them. If she went back to Illinois she wouldn't hear what Bubbles was up to each day. She wouldn't have a chance to help Otto or to see Willis again. The thought dragged her spirits lower. What should she do?

Danny came up behind her and placed his hands on her shoulders. "Don't worry about it, Eva. I am here simply to visit my sister and have her show me around the wild woods of Maine. Are there really bears?"

He dismissed her decision so easily. If only she could do the same. "There are and also moose. I haven't seen a moose yet, but I understand they are plentiful and can be as dangerous as a bear. If you go hiking in the woods, take bear repellent and give moose a wide berth."

"Listen to you with your backwoods lore. I will tell you one thing, Eva, I have missed your cooking. Corinne's cooking is passable. That's the kindest thing I can say about it."

"If you can't say something nice it's best not to say anything."

He chuckled. "Words of advice that Corinne never took to heart. She thinks you moved away simply to make things more difficult for her."

Eva stared at him, aghast. "Did she say that?"

"She has. More than once."

"Well, perhaps I did hope that she would take on more responsibility around the house if I wasn't there."

"Gene spoiled her at your expense. You deserve a life of your own. How many times have I told you that?"

"Often enough." She glanced across the street at the Gingrich home. "Now that I have had a taste of it, I'm not sure I can give it up."

"I like Eva a lot, don't you, Willis?" Maddie was pulling the pepperoni slices from her pizza and stacking them on the edge of her plate for Bubble. One by one, she slipped them over the edge of the table to Sadie who was lying under her chair.

"Sure, I like her."

"Bubble says if you ask her to marry you she'll say yes. I wish she could eat with us. Can I go invite her?"

"Not today. She wants to visit with her brother. What

did she say his name was?" He ignored the suggestion that he should marry Eva. She wouldn't have him even if he asked. She would want a smart husband. One who used fine words and read books.

"Her brother's name is Danny. He's nice, too. I think Sadie would like more pizza."

"Sadie has had enough. Did Eva's brother say why he was here?" It seemed odd that a family member would visit when she had been here less than two weeks. It made him wonder if something was wrong back home. He didn't want to come out and ask. He was used to minding his own business. Until Eva had arrived in New Covenant, he'd seldom given his neighbors a second thought.

Now he found it impossible to stop thinking about her. She had somehow wormed her way past the defenses he kept around his heart. He cared for Eva a great deal.

Maddie took back one slice of pepperoni and ate it. "Why do people get married?"

"Because they love each other, I reckon."

"What if someone matchmakes them together? Will they love each other then?"

He was sorry she'd ever heard the term. "A matchmaker is just a person who introduces two people in the hopes that they will fall in love. I don't think it works out all that often."

Maddie sighed. "I hope it works out for you."

Otto nudged Maddie. "You talk too much."

"I don't. I talk just enough."

Willis realized something was going on between the two of them. "What do you want to work out for me?"

"Nothing," Otto said quickly. He scowled at his sister.

Willis glanced between them. "I don't think *nothing* is the right word. What's going on?"

"We gave Eva a list of things we want your wife to have," Maddie said proudly.

Harley rolled his eyes. "Girls can't keep a secret."

Maddie stuck out her lower lip. "Nobody said it was a secret."

"It's not anymore." Otto got up and left the table, carrying a piece of pizza outside.

Willis shook his head. "I'm not going to find a wife, so it doesn't matter what you and Otto told Eva I needed."

"Okay." Maddie gave Sadie her last piece of pepperoni. "I'm done. Can I go out and play now?"

"It will be time for bed soon. Don't forget. Harley is going to read us a story tonight. Send Sadie home."

"Okay."

Harley cleared the table without being asked. Willis washed what few dishes there were. When the kitchen was clean, Willis sat down in his chair by the window. Maddie climbed onto his lap while Otto and Harley sprawled on the floor. Harley turned the pages of a book and stopped when he found what he was looking for. "This is the story *Mamm* liked to read to us. It's about Joseph and his brothers."

Willis knew the tale, but he listened to Harley read it with a new appreciation. No matter what he made in his forge it couldn't convey the message of God's love and the power of forgiveness as clearly as the words in Harley's book did. Eva understood that.

After the children were in bed Willis finished a set

of horseshoes for his draft horses at his forge. When he was done, he stepped out into the cool night air, relieved to leave his hot workplace. The moon wasn't up yet, but the sky was littered with millions of brilliant stars. His gaze was drawn to Eva's house. The light in her sitting room was on. She was still up. He was tempted to walk over and visit for a while but stopped himself before he made such a foolish mistake.

Eva's light went out as he watched. Maybe it was her brother who was restless. And what business did he have spying on her even from a distance? He was about to turn away when he saw her front door open. She came out onto the porch, drew a shawl around her shoulders and started across the lawn to the school. She didn't go inside the building; instead, she passed behind it.

Curiosity got the better of him. Where was the new teacher going this time of night? Although there hadn't been any reports of bears in the area since Maddie's adventure, it wasn't particularly safe to be wandering alone in the dark. It was still wild country. Potato farms and towns covered the floor of the valley, but the hills on either side were timber. He started walking in that direction just to make sure she got safely to wherever she was going.

When he came around the corner of the school building, he saw her sitting on the playground swings. She pushed off and began to move back and forth.

She was safe enough where she was. He should go home, but he didn't move. Why was she out here? Was something troubling her? Drawn to her almost against his will, he crossed the lawn and approached the swings.

"Good evening, Willis. Isn't it a beautiful night?" She had seen him coming. She must have eyes like a cat.

"I reckon you're right. It's a downright pretty night."

The thick trees kept the lights from the nearby town blocked. Overhead the Milky Way stretched like a glittering gauze scarf thrown down on the floor of heaven. Across the night sky the constellations looked so close a man could almost reach out and touch them. A soft breeze brought the ever-present scent of pine to him, and underneath that the odor of the potato plants that covered much of the valley.

"What are you doing out here?" he asked.

"I'm practicing how to swing." She leaned back and pumped her legs to gain height.

He chuckled as he leaned against the A-frame metal crossbar. "I didn't know swinging required practice. I thought it was like riding a bicycle. Once you learned you never forgot."

"That might be true for you, but I need to practice. I may want to impress the children with my skills."

"Somehow, I don't think that's the whole truth. I suspect you are out here because you have something on your mind."

She gave a big sigh and leaned back as far as she could. "Mr. Gingrich, you are every bit as perceptive as Bubble."

"I'm not sure if I should take that as a compliment or not." He moved to sit in the swing beside her.

"That was meant as a compliment. I do have something on my mind."

"Does it have to do with a list?"

She frowned. "A list? *Nee.* Oh, you mean the list the children gave me. I almost forgot about it. I'm surprised they told you."

"Maddie isn't good at keeping secrets. What is contained in this list?"

"I have kept it in my pocket to share with you if you'd care to read it?" she offered.

"It's too dark. Tell me what they said."

"It's a well-thought-out list of requirements for your wife-to-be."

"From Otto and Maddie? I can't wait to hear it."

"Oh, Harley added one requirement. She should be pretty."

"At least Harley has my best interest at heart. What else?"

"She has to smell nice, be a good cook and not make them take a lot of baths."

He chuckled. "That last requirement came from Otto, didn't it?"

"It did. Oh, and she shouldn't be old but fifty like me is acceptable."

"Ouch, that had to hurt."

"They are such amazing children. I haven't been bored for a minute since I met them." She sighed deeply and fell silent.

"You said you had something on your mind. Would it help to talk about it? I can listen and swing at the same time."

She giggled. "I knew you were a man of many talents when I first laid eyes on you. Next, you will tell me you can walk and chew gum."

"I've been able to do it for years. What's troubling you, Teacher? Tell ole *Onkel* Willis."

She stopped swinging and sat still. "I have a decision to make."

He waited but she didn't say anything else. He began

turning himself around until the chains were tightened. When he picked his feet up he whirled rapidly as the chains unwound.

"Don't you want to know what decision I have to make?" she asked.

"Only if you want to tell me."

"Do you know what I did before I came here?"

"I know you didn't teach school. You told me this was your first teaching job. If you want me to guess, I'll start with the A's. Were you an arrow maker?"

He heard her soft chuckle. "I lived with my brother and his wife and I took care of my grandparents. Grandmother was very frail. She was bedridden for most of the last five years."

"She was blessed to have a granddaughter willing to care for her."

"That's what everyone said. 'Isn't it wonderful that Gene and Corrine have Eva to take care of the old folks? She is such a blessing to them. What would they do without her?' When my grandparents passed away I suddenly found myself without a purpose. Do you know what that feels like?"

"I never gave it much thought. I believed my purpose was to beat hot iron into useful things."

"And a fine purpose that is."

"Is that what's troubling you? That you don't have a purpose now? What about teaching?"

"My sister-in-law's mother has had a stroke and she is going to need someone to take care of her. My brother and his wife want me to return to Illinois and be that someone."

"I see. Will you go?"

"I want to stay and teach school. Is that being self-ish?"

"What if I said that I want you to stay?"

Chapter Ten

Eva turned to stare at Willis with her heart thudding rapidly. What was he implying? That he cared for her? Or was she reading something into his statement that he didn't mean? They had only known each other a little more than a week although it felt as if she had known him longer. She wished she had gone out on more dates. Nothing she had read in her books prepared her for a moonlight conversation with a man she was beginning to care for.

"What I mean is that my brothers and sister like you and they would be upset if you left." Willis ran his words together so quickly she almost laughed. "Particularly Maddie," he added.

It was foolish to think he might have meant something else. He'd made it plain from the start that he wasn't interested in dating or marriage.

"I would miss all of you terribly if I went back to Illinois."

"Then don't go."

"Isn't it my duty to return and do as my older brother wishes? He has taken the place of my father who died when I was fifteen. I lived in his household until I came here."

"Then go back and be miserable."

"What a terrible thing to say. What makes you think I'll be miserable?"

He stood up and let the swing undulate on its own. "Because you sound like it will make you miserable to return. If your brother has truly replaced your father in your life, then he will understand that at some point you need to leave the nest. I see that you have two choices. Sit on your brother's roost and squawk about your difficulties like a chicken or take off like a dove and look for your own nesting ground. Good night, Eva."

She watched him walk away. "Good night, Willis. You've been extremely unhelpful."

"That's what friends are for," he shot back.

She smiled as she watched him cross the road and enter his home. A man she could talk to without even mentioning books. Willis was a rare fellow indeed. He was turning out to be the best friend she had never had.

She would cherish that friendship and keep her girlish emotions in check. He didn't want a romantic relationship. Nor did she. Letting him suspect she felt otherwise might destroy their wonderful camaraderie.

Maddie appeared at Eva's door the next morning just before six o'clock. She cupped her hands around her eyes and pressed her face to the screen door. "Hello? Is anybody home?"

Eva walked out of the kitchen. "My, you are here early."

"Willis is fixing oatmeal for breakfast. Bubble

doesn't like oatmeal so we came to see what you're having."

"I was about to fix some French toast. How does that sound?"

"Yummy."

Danny strolled to the entryway and held open the door. "I have got to get me one of those."

Maddie tipped her head to the side. "You want a bowl of oatmeal?"

"I want an imaginary friend who will check out what everyone is having for breakfast and take me to the best house."

Maddie shook her head. "Bubble didn't check with everybody. Just Willis and Eva."

Eva chuckled. "I love to cook for my friends. Real and imaginary. Go wash your hands, Maddie, and breakfast will be ready in a few minutes."

"I have to do something first." Maddie raced out the door toward her home.

"I don't believe I've ever met anyone quite like that child." Danny poured himself a cup of coffee from the percolator on the stove and sat at the table.

"I don't believe there is anyone quite like Maddie anywhere," Eva said as she began cracking eggs.

"You were out late last night." Danny cast a glance at her over the top of his mug.

"Was I? I guess I didn't notice what time it was."

"If it was me coming in that late you would be right in thinking I was out with a girl."

"What are you suggesting, brother dear?"

"I'm not suggesting anything because I have known you to burn the pancakes of someone who's getting on your nerves. I assume the same applies to French toast."

"It's amazing how well you understand me. Gene was never able to put two and two together."

"He ate a lot of blackened pancakes over the years. I take it that you've made up your mind."

She smiled at him. "I wish I could say that I have. I'm praying about it."

"*Wunderbar.* Now I can enjoy a few carefree days with my sister. Will you show me around your school this morning?"

"I'd be delighted to do that. We can go over after breakfast." She began whipping her eggs. "I wonder what's keeping Maddie?"

"I'll take a look." He stood and stepped out onto the porch. "You might want to put a few more eggs in that bowl. I hope you have enough bread."

"What are you talking about?"

He stepped aside and held open the door as Maddie came in followed by Willis, Otto and Harley.

"What did you need to see me about?" Willis asked, worry creasing his brow.

Eva fisted her hands on her hips and leaned down to address Maddie. "What do you think you are doing, young lady?"

"No one in my family likes oatmeal, so Bubble invited them over here to have breakfast with you."

Willis looked confused. Eva didn't blame him. He scowled at his sister. "You said Eva needed to see me right away."

Eva straightened. "Well now that you're all here you might as well stay. Please have a seat. Boys, there are extra chairs in my sitting room. Go ahead and bring them in here."

Maddie climbed into the chair she liked best. It was

the one next to where Eva normally sat. Otto sniffed the air near the stove. "That sure smells a lot better than oatmeal."

Willis glared at Eva as he pulled his hat from his head. "You shouldn't let her get away with this. One of these days her tall tales are going to get her in more trouble than she can handle."

"You're right of course, but I find her too charming to scold."

His eyes narrowed. "You're going to make me be the stern one, aren't you?"

"Indeed I am. That's what friends are for."

"I knew I'd regret that crack," he muttered. He sat on a chair and lifted Maddie to his lap. "You can't make things like this up, Maddie. Have you heard the story of the boy who cried wolf?"

She fastened her gaze on her bare toes. "Maybe."

"We've all heard it," Harley said. "It was one of *Daed*'s favorite lessons."

"It means if you tell a fib often enough people will stop believing you when you need them to listen to the truth."

Maddie raised her head and started to say something but Willis cut her off. "You can't blame this on Bubble."

Her shoulders slumped. "Okay. I'm sorry I said Eva needed to see you right away."

"I was frightened that something was wrong. You are forgiven but don't forget what I've said."

She looked at him from beneath her lashes. "But I'm not sorry we're going to have French toast for breakfast."

"Neither am I," Otto chimed in.

"Then enjoy the treat today because it will be oatmeal again tomorrow and no complaining. Understood?"

"Understood," they all replied.

He put Maddie down and looked at Danny. "My advice is to avoid having kids until your hair is already starting to turn gray because they surely speed the process."

Danny chuckled. "Good advice."

"What do you do back in Illinois?" Willis stepped to the cupboard and brought out more plates. He handed them to the boys and Maddie.

"I'm a cabinetmaker by trade. I work in a factory with about thirty other Amish fellows. I also farm with my brother."

"Is the factory Amish owned?" Willis asked.

"It's not. An *Englisch* company owns several plants across the state. We make everything from kitchen cabinets to dressers and nightstands. The *Englisch* like tacking on a label that says 'Amish Made.' They can push up the price that way."

"Danny is a supervisor in the plant near our home. He has done well for himself." Eva couldn't keep a touch of pride from creeping into her voice.

"We could use a good tradesman up here if you get tired of working for the *Englisch*. Our bishop owns a backyard shed-building business, but he is branching out into building tiny homes. I understand they are all the rage."

"I've heard that. I wish him success, but I can't see moving here to do the same thing I do back home only for less money."

"Money isn't everything," Eva said, wondering why

she hadn't thought to ask Danny to stay. It would be wonderful to have him close by.

"It can buy happiness," Maddie said with a grin.

"Money *can't* buy happiness," Otto said, shaking his head at her mistake.

"Well, if there was a puppy named Happiness, money could buy her." Maddie stuck her tongue out at her brother.

"That's not the same thing," Otto snapped.

Maddie crossed her arms and glared at him. "If I had money I'd buy you some happiness 'cause you're grumpy all the time."

"Children, be nice to each other," Willis cautioned, "or I will take you home before Eva puts food on your plates."

"Sorry, Otto." Maddie's overly contrite expression made Eva choke on a laugh.

"Me, too," Otto added, but he didn't bother trying to sound sincere.

"Put some happiness in Otto's food, please, Eva," Maddie said in a tiny voice sweeter than the maple syrup she was pouring over her toast.

Eva saw Willis struggling not to laugh. She covered her mouth with her hands in an attempt to stay quiet but lost the battle as soon as her eyes met his. A second later everyone was laughing.

Willis couldn't remember a time when he had enjoyed a meal more. Eva was unfazed by the arrival of four hungry guests first thing in the morning. She turned out piece after piece of golden-brown French toast with a smile and some funny comment. Willis even liked her brother. He was an unassuming fellow with the same honey-brown hair and gray-green eyes. It was how a family meal should feel.

Maddie enjoyed being the center of attention. She didn't mention her friend Bubble for the entire meal. Even Otto and Harley seemed to come out of their shells when Danny started discussing baseball. He occasionally attended a Chicago Cubs game and was able to discuss batting averages and the Cub's up-and-coming pitchers with the boys. Harley followed the Cubs in the newspapers and on the radio when he was able to listen to a game. The local feed store back in Maryland broadcast baseball games over their sound system for their Amish customers and in the process sold more feed.

"What are your plans for today?" Eva asked him.

"The same thing I have planned every day. Take a piece of iron, get it real hot and then bang on it until it looks like something."

"Don't let him fool you," Eva said to her brother. "He's very skilled at what he does."

"What will you do with my siblings while I'm working?" Willis asked.

"I have plenty to keep me busy at the school. I'm making folders for each of my scholars in case I need a substitute teacher for any reason. That way another teacher can quickly see each child's strengths or challenges. I was hoping that Maddie could give me a hand."

"Will I get to color again?" Maddie asked.

"Absolutely," Eva replied. "I have colored chalk you can use on the blackboard."

"*Danki.* Can we go now?"

Willis shook his head. "No one goes anywhere until the dishes are done. Eva was kind enough to cook for us. The least we can do is clean up after ourselves."

Eva gave him a sweetly grateful look. It made him realize how much more he would like to do for her. A little voice in the back of his mind told him he was becoming too attached to her, but he ignored it for now.

It only took a few minutes to get the plates washed and put away. Although Willis had work to do he tagged along as they walked to the school to hear what Danny had to say.

The first thing Eva's brother noticed was the boarded-up window. "What happened here?"

"Otto broke it," Maddie said, earning a sour look from her older brother.

Willis could tell that Otto was embarrassed, but he chose to own up to what he had done. "I hit a rock through it."

"Line drive or high fly foul ball?" Danny was trying to look serious.

"Line drive," Otto said quietly.

"On purpose or was it an accident?"

"It was sort of an accident." Otto looked up to judge Danny's reaction.

"How much did that set you back?"

"Enough. Your sister said I have to work after school for two months."

"The time will go by quickly enough."

"Danny is an expert on broken windows," Eva said, a sly grin curving her pretty lips.

"That was a long time ago, Eva." A wave of red crept up Danny's neck.

"He and some friends broke four windows in Arthur, Illinois, one night."

"Four? This many?" Maddie held up the correct number of fingers. "Did you get in trouble for that?"

"Lots and lots of trouble," Danny admitted.

Otto looked impressed. Willis thought he saw a gleam of hero worship in his young brother's eyes.

Danny must've noticed it, too. "Three of my friends came up with the idea to scare a couple of bully boys who picked on us whenever they could. They were older and they ran with a tough crowd. We didn't mean any harm but one of the rocks hit a boy in the head. He ended up in the hospital and almost lost the sight in one eye. It turned out okay, but that was the last time I followed a stupid suggestion from one of my friends. Now I think of the consequences before I act. God gave us a conscience for good reason. I would've saved everyone a lot of grief if I had listened to it back then."

Willis could see Otto mulling over Danny's comment. If even a little of it sank into the boy's head, Willis would be grateful to Eva's brother. Willis caught Eva's eye and she winked. It was exactly why she had wanted him to tell the story.

Inside the school, Eva happily showed off her desk, the supplies that had been donated and the chair that had upended her dignity the first day she arrived. Willis hung back near the outside door. Danny took a closer look at the cabinetry. He opened and closed the doors and drawers and gave Willis a thumbs-up sign. "Someone put a lot of care into this work. It should last a long time. I really like the heavy hinges and the big cabinet pulls. Are they your work, Willis?"

"Jesse Crump and Bishop Schultz made the cabinets. I did all the hardware."

"From scratch?"

"That's what I do. I hammer on a piece of hot metal until it makes something."

"Do you sell these?"

"If someone orders a set, sure."

"Do you have a few lying around?"

"I don't but I will be happy to make you some."

"Go ahead and make me a sample of a dozen different styles. I know someone who might be interested in purchasing them in bulk."

"I don't make things in bulk. I make them one at a time. Each one is a little different."

"As the owner of the company I work for would say, that's the charm of an object handmade by Amish craftsmen."

"This Amish blacksmith should get back to work," Willis said. "The potato harvest will start in a few weeks and everyone needs some sort of part made or repaired for their old potato digger. They don't appreciate the charm of my work, only that I get it done as quick as possible."

Harley, who was standing by the windows, turned to look outside. "The Fisher family is here. Do you want to get your hands dirty, Danny?"

"What do you have in mind?" Danny crossed the windows to look out. Willis followed him. Ezekiel Fisher and his four sons had rolled up in a large wagon pulled by a pair of gray draft horses.

"They are going to dig and pour the foundation for the new barn," Willis said.

"Mr. Fisher looks like he has plenty of help. If those are his sons, they are a strapping bunch. Are those two twins?"

"Triplets." Willis grinned at Danny's surprised expression. "Asher, Gabriel and Seth. Moses is the youngest. They are wheelwrights and buggy makers. The Lord has blessed us. Our community is growing rapidly."

Danny grinned. "The Lord has certainly blessed that father. I'll be happy to lend a hand today. All I need is a shovel and a pair of gloves."

"I can get that for you," Otto said.

When Otto, Harley and Danny went out the door Maddie followed them and Willis turned his attention to Eva. "I like your brother."

"I like him, too. He's a lot different than my older brother."

"So have you made your decision?" He prayed for her to stay but he wanted her to be content wherever she went.

She shook her head. "I haven't. I want to stay here. I want to become a fixture in the community of New Covenant. I had hoped to grow old and gray and have my students come back and visit me for years after they've graduated to tell me what a wonderful impact I made on their lives."

"So why not stay?"

"I'm trying to figure out *Gott*'s plan for me. I'm praying He will show me the answer I need soon."

It was hard not to admit how happy he would be if she stayed and how sad he would be if she left. "I hate the idea of losing a *goot* neighbor."

Eva chuckled. "Are you afraid the next teacher might complain about your hammering at all hours of the day and night?"

"It's rare that I work at night."

"Then she'll complain about your noisemaking while her scholars are trying to study but she still might make you some blackberry jam."

"What faults do you have that I can complain about?"

"Ha. That's a trick question if I've ever heard one. If you haven't noticed my faults, I'm certainly not going to point them out to you."

He cupped one hand over his chin. "I'll have to study on that for a while. I'm sure you have them."

"And it would be un-Christian of you to point them out. Speaking of, I know this coming Sunday is our prayer meeting, but I haven't heard where it's going to be held."

"I believe the Fishers are hosting this time."

"I hope the weather stays fine."

"If it is raining, I will take you up in my buggy."

She inclined her head, and the ribbons of her *kapp* fell forward. "Why, thank you, neighbor Willis. That's very generous."

"I didn't say for free. I will expect two jars of jam as payment."

She laughed. "One jar of jam and one loaf of fresh bread."

"It's a deal." He realized he was smiling foolishly but he didn't care.

She opened her desk drawer and pulled out a stack of papers. She looked up at him. "Don't you have to go to work?"

He did, but he didn't want to leave. It was too much fun to spend time teasing her and laughing with her. Neighbors until they were both old and gray. It didn't sound bad.

But would he be able to keep his secret from her for years or would she discover how dimwitted he really was? And then what would she think of him?

Chapter Eleven

Eva saw the smile on Willis's face fade and wondered why. Was he unhappy that she might be leaving New Covenant? Maybe she assumed he was thinking about her when he had something else on his mind.

"What's wrong, Willis?"

"Nothing. I was thinking about what your brother said. That he knows someone who might buy hardware from me.

"Do you think they will purchase some of your work?"

"I think it's worth a try to find out."

"When could you have enough pieces ready to show them?"

"Two weeks maybe."

"That's exciting. Why aren't you smiling?"

He did smile at her then. "It's a pretty big *if*."

Her heart grew lighter once more. "I think when the Good Lord inspires us we should hold on to that hope."

After Willis left the schoolhouse she went to work on making folders for each student where she could keep their information handy. That way, another teacher could quickly read up on each scholar. Once the folders were finished, Eva found herself struggling to concentrate on her lesson plan for the first week of school. More and more, her thoughts were drawn to Willis. His brothers and sister were delightful, but Willis had a stronger hold on her emotions. As much as she wanted to rationalize it away, it wasn't working. She was falling for her friend. If he didn't return her feelings then staying in New Covenant would become much more difficult.

She got up and went to check on Maddie. The little girl was busy building mud pies and cookies. Otto, Harley and Danny were helping the Fisher brothers string chalk lines in a large rectangle to make sure the building would be straight and square. Maddie got up from her play kitchen and carried several pies on a piece of bark to the Fishers. They each stopped what they were doing and made a production out of sampling her offering. They were too old to be Eva's students but none of them appeared to be married as they were all clean-shaven. Maddie was doing her best to impress them with her pie-making skills.

Eva was ready for a break by midmorning. She went back to her house to fix some lunch for herself and the Gingrich kids. She was dicing celery for chicken salad when Constance Schultz and Dinah Lapp stopped in.

"I had to see how you were getting along," Constance said as she came in.

"I'm fine. Just anxious for school to start. Everything seems to be in place. The only things I don't have are my library books but I should get them any day."

"*Goot.* I see they are working on the barn foundation. You were told we are having a frolic to raise it on Monday, right?"

"*Ja*, I heard."

"I also came to let you know we have another new family that arrived a few days ago. A young widow, her father-in-law and her daughter. She is the granddaughter of Samuel Yoder. He convinced them to settle here. Her name is Becca Beachy. I believe the child will be in the first grade. They purchased the old Kent farm on Pendleton Road."

Dinah made a sour face. "That house hasn't been lived in for years."

Constance nodded. "That's why I intend to organize a frolic for tomorrow. With all of us working we can get the house in shipshape in no time. We are spreading the word and you may do so, as well, Eva. So far Bethany, Gemma, Penelope Martin, myself and Dinah are going."

It was her first opportunity to join the women of the New Covenant congregation in a charitable endeavor and she was pleased to be asked. Taking care of each other was as important to the Amish as taking care of family members. Eva was beginning to feel she truly belonged among these North Country Amish and she gave thanks for the many gifts the Lord had given her since she arrived. Especially for the friendship Willis had extended to her. If only she could be sure she would be staying.

Bright and early the next morning, Constance turned her buggy into the schoolyard. Eva and Maddie had been waiting for her and hurried out with a basket of supplies. "Does the family know we are coming?"

"*Nee*, I thought we would make it a surprise."

The shocked expression on Becca Beachy's face

when she opened the door proved Constance right. The women all introduced themselves. Dinah gestured to Eva. "This will be your daughter's teacher when school starts."

Becca, a soft-spoken woman in her early twenties with dark hair and dark eyes extended her hand to Eva. "My daughter is looking forward to school." She smiled at Maddie who was uncharacteristically quiet. "I hope there will be other children her age attending. Will you be in school?"

Maddie didn't say a word. She had her face against Eva's skirt.

Eva patted her head. "This is Maddie Gingrich. She is also a first grader. Is your daughter here?"

Becca shook her head. "She's gone with my father-in-law to purchase some dairy cows, but they should be back soon. Please come in. I'm afraid I'm out of coffee, but I can offer you some tea."

Constance walked past Becca into the kitchen and set her basket on the table and pulled out a coffee tin. "I brought some with me. We're here to tackle the dust so let's get started, sisters."

The other women gathered around the table, each one with a basket or pail filled with cleaning supplies.

Becca pressed a hand to her cheek. "I hadn't expected this much help from the community so quickly."

Eva carried her pail to the sink and began to fill it with water. "I can start on the windows."

"I'll get this food put away," Bethany said as she opened her basket. She brought out two loaves of bread, butter and a cheese spread and finally a cherry pie with a golden lattice crust. Penelope Miller began unpacking pint jars filled with canned fruits and vegetables.

Becca shook her head. "This is overwhelming. *Danki*. I've already cleaned two bedrooms and this kitchen. If you could help me drag the mattresses outside from the other two bedrooms so I can beat the dust out of them I would appreciate it."

The house quickly became a flurry of activity as the women attacked the floors, walls and even the ceilings with pine-scented cleaner and elbow grease. Eva was amazed at how quickly the dilapidated farmhouse took on new life as grimy windows were cleaned, rubbish hauled out and the floors scrubbed and polished. Even Maddie was given the task of polishing the kitchen cabinet doors that she could reach.

The group broke for lunch at noon and decided to eat outside. Eva was shocked when Willis walked in the door with the bishop while she was fixing a plate. Willis wrinkled his nose. Eva smiled at him and chuckled. "We are about to eat outside where the scent of real pine trees isn't as overpowering as the cleaner we have been using. What are you doing here?"

Bishop Schultz smiled at her. "I asked Willis to come take a look at some machinery Mr. Beachy purchased along with this farm. He's not sure it's in working order."

Willis pushed the brim of his straw hat back with one finger. "I can usually make a part for less than what the owner would have to pay to buy one. I won't know if it's something I can fix until I get a good look at it."

"The property has been planted in potatoes and hay," the bishop added. "The church will help Mr. Beachy get his first crops harvested. I just wanted to know if we should bring our own machinery. Is your father-in-law about?" he asked Becca.

"I think that is him now." A pickup pulling a silver cattle trailer turned into the drive. An elderly Amish man who walked with a cane got out of the truck and helped a little girl out. She came running over to see her mother. "We have four cows now and *Daadi* is going to show me how to milk them."

Becca put her arm around the child. "This is my daughter, Annabeth. These nice women have come to help me clean the house and this is our new bishop. And this little girl will be in the first grade with you when school starts. Her name is Maddie."

The two girls sized each other up. Annabeth spoke first. "Do you want to come see our new cows?"

Maddie nodded and the two girls started toward the barn. "Stay away from the truck and the trailer until they have the cattle unloaded," Becca called after them.

"We will," they replied in unison.

Becca pressed a hand to her chest. "That went better than I was hoping. She hasn't had anyone her own age to play with for ages."

Willis raised both eyebrows. "I'm happy to have someone for Maddie to play with, too. She has an imaginary friend if Annabeth should mention meeting someone called Bubble."

Willis and the bishop went out to speak to Mr. Beachy.

"Tell us a little about yourself," Constance said as she handed Becca a plate with a sandwich, some grapes and wedges of cheese.

"There isn't a lot to tell. I'm from Pinecrest, Florida."

"What?" Dinah looked ready to fall over. "You moved from the beautiful beaches of Florida to the northernmost county in Maine? Are you out of your mind?"

Everyone laughed. "Pay her no attention," Constance said. "Dinah has been trying to get her husband to take her there for years."

"I lived in Pinecrest for a short time," Gemma said. "I worked at the Amish Pie Shop. Do you know it?"

"I do. Perhaps we saw each other there. My husband loved their rhubarb pie."

The sadness in her eyes told Eva it had been a love match. Eva wondered how the young husband lost his life but she didn't ask. The Amish rarely spoke of the dead or of their grief. The passing of a loved one was the will of God and not to be questioned.

Becca and Gemma began talking about people and places they both had known in Florida. The beginnings of a new friendship seemed to be flourishing between the two. Eva had been involved in frolics before, but today she felt she truly belonged in the community of New Covenant. She glanced out the kitchen window. The bishop stood beside Mr. Beachy while Willis was on his knees looking under a rusty machine. He lay down on his back and wriggled beneath it. She grinned at the sight. A wife would have trouble keeping his clothes clean. The kids should have added being a good laundress to their list.

"What are you smiling about?" Bethany asked.

Caught off guard, Eva stumbled over her reply. "Am I smiling? I reckon I'm just happy to be useful today."

Bethany tipped her head to the side. "That was more of a daydreamy smile."

Eva felt a blush heat her cheeks. She wanted to deny it but she couldn't.

"Do I detect a hint of romance in the air?" Dinah

asked. All the women looked at Eva, waiting for her answer.

"*Nee*, you are mistaken." Willis's affection for her was that of a friend. If hers was something more she was the one who had to deal with that.

Dinah walked over and looked out the window. "It's Willis Gingrich, I'm guessing."

"Ah, that makes sense." Bethany nodded. "A helpful neighbor, adorable children, a strong, hardworking blacksmith. What's not to like?"

"Has the date been set?" Constance asked and everyone giggled.

Eva shook her head. "*Nee*, nothing like that. We get along well. We are friends. I look after the children for him sometimes. Don't make it out to be something that it's not."

Dinah let out a long sigh. "This means we'll be looking for another teacher soon."

"I fully intend to keep teaching for as long as the good Lord wills."

Annabeth and Maddie came in together. Annabeth tugged on her mother's sleeve. "Maddie told me a secret. Can I tell you?"

"I'm sure it involves her imaginary friend Bubble," Eva said with a smile.

Annabeth shook her head. "Maddie is getting a new mother and it's her teacher."

Everyone turned to stare at Eva. She wanted to sink into the ground. "Maddie is mistaken."

No one looked convinced.

It wasn't until Willis and Maddie came over with their plates that Eva had a chance to speak to the child. "Maddie, I'm very disappointed in you."

"What now?" Willis asked, eyeing his sister.

Eva kept her gaze on Maddie, too embarrassed to meet Willis's eyes. "You can't make up things that aren't true. Why would you tell Annabeth such a story?"

Maddie shrugged her small shoulders. "I don't know."

"I'm not going to like this, am I?" Willis asked.

"That is not an explanation, Maddie. She told Annabeth that I was going to be her new mother. Annabeth told everyone else in the room." Eva could barely get the words out because as upset as she was with the child she was even more upset that it could never be true.

"What?" Willis looked around. "No wonder everyone is staring at us."

Maddie looked down at her feet. "I said it because you're so nice. You like me. And you remind me of my *mamm*. I started wishing it was true and then I started thinking it was true. I'm sorry."

It was hard to be angry with someone who looked so dejected. "I know you're sorry for what you did but this storytelling has to stop. You can't make something come true by wishing for it, or by making up stories about it."

Maddie started crying and it almost broke Eva's heart. Willis lifted her onto his lap. "We talked about this, Maddie. I thought you understood that it was wrong to make up stories."

"Bubble said…"

Eva shook her finger. "None of this can be blamed on Bubble. I just vehemently denied that we were in a romantic relationship, which by the way every one of those women approves of, so what do we do now?"

He rubbed his knuckles on his cheek stubble. "Talk

will die down eventually. I'm afraid the more we deny it the more they will think it's true. That's the way of human nature. I'm going to take her home. You will spend the rest of the day in your room, Maddie. Go get in the buggy."

The child walked away with dragging footsteps. When she reached his buggy, she glanced back but she didn't say anything. After she climbed inside, Eva pressed a hand to her heart. "She looks so sad."

"Do you think I was too tough on her?"

"I don't think so. I hope she has learned her lesson. If Samuel Yoder gets wind of this story he could say I'm not fit to teach the children."

"You don't think he would take it to heart, do you? She's just a little kid."

"Who can say."

"Well, there is one good thing about this," he said, rising to his feet with his back to the other women.

"Tell me quickly. I need to know."

"You check a couple of items off the wife-to-be wish list. You're only fifty and you're a good cook."

"Go away."

"Guess I'll see you tomorrow at church. Remember I'm happy to give you and Danny a lift if the weather is bad."

"I remember. *Danki*." She hoped it would rain and she could travel to the Fisher farm seated beside Willis. It wouldn't stop any gossip about them, but she was willing to risk a few knowing looks and awkward questions in order to spend more time with him. Such brief moments together were all she could expect, but she was rapidly growing to believe they would never be enough.

* * *

It was raining when Eva woke. She sprang from bed and hurried into her best Sunday dress. It was a deep maroon with an apron of the same color. She put up her hair and pinned her *kapp* in place. Although it was vain, she took a moment to pinch some color into her cheeks. She shook her head sadly. Was she trying to check "being pretty" off the list? That was a hopeless task.

At least Willis didn't seem to mind her appearance. Would riding to church with him fuel the gossip she was sure would circulate today? If it did, it would be a small price to pay for time spent in his company.

She had to admit she was falling for Willis, but it was a secret she would guard closely lest it ruin their friendship.

Willis pulled his buggy to stop outside her front door. She gathered together the food she had prepared for the noon meal and went to the end of the hallway. "Hurry up, Danny. Willis is here."

Her brother came out of her guest room dressed in his Sunday best. He wore a black suit coat over a vest, a white shirt and dark pants. He carried his black, flat-crowned hat in his hand. "The rain is letting up. We can take the cart."

"We will be more comfortable in Willis's buggy. It might start raining again and I have no wish to arrive at my first church service here looking like a drowned rat."

She hurried outside. Willis wore a suit almost identical to her brother's. He looked particularly handsome. She was so used to seeing him with a leather apron and rolled-up sleeves that she almost didn't recognize him.

He helped her into the front seat. Maddie sat quietly in the back, wearing a pretty green dress with a white apron and a white *kapp* on her head that Eva had finished the night before last. Otto and Harley looked clean and uncomfortable in their Sunday best.

Danny climbed in the back. "Morning, Willis. Boys. Maddie, you seem quiet today. Is something wrong?"

"I got in trouble for telling someone Eva was going to be my new *mamm*."

"Which isn't true," Eva and Willis said at the same time.

"Good to know," Danny said with a smirk and a wink at his sister. She turned to stare out the windshield.

The trip to the Fisher farm was less than a mile. It started raining again, and Willis didn't hurry. What was he thinking about? Was he as happy to ride beside her as she was to be sitting beside him? Their times on the swings together made her believe he was. Good friends enjoying each other's company. If she was courting a heartache in the future she pushed that thought aside.

He leaned closer. "You smell nice. Like cinnamon and fresh bread. Have you been baking?"

"Check, check," she said, knowing it would make him laugh to refer to the list. It did.

She turned to the boys in the back. "I hope you enjoy my rolls after the service."

"What if they are all gone before we get through the line?" Otto asked.

"I kept a second pan at the house in case you wanted some for breakfast tomorrow."

Willis grinned. "You are spoiling them."

"Nonsense. I intend to teach Otto how to make them so they can enjoy them whenever they like."

"You're going to teach Otto to bake?" Harley moaned. "Argh, I'm never going to eat a cinnamon roll again."

In spite of their slow place, they soon turned into the Fisher farm. The service was to be held in the barn. Eva and Maddie took the food up to the house where Mrs. Fisher and the older women of the community were preparing to serve the meal when the preaching was done.

After visiting briefly and getting a few sidelong glances but no direct questions about her marriage plans, Eva walked into the barn. The sun had come out and shone brightly beyond the open barn doors at the other end. Rows of wooden benches had already been set up and were filled with worshippers, men on one side, women on the other, all waiting for the church service to begin. The wooden floor had been swept clean of every stray straw.

Eva and Maddie sat with the single women and girls while the married women sat up front. Glancing across the aisle to where the men sat, she caught Willis's eye. He was near the back among the single men and boys along with his brothers and Danny. He smiled at her and she smiled back shyly.

As everyone waited for the *Volsinger* to begin leading the first hymn, Eva closed her eyes. She heard the quiet rustle of fabric on wooden benches as the worshippers tried to get comfortable. The songs of the birds in the trees outside came in through the open door. The scent of alfalfa hay mingled with the smells of the animals and fresh pine as a gentle breeze swirled around her.

The song leader started the first hymn with a deep, clear voice. No musical instruments were allowed by their Amish faith. More than fifty voices took up the solemn, slow-paced cadence of the song. The ministers and the bishop were in the farmhouse across the way, agreeing on the order of the service and the preaching that would be done.

Outsiders found it strange that Amish ministers and bishops received no formal training. Instead, they were chosen by lot, accepting that God wanted them to lead the people according to His wishes. They all preached from the heart, without a written sermon. They depended on the Lord to inspire them in their readings from the Bible.

The first song came to an end. After a few minutes of silence, the *Volsinger* began the second song. It was always *Das Loblied*, the hymn of praise. When it ended, the ministers and the bishop entered the barn. As they made their way to the minister's bench, they shook hands with the men they passed.

For the next several hours Eva listened to the sermons delivered first by each of the ministers and then by the bishop interspersed with long hymns. She glanced over at Danny and Willis. Danny had his hymnbook open. Willis didn't, but he was singing. She wondered how many of the songs in the large *Ashbund* he had committed to memory. She knew only a few by heart. Maddie was surprisingly quiet.

When the three hours of preaching and singing came to an end, Bishop Schultz announced the school barn raising, and listed what supplies were still needed and then gave a final blessing. The service was over.

The scrabble of the young boys in the back making a quick getaway made a few of the elders scowl in their direction. Harley and Otto were among the first out the door. Eva grinned. She remembered how hard it was to sit still at that age. Although the young girls left with more decorum, they were every bit as anxious to be out taking advantage of the beautiful day. Winter would be upon them all too soon. She let Maddie follow them out.

Eva happened to glance at Willis again and caught him staring at her. All the other men were gone.

Gemma stopped by with her baby in her arms. "You should stop looking at that man like you are a starving mouse and he is a piece of cheese. No point in denying it."

Eva rose to her feet. "I'm not a starving mouse."

"You're doing a good impression of one." The two of them went out together and soon joined the rest of the women who were setting up the food. The elders were served first. The younger members had to wait their turn. When Willis came inside to eat, Otto and Harley were with him. He walked past Eva without a word. At first she was hurt but she soon realized they were both under an unusual amount of scrutiny. Ignoring each other was one way of putting the rumors to rest. She was thankful for his thoughtfulness. She accepted a ride home from Jesse and Gemma, leaving her brother to return with Willis and his family. She could do her part to limit the gossip as well as he could.

Later that night she took a stroll and ended up at the swing set on the school playground. It wasn't long before a lone figure stepped out of the shadows and her heart began to hammer in her chest.

Chapter Twelve

Willis walked slowly toward the swings. He had tried to talk himself out of coming tonight. Things were becoming too complicated for him. And it was all because of her. He had no idea what to do about it. He knew what he wanted; he wanted Eva in his life. Not just to give her a ride to church on a rainy morning or to spend a few stolen moments on the schoolyard swings at night. He wanted more, and he was heading for a heartbreak if he thought he could have it.

He saw her waiting for him, and his breath quickened as a surge of happiness slipped through his veins. Even though he knew he should turn around and go home he kept walking until he reached her. "Can I give you a push, Teacher?"

"That would be lovely."

She was lovely both inside and out. He knew he wasn't smart but the men in her community must've been blockheads not to have snapped her up.

He gave her a few gentle pushes before taking a seat on the swing beside her. She let her momentum slow gradually until she was stopped. "Was your day awkward?"

"I got some razzing from my friends. Jesse and Michael mostly. They are happily settled down and think I should be, too. How about you? Were there any more questions about who you are seeing?"

"Gemma was the only one who made a comment. Why can't people accept that a man and a woman can be friends without any strings attached?"

"I'm sure it happens but it's rare. Especially among us Amish. The bishop says it is the duty of men and women to marry and have children. Our people don't look for careers. God, family and community are what we value."

"At least you got it half-right. You don't have a wife but you've got three wonderful kids. I don't have anything to show for my years on this earth. I guess that's why I hope I make a good teacher."

"You will. You'll make a wonderful teacher."

"Maddie was very subdued today. She must've taken our scolding to heart."

"I noticed she didn't have much to say. Will you hate me if I say I rather enjoyed it?"

She chuckled, and he wished he could see her face. He loved the way her eyes lit up when she was excited about something. The way she chewed on her thumbnail when she was deep in thought. He was getting to know her better than most other people in his life. And he wanted to know more. He wanted to know everything about her.

"What's the best book that you read this week?" he asked, knowing she would happily chatter away about some novel or other.

"I've been reading about dyslexia and how to help little children overcome their inability to read."

"And did you learn anything new?"

"I think maybe I did. I'm going to see if I can use any of it to help Otto improve."

"What if he doesn't want to get better?"

She sighed. "Then I will consider myself a failure as a teacher."

"I don't see that. Overeager maybe but not a failure. Otto is a sensitive kid. He'll understand that you're only trying to help."

"I hope so. I can't imagine going through life without being able to read. Books aside, if you can read, you can do just about anything. With a cookbook you can create wonderful meals. You can read the weather forecast and the baseball scores in the newspaper. You can see who's having babies and what land is for sale." Her voice rose with excitement. "You can even see what's in the cat food if you're dying of curiosity and want to read the label."

"Oh, every fella needs to know what's in Tabby's treats. Imagine the horrible life Otto will have without knowing that."

She slanted him a sharp look. "Now you're making fun of me."

"Just a little. You get so passionate. You make it easy for me to get your goat. It's fun watching the steam coming out of your ears."

"If by that you mean I get angry, maybe I do a little. I know that advanced education is not necessary to our way of life. But I do believe there are students who should go on to higher learning. Samuel Yoder would

have a fit if he heard me say that, wouldn't he? The
bishop might have me shunned."

"I don't think so. Did you want to be one of those
kids? Ones that went to high school and on to college?"

"Not really. My eighth grade education was enough
because I found solace in reading. I discovered I never
have to stop learning. What about you, Willis? Is there
something you wanted to do but never had the chance?"

"You're going to laugh."

"I won't. I promise"

"I always wanted to learn to fly an airplane."

"Is that so? I never would've guessed that about you.
You seem to me to be a man with his feet planted firmly
on the ground."

"It just goes to show how well I can hide my feelings."

"That's something I'm not very good at. But I have
been getting some practice lately."

He tipped his head to study her face. "What do you
have to hide, Eva Coblentz?"

That I'm falling in love with you.

If she answered his question honestly, she wouldn't
have anything left to hide and she might lose the friendship she cherished.

She stared at the ground. "I'm trying to hide how
afraid I am that my brother and his wife will make me
go back to Illinois."

"They can't really do that if you don't let them."

"When I think how hard it will be to cut myself off
from them I'm not sure I can make that choice."

She could leave New Covenant when Danny went
back and take up her old life. Or she could stay and try

to make a satisfying life across the road from Willis Gingrich. Neither of her choices appealed to her. She didn't want to exist on the fringe of Willis's life. That was all she had done until now. Exist. If only she could discover what he thought about her, not as a neighbor or as a friend, but as a woman.

If he gave her any kind of encouragement she was liable to throw caution to the wind and tell him exactly how much she thought of him. She was falling head over heels for the blacksmith. He had forged a band around her heart that might never be broken.

He was amazing with the children. He had a craft that he had honed to near perfection. If he could cook he would be the perfect husband. For a second she thought she had said it out loud but his expression had changed.

"So what are we going to do?" she asked.

"About what?"

"About the stories that Maddie spread about you and me?"

He shrugged. "Ride it out, I guess and hope our reputations can take the heat and make sure she understands she can't tell people we're planning to wed. I can't understand why that is important to her."

"Do you think she is afraid of being left alone again?" Eva asked.

"Maybe so. It would make sense. I'm not sure there's anything we can do to change that. When she's old enough she will have her faith to sustain her. I reckon I can reassure her that the boys and I will always take care of her and she doesn't need to be afraid."

Eva reached across the space between them and laid her hand on his shoulder. "You're a *goot* brother, and she is blessed to have you."

He covered her hand with his. "I'm glad you think so."

She pulled her hand away from his tender touch. "It's getting late. I should go in."

She stood up and so did he. They walked side by side toward her porch. She kept her fingers clasped tightly in front of her because she wanted him to take her hand more than anything. A simple stroll while holding hands wouldn't hurt anything, but it would change everything and she couldn't risk it. The last thing she wanted to do was to drive him away with her unwanted attention.

"Good night," she said then rushed inside without waiting for his reply.

The workers clattered into the schoolyard before dawn. Eva watched from her kitchen window as wagonloads of lumber were parked where there would be easy access to their cargo. Otto and Harley took the horses over to Willis's place. It was the closest corral.

Bishop Schultz was the one in charge as events unfolded. Eva kept a big pot of coffee hot and served anyone who asked for a cup. When a busload of Amish men arrived from a settlement in Pennsylvania to help she quickly put on another pot.

The bishop never appeared hurried or at a loss. To her it looked as if everybody knew exactly what to do. Danny and Harley were among those getting the walls in place. Willis was putting the new window in the school. Otto stood by with a caulk gun, ready to seal it when Willis got off the ladder. It made her smile to see the two of them working together.

By ten o'clock the framing for the four outer walls was going up. A long line of men hefted the first wall off the ground at a sign from Bishop Schultz. Some men used long poles to hoist it upright while an equal number of them quickly fastened it to the foundation. The ring of hammers filled the air.

A few minutes after ten the first buggy full of women arrived, followed by the bench wagon driven by Constance Schultz. The women quickly set out tables on the schoolhouse lawn and covered them with bright checkered cloths. Baskets of food were unloaded next.

Becca Beachy arrived with her daughter and her father-in-law. He walked with a pronounced limp and used a cane, but he soon had the young boys applying paint to the first finished wall. Annabeth and Maddie took their places on the swings until Dinah called them over to babysit the infants while their mothers began serving food.

Danny collided with Becca coming out of the house. She blushed and murmured an apology as she hurried away. Danny stood staring after her. Eva took note of the bemused expression on his face when he turned to her. "Who was that?"

"That is Becca Beachy. She and her father-in-law recently moved here."

"Oh, she's married, then."

"She's a widow. She has a little girl Maddie's age. Dinah said she is one of Samuel Yoder's grandchildren."

"Is that so? Well, I hope they like it here." He walked back out to the barn.

Eva glanced at him and then at Becca, who was watching him, too. Should she drop a hint that Danny wasn't a resident of New Covenant and that he would be leaving soon? She decided against it and went back inside to make more iced tea for those who wanted it instead of coffee.

Everyone was sitting down to eat when Dale Kaufman pulled up in his yellow pickup. Jesse and Willis went down to the street to see what he needed. Willis came back to Eva a few minutes later. "Dale says he has a delivery for you. Four large crates. Where would you like them?"

Eva clasped her hands together in excitement. "They're here. My books are here. Take them inside the school, please." She wrapped her hands around Willis's arm and pulled him into the school. "I'm so excited to be able to share them with my students. I may even start a lending library so that the adults in this community can borrow them."

Dale brought in a crate and pried the top off. "Are these what you're waiting for?"

"Ja."

"I'll get the rest."

He went out and Eva grinned at Willis. "You may have the first pick and don't tell me you don't have time to read. You will this winter."

He slipped her hands off his arm. "Okay. I'll do that. Um, I know Harley likes to read. The kid always has his nose in a horse magazine. Maybe you could pick one out for him about horses."

"We'll each pick one for him." She drew her hand along the spines of the books. "Let's see I have *The Black Stallion, Black Beauty* and several Westerns featuring horses." She picked out one.

"Okay." Willis rubbed his hands on his pant legs.

She waited for him to look through her collection. What was wrong? He took a step back. It was almost as if he was afraid of them.

"I'm sure Harley will like whatever you choose. He can bring it back if he doesn't and pick another."

Willis swallowed hard and shook his head at Eva's excitement. All for a couple of crates of books. The joy on her face was unbelievable. There was no doubt about it. Eva didn't just like books. She loved them. Any man who wanted to woo her would do well to come visiting with a new book under his arm each time he stopped in.

And that man wouldn't be him. He could carry a crate of them, but he couldn't choose one. He wouldn't know if it was one Harley would like. If he picked the wrong book, would she guess he didn't know what he was looking at?

She was waiting for him to look them over. Watching him to see what he would do. He read the confusion in her eyes. She didn't know why he was hesitating. He rubbed a hand across his dry lips and leaned down.

He ran his fingers along them as he had seen her do. "I'll surprise him with this one." He pulled a book out and tucked it under his arm. "Now I've got to get back to work."

"Are you sure that's the one you want him to have?"

"Yup. See you later." He stumbled a little as he turned to go. His legs were stiff with fright.

Harley came through the door. "I heard the books came in."

"They did. I picked one out for you already. I hope you enjoy it." He pressed the book into Harley's hands, praying it was something that might interest him.

Harley took the book, looked around Willis to Eva and back to the book in his hands. He frowned slightly.

"*Danki, bruder.* You must have heard me say I wanted to learn more about the history of Scotland."

Willis didn't realize he was holding his breath until his brother finished speaking. He drew in a ragged gasp of air. "I did. Make sure you get it back to Eva when you are done with it."

He left the school thanking God that he had survived such a close call but his time was running out.

The exterior of the barn was finished by four o'clock. It was the traditional barn in shape but not in size, being only about one-third as big as the usual structures. When the interior was finished, it would hold ten horses or ponies in roomy stalls. The parents of the schoolchildren would be responsible for keeping hay and grain available. The older children in Eva's class would keep the stable clean and make sure there was water available for the animals during the day.

People were starting to leave when Willis went in search of Eva again. He found her sitting on the floor beside her bookcases with stacks of books surrounding her. "I came to tell you that I'm going home. Most of the workers have already left. What are you doing?"

She gestured to the stacks around her. "At first I put them out in alphabetical order but then I realized it would be better if I separated them into age-appropriate categories. Upon sorting, I realized that some of them are very hard to decide which age group would enjoy them the most."

She held up one of the books with a deep blue cover edged in gold. "Take *Anne of Green Gables.* Any age would enjoy this story."

"Decisions, decisions. All in a day's work for the schoolteacher. If you ask me, which you haven't, but I'm going to give you my opinion anyway, put the books that might fit any age on their own shelf. That way someone younger who reads it will feel quite an accomplishment and someone older who reads it won't feel like he or she is taking a book from the baby section."

"I don't have a baby section. Should I get one?"

"You should finish up and go take a look at your new barn."

"I believe it is actually the school's barn. Are you going to bring Dodger over tonight?"

"The corral isn't finished. He can stay with me a few more days."

"I appreciate all you have done for me, Willis."

He stood and hooked his thumbs under his suspenders. "Save your appreciation until after you get my bill." He held out his hand. She grasped it and he helped her to her feet.

It was a mistake on his part. Once her hand was nestled inside his, he didn't want to let go. The urge to draw her closer and kiss her sweet lips was overpowering.

How had he fallen so hard for this woman? He knew it couldn't work. Eva might not view him as a laughingstock the way the last woman he cared for had done, but she would be repulsed by his ignorance, and he couldn't stand seeing that in her eyes.

He made himself release her hand and he turned away from her. "The barn has plenty of room. You will be able to store your buggy inside when you get one. I'll keep an eye out for a used one if you don't have the funds for a new one."

"You must be joking. I don't have the funds for a new book let alone a new buggy. Does your *Ordnung* allow baptized members to ride a bicycle or a scooter?"

"Bicycles. But nobody rides them in the winter."
They stepped outside of the school and the last of the building crew were out on the road walking home. A line of six men dressed in dark blue pants, matching jackets and straw hats.

"Hopefully, I will have a buggy before the first snow."

"That could be next week."

Her eyes grew wide. "Are you serious? You can have snow here in September?"

His gaze was drawn to her lips parted in surprise. And he wasn't going to think about kissing her. He wasn't. "It's happened. Late September, but we almost always have snow before Thanksgiving. Do you have snowshoes?"

"*Nee*, but I have big feet. Will that help?"

He checked out the small sneakers she was wearing. He wouldn't say she had big feet by any stretch of the imagination. "Buy snowshoes. I'll see you later." He started toward his house.

"Aren't you going to show me the barn?" she asked.

He turned around and pointed. "Behold. The barn. See you tomorrow."

He could make a joke out of it, but he wasn't laughing inside. He needed some distance between them. He needed to get his head straight and stop thinking about what it would be like to kiss the teacher.

Willis seemed in a big hurry to get away from her. Of course, she had no right to monopolize his time. It was simply that her world seemed empty when he wasn't in it. Instead of going into the house she chose to walk to the small grocery store at the other end of the community. New Covenant wasn't a true town. It was a string of Amish homes interspersed with a few *Englisch* ones along a narrow-paved road.

At the grocery store she purchased an array of fresh vegetables and fruit. The prices were higher than what she was used to paying. Mr. Meriwether, the owner of the grocery, was a likable fellow who enjoyed visiting with his customers. As she was paying she noticed a small flyer on a bulletin board behind the cash register. It was for a cabinetmaker in Presque Isle, the largest city in Aroostook County. The phrase that caught her attention was "handmade cabinet pulls and knobs produced by local artisans."

"Mr. Meriwether, could I have that card?" She pointed out the one. "I'd like to write down their contact information."

He pulled the thumbtack out and handed the flyer to her. "The fellow's name is Ray Jackson. He comes here once or twice a month. I can easily get another one."

"Thank you. Is he local?"

Mr. Meriwether shook his head. "He's from Portland. He owns a couple of stores there, and one in Presque Isle. He comes out to get wood from your bishop. The one who makes backyard sheds and those ridiculous little houses. Bishop Schultz gets his wood from an Amish fellow who runs his own sawmill."

"Thank you again." She left the store and headed home. Perhaps Willis could sell his handmade cabinet knobs and pulls to this man. If he came to New Covenant monthly, Willis might not even have the expense of shipping his products to Presque Isle or Portland. She would suggest it. Perhaps the bishop could introduce the two. Feeling quite pleased with herself, Eva walked briskly all the way home.

Her brother was sitting at the kitchen table with a glass of milk and a sandwich. She grinned at him. "A man who knows how to make his own supper is a welcome addition to any household. I think I may have found a place for Willis to sell some of his ironwork."

Danny had an odd expression on his face. He didn't ask about her discovery. Instead, he held out an envelope. "You have a letter from Gene."

She put the brown paper bag with her groceries on the kitchen counter and took the letter from him. Was she being summoned home? She looked at Danny. "I don't want to read it. I don't want to go back to Illinois."

"I understand that but I'm not sure Gene will."

"Why? Why can't my life come first for a change?"

"I can tell you what he will say. Because we are commanded by our Lord to care for others. There isn't a commandment to make thyself happy first."

"There should be. Is there anything else?"

"A packet from a school in Maryland."

"*Goot.* Those must be the records for Otto and Harley." She laid her brother's letter on the counter. She picked it up and turned it over so she couldn't see her brother's handwriting. "I don't have to read it right away.

"I'm not going to be the one who tells you what to do. I can see how much you love—it here. I like it here."

She sat down at the kitchen table and clasped her hands together. "I appreciate that."

"So you found someplace for Willis to sell his ironwork?"

She turned away from the letter and smiled. "I saw

this flyer in the grocery store. It is for a cabinet-making business. They have hand-wrought hardware. It would be helpful to the family if Willis could sell items on a regular basis and not just when a horse throws a shoe or a potato digger has a broken nose."

"Potato diggers have noses?"

"Sure." She put her hands together in front of her face. "It's the part that pushes into the ground underneath the potatoes and brings them up to the surface."

"Since when are you an expert on potato diggers?"

"I read about them when I knew I was going to come to this part of Maine. The potato is their main agricultural crop, but I don't want to talk about potatoes. I want to talk about finding a market for Willis's skills."

"I grant you the man knows how to work metal. I was thinking of taking some of his pieces back to Illinois to see if our company would be interested in using them. The downside of that will be the shipping cost. Finding a local market is a much better idea. And now you're going to open that letter from your brother so that I don't have to stay in suspense any longer."

"Very well, but if he wants me to come home, I'm not going to do it. I have a contract with the school board to be their teacher."

"I heard it was month-to-month, not a full year."

"So what? It's a contract." She stood up and picked up the letter. She slipped her finger under the envelope lip and ripped it open. She read the brief missive and burst into tears.

Chapter Thirteen

"Eva, please. You know I can't stand to see a woman cry." Danny was pushing a box of tissues into her hands. Eva dabbed her eyes with a handful and then blew her nose.

"Gene says I must come home at the end of this month. Corinne's mother is in a rehabilitation hospital. They expect her to return home by then." Eva struggled to control her sobs. "A month. That's all I have? It isn't fair."

"No one said life would be fair. I'm sorry. I really am. I think you would make a marvelous teacher."

"If I only have a month, then I will be a marvelous teacher for one month." She wiped her eyes and threw the tissue at the trash can. She missed. She bent over, picked up the tissue and dropped it in.

She pressed her lips together and looked at Danny. "*Nee*, I'm not going back. Gene will have to hire someone to take care of Corrine's mother. I will write him today and explain my reasoning."

"He's not going to like that. When have you ever known our brother to spend a penny more than he has to?"

Eva's bravado faded. "He can't force me to return."

"He can put a lot of pressure and guilt on you. Are you prepared for that?"

"I can't believe *Gott* would lead me all the way up here to simply send me home at the end of thirty days."

"I admire your spunk, but Gene won't. I'm sure he'll appeal to the bishop here."

She hadn't thought of that. If Bishop Schultz took Gene's side she would have no choice but to return home. Her job would vanish and her relationship with her family would be strained. Tears pricked her eyes again. Was her stubborn pride worth a rift with her family? She had aunts, uncles and cousins who would side with Gene because they believed that family came first.

Danny put his arm around her shoulder and gave her a hug. "A lot can change in a month. Maybe the good Lord will decide you belong here."

"Maybe. I'm going to write to Gene anyway." She wasn't going to lose hope.

"Will you tell Willis that you have been ordered home?"

Eva shook her head. "Not yet. He has been such a good friend to me. I will miss him more than I can say."

"He seems like a fine man."

She stepped to the sink and splashed water on her face. "I have a lot to do and not much time to do it in."

Would she be able to face Willis without breaking down? She had to. For his sake as well as for hers.

That evening she wrote a lengthy letter to Gene explaining why she needed to stay in Maine and continue teaching. She didn't mention Willis or how moving away from him and his wonderful family would break her heart.

After a troubled night's sleep, Eva was ready to face the day, determined to enjoy what was left of her time in New Covenant if Gene's mind wasn't changed by her letter. The three children arrived in time for breakfast but Willis wasn't with them. Eva was grateful for the reprieve. She wasn't sure she could keep from crying. She made cinnamon rolls as a special treat for the children. A few minutes before eight o'clock, Harley left to go wherever Harley went. Eva, Otto, Danny and Maddie all went over to the schoolhouse.

She put Danny in charge of shelving the books and making note cards and note card holders so she could keep track of who had the books checked out. At least her books would be here if she was forced to leave. She prayed the children would find some solace in knowing she cared enough to leave her most prized possessions in their care.

"When is the first day of school?" Danny asked. He was on the floor thumbing through some of her books for the older students.

"It starts tomorrow at eight o'clock," she said, wondering if she was ready. "When will you be leaving?"

"The middle of the week."

She walked outside and returned a short time later with a shoebox lid. It held an inch of sand in the bottom. She sat down at her desk. "Otto, can you come here, please?"

He came over, looking at her with suspicion. "*Ja*, Teacher?"

"I know that you have had trouble reading and writing in school. Your records from you last school show it. I've consulted with some other teachers and we believe you may be suffering from dyslexia. It's a condition that makes it very hard to learn to read or write. We can't say for sure that you have it but there are tests that can tell us for certain that you do. Would you be willing to be tested?"

"I don't know. Maybe. I should ask Willis."

"That's a good idea." She held up the little box. "In the meantime, I would like you to practice writing some letters in this sandbox instead of with paper and pencil. I want you to spell sand one letter at a time."

She scooted over to make room for him. "Come sit beside me. I'll help you."

"Is this the test?"

She smiled to reassure him. "*Nee*, this is a way to make learning easier for you."

"Why write them in the sand?" Danny asked.

"With dyslexia, a child's ability to identify a sound when they see the letter is impaired. This lets you see and feel the grains of sand as you work. It helps a different part of your brain remember the letter. Want to try it, Otto?"

Otto shrugged but he sat down with the box beside her desk. Eva smiled at him. "Let's start with the letter S." She drew it for him and she let him trace it over and over through the sand.

While Otto was doing that, she took Maddie to the bookshelf and allowed her to pick out a book for herself. She eagerly chose one and opened the book but there were words along with the pictures. She looked up at Eva. "I can't read this."

"I'll help you read it," Danny said.

"Are you as excited for school to start as I am? Can you believe it starts tomorrow?"

"I'm gonna walk to school. I don't think Willis is ever going to shoe my pony."

Eva felt she should defend him. "He's had many things to do. Some that you don't know about. He has to work hard to make enough money so you can eat and have a place to live."

Maddie mulled that over and nodded. "I guess my pony can wait. Will you remind him?"

"I will."

They had a lunch of peanut butter and jelly sandwiches along with fresh apples and some of the leftover cinnamon rolls. It was a little before four o'clock when Willis walked in the door.

Eva's heart expanded to fill her chest at the sight of his grimy face. Tears sprang to her eyes but she blinked them away. She didn't want to ruin any of their time together.

He looked around the room. "Where is Danny?"

She smiled. "He is out at the barn helping dig the post holes for the corral fence."

"Sounds like tough work. I should go help."

"Before you go I have something I want to show you." She handed him the flyer. He looked at it and turned it over once. "So?"

"This man sells hand-forged hardware and brackets for the kitchen cabinets that they make in their shop. He buys his lumber from Bishop Schultz. You should ask the bishop to give you an introduction. If this man likes your work, he can pick up the hardware when he comes to pick up the lumber. That way, neither one of you have to worry about the cost of shipping. What do you think?"

"I already have a lot to do, but I'll check with the bishop."

He didn't seem excited at the prospect. Eva dropped the subject. He scrutinized her face and she worried that some traces of her tears from last night might be remaining. "Are you okay?"

She managed a big smile this time. "Of course I am. I'm just stressed about starting school."

"You'll be fine. The kids will love you." He waved away her concern. Her fake grin faded. She longed to tell him she might be leaving but she kept silent. One of them hurting inside was enough.

Willis glanced at Otto as the two of them were cleaning up the kitchen after supper that evening. "The first day of school is tomorrow. Are you excited?"

"Not really." Otto slowly dried the plate in his hand.

Willis grunted. "I didn't care for school, either."

Otto looked at him. "Why?"

"It was hard for me. A lot harder than it was for my friends."

Otto went back to drying the plate. "That's the way it is for me, too. I'm just dumb, I guess."

"I've heard you described a lot of ways but I have never heard anyone call you *dumb*."

"Eva thinks I have something called dyslexia. Do you know anything about it?"

"I don't. What does Miss Eva say about it?"

"She wants me to have some tests to see if I've got it. I don't know. What good would it do?"

"Maybe they can cure it if they know what you've got." Was he giving the boy false hope?

Harley came into the kitchen. "I heard about it from

one of the *Englisch* kids back home. He said his older brother had it. He was going to be tested because his grades weren't very good and sometimes it runs in families."

Willis turned to look at Harley. "You mean more than one person in the family can have it?"

"That's what he said."

"Did he get tested? Did he have it?" Otto asked.

"I never found out. We moved here, and I never saw him again."

Willis mulled over Harley's information. Was it possible he had this dyslexia thing along with Otto? It would explain a lot.

Maddie came out of her bedroom in her pajamas. She had a book under her arm. She held it up to Willis. "Eva gave me a book from her library. Will you read it to me, Willis?"

"I'm busy, not now." It was the same excuse he always used when he was confronted with something to read.

Her lips turned down in a frown. Willis wanted to read to her. He often made up stories for her. She didn't know they weren't the same words that were printed in the book he was looking at. But soon she would know and she would realize how ignorant her big brother was.

Harley reached over and took the book from her. "Come on, sprout. I'll read it to you." He looked at Willis and winked.

Willis's mouth fell open. He knew. Harley knew that Willis couldn't read. Shame left a bitter taste in his mouth. He had tried so hard to keep it a secret but a thirteen-year-old boy had figured it out. It made him wonder if Eva knew, too. He didn't think he could bear that.

"Do you think I should be tested?" Otto asked.

"I don't know."

"Harley, me and Maddie, we all like Eva a lot."

"I like her a lot, too." He sensed that there was something more to Otto's comment.

"Do you think you'll ever get married?"

"Why is everyone so concerned with my marital status? If I don't want to get married, I am not going to get married. That's the end of it." He hung his dish towel over the faucet and walked out of the room and out into the evening air.

The lights were off at Eva's home. He wanted to see her but he decided against it. He began walking out to the road and instead of following it, he crossed it and went up to the school. He laid a hand on the building. It had been built to last. Harley's grandchildren and great-grandchildren would stick their gum to the bottom of the seats, sing hymns and put on a Christmas play for their friends and family. He wished his experience had been different, but his childhood memories of school were mostly unhappy ones. He didn't want that for Otto or for Harley and certainly not for Maddie.

Willis turned his footsteps toward home but he didn't have enough willpower to pass by the schoolyard without checking to see if Eva was waiting on him on the swings.

She was.

He could still change his mind. He hesitated, but in the end he followed his heart and not his head. He sat down in the swing beside her. "You're up late."

"A little. I can't sleep."

"Nerves?"

She chuckled. "Exactly. That feeling of oh-what-have-I-gotten-myself-into? What has you walking the playground at this time of the night?"

"I have a lot of things on my mind." He got up and walked a few steps away. Then he turned to her again. "You are one of them."

"Me? Why do I trouble you?"

"Because I can't stop thinking about you."

"I think of you often, too."

He took a step closer. "I don't just think about you. I see you everywhere. I see you when I'm awake and I see you in my dreams. You're in all the things the kids tell me. I can see your eyes smiling at me from across the road."

She stared at the ground. "I'm sorry. I don't mean to be a distraction."

"That is exactly what you are." He walked toward her, bent down and kissed her. It was every bit as sweet as he had imagined it would be.

He moved his hand to the back of her head but she didn't draw away. She pressed her lips against his and slanted her face just enough to make their mouths fit together more perfectly. His heart started pounding so hard he knew she must hear it. Nothing had ever felt as right and as wonderful as her fingers when she laid her hands against his cheeks and let them slip into his hair. He thought he might die of happiness when she curled her fingers in his locks and held on.

Why couldn't he have been smarter, more deserving of her?

When he drew back he looked at her stunned face. She was so lovely, so kind and funny. Everything he ever dreamed of finding in a wife. Everything he knew he couldn't have.

He was struck with remorse. He couldn't give her false hope. "I'm sorry. I shouldn't have done that."

Eva pressed a hand to her mouth. "Don't say that. It was nice." She rushed away without another word.

Why did he have to do that? Eva hadn't been prepared. She stumbled toward her house. He wasn't supposed to kiss her. They were friends. Only it wasn't friendship that drew her to deepen the kiss and hold his face in her hands. She loved him. He had to know it now.

He wasn't supposed to say he was sorry afterward. How was she going to act from now on? He had changed everything.

It was her first kiss. He shouldn't have said he was sorry.

She could still feel the tingle on her lips. She stopped and looked back. He remained standing by the swings.

She rushed into her house being as quiet as possible. She didn't want Danny's sharp eyes noticing something was wrong. She didn't want to explain what had happened because she didn't understand it herself.

In her room, she sat down on the edge of her mattress and slowly took down her hair. What reason did Willis have for kissing her? She wasn't foolish enough to think her beauty had robbed him of coherent thought. Was she reading more into it? Had he simply followed an impulse because he felt sorry for her and then regretted it? Poor Eva, never been kissed?

That would be the most logical explanation. It didn't help her bruised ego. Tears filled her eyes. She was in love with Willis Gingrich and he was sorry he'd kissed her.

* * *

The sky was overcast but the rain held off for the first day of school. Some of the children arrived early enough to play outside on the playground equipment before coming in. The air was full of excitement, childish laughter and happy voices.

Eva greeted each of the students as they came in and introduced herself. Becca Beachy walked in with Annabeth. The little girl clutched her mother's hand. She did not want to go to school.

"I hope you don't mind if I sit in today," Becca said.

Eva shook her head. "Of course I don't mind. You may come as often as you wish."

Maddie came running up the steps, eager to choose her desk from the ones in the front row. "Morning, Teacher. Willis said Bubble had to stay at home or at least outside. He said a girl my age doesn't need an imaginary friend. I'm supposed to make real ones. Will you be my friend?"

Eva smiled and nodded. "I would love to be your friend. And I think Annabeth would also enjoy being your friend. Why don't you go sit by her? She's sort of scared today."

"There isn't anything to be scared of." Maddie tromped to the front of the room.

Eva was as prepared as she could be. She had written out exactly what needed to be done for every part of the morning and afternoon on a long list. That sheet of paper sat squarely in the middle of her desk so she could refer to it as needed. At exactly eight o'clock she rang the bell and everyone took their seats. The murmur of voices died away.

She wrote her name on the blackboard and turned

around to face the class. She had never been more nervous in her life. Fifteen eager children watched her every move. Her mouth went dry. She wasn't going to be able to do this. What came next? She walked over to her desk only to discover her sheet of paper was gone. She checked underneath the desk and the chair but her list was nowhere to be found.

What next? She was going to blame Willis for making her so scatterbrained this morning. "Let's begin the day with a song."

One boy in the back held up his hand. "Shouldn't you begin with a prayer?"

"That's what I meant to say. A prayer. The Lord's Prayer."

Two of the girls from a newly arrived family rose to their feet. "*Daed* said we should all stand for a prayer."

"Of course. Everyone stand, please." As the class recited the prayer Eva prayed as hard as she could that she would make it through the day. What came next? Arithmetic assignments or reading with the first graders? When was recess?

"Amen," they all said in unison. Then they were all staring at her, waiting for directions and her mind was blank.

Eva sat on one of the swings in the schoolyard after the last of the children went home. She didn't want to return to Illinois, but she might not have a choice after this. Once Samuel Yoder heard about her first day of school, he was sure to start looking for a teacher who knew what she was doing.

"How did it go?"

She wasn't surprised when Willis came over and took

a seat beside her. She had been hoping to see him. The need to confide her failure was overpowering as was the need to find out why he had kissed her.

"My first day on the job was a complete and utter disaster. I don't know why I ever thought I could be a teacher."

"Were the students unruly? Was Otto part of the problem?"

"I was the only problem. I had made a list of all the things I needed to do throughout the day and I lost that list five minutes after I rang the bell. I looked at all those faces waiting on me to do something and I panicked."

"That doesn't sound like the Eva I know."

"Before the first hour was up, two of the boys were involved in a paper wad fight, Annabeth was crying because she didn't want to be there and Sadie kept running into the room and barking at everyone."

"Keeping the door shut might have kept the dog out."

"Oh I tried that, but someone kept opening the door when my back was turned."

Tears stung her eyes. "I thought I could do this. I thought it would be easy. School was always easy for me. I never had to struggle over a problem the way Otto has to struggle. I don't know how to help him."

"You help him just by caring about him."

"I wanted all the children to love school the way I loved it."

"I hate to say this but maybe it's not about you."

She turned to gape at him. "I was the only one at the front of the schoolroom. How can it not be about me?"

"Shouldn't it be about your scholars? About what they need and not about what you used to do? Maybe your expectations were too high."

She pushed back and began swinging. "Well, they're not too high anymore. I'll be thrilled if any of the parents let their children come back for a second day."

"I think you're being too hard on yourself. Every big change takes some getting used to."

"I'm afraid I will give the children a disgust of education. I can imagine how the public school teachers will laugh at me when they hear about this. They go to four years of college or more to become teachers. I thought I could do it with a sharp pencil and a book of hymns."

He started swinging back and forth. "Maybe you're looking at teaching from the wrong angle."

"What's that supposed to mean?"

"What's the big picture?"

"I want Otto to be able to read. I want Maddie to learn her letters and numbers. I want the Yoder twins to stop shooting paper wads at each other and the other children."

"Those are all the little parts. You are looking at the cogs. You aren't looking at the driveshaft."

"Now you're talking over my head. What is the driveshaft?" She had been afraid she couldn't talk to him anymore but they were right back where they had been before the kiss. Or almost.

"A driveshaft is the big piece that turns all the small ones. Our Amish faith is the driveshaft. The Amish want to educate our children to be good stewards of the land and to care for each other. We want God first, family second and our community third. You need to look at your students in that light."

She stopped swinging. "How do I become a driveshaft?"

He chuckled. "First, you need a backbone of steel. The driveshaft has to be strong or it breaks and the whole machine becomes useless."

She wrapped her arms around the chains and rolled her eyes. "I can talk a good game but I'm not tough enough to say I have a backbone of steel."

"You're going to have to get one."

"Do you have a spare in your junk pile?"

He stopped swinging. "If I did I would give it to you in a heartbeat. I'm afraid you're going to have to forge your own. It takes heat, time and patience before metal can be shaped. I'm going to guess it takes the same thing to shape scholars. You can't do it in one day. Just as I can't turn out a horseshoe with a single mighty blow of my hammer. It takes a lot of small strikes in just the right places to bend steel. You didn't have your iron hot enough today. It's a mistake all new blacksmiths make."

She drew a deep breath, buoyed by his words. "I'm going to find my list and stick to it tomorrow."

He got out of the swing and stood in front of her. He leaned down and tapped one finger against her forehead. "The knowledge you need is already in here. Your list is a useless crutch that can blow away in the wind. Your scholars need to believe you know more than they do." He stood up straight.

She nodded slowly. "I think you should be the teacher and I should go pound metal into crooked horseshoes."

He laughed. "If I find a horse with a crooked hoof I will call on you." He stopped laughing and grew somber. "Eva, about last night."

"I was wondering when that would come up."

"Can we forget it happened?"

"No."

He arched one eyebrow. "That wasn't the answer I had hoped for."

"You shocked me beyond belief."

"I shocked myself. I value you as a dear friend. You are an attractive woman and I got carried away. It won't happen again. You've heard me say I don't want to marry and that is true. I didn't mean to give you false hope or treat you poorly."

"Then I will say that I forgive you."

"*Danki.* Good night, Teacher."

"Good night." Eva was sorry to see him leave. She sat on the swing until the moon began to rise. Somehow, everything seemed better when she could talk it over with Willis. He had quickly become important in her life. That one kiss had opened her eyes to what she wanted and it was much more than friendship. She wanted his love in return. Foolish or not, she wanted to be held in his arms and kissed without an apology to follow. Was it possible? Or would she be gone before that happened?

Chapter Fourteen

The next school day Eva faced the classroom with new determination as she kept Willis's advice in mind. "Good morning, students."

"Good morning, Teacher," they said in unison.

"Let us stand and pray." She bowed her head.

When she finished she smiled at the classes. "Yesterday wasn't the best start to your new school year. Today will be better. Jenny Martin is going to be my helper. Jenny, I'd like you to assist the third and fourth grade students to do page one and two in their math workbooks. And make sure Sadie stays outside today."

"Yes, Teacher."

Eva looked to the two boys in the very last row. "If the dog comes in today we will all forgo recess. Do I make myself clear?"

The twins looked at each other and nodded. She smiled "*Goot*. Take your places for our singing."

Willis dropped by after school the next day to see how Eva was getting along. Maddie was playing with Sadie and Jenny in the schoolyard. He found both his brothers still inside at the blackboard. Eva looked up and smiled when she caught sight of him, and it warmed his heart. "How did things go today?" he asked.

"I took your advice and the day went better. It's going to take more than a few days for everyone to learn their schedules and to behave in a single classroom while I'm busy with other students."

She quickly changed the subject. "Have you contacted the cabinetmaker I told you about yet?"

"I spoke to him on the phone this morning. I have a meeting with him tomorrow. He has asked me to visit his businesses in Portland and bring samples of my work.

"That's wonderful."

It was and he was going to do his best to secure a new line of income to support his family. The thought of being away from Eva for two days was already depressing him. How was he going to go through life without kissing her again?

He cleared his throat. "Dale has agreed to drive me. We leave this afternoon. I'll be home late tomorrow night. I've arranged for the children to stay with Michael and Bethany while I'm gone and don't say you will keep them. You have enough to do."

He watched a wry smile curve her pretty lips. "I would happily take care them, but it would be a bit crowded with Danny here."

She was kind and generous, and he loved her. If he told her that he couldn't read would she react with compassion or recoil from his stupidity?

He needed to tell her. He didn't want any secrets between them.

He gazed at her sweet face and knew he would do

it. He would find the courage. When he was back from Portland with a contract for more work and a chance at a future together he would tell her when they were alone.

"I appreciate that you want to help," he said softly and pushed his hands into his pockets to keep from touching her face. She gazed intently into his eyes and then looked away as a faint blush rose to her cheeks. Was she remembering that evening? He wished he knew how she felt about him. When he found the courage to tell her about his problem, would she be as understanding and as kind to him as she was with Otto? How could he doubt that?

"I have work I must get done." Eva left his side to go back to her desk.

Harley was helping Otto write letters in colored chalk on the blackboard. The sound of someone calling outside caught his attention. Willis walked to the door.

"Who is it?" Eva asked from her desk.

"I don't know them. Two *Englisch* women."

Eva moved to stand beside Willis. "The shorter one is Mrs. Kenworthy. She teaches at the public school. I don't know the other woman."

Mrs. Kenworthy waved when she spotted them standing in the schoolhouse door. "It's good to see you again, Eva. This is a friend of mine, Janet Obermeyer. She's with the Early Learning Center. I was telling her about the child we believe has a learning disability and she wished to speak to you."

Janet was tall and slim with short, straight red hair. She wore a lavender pantsuit and carried a briefcase. Willis turned to Eva. "Is she talking about Otto? He doesn't have a learning disability. It doesn't help the kid to have folks tell him he's not as good as everyone else."

"You are right, sir," Janet said. "Labels are not useful. A proper diagnosis is."

"There's nothing wrong with my brother. He's as smart as anyone. Maybe smarter." He glanced at Otto. The boy looked ready to bolt.

"From what Mrs. Kenworthy has told me, I suspect your brother may be affected by dyslexia. Many people with dyslexia are of above-average intelligence. I have brought some educational materials with me."

She looked directly at Otto. "The problem isn't a lack of intelligence. The problem lies in the way the brain fails to interpret the connection between letters and words with the sounds that they should make."

"So I've got a bad brain. Is that it?" Otto scowled at her.

Willis heard the pain in his voice and wished he knew how to help. Had he been blind to Otto's struggle because of his own shame?

"Not at all," Janet said. "Some children excel at math, others don't. Some children are good at art, others are not. Those are only a few examples of how our brains function differently. None of which are bad."

"Exactly what is dyslexia?" Danny asked from behind Willis. He hadn't heard him come in.

"A good question but one without an easy answer," Janet said.

"This is my brother Danny," Eva said.

Janet handed several books to Eva and then turned to Danny. "Reading isn't natural. Speaking is. Reading requires our brain to match letters to sounds, put those sounds together in a correct order to create a word, and then form words together into the sentences we can read, understand and write again. People with dyslexia have trouble matching the letters they see with the sounds the letters and combinations of letters make."

"Can it be cured?" Eva asked.

Janet shook her head. "It can't be cured. It is a life-long problem, but with the right supports, dyslexic children can become highly successful students and adults."

Eva leaned forward eagerly. "How do I accomplish that?"

"The first step is by having a dyslexia-friendly classroom, one that encourages dyslexic students to find their strengths and follow their interests."

Eva sat back. "All this is new to me. Can you explain what you mean?"

"Dyslexic-friendly means things like using colors to highlight different parts of speech. One thing that has been found to be effective is tactile learning. By using something as simple as a tray of sand the student can say the letter and write the letter in the sand with his finger over and over. It reinforces learning in a different part of the brain."

"Teacher has been having me do that," Otto said.

The woman smiled. "Excellent start."

Willis listened intently to what the women were saying. What did it mean for him if he had this problem, too?

Mrs. Kenworthy looked straight at Otto. "Children with dyslexia often believe they are stupid, but they aren't. Not by a long shot."

Willis fought against the hope rising in his heart. Was it possible that he had dyslexia and that was why he couldn't read? Maybe he wasn't ignorant or stupid. Maybe it was because his brain didn't recognize the squiggly lines as words. After all the years of believing he was inferior it was hard to wrap his mind around the fact that he might not be.

If he could learn to read, he could hold his head up in front of a congregation and preach from the Good Book. He could take a wife and not worry that she would be ashamed of him. It would mean he could keep better records for his business. It meant he could admit his love for Eva. The hope unfolding in his chest was almost painful.

"What else should I do?" Eva asked.

"Read aloud to your students. Show them your love of reading and books. Make it part of every school day. Encourage the parents to do the same."

Danny leaned against the corner of Eva's desk. "Are there some things that a teacher shouldn't do?"

"Never ask a dyslexic child to read aloud in front of classmates. It only serves to shame and embarrass them. We are learning more about this problem every year. Thousands of people live with this disorder. Most of them go on to become successful individuals. But it takes a lot of work."

"What about a grown-up who has dyslexia?" Harley asked. "Can they learn to read?"

Janet nodded. "Many young adults with dyslexia do learn to read but not rapidly or easily."

Harley frowned. "But if they can't read at all, can they learn with help?"

Janet smiled sadly. "It is much more difficult to re-train an adult brain. It can be done but it takes years of work and therapy. Even with that it is unlikely that they will be proficient readers."

Willis swallowed hard. The memory of the humiliation he had endured in school and from his so-called friends burned in the pit of his stomach.

"But it is possible?" Harley asked looking at Willis. Janet nodded. "It is possible."

Willis rubbed his hands on his pant legs. He wasn't afraid of hard work. Not if a life with Eva was his reward.

Eva caught Willis smiling at her and she had to look away from the warmth in his gaze for fear she would start blushing. She was afraid the others would notice so she hugged the books Janet had given her to her chest.

Willis cleared his throat. "I'd better get going."

Eva followed him to the door. "When you get back from Portland will you put shoes on Maddie's pony? She is constantly asking me to remind you."

Willis's smile disappeared. He looked at her with sorrow-filled eyes. "Maddie doesn't have a pony anymore. Her pony was pulling the cart when her *Mamm* and *Daed* were struck by a semi. Her pony was killed, too."

Eva pressed a hand to her heart. "The poor baby. No wonder she has a make-believe friend. Bubble can't be hurt."

"Thanks to you she is making real friends again. When I get back I have something I need to tell you."

She tipped her head to the side. "Can't you tell me now?"

"*Nee*, when we are alone," he said quietly with a glance at the others watching them. He settled his hat on his head and left.

That evening Eva went to the swing set instead of staying at home. She knew Willis was gone. She had seen him leave with Dale in his yellow pickup an hour ago. She prayed Willis's trip would be successful. He was determined to provide for his family, and she loved him for it.

She pushed herself back and forth with one foot as darkness descended. The swing was the place she felt closest to Willis. She missed his engaging conversations more than anything. She missed the way he looked her and the way he smiled at her. She touched her lips with her fingertips. Would he ever kiss her again? He cared. She knew that, but was it love? Was that what he wanted to tell her? She hugged her secret hope close to her heart.

When she entered the house sometime later she found Danny raiding her cookie jar with a tall glass of milk in one hand. His eyebrows drew together. "Where have you been?"

"Enjoying the evening. Why are you still up?"

"I just wanted to tell you I understand why you are drawn to teaching, Eva. I never thought about it before, but I see how rewarding it can be. You have opened my eyes."

"*Danki*. Hand me a cookie, please."

He held one out. "Eat it first, and then I'll tell you about your letter."

"From Gene?"

"Yup."

"Put my cookie back. I've lost my appetite. Where is it?"

"On the table by your rocker."

"Did you open it to see what he says?"

"I don't open other people's mail. What kind of snoop do you think I am?"

"I'm sorry. When will you be leaving?"

"The day after tomorrow."

"I'll miss you."

"Look on the bright side. You might be coming with me."

His joke wasn't funny. She went into her sitting room and picked up the letter. Drawing a deep breath, she slit it open and read her brother's brief note. He was expecting her to come home with Danny as soon as possible. He had included the money for a bus ticket this time.

"And?" Danny asked.

"I made myself plain in the letter I sent him. I want to stay. He's enclosed the money for our bus tickets and says he has written to the bishop and the school board detailing why I shouldn't be a teacher and why I'm needed at home. I lose. Gene wins."

"Gene's going to be eating burnt pancakes for the rest of his life, isn't he?"

"Very likely."

"I'm sorry, sis."

"I know."

He walked away. Eva stared at her letter. Danny might calmly accept Gene's order to return home, but she wasn't going to leave unless she had no other choice.

The next day started off well at school. She confiscated the rubber bands from the Yoder twins and made Sadie go home the first time she poked her nose in the door. Both Harley and Otto were quiet but that was a good thing. The children went out for the morning recess and Eva stayed in to grade papers.

She didn't see what started the fight. One moment the children were playing a game of softball and when she looked up again there was a fistfight in progress. Otto and Harley were pummeling the Yoder twins.

She rushed out the door to break up the fight. She stepped between the two boys to push them apart. The next second she found herself in the dirt between them. Otto tripped over her legs and fell on top of her.

Before she could get up, the boys were pulled apart by Bishop Schultz and Samuel Yoder. "What's going on here?" Yoder demanded.

"I haven't the least idea," Eva said breathlessly as she scrambled to her feet. The bishop had a hold of both Harley and the older Yoder boy.

"Grandson, what is the meaning of this?" Samuel demanded.

"Nothing." The boy couldn't look his grandfather in the eye.

Harley's face was beet red. "He called my brother an idiot, and he wouldn't take it back."

Samuel glared at Eva. "Is this the sort of behavior you are teaching our children?"

Her temper flared. "It is not. Your grandsons had learned to throw insults and punches long before I came."

"Woman, where is your *demoot*?"

She forced herself to calm down. "I beg your pardon. My humility is in short supply at the moment."

The bishop turned to the children gathered in a semi-circle. "School is dismissed early today. Go home."

They all filed away except for Harley, Otto and Maddie who gathered close to Eva. Jenny and little Annabeth waited by the school steps.

Eva managed a smile for the Gingrich children. "Go to the house, get cleaned up, do your chores then go home with Jenny. Bethany and Michael are expecting you to stay with them another night aren't they?"

Harley nodded. "Willis said he wouldn't be home

until after midnight and he didn't want to get us so late on a school night."

"Okay, I will see you all tomorrow and we'll discuss what happened with him. Harley, my brother Danny is working in the new barn. Tell him Annabeth needs a ride home. She's too small to walk so far alone."

Samuel scowled at her when the children were gone. "It is as your brother Gene stated in his letter to us. You are not a proper teacher if you allow the *kinder* to engage in fistfights. You were warned that your contract would run for one month at a time, but an exception must be made. Consider yourself terminated."

"What?" Her jaw dropped.

"Samuel, I think you are being hasty," the bishop said calmly.

"I don't believe I am. Your pay will be forwarded to your home in Illinois. I will take over your duties until a suitable replacement can be found."

The two men walked off, leaving Eva reeling. She had lost her job and her home in one fell swoop. Her days in Maine had come to an end. All that she had feared was coming true.

She went back inside the school and stared at the blackboard. What was she to do? She needed to talk to Willis, but he wouldn't be back until late. She didn't want to wait until tomorrow to speak to him.

She grabbed a pen and a sheet of paper. The time for maidenly reserve was past. She was in love with Willis. If he cared for her, she would defy Gene and find a way to stay in Maine but she had to know for sure.

My dearest Willis,
I have been fired from my position as teacher. I

don't want to leave you and the children. I love you Willis. I love Harley, Otto, Maggie and even Bubble. If you hold any feelings for me in your heart please meet me tonight at the swing set no matter what time it is. I'll be waiting. I can't leave without knowing how you truly feel. Your kiss gave me hope even if that wasn't your intention.

If you don't come, I will know my hope was in vain and I will leave.

Eva

She sealed the letter and went to Willis's house. The children had already gone. She placed the note on the counter under the kerosene lamp where he couldn't miss it and left.

She told Danny what had happened when he returned from taking Annabeth home. He was as astonished as she had been. "What are you going to do?" he asked.

"I'll let you know in the morning." It all depended on Willis.

Time dragged until it was almost midnight. She hurried to the schoolyard and waited.

It was long before she heard Dale's truck pull in. She saw Willis enter his house. The light came on in the kitchen. Her heart began hammering in her chest. He had to be reading her letter. What was he thinking? Had she been too bold? The chains of swing bit into her palms as she waited. He must love her. She loved him so much.

He came out a short time later and went into his smithy without looking her way. She waited, afraid to breathe. When he came out of his workshop he went back into the house. Was he ignoring her request? His light went out.

She waited for another half hour and then bowed her head as the bitter truth sank in. He wasn't coming. He didn't love her. The tears she'd been holding back slipped free.

She made her way home, drying her eyes when she saw Danny was waiting up for her. "Well?"

"I'm going back with you."

"Tomorrow?"

"The sooner the better." She had been such a fool.

Chapter Fifteen

Willis couldn't wait to share his good news with Eva, but he didn't want to interrupt her during school. He'd been hired to supply all the hand-forged hardware for Ray Jackson's shops in Portland and for his new store in Boston. Willis decided to wait until he knew Eva would be free at lunch. In the meantime he got busy on Mr. Jackson's first order.

It was almost noon when he crossed the road and headed for the schoolhouse. He noticed a van stop in front of Eva's house. Bethany and Michael's buggy pulled up behind it. Dinah and Gemma got out along with Bethany and Michael. They went up to Eva's house. Was Danny heading back today? Willis would make sure to tell him goodbye, but he had to see Eva first.

He opened the door of the schoolhouse and stepped inside. Samuel Yoder sat at the desk up front. Otto was standing beside him with his hands clenched into fists at his sides. He was shaking and there were tears on his cheeks.

Willis strode to the front of the room. "What's going on? Otto, what's wrong?"

"Your brother is being stubborn. He has refused to read his assignment out loud."

Otto looked at Willis. "I can't."

Willis nodded. "I understand. It's going to be okay." He looked at Samuel. "Where is Eva?"

"Eva Coblentz no longer teaches here."

Willis wasn't sure that he heard right. "What do you mean she doesn't teach here? Where is she?"

"Preparing to return to Illinois with her brother."

"She wouldn't leave without telling me."

But maybe she had told him. He thought of the note he'd found on the counter last night. He had brought it with him to have Harley read it when they were alone.

Willis pulled the envelope from the pocket of his jacket and stared at it. She wouldn't have written a good-bye letter. She would've come to see him in person. Wouldn't she? He had to know if the note was from her. He held it out to Harley. "Read it."

Samuel scowled at them. "Willis, I am trying to conduct class here. If you have business with your brother, please step outside. Otto, read the statement on the board. You will not return to your seat until you have done as I asked, even if you have to stand here all day."

Harley came to Willis's side, pulled the letter out of the envelope and opened it. "My dearest Willis." Harley's eyes grew round. "I don't think I should read this. It's kind of personal."

"Is it from Eva?"

"*Ja.*"

Willis took the page from his brother. "*Danki.* Otto, Maddie, we're leaving."

Samuel rose to his feet. "Willis, you are interfering with the discipline of this classroom. Your brother is not dismissed."

"If you were half the teacher that Eva Coblentz is, you would know that Otto suffers from dyslexia. Did you even bother to read her notes about the boy? He can't read his assignment. With special tutoring he will be able to someday, but humiliating him will not hasten that day. Come on, kids, we have to stop Eva."

Maddie was already headed for the door. Willis, followed closely by Otto and Harley, hurried to catch up with her. Outside he saw Danny loading a pair of suitcases into the van. Eva stood beside him. She was hugging Bethany. Michael shook hands with Danny while Dinah and Gemma looked on.

Fear choked Willis and closed his throat so he could barely breathe. What if she didn't want to stay? Why would she consider marrying a man as dimwitted as he was? She could have the choice of any man. A man who could read the books she loved and talk to her about them. He didn't deserve her.

Maddie tugged on his hand. "Come on. What are you waiting for?"

"I guess I'm waiting for my courage to show up."

"I don't think you're gonna find it standing here. You have to make Eva stay."

He smiled at his little sister. "I think I would rather face a bear than tell her what's wrong with me, but she has to know."

Eva had her black traveling bonnet on. She hadn't seen him. Willis crossed the strip of grass and ran up to the van where Danny was loading her belongings. "Eva, wait. What are you doing?"

When she looked his way, he saw her eyes were red from crying. He wanted to take her in his arms and comfort her but he didn't know if she would allow it.

Tears glistened on her lashes. "I'm going home."

"But why? I thought you liked it here. I thought you loved teaching the children." He took hold of the van door.

I thought maybe you loved me.

She closed her eyes. "I explained why in my letter. I said everything there was to say. I don't want to rehash it here. Please, just let me go. You've been a fine friend and I'm sorry I expected more than you could give. Goodbye, Willis Gingrich. God be with you, always."

She was going to leave him unless he could put his pride and fear aside and make her understand. Her friends stood a few feet away watching him. Willis swallowed hard. Everyone would know what a failure he was, but he was more afraid of losing Eva. "I couldn't read your letter."

"I'm sorry if it embarrassed you. The feelings are my own and I understand that you couldn't return them."

He held the paper out to her. "You didn't hear me, Eva. I wasn't embarrassed by your letter because I couldn't read it. I can't read." He closed his eyes and hung his head.

Please, dear God, don't let her laugh.

The silence stretched on so long that he finally looked up. There were tears running down her cheeks. "Oh, Willis, why didn't you tell me?"

"I was ashamed. I didn't want anyone to know. I've hidden it for so long I didn't know how to tell you. I didn't want you to feel sorry for me. I didn't want you to know how stupid I was."

"I'm sorry you didn't feel you could trust me."

Willis gazed into her beautiful green eyes. "I wanted to."

This was the hard part. He stared at his feet. "When I was twenty, I started seeing a girl who wasn't Amish. She ran around with a cool bunch of kids. They had fast cars and money to spend, they liked loud music, but I think they were bored a lot of the time."

He stared at his hand on the car door. His knuckles were white from gripping the steel. Even now it hurt to repeat what happened. "I confided to that young woman that I couldn't read. I didn't want to keep a secret that big from someone I thought I was serious about." He swallowed hard.

"Go on," Eva said gently.

"She laughed a little. She thought I was kidding. She told the others. They laughed a lot. Of course I laughed, too. I pretended it didn't matter. A few days later we were coming back from a party when the boy driving pulled into a convenience store parking lot. He said he needed a few things, some candy, some crackers and soda. He gave me a twenty-dollar bill and a list of what he wanted. He said give it to the clerk and he'd get the stuff for me. So I went in and handed the young woman behind the counter the note." Willis stopped talking. Humiliation burned deep in his chest.

He felt a hand on his arm. Eva was staring at him intently. "It wasn't a list of grocery items, was it?"

"It read, *This is a holdup. Give me all the money in the cash drawer.*

"The clerk was just a kid. She went pale as a sheet,

started shaking and crying. An alarm went off. I didn't know what was going on. Then my friends rushed in, laughing like a bunch of fools." He could see their red faces, hear them howling with mirth while they clapped him on the back as if he was somehow privy to the gag.

"They bolted when the police came." His girlfriend had been the first one out the door.

"I spent the next twelve hours explaining to them that I had been duped. I was fortunate that I didn't get arrested. I knew the story would be all over the county in a few days. I decided to leave before I had to face everyone. I ended up here. I never told anyone else, although recently there was someone that I wanted to confide in. The trouble is that she's so smart I was afraid she would be ashamed of me."

Eva stepped forward and cupped his face with her hands. "Willis, you are one of the finest men I have ever known. I love you. Do you hear me? I could never be ashamed of the man I love.

"You are not ignorant. When I think of all the times I criticized you for not caring about Otto's education I'm the one who is ashamed. I'm so sorry. Please forgive me."

He drew her into his arms without caring who saw. "There's nothing to forgive unless you leave this brokenhearted fellow behind and return to Illinois."

"Danny, take my things out of the car, please." Her eyes never left Willis's face. He started to believe she truly did love him.

Danny set her suitcases aside. "Why don't I take the kids to the bus station with me? The driver can bring them back here after we've said our goodbyes and had some ice cream. Who wants an ice cream cone?"

Maddie held up her hand. "I do. I do."

Harley put a hand on her head and turned her toward the van. "We all want some. Come on, Otto."

"Did you hear what Willis said? I'm not the only one. He's like me."

Harley ruffled Otto's hair and winked at Willis. "Yeah, I heard. I think our big brother's a mighty fine fellow. I hope he knows how blessed he is to have found a good teacher." The children got in the van with Danny and drove away.

Willis suddenly realized he was holding Eva in his arms in plain sight of the school, and a number of their church members. He looked over Eva's head at Michael. "I'd like to continue this conversation somewhere more private."

"We're going. Eva, you are welcome to stay with us for as long as need be," Michael said.

Dinah was grinning from ear to ear. "Leroy and I will make the same offer."

"*Danki*. You are all very kind."

They left and Eva turned to Willis. "Come into the house. I can make us some coffee although it actually belongs to the school and not to me. How did your meeting with the Bartlett people go?"

"I almost forgot. I have a standing order for two hundred cabinet pulls and hinges for the next two months. If they sell well, there will be more orders. They like them."

"I don't see why not. You do beautiful work."

As soon as they were in the house, he closed the door and pulled her into his arms again. "I'm going to kiss you, Eva Coblentz, unless you tell me I can't."

"I thought you'd never ask, Willis." She slipped her arms around his neck and closed her eyes.

Eva had dreamed about this moment since the first time they sat on the swings together. She knew then that she was losing her heart to this amazing man, though she had been too afraid to admit it. Their first kiss had been amazing. This kiss was far more wondrous.

His lips were firm and gentle as they touched hers. A shiver raced down her spine and she leaned closer, melting against him, loving the way he made her feel cherished and as giddy as any teenager. He pulled away with a sigh and tucked her head under his chin. "Have I told you how much I love you?"

"I'm not sure. I don't think you mentioned it."

"Eva darling, I love you. Today, tomorrow, for the rest of my life and into eternity, I will always love you."

She would never tire of hearing those words or of saying them. "I love you, too. What did I do to deserve such happiness?"

"I am asking myself the same question. I reckon only God knows for sure. Or maybe Bubble does."

"*Gott* has truly blessed us." She rose on her tiptoes to press a kiss to his lips. "What does Bubble have to do with any of this?"

Wrapping his arms around her, he pulled her closer and kissed her until her head was spinning and she was breathless all over again. Pulling away, he took a deep breath. "Bubble gave me some interesting encouragement."

Eva settled her face against the side of his neck. He smelled of smoke and leather and the pine forests all around them. She breathed in the scent knowing she would never forget it. "What sort of encouragement did an imaginary girl give you?"

"You'll laugh."

"At you? Never. With you? Every chance I get."

"Bubble told me you would say yes if I proposed to you."

"She did? Isn't she a bold child?"

He leaned back so he could see her face. "Maybe, but sometimes she spouts the truth when I'm least expecting it. Was she right?"

"I don't know."

"What do you mean you don't know?"

She looked up and tapped his nose with her finger. "You have not asked me."

He held her at arm's length. "Teacher, will you do me the honor of becoming my wife?"

"To have and to hold?"

He cupped her face with his hands. "In sickness and in health, *ja*, all of that. Will you please marry me? I desperately need someone to help me with the children and I need a good cook."

She pulled his hands away. "I knew you had an ulterior motive."

"I'm simply going down the list the *kinder* made. You're pretty and you aren't too old."

She laughed out loud. "I love you, Willis Gingrich and all your family."

A knock at the door startled them both. Willis moved a few steps away. Eva straightened her *kapp* and smoothed the front of her dress. She opened the door. Samuel Yoder stood there with a manila folder and his hand.

He cleared his throat. "I believe there has been a mistake. And I'm afraid that I am the one who has made it."

"Won't you come in?" Eva said. What was this about?

Samuel stepped to the door and nodded to Willis. "I finished reading your file on young Otto."

"I see. Please have a seat." She led the way to her sitting room and sat down in her rocking chair. Samuel sat on the edge of the sofa while Willis stood in the doorway, leaning one shoulder against the doorjamb.

Samuel looked from one to the other. "I was unaware of Otto's difficulties and I humiliated him in front of the other children. I want to apologize. In looking through your desk I saw numerous articles about dyslexia. Clearly, you have a plan to help the boy. I don't want to rob him of his chance to learn. I hope that you will consider returning to your teaching post. I will write to your brother and explain that you can't be spared at this time. If you want to stay?"

Eva's heart gave a little leap of joy. She glanced at Willis before replying.

"Your decision," he said with that adorable little half smile on his lips.

She folded her hands together tightly. "I will consider it."

The outside door opened. The children followed by Danny tripped into the kitchen with ice cream cones in their hands. They made themselves at home around the table. Danny looked into the sitting room. "Are we interrupting?"

Eva stared at him in amazement. "Did you miss your bus?"

"Nope. I saw it. I bought my ticket. I put my suitcase on it and then I changed my mind. Fortunately, I was able to get my suitcase off before the bus left. And I got a refund for the ticket."

"You're staying here? In New Covenant? Why?"

"I had a sneaking suspicion that there was going to be an opening for a new teacher soon. Also, Bubble mentioned that you were getting married. Can I guess who the poor fellow is?"

"Willis," Maddie called out. "Bubble said so."

Willis wagged his eyebrows at Eva. "Bubble is right again."

Danny handed his melting cone to Eva. "Brother Yoder, I'd like to talk to you about a teaching position. Have you considered hiring a man?"

"Having a man as a teacher is most unusual." Samuel stroked his beard. "But I will bring this to the attention of the school board."

"Fine. And is your granddaughter Becca seeing anyone?"

Samuel frowned. "My granddaughter?"

"I was just curious. Come, I'll walk you out." The two men went out the door, leaving Eva and Willis with the three children.

Willis tipped his head toward the kitchen. "I have some explaining to do. Care to listen?"

She walked up to him and laid her hand on his cheek. "If you are sure you don't mind?"

"I never want to keep secrets from you again."

Willis took a deep breath and sat down at the table with his brothers and his sister. "You heard me tell Eva that I can't read."

"Is it true?" Maddie asked.

"It is."

"But you read me stories at night sometimes."

"I only look at the pictures in your book and I make up the story as I go along. I'm not reading."

"You could have fooled me," she declared and licked her ice cream.

He saw Eva struggling not to laugh. "I fooled a lot of people. In school I could memorize what the other children read and then repeat it when my turn came. If I had to go first, I couldn't do it. Like Otto, I misbehaved a lot, hoping the teacher wouldn't notice. It worked for a while. She thought I was lazy and so did our *daed*."

"I guess he yelled at you a lot. He did me," Otto said quietly.

"He didn't understand what was wrong with us but he wanted the best for you and for me. I believe that. I wish he was still here so Eva could explain."

"He understands now," she said softly.

Willis nodded. "I started skipping school before the end of my last year and went to work in the smithy with my uncle. I didn't need to read there, and I liked it."

Harley walked to the front door. "I've got to go. Maddie, wait here. I'll be back in a minute." He took off at a run.

"What is that boy up to?" Willis asked.

The other two children shrugged. They all walked out onto the porch. Willis slipped his arm around Eva's waist and pulled her close. She pushed his arm away. "Not in front of the children," she whispered but she was smiling.

Harley came walking up the drive, leading a black-and-white pony. He stopped at the foot of the steps and waved to Mrs. Arnett. She waved back and pulled away in her truck with a horse trailer hooked on behind.

Harley handed the reins of the pony to Maddie. "I know you miss Popcorn. This is Zip. He's as sweet as they come and he's for you."

"For me?" Maddie squeaked.

"I've been working over at her farm so I could buy him from Mrs. Arnett. Willis put shoes on him not long ago so you can ride him now if you'd like."

Maddie threw her arms around him. "You are the best brother ever!"

"I know. It was Otto's idea. He can't read well but he's the thinker in this family."

Maddie hugged Otto. "You are the second-best brother in the whole world."

"Sure, sure. Get up on him and go for a ride."

Willis lifted her to the pony's back and settled her feet in the stirrups. She beamed at him and Eva. "I'm going to go show Annabeth."

Eva pointed up the road. "Fourth farm on the left. There is a path along the edge of the woods so you don't have to ride out on the highway."

Willis nodded. "*Goot*. Okay. You and Bubble have a nice ride."

"She can't come. She's gone to visit her sister in Texas." Maddie turned Zip around and trotted him along the path that led past the school.

Harley tugged on Otto's arm. "Come on. We should keep an eye on her in case she decides to ride to Texas and show Bubble her new horse."

"Where is Texas?" Otto asked as he followed his brother.

Willis didn't hear Harley's reply. He turned to Eva

and took her hand. Together they walked to the swing set beside the school. She sat down and he gave her a gentle push. He kept her swinging for a few minutes. "Do you want to continue teaching this year?"

She titled her head back to see him. "How did you know?"

"Bubble told me."

"How could she? She's in Texas."

"She mailed me a letter. Speaking of letters, do you want to read the one you wrote to me?"

"No."

"Why not?"

"Because I said some very personal things. I want you to read it for yourself someday."

"What if I can't ever do that?"

She put her feet down, hopped off and twisted around to look at him. "You will. It may take a long time and it won't be easy but I know you will."

"How can you be so sure?"

"Because you have a teacher who loves you. Do you mind if I finish out the school year here?"

"Maybe just a little but I know you had your heart set on it. I've waited for you my whole life. I can wait until school is out in the spring. But not one week more."

"I love you for that!" She leaned forward and he had no choice but to kiss her again.

It was much too brief. He foresaw a long winter ahead. "Was your brother serious about becoming a teacher?"

"I think he is. I'll have him be my helper this year and he can take over next year."

Willis moved the swing out of the way. "It's hard to believe this is real." He reached out and drew his fingers along the curve of her cheek. "I'm afraid I will wake and find it has all been a dream. Promise you won't vanish with the dawn."

She captured his hand and pressed a kiss into his palm. "I am not a dream. I love you, Willis, with all my heart. For now and forever. I thought this kind of love was found only in books but I was wrong. It's found in the heart. My heart."

She slipped her arms around his waist and laid her cheek against his chest.

He sighed deeply as he pulled her close. "I don't know anything about books or poems. All I know is iron and roaring hot coals. What will we talk about?"

She giggled and rose on tiptoe until her lips were only an inch away from his. "Silly man. Who says we're going to be talking? I plan on a lot of kissing and being kissed. Like this." She proceeded to show him just how wonderful a conversation with the teacher could be.

* * * * *

HEALING THEIR AMISH HEARTS

Leigh Bale

This book is dedicated to all those faithful couples who love, adore and cherish one another with a loyalty that surpasses anything this life or the dark forces can throw at them. They cling to one another and put the other first, second only to God, and love one another as the Savior taught us to do.

Lo, children are an heritage of the Lord.
—*Psalm* 127:3

Chapter One

Starting a new job was never easy. But for Rebecca Graber, it seemed her first week as the interim teacher of the Amish school in Riverton, Colorado, might also be her last.

Standing beside her desk in the one-room schoolhouse, she picked up her McGuffey reader. Thirty old-fashioned wooden desks sat lined up in orderly fashion with a black potbellied stove at the front of the room. A wide chalkboard covered the front wall, topped with English and German penmanship charts and several pull-down maps and illustrations for lessons. Poetry, artwork and Amish proverbs dotted the other walls. Becca had plenty of paper, crayons and flash cards for the children to use. And sitting on her desk was a large handbell she rang when she called the children in from recess.

"First and second grades, please take out your reading books. All other grades will study quietly in their workbooks," she said.

There was a slight rustling as the twenty-four scholars did as she asked. She didn't have a lot of students but since this was her first week teaching here, it felt closer to forty. On Monday morning, her first day here, her lesson plans had mysteriously disappeared. On Tuesday, she'd sat on a tack that had appeared on her chair. And the day after that, she had to break up a fight during recess when Caleb and Enos were teasing Sam. Yesterday, she'd found a paper taped to the back of her sweater that said *kick me.* No wonder the children had snickered every time she'd turned away. If she couldn't get control of her class soon, she had no doubt the school board would dismiss her as a complete and utter failure even before the first of May when school let out for the summer.

The room was tidy, with dark tan walls and wooden floors. The red log building had been a specially ordered kit that was built by the fathers of the scholars. Bike racks and a hitching post were situated out front in the graveled parking lot. A small barn stood near the outhouse where the children's horses and ponies were kept until it was time to go home. A spacious dirt area served as a baseball field. Although the school possibly needed a couple of swings and teeter-totter, Becca couldn't ask for more and wished this was a permanent position. But the regular teacher would return next fall, after she healed from the buggy accident that had crushed her pelvis and broken both her legs. The young woman was blessed to still be alive.

As she waited for the students to settle themselves, Becca glanced out the wide windows. The afternoon sun sparkled against the dusting of snow they'd received early that morning. The azure sky looked crystal clear but the February temperatures were downright frigid.

Becca added another piece of wood to the fire, then called on a student to begin.

"Samuel King, would you please read out loud for us?" she asked with a kind smile.

Sam's soft brown eyes widened in panic, then he looked down at his book, his hands folded tightly in his lap. Becca waited patiently but the six-year-old boy didn't speak. Not a single word.

"Excuse me, Teacher Becca." Andy Yoder, the bishop's youngest son and another first-grader, held up his hand.

"Yes, Andy?" Becca asked.

"Sam don't talk, teacher. Not ever," Andy said.

"Sam *doesn't* talk," she said, correcting the boy's grammar.

And she wasn't willing to accept that. But first things first. She reached for a piece of chalk so she could write the correct sentence on the board. Finding no chalk, she pulled open the drawer to her desk…and quickly jerked back as a shrill cry escaped her throat.

A snake! In her desk drawer.

She stepped back so fast that her chair toppled to the floor. All the scholars gaped at her in surprise. A few snickered. Becca blinked, expecting the snake to move. But it didn't. And after closer inspection, she realized it was made of rubber.

A toy snake! In her desk drawer.

With a quick twist of her hand, she flipped it out onto the floor. It landed near Caleb Yoder, the bishop's eleven-year-old son. He scooped it up before shoving it into one of the girls' faces. Absolute pandemonium erupted. The girl reared back and screamed as Caleb tossed the fake reptile to Enos Albrecht, who laughed and waved it in the air.

"Enos! Stop that," Becca called in a stern voice, trying to restore order.

Screeching madly, little Fannie Albrecht jumped up on her chair, her fisted hands pulled to her face in absolute terror. Shrieks and shouts filled the air.

"Stop that!" Reuben Fisher cried.

Reuben was the son of Becca's cousin and lived in the same house with her and her aunt Naomi. He tried to snatch the toy away from Enos but wasn't tall enough. In the struggle, the fake serpent bounced against the boy's hand and landed on the wooden floor in front of the door.

There was a loud gasp and the room went absolutely still.

Jesse King, Sam's father, stood in front of the open door, holding his black felt hat in his hands. His gaze swept the room, his shrewd eyes showing that he understood exactly what had transpired. A corner of his mouth twitched and Becca thought he might laugh. But no. He looked too stern to find any humor in the moment. A chilly gust of wind accompanied his entrance and he pushed the portal closed with the point of his black work boot. Becca stared, thinking she imagined the man. When had he come inside? Probably during the chaos.

Oh, no! Why did he have to show up now? What must he think of her?

A moment of confusion fogged Becca's mind. She couldn't move. Couldn't breathe. She watched as if in slow motion as Mr. King leaned down and picked up the rubber snake. It dangled from his large hand and Becca couldn't contain a shiver of revulsion.

"Is this yours?" Looking directly at Becca, Mr. King spoke in *Deitsch*, the German dialect their Amish people used among themselves. His voice sounded low and calm and he seemed completely unruffled by the horrible snake.

Mortified beyond words, Becca hurried toward him. Her face heated up like road flares. The fact that one of the fathers of her scholars had witnessed this shameful moment almost undid her.

"No, but I'll take care of it." She spoke in perfect English, the language they used in the classroom.

She forced herself to take the toy snake between two trembling fingers. With disgust, she returned it to the front of the room and shut it up in her desk drawer again. Out of her peripheral vision, she saw Lenore Schwartz help little Fannie climb down off her chair and the children all took their seats. And just like that, order was restored.

Gathering her composure, Becca patted her white organdy prayer *kapp* and smoothed her lavender skirts before she faced Sam's father again.

"Mr. King, was there something you wanted?" She lifted her chin higher, forcing herself to meet Jesse King's solid gaze. For just a moment, she thought his eyes looked sad and…haunted.

This was the first time she'd met him, though she'd seen him from afar on several occasions. Since she'd only arrived in Riverton eight days earlier, she hadn't had the opportunity to attend church yet but she'd tried to speak with him yesterday when he'd picked up Sam from school. He'd driven away before she could catch him and, if she didn't know better, she'd think he'd been trying to avoid her.

Up close, she realized he was a tall man with dark brooding eyes, high cheekbones and a narrow chin. His black hair was overly long for an Amish man and curled against the sides of his face. His beard indicated he was married, though Becca had been told by a member of the school board that he was a widower. Becca figured there was no one at home to cut his hair for him. If only he would smile, she might find him ruggedly handsome. But just now, his angular face showed no emotion whatsoever and only his eyes indicated an active mind hidden beneath his tranquil exterior.

"I've come to pick up Sam," Jesse said. His voice sounded low, his dark eyes unwavering.

Like her, Jesse and Sam were newcomers to this *Gmay*, their Amish community. They had moved here from Lancaster County in Pennsylvania just two months earlier. Apparently Jesse had lost his wife and two young daughters in a house fire a year earlier. The poor man. No wonder he looked so sad. And since that time, little Samuel hadn't spoken a single word. Becca knew no more than that. But she kept giving Sam opportunities and hoping that one day he would surprise her and finally read out loud.

Trying to be professional, she glanced at the clock on the wall. "But school isn't out for another twenty minutes. If you'd like to wait, perhaps I can speak with you afterward."

Jesse inclined his head. "*Ne*, I'm afraid I don't have time to wait. This afternoon, I need to move a boulder from my south field and won't be finished before it's time to return and pick him up from school. I'll have to take him home now."

Becca blinked. She was trying to be understanding. Trying to be a good teacher. But the truth was, she was highly inexperienced. Though she'd served four months as a teacher's apprentice in Ohio, this was her first time teaching solo. It was bad enough to come into a classroom full of scholars she didn't know but she had also entered this class midway through the school year. She wanted to do a good job. She really did. In fact, her future depended on it.

"Of course." She glanced at Sam, stepping over to help the boy gather his lunch pail and put on his warm winter coat.

For just a moment, Becca wished she was anywhere but here. She should be married and looking forward to raising a *familye* of her own, but that wasn't possible now. Not since her ex-fiancé had broken off their engagement. She'd known and loved Vernon all her life, yet he'd chosen to wed another girl they'd grown up with. If Becca failed in this position, she'd be forced to return to her *familye* in Ohio in shame. She was hoping for a good job reference so she could go elsewhere. She couldn't bear to go home and watch Vernon and Ruth marry and raise a *familye* together while she became a dried-up old spinster.

As she accompanied Sam to the door, she walked with him outside onto the front steps. "Mr. King, I really need to speak with you about Sam. Did you receive the letter I sent home with him two days ago?"

Jesse nodded. "*Ja*, I received your letter."

"*Gut*. Then you know I'd like to discuss Sam's problem…"

"Not now." Without another word, Jesse placed his hat on his head and hurried down the steps. Sam trailed behind.

Becca shivered and wrapped her arms around herself. Something hardened inside of her. She was Sam's teacher and must look after his education. Determined not to be ignored, she followed Jesse.

"If not now, when? I'm concerned about Sam. He's not speaking. I'd like to help," she called to Jesse's back.

Without a backward glance, the man climbed into his black buggy and closed the door. Sam scrambled into the buggy on the opposite side with a little difficulty. Becca helped him in, thinking it a bit derelict for a parent to let their six-year-old son fend for himself. She rounded the buggy, intending to confront the boy's father.

"Mr. King, please," she said.

Jesse took the leather lead lines into his large hands. Becca noticed several ugly, purple scars on his skin before he gave a little flick and the buggy lurched into motion. She had no choice but to step back or be trampled as he directed the horse down the muddy road. Within moments, they disappeared from view.

Well, of all the nerve! What a rude man.

Trying to hide her frustration, Becca turned and went inside. She was surprised to find the classroom so quiet. Every student had their head ducked over their books, the younger children studying their McGuffey readers while the older children wrote out vocabulary words.

No doubt the culprits of the snake incident must fear her wrath. She thought Caleb Yoder must be the ringleader. But without proof, she couldn't accuse him openly. Still, after the events of the past week, this wasn't the first time. And now there was a toy snake in her desk drawer. What would the school board say about that?

Being more cautious, she glanced at her chair before sitting down, then breathed a silent sigh of relief. Only ten more minutes and she'd be free for the weekend. Most of the children were bright, helpful and quiet. But Caleb and Enos had a penchant for causing enough trouble that Becca was seriously considering speaking with their parents. The only problem was that Caleb's father was Bishop Yoder. And she hated the thought of approaching the bishop of her new *Gmay* about his wayward son. No, she must handle this on her own. She had to get control of the school. And fast.

Standing again, she was determined to say something to the students. After all, it was her job to correct poor behavior. Choosing her words carefully, she folded her hands in front of her starched white apron.

"Scholars, I must tell you that I'm ashamed of you today. When Mr. King came to our school, we showed him what poorly behaved children you are. You embarrassed yourselves and I have no doubt your parents will hear all about it."

There. That was good. Maybe the fear of their parents finding out might make the children behave better. From the front of the room, Caleb slid lower in his seat. Perhaps the thought of his father hearing what had happened didn't appeal to him. Good! Maybe he'd think twice before putting tacks on her chair or rubber snakes in her drawer again.

"I hope as you go home this afternoon, you'll think about what your parents expect from you," she continued. "And I hope you won't let this happen again. Now, it's time to go home. Please tidy your desks and get your coats on. School is dismissed."

The students did as asked, hurrying toward the door. Out of her peripheral vision, Becca saw Caleb's elder brother nudge his arm, a look of disapproval on his face. Karen, who was Caleb's older sister, frowned as well.

Great! Becca wanted to cry out in victory. If Becca's admonitions wouldn't work, perhaps sibling pressure might help correct Caleb's poor behavior.

The last student headed out the door. Through the wide windows, Becca saw several black buggies waiting. Since the school was situated in one corner of Bishop Yoder's hay field, his farm was nearby. But this certainly wasn't like her home in Ohio where everyone lived within walking distance of the school. Many of the children here in Riverton lived as many as nine miles away and needed a ride home. Some children brought a small pony cart to school, while others waited for their parents to pick them up with their horse and buggy.

Returning to her desk, Becca stared at the place where she'd stowed the toy snake. With a quick jerk, she pulled the drawer open and recoiled in anticipation. But there was no need. During the brief time when she'd been outside speaking with Jesse King, the snake had disappeared.

Hmm. No doubt one of the children had taken it. And honestly, Becca was happy to have it gone. Hopefully it didn't make a reappearance. Because she desperately wanted the school board to write her a nice reference when she finished her assignment in May. She needed to serve as a substitute teacher for three full years before being eligible to teach at any Amish parochial school. As a teacher, she was a late bloomer. She hadn't done any student teaching earlier, when she'd first achieved her certificate of completion from the Amish school she'd attended as a girl. She thought she'd be getting married, so she hadn't even considered it at the time. But if she did well here in Riverton, she could get an Amish teaching job anywhere. This position was only a beginning, but she'd do almost anything to keep from returning home to Ohio.

Now, if she could just figure out a way to handle Jesse King and little Sam's lack of speech, she might have a chance.

Jesse patted the side of his black-and-white Holstein and picked up the two buckets of fresh milk. Carrying them outside the barn, he noticed the skiff of snow they'd had that morning had almost melted off. It'd be dark soon. The afternoon sun was settling behind the Wet Mountains to the east. The fading beams of light sprayed the sky in creamy pink and gold, glinting off the jagged spikes of granitic rock. Jesse had been reading up on his new home. The Wet Valley sat at an elevation of just under 8,000 feet. With the cooler elevation and much shorter growing season, he'd never be able to successfully grow anything but hay, some barley and maybe some sugar beets. In his summer garden, the snap peas and carrots should do fine, but some other Amish farmers at church had told him not to bother growing celery and he'd have to cover his tomato plants at night or they'd freeze. But his farmland was fertile and located ten long miles outside of town. Because his new home was isolated and lonely, he'd gotten it for a cheap price. And the solitude was just what he wanted to soothe his broken heart.

Still holding the milk buckets, he paused, remembering the last time he'd shared a similar sunset with his sweet wife, Alice. Back then, they'd been living in the overly populated area of Lancaster County. They'd been walking from the barn to their house when he'd pulled her close as they'd admired the beauty of *Gott's* creations. They'd heard about this new Amish settlement in Colorado and talked about moving here. It'd provide more opportunities for growth. A place where they could expand and their *familye* would have a better future. They were happy and filled with anticipation. Life was so good then.

Alice and their two daughters had died three days later, taking all of Jesse's joy with them.

The rattle of a horse and buggy drew his attention. He turned and groaned out loud. Rebecca Graber, Sam's schoolteacher, was just pulling into his graveled driveway.

He thought about rushing inside and pretending he didn't know she was here. He could ignore her knock on the door. But no. He'd have to face her sooner or later.

Setting the buckets of frothy milk on the back porch, he tucked his thumbs into the black suspenders that crossed his blue chambray shirt and waited. Becca pulled up right in front of him and climbed out of her buggy. Wearing a heavy black mantle with a gray scarf wrapped around her neck, she tugged off her gloves. Taking a step, she tucked several golden-blond strands of hair back into her black traveling bonnet. Other than her bright pink cheeks and nose, her skin looked smooth and pale as porcelain. Her startling blue eyes sparkled with a zest for life, her heart-shaped lips creased in a tentative smile.

"*Hallo*, Mr. King," she called.

"*Hallo*. What can I do for you?" he returned with little enthusiasm.

Slightly breathless, she joined him next to the back door. "I was hoping to speak with you briefly about Sam. I'm guessing you've noticed he doesn't speak. I'd like to help. And I think if we team up, we can be more effective."

Something hardened inside of Jesse. Who did this woman think she was? Coming to his home to tell him how to raise his son.

"How old are you?" he asked.

She blinked at his odd question. "I'm twenty-two. But I don't see what that has to do with Sam's reluctance to speak."

Hmm. She was just four years younger than Jesse. Since age eighteen was the norm for schoolteachers, he thought her quite old. And he couldn't help wondering why she wasn't already married. A pretty little thing like her should have no trouble finding a willing groom. Especially here in Colorado, where Amish women were scarce. But he told himself he didn't care. It wasn't his business and he had bigger problems on his mind right now.

"I'm a fairly new teacher but I do know my subjects quite well. I just want to help," Becca said.

"I doubt anything can be done for Sam," he said, trying to keep his voice even and calm. "He'll speak again once he's *gut* and ready."

Becca shook her head. "I don't think so, Mr. King. When did Sam stop speaking?"

A rush of sad memories flooded his mind and he looked away. Her question seemed too personal. The pain was still so raw that it felt like it had happened just yesterday. "It started the afternoon of his mother and sisters' funeral."

She made a sad little crooning sound, like the coo of a dove. "*Ach*, I'm so very sorry. I have no doubt that was traumatic and difficult for both of you."

She didn't know the half of it. Sam had started the fire. It was his fault his mother and sisters had died. His fault they were now alone in this cold, ramshackle house. But Becca's compassion was more than Jesse could stand. Over the past year, so many people had expressed their condolences. Then they'd introduced him to another eligible woman, as if anyone could take Alice's place in his life. And that was just the problem. He didn't want another wife. He didn't want to ever marry again. He just wanted to be left alone. That was the whole reason he'd relocated to Colorado in the first place.

"I really don't think there's anything you can do for Sam. It'd be best if you just leave him alone and he'll start to speak again when he's ready." Jesse turned to go inside but she stopped him, placing a gentle hand on his arm for just a moment.

"I don't think so, Mr. King. I'm sure there are things we can do to help," she said.

"*Ne*, I've already had two doctors take a look at him and there's no physical reason he can't speak. He's just decided to stop talking," Jesse insisted.

"It's *gut* that you've had him visit some doctors but there's obviously something wrong. Though I've never dealt with a traumatic problem, I worked with a couple of special needs children in Ohio and I believe Sam needs some extra help."

So. She wasn't going to let this go. Though Jesse was a new member of the *Gmay* here in Riverton and had attended Sunday church meetings, he'd stayed apart and hadn't yet developed any real friendships with the other Amish families. Instead, he'd buried his heartache in hard work. Easy to do, considering the dilapidated condition of his new farm. Since he'd moved here two months earlier, he'd spent every waking moment mending the house, barn and broken fences. He still needed to repair the leaky roof and build furniture for his cold, ramshackle home. Having lost most of his possessions in the house fire, he'd had to start from scratch. And amidst all of that, he'd had to look after Sam, driving the boy back and forth to school, preparing meals, washing laundry and a myriad of other chores his wife used to do. There'd been a lot to deal with on his own.

Thankfully, he'd been able to sell his smaller farm in Pennsylvania to a neighbor, which had allowed him to purchase this new, bigger place in Colorado. And right now, he needed to get back to work.

The screen door on the back of the house clapped closed as Sam came outside. Jesse barely glanced at the boy, trying to think of something to say that would make Becca Graber go away and leave him alone. Instead, she smiled at Sam, so brightly that Jesse could only stare at her for several seconds. Bending at the waist, she looked the boy in the eyes.

"*Hallo*, Sam. How are you?" she asked.

The boy's eyes widened, his face creased with worry. He shuffled his feet, looking anxious. A few gurgling sounds came from the back of his throat but he couldn't seem to get any words out. Finally, he jabbed a finger urgently at the house and Becca gasped.

"*Gucke!* Something is burning," she cried.

Jesse turned and saw billows of black smoke rushing from the open doorway of the kitchen. Oh, no! The pork chops. They must be burning. He'd completely forgotten all about them.

"Stay here," he commanded as he raced into the house.

A thick fog of black smoke emanated from the metal frying pan sitting on top of the gas stove and filled the kitchen. As a certified firefighter, Jesse knew what to do. He reached into the cupboard beneath the sink and pulled out a Class B kitchen fire extinguisher. Aiming the nozzle, he blasted the burning pan with a fog of fire retardant. Then, he picked up the metal lid and, angling it to protect his face, slid it over the top of the pan to snuff out the grease fire. Lastly, he switched off the burner and slid the pan away from the source of heat.

A light tapping came from the open doorway and Becca poked her head in. "Is it safe to come in now?"

She stood there holding Sam's hand, waiting for Jesse's permission to enter. He nodded, wishing she'd go away. This had been a simple grease fire but it had brought the past right back for him. The night Alice and their two daughters had been killed, he was off fighting a house fire somewhere else. If only he'd been home that night, he might have saved them. It was his fault they were gone. It had been his job to protect them. His job to keep them safe.

And he'd failed.

His body trembled as he stood looking at the charred remnants of the four pork chops. He'd put the meat on the lowest heat, thinking they'd be fine until he returned from the barn. Now, he had nothing to feed Sam for supper.

He glanced at Becca and saw her gazing at his hands. Reddish-purple scars covered his skin, extending up both of his forearms. A cruel reminder that he'd run into a burning house to try and save his wife and daughters.

He folded his arms, hiding the ugly scars. Without speaking, Becca quietly opened all the windows and doors, allowing the chilly breeze to clear the house of smoke. As if from a distance, Jesse watched her silently. No matter how hard he clenched them, he couldn't stop his hands from shaking.

Becca directed little Sam to put on his coat until the room could be warmed up again. With rapt attention, the boy followed her every move as she built up the fire in the potbellied stove.

She glanced at Jesse and hesitated. From her sympathetic expression, he was certain she could see the truth inside him. That he was upset. Shaken by the grease fire. He felt suddenly exposed. The moment was too personal. Too private. Because it hit too close to home. A reminder of what had happened a year earlier when he'd lost everyone in his *familye*, except Sam. And he didn't want Becca Graber to see that. Or to know what he tried so hard to hide.

"You should leave," he said, feeling grouchy.

"You'll need something else for supper." She spoke in that soft, efficient voice of hers.

Without permission, she stepped over to the cupboards and opened the doors, peering inside. He knew she would find them as empty as his broken heart. She opened the fridge before lifting her eyebrows in a dubious expression.

"Is this all the food you have in the house?" she asked, gesturing to the skimpy remnants of a ham and a small chunk of Swiss cheese.

"That and the milk." Jesse retrieved the two buckets and set them on the counter by the sink. Having a chore to do helped soothe his jangled nerves.

Alice had always made their butter and cheese. Jesse knew the process but didn't have time to sit and churn milk into curd. And the few times he had done so, it didn't taste right when he finished. Something was missing.

Alice, Mary and Susanna were gone.

Pulling the ham and cheese from the fridge, Becca set them on the counter. She paused for just a moment, looking at the sink filled with dirty dishes. Without recriminations, she picked up a horse harness he had been mending and carried it to set beside the back door. Then, she rolled up her sleeves and quickly washed two plates and glasses.

"I noticed you have a coop but it doesn't look like you have any chickens on your place, so you don't have any eggs." She spoke as she worked. "Maybe in the spring you can get some baby chicks. But this will do for tonight."

Yes, he planned to buy some chickens next week. He also wanted to buy pigs, draft horses and another milk cow once the weather warmed up. But for now, he'd have to make do. A trip to the grocery store in town was definitely on the agenda for the morning. He'd stock up so this didn't happen again.

Becca shivered and Jesse placed another stick of wood in the potbellied stove. His home wasn't much to look at. The walls were dingy and scarred, the rooms devoid of furniture. Upstairs in the bedrooms, he'd laid two mattresses on the bare wood floors for him and Sam to sleep. No chairs. No chests of drawers. No armoires, curtains, rugs or wall hangings. The house had been uninhabited for six years. He'd been told the previous owner was *Englisch* and couldn't make a go of the place. But Jesse was willing to work hard and didn't need much to earn a simple living for him and Sam. He'd bought the farm cheap from a foreclosure sale and was glad to have it.

Becca set out the last six slices of his store-bought bread and layered them with wedges of ham and cheese for sandwiches. It'd be a dry meal but they could wash the food down with plenty of milk.

Watching her slender hands work, he thought about how much he missed Alice's homemade breads, biscuits, pies and cakes.

"Here you go." Becca set the two plates on the table and directed Sam to sit.

The boy gave her a questioning glance, his eyes wide, his little face so sweet and innocent. Jesse dearly loved his son. He truly did. But Sam was a constant reminder of all that they'd lost. Because Sam had set the fire. And though Jesse knew it wasn't right, he couldn't help blame the boy. He'd tried to forgive his son just as he'd tried to forgive himself. He really had. But he hadn't been able to do so. Not yet, anyway.

"Ahem, will you join us?" Jesse asked, trying to be polite but wishing she'd go now.

"*Ne*, I'll eat when I get home. This is for you," Becca said.

Surprised by how she seemed to have taken over his home, Jesse joined Sam at the table. Within a few moments, they had bowed their heads and blessed the food. Jesse didn't know what else to do. While Becca poured his son a glass of milk right from the pail, Sam immediately picked up his ham sandwich and took a big bite.

"I'm going to head home now." Becca spoke to Jesse. "It's getting dark outside and the roads will turn icy. I think you and I should speak more in depth at another time when you aren't so...indisposed."

Jesse nodded eagerly. "*Ja*, another time, perhaps."

But she didn't move. Didn't take a single step toward the door. Instead, she closed the windows above the sink, seeming satisfied that enough smoke had dissipated from the house. Since it was wintertime, the days were shorter and it was already getting dark outside. She lit two kerosene lamps. The wicks flickered, sending eerie shadows to chase around the room. He could see her curious gaze as she peered into every corner. A feeling of mortification washed over him. He was highly conscious of the run-down condition of his home. And more than ever, he missed Alice's home bottled beans, corn, peaches and tomatoes. She'd cared for their children and kept their home running with methodical order. But like everything else, it had all gone up in smoke.

"I... I've been kinda busy. I haven't had time to go into town to the grocery store. And I haven't had time yet to repair and paint some of the holes in the walls." He sat there, his thumbs looped through his suspenders.

She brushed past him. He caught her scent...a clean, citrusy smell that he kind of liked. "I understand completely. It must be difficult being on your own in a new place with a little boy to raise. But don't worry. You'll get things in order soon." She spoke in a cheerful, positive voice as she picked up the pair of gloves she'd set aside earlier when she'd prepared their supper.

Finally. Finally she stepped toward the outside door. Jesse stood and followed, breathing a silent sigh of relief. She was really leaving this time. But she stopped at the door and turned, catching him unaware. As he gazed down into her beautiful blue eyes, he couldn't help comparing her to Alice. The two women were so different. Alice had been filled with inner strength but she'd been shy, quiet and unassuming. So different from Becca, who was rather bossy, outgoing and quick to take matters into her own hands.

"Mr. King, until we can make a more formal plan of action, I'd like to suggest that you read to Sam each evening. Try to get him to read to you as well. I really think that would help for the time being," she said.

Read to Sam? Jesse didn't have time for such nonsense but didn't say so. He wasn't interested in taking advice from an inexperienced schoolteacher like Becca Graber, no matter how attractive she was. But he nodded.

He accompanied her outside but didn't help as she climbed into her buggy. He didn't think it would be appropriate to touch her. With a wave of her hand, she bid him farewell and her horse took off at a jaunty trot.

Jesse stood there, watching her go. And as she turned onto the main county road, he breathed a deep sigh of relief. He couldn't help feeling as if a tornado had just swept through his home. Rebecca Graber. What a dynamo. Jesse chuckled, thinking that another fire wouldn't dare invade his new house. Because if it did, Tornado Becca would just sweep it away.

Chapter Two

Becca pulled another dusty book off the shelf and promptly sneezed. Flipping through the front table of contents, she read each topic, searching for anything that might help Sam King. After a few moments, she added this text to her growing pile. She had chosen at least six good books on vocabulary and selective mutism and how to help children who wouldn't speak.

Standing inside the town library, she perused a bulleted list on a tip sheet, her mind churning. The little bit she'd learned that morning was not what she'd expected. Not at all. Selective mutism wasn't a problem where a child refused to speak in order to get attention. Nor was the child acting naughty. Rather, such children had an anxiety disorder wherein they couldn't speak because their apprehension was so severe they were actually scared silent.

Flipping to a chapter on treatment, she braced the book against the shelf and continued reading. It was Saturday morning and she'd taken advantage of the clear weather to come into town and see what she might find. She could check out library books, as long as they magnified Jesus Christ. Jakob Fisher, her first cousin, had driven her here but she'd have to walk back to his farm. She lived with Jakob, his wife and three children, her aunt and grandfather. If she found some help for Sam today, the nine-mile walk home would be worth it.

An hour earlier, she'd paid a quick visit to Caroline Schwartz, Sam's permanent teacher. The poor girl was still in the hospital, her legs and hips in traction. If Caroline hoped to walk again, she'd be restricted to bed for the next four months. At barely eighteen years of age, Caroline seemed even more inexperienced at teaching than Becca. And since the accident had happened about the same time Jesse and Sam had moved to the area, Caroline hadn't yet been able to do anything about the boy's problem. She'd explained to Becca that she'd ordered a newsletter written by Amish parents of special needs children titled *Life's Special Sunbeams*. That might be of some help but Becca doubted it. Still, she had the address of the national publication and planned to subscribe as well.

Caroline had also tried to speak with Jesse King but the man had terrified her with his offish manner. No surprise there. Jesse didn't seem to like anyone. But Becca wasn't about to let the oafish man scare her off. She was determined to do something to help Sam, with or without his father's cooperation. She believed Sam's unwillingness to speak had everything to do with his mother and sisters' deaths.

Lifting the pile of books, Becca carried them back to the open area of the library. Her mind buzzed with a number of techniques she'd like to try with Sam. Ritual greetings every morning at school, including him in activities even if he didn't speak and some other techniques to reduce his anxiety while at school. She had some flash cards she could use but thought she might need to spend extra time working one-on-one with Sam when the other children weren't around to distract or startle him. And she wasn't sure how to build that time into the school curriculum. It wouldn't be prudent to ignore the other children's needs because Sam required so much extra attention but she'd figure it out.

Making her way back to the table where she'd been jotting down notes, she thought of a possible solution… and promptly bumped into someone.

"Oof!"

She looked up and blinked. "Mr. King."

He stared down at her with widened eyes, seeming just as surprised as she was. "*Hallo*, Miss Graber."

"Wh…what are you doing here?" she asked, thinking how nonsensical she sounded.

He shifted his weight and she saw that he held a book in his hand. He quickly lowered his arm, shielding the text behind his thigh. From his nervous gesture, she thought he was trying to conceal it from her. But he didn't know her very well. Reaching behind him, she took the book from his hand and read the title out loud.

"The Silent Child."

His face flushed red as a sugar beet. Ah, he wasn't as withdrawn from his son's problem as he made it appear. In fact, it looked as though he was actually trying to do something to help Sam. And right then and there, Becca's opinion of Jesse King improved just a tad. Up to now, she'd had little respect for the man but realized he wasn't the uncaring, brutish father he appeared to be. But why did he have to be so difficult about it? Why did he have to hide his concern? It seemed as though he were fighting against himself. As though he didn't want to care about Sam, yet he did. Very much.

She met his gaze, noticing the irritated glint in his eyes. She could tell that he didn't like meeting her here. She held the book out to him and he took it reluctantly.

"It looks like you're reading up on Sam's problem." She spoke the obvious.

"*Ja*, I thought maybe…" He didn't finish the sentence. "What are you doing here?" he asked instead.

She held up several books on the same topic. "The same as you. Looking for ways to help Sam."

He snorted. "I doubt it'll do any *gut*. I've already tried everything I can think of and Sam still won't talk. He hasn't said a single word in almost a year."

"I'm sorry."

He shrugged and looked away but not before she saw the pain written in his eyes. Her heart gave a painful squeeze. The poor little boy. And the poor man too! This couldn't be easy on Jesse either.

"But we have to try, don't we?" she asked.

He glanced at his son, who sat a short distance away at another table, poring over several children's books. The boy's lips were moving and Becca got the impression he was reading to himself. She'd seen him do this in school before but what it meant, she had no idea.

"It appears that he can read," she observed.

"*Ja*, his *mudder* taught him. She…she used to read to all our *kinder* all the time. Sam can definitely read."

Hmm. Was that why Jesse seemed so against reading to Sam each night? Because it was something his wife had done before she died? Or was it simply because he was busy and thought reading to his son was a woman's job? Well, it was time to teach him differently. Fathers could read to their kids just as well as mothers.

"Are you planning to read to Sam each night, as we discussed?" she asked.

"I... I don't have a lot of extra time. By the time I finish my barn chores, Sam's usually half-asleep. And I've been trying to make us some furniture in the evenings," he hedged.

Becca didn't argue. She sensed that she couldn't push Jesse King any more than she could little Sam. But still, Jesse had come to the library to check out some books. That was a good start.

"Any idea how well Sam can read?" Becca asked.

He shrugged those unbelievably wide shoulders of his. "*Ne*, I have no idea. I just know he can read. He was always a bright little fellow before..."

Before his momma died. That was good. If they could just get Sam to speak again, it could open up a whole new world for the boy. And possibly open the world again to Jesse King too.

He sidestepped her, edging toward his son. "Um, we were just leaving. We have to get home soon."

"But I was hoping to meet with you at length. Is there a time when you and I can sit down and develop a plan of action for Sam?"

He shook his head. "Not today."

"But, Mr. King!" She took a step after him.

"Shh!" The librarian appeared out of nowhere, pressing a finger to her lips. From the stern lift of the woman's eyebrows, Becca realized she must have spoken too loudly.

Without another word, Jesse turned and hurried over to Sam. The man's black felt hat sat on the table top and he picked it up and placed it on his head. Becca watched in frustration, longing to go after him. Wanting to make him listen to her. But she knew she couldn't force him to do what he didn't want to do. And that's when something else occurred to her.

Sam didn't speak because he was traumatized by the deaths of his mother and sister. But Jesse King was just as traumatized in his own way. And he obviously didn't want to talk about it. She could empathize with the man. Losing his wife and daughters must have scarred his heart as much as it had Sam's. And that's when she decided to give Jesse some space. He'd been reluctant to help, yet he'd come to the library on his own. With a little more time, maybe he would seek out her assistance as well. But for Sam's sake, she hoped Jesse didn't wait too long.

"Come on, Sam." Jesse spoke low as he took the boy's arm and tugged gently.

Sam had no choice but to follow and he reluctantly left his books behind. As they headed toward the front door, he looked back at the texts with such longing that Becca knew he wasn't finished with them yet. She couldn't help wondering why Jesse seemed so antisocial. Every time she tried to talk to him, he acted skittish, like he wanted to get away. Or was it just her he didn't like? She wasn't sure but it seemed to her that Jesse fought against himself. Some inner strife seemed to wage a battle inside of him. She figured it all must relate to his deceased wife and daughters.

She watched as they hurried out of the library without a single book in tow. Even Jesse had abandoned the text he'd been holding. It was such a shame. Both the father and son could benefit greatly from those texts.

Becca decided to do something about it. Stepping over to Sam's table, she scooped up most of the plethora of books the child had been reading and carried them over to the checkout counter with her own selections. She added Jesse's book to the pile. No matter how hard he tried, Jesse King was not getting rid of her.

Jesse flicked the leather lead lines at his horse's rump and settled into his seat. After leaving the library, he'd taken Sam over to the grocery store and stocked up on numerous cases of canned and boxed goods. Soup, chili, corn, string beans, peaches, pears and oatmeal. Now, even if he did burn their supper, he'd have something in the house to feed his son. It wasn't that he didn't have money to buy food but rather he had too many chores to carry alone. He needed his wife and daughters back. He needed Alice more than ever.

The buggy-wagon swayed gently as he turned the horse off Main Street and headed along the county road. The clop of the horse's hooves hitting the black asphalt soothed his jangled nerves. He didn't know why he'd gone to the library in town. Sam had been delighted. Though the boy didn't speak, Jesse could see his pleasure written across his face and in the little skip in his stride. It had been a lapse in judgment and Jesse had been mortified to be caught there by Becca Graber. Having been raised by a strong, domineering father, Jesse didn't like feeling out of control. And that's how Sam's problem made him feel. Out of control.

Sam sat silently beside him on the front seat. Jesse knew his son wasn't happy to leave his books behind. Maybe he should have checked them out for the boy. Even if he didn't read to Sam, there was no reason to keep the child from reading on his own. They both already lived such a lonely, isolated life. The books might open up the world to Sam. They might help him speak again.

Maybe on Monday, Jesse could make another quick trip into town and check out the books for Sam. Wouldn't the boy be excited when he came home from school and found a pile of texts waiting for him?

The thought made Jesse go very still. He'd been so angry at Sam for so long now that it was a novelty for him to want to make the boy happy. But he did. In fact, Jesse longed to hear his son's laughter again. How he wished his son would speak.

At that moment, Sam lifted an arm and pointed. Jesse could just make out a lone figure, walking ahead of them on the side of the road. From her plain dress, black tights, heavy shawl and bonnet, he could tell she was Amish. She carried a heavy bag in each hand. Probably walking home after shopping in town. But then he saw a flash of purple skirts and knew exactly who she was.

Becca Graber.

His shoulders tensed and he thought of driving on by without acknowledging her. But that would be too rude, even for him.

As his buggy-wagon neared, she glanced over her shoulder and moved a safe distance off the road so she wouldn't be trampled. He instantly regretted making her move as he watched her sidestep the muddy ground.

When he pulled up beside her, she stopped and nodded, her hands too encumbered by the heavy bags to wave.

"*Hallo*! Fancy meeting you out here on the road," she said.

Her voice held a happy lilt and he wondered vaguely if anything ever got her down.

"*Ja*, fancy that. You look as though your arms are quite full. Can we offer you a ride home?" Though his voice held little enthusiasm, Jesse forced himself to say the words, knowing it was the right thing to do.

She hesitated, glancing at the long road ahead. "Are you sure it's no trouble?"

He'd heard that she lived with the Fishers, who were her relatives. *Dawdi* Zeke, the eldest member of the *Gmay* at ninety-six years, was her grandfather. They lived nine miles outside of town and Jesse would pass right by their farm on his way home. Ironically, the Fishers were his neighbors. A fact that made it much too easy for Becca to drive over to their place whenever she wanted. He just hoped she didn't make a habit of popping in during the supper hour.

"*Ne*, of course not. We pass by your place on our way home. Climb in." The moment he made the invitation, he regretted it. He didn't want to give Sam's schoolteacher a ride home. He wanted to be left alone.

"*Ach, danke* so much. I didn't realize how heavy these books would be when I was sitting in the library." She handed the bags to him and he set them on the floor of the back seat.

As she climbed up to sit with Sam in between them, Jesse saw her glance back at the wagon. It was filled with boxes and bags of groceries, shingles and other roofing supplies, as well as a large crate of live chickens. The hens had fluffed their feathers and huddled together for warmth as they clucked with impatience. He didn't get into town often and had made the best of this trip.

"I see you've been to the grocery store and got some hens too," she said as she settled herself.

"*Ja.*" He flicked the leads at the horse's rump and they lurched forward.

"That's *gut*. At least you'll have fresh eggs to eat if you burn the pork chops again." She laughed, the sound high and sweet. There was no guile in her voice but simply a gentle sense of humor.

Jesse would have smiled but he still couldn't decide if he liked this woman. She was definitely likeable, if he weren't still missing Alice so much.

"Sam, I have something special for you." She reached around and rummaged inside one of her burlap bags before pulling out the pile of books the boy had abandoned at the library.

Sam made a happy sound in the back of his throat and took the books onto his lap.

"And this is for you." She pulled out the book Jesse had been perusing and held it up for his inspection.

Jesse went very still. He wasn't sure if he should be happy or sad. He'd wanted to check out the book but he didn't want it forced down his throat by the pretty schoolteacher.

"I know you were in a big hurry to get home, so I thought I could check them out for you," she said.

Hmm. Interesting how she was making this easy for him, as if he'd been indisposed so she'd done him a favor.

"I had planned to bring them to you at church tomorrow. Now you can read this evening. But you'll only be able to keep them for two weeks before they're due back at the library," she warned.

She smiled and spoke so happily that Jesse didn't

have the heart to scold her for being presumptuous. Her gesture was kind and he realized she only had their best interests at heart.

"Danke." He spoke low, forcing himself to say the word.

"You're *willkomm.*"

Turning in her seat, she perused the clear but chilly day. The afternoon sun had done its best to melt off the snow but slushy spots on the road would soon ice up as evening came on and he was eager to get home. Driving a horse and buggy at night was not safe. Cars and trucks traveled way too fast and might come upon them without seeing their reflective lights. He'd heard that Caroline Schwartz, the regular schoolteacher, had been driving a buggy at night when she was hit from behind. The accident had nearly killed the poor girl and they'd had to put her horse down.

"Isn't it a nice day?" Becca asked, then gave an exaggerated shiver. "But brrr, it's so cold. Still, it could always be worse. At least it isn't snowing again."

Jesse agreed but didn't answer. He just listened as Becca talked on and on about inconsequential things. The weather. Their church meetings tomorrow. The end-of-year program she was planning for the school. The box social fund-raiser she'd been asked to coordinate so they could purchase playground equipment for the school. He glanced at her pretty profile, thinking once again that she was like a whirl of wind. And he wasn't sure he liked that.

"Did you walk into town this morning?" he asked.

"Ne, my cousin, Jakob, gave me a ride. He needed to buy supplies too. But I wanted to stay longer and told him I'd walk home this afternoon. Since the weather

was clear, he agreed." She gazed out at the damp countryside. "I think at that time, I underestimated how cold it is outside. I walked everywhere when I lived in Ohio but I'm still not used to the colder weather in Colorado. And everything is so spread out here. My cousin's farm is much too far from town to walk in the cold and I won't make that mistake again."

He agreed. If she had been his cousin, he would not have let her walk nine miles on such a cold winter's day. And though he would never admit such a thing, it kind of upset him that Jakob Fisher had been so derelict in her care. Since he'd lived here for a number of years already, the man should have known better.

"I'm sorry. I'm talking too much, aren't I?" she said suddenly.

Yes, but he didn't say so. He would never admit that he liked her incessant chatter. It had been so long since he'd listened to a woman talk about everything and nothing and it filled up the lonely void of the ride. With Sam not speaking, Jesse's life had become overly quiet and he realized he was hungry to talk to someone. Anyone! Even if that someone happened to be Sam's pushy schoolteacher.

Before he knew it, they had arrived at the turnoff to the Fishers' farm. Jesse wasn't about to make Becca walk the muddy road leading to the house and he turned the horse down the lane. The two-story log structure looked just the same as his, except that it was in pristine repair. So was the large, red barn. The tidy property was outlined by long barbed wire fences and fallow fields waiting for spring plowing. Black-and-white milk cows stood in a corral, chewing their cud. Several draft horses stood together near a cluster of barren trees. In the summertime, he had no doubt the place would be burgeoning with green life.

One day soon, Jesse hoped his own farm looked in this good a shape but he knew it would take time and lots of hard work for it to prosper. But he intended to do just that. Bishop Yoder had offered to coordinate a work frolic to help with some of the repairs but Jesse had politely refused. He'd come here for isolation and didn't want a lot of people around his place asking a lot of questions about Alice and their girls. For now, he wanted to be left alone.

"*Danke* for the ride. I'll see you tomorrow at church." Becca hopped out after he pulled the horse to a stop in front of the house.

She reached up as Jesse handed her the bags. Their fingers brushed together for just a moment and he felt the warmth of her soft skin against his. Sam waved, but Jesse didn't speak. He didn't want to see Becca Graber again. And yet, he did. Not because he was interested in her as a woman. But rather, she was so different from Alice. So filled with ideas, so talkative and bright, like a shiny new button. Becca Graber was a novelty to him. A glimpse of normalcy that he hadn't enjoyed in a long, lonely time. And no matter how hard he tried not to, he liked her.

Chapter Three

Jesse awoke slowly, pulled out of a deep sleep. Opening his eyes, he blinked into the darkness. It was way too early to get up for morning chores. Over the past year, he hadn't been sleeping well. Tonight was no exception. He'd gone to bed late after working on another chair to go with the kitchen table. After tossing and turning for what seemed like hours, he'd fallen into a dreamless sleep. So, what had awakened him?

He rolled over, pulling the warm quilt with him. He gazed through the shadows at the empty pillow next to him. How he missed Alice and her warm, gentle touch. Just knowing she was there, lying beside him, had brought him joy. But now, the house felt cold and empty. He must have forgotten to stoke the fire in the stove before he went to bed. But honestly, he'd become skittish about adding kindling at night for fear it might start another house fire. Although he'd lost his previous home because Sam was playing with matches, he'd become overly cautious when it came to fire.

There! The sound came again. A low cry from the

outer hallway followed by muffled crying. Sam must be having another nightmare.

Throwing back the covers, Jesse sat up and placed his bare feet against the chilly floor. Alice wasn't here to make one of her large rag rugs to cover the bare, scarred wood. He'd resisted buying one, trying to conserve his funds until the priority expenses had been met, such as repairing the leaky roof and buying more livestock. His future livelihood depended on him making this farm prosper and he intended to do just that.

Standing, he reached for his discarded shirt and pulled it over top of his undershirt. Raking a hand through his disheveled hair, he walked out onto the landing at the top of the stairs. He paused beside the door to Sam's bedroom and listened. Another scream and then pitiful weeping came from the room and he raced inside. Sam lay upon the mattress, his arms and legs tangled in the bedding. His eyes were closed in sleep but he thrashed around, as if he were trying to escape some unknown predator.

Definitely another nightmare. The boy had been having such bad dreams ever since the fire, though their occurrence had diminished once they'd arrived in Riverton. Over time, Jesse had hoped the bad dreams would disappear entirely.

He pulled the covers away and rearranged them before lying on the mattress with his son. Blanketing them both against the frigid night air, he pulled Sam into his arms, aware that the boy had awakened and was silently weeping. His slim body trembled, his shoulders quaking. Holding the child against his chest, Jesse rubbed his back the way Alice used to do whenever one of their children was sick or upset about something.

"Shh, *Daed* is here now. You're safe. It's going to be all right," Jesse soothed, copying her words.

Alice had always known what to do, what to say. Her kind, quiet nature had brought him comfort whenever he was worried about something too. She was the most caring, prim and proper woman he'd ever known. So different from Becca Graber's outgoing nature. And yet, Becca seemed no less kind and giving. She just went about it in different ways.

Sam's back and shoulders trembled, his tears wetting Jesse's neck. The boy curled his tiny hands into the folds of Jesse's shirt, as if he were clinging to a lifeline. Jesse continued to reassure the boy, speaking sentiments of comfort.

How he wished he could believe what he said. That everything would be all right. That the painful ache lodged inside their hearts would somehow ease and go away. But it hadn't. Not one bit. Because Alice, Mary and Susanna were all gone. And Jesse couldn't bring them back. He thought that relocating his son to Colorado would diminish the tender memories they each suffered from. That somehow, they could forget. But it was still there, raw and painful. Haunting them every day.

Jesse had been taught all his life to accept *Gott's* will. That he should be accepting of where divine Providence had placed him. It wasn't right for him to question *Gott's* motives in anything. But he did. He couldn't help asking why Alice and his little girls had to die. Why?

Now, Jesse had only his faith to rely on. The belief that *Gott* had taken his *familye* into His hands and would love and care for them until they could all be reunited once more.

"Gott verlosst die Seine nicht." Jesse spoke the

phrase softly, trying to believe that God would never abandon them.

Sam didn't respond. Didn't move a muscle or say a single word. But Jesse knew he heard and understood. Now, if only they could both believe his words, they might have some hope of healing.

An hour later, Jesse still lay there in the dark, staring up at the ceiling, wondering if it had been a good choice for him to bring Sam to Colorado. It was what he and Alice had talked about. What they had planned for some time. Their home and *familye* in Pennsylvania was gone and he'd thought to give them a fresh start somewhere that didn't remind him and Sam of all they'd lost. But even here, in a house that Alice and his girls had never lived in, Jesse still saw them every day in his mind and in his heart. The memories haunted him. And he realized then that they were such a part of him and Sam that neither of them could ever forget. Jesse couldn't seem to let them go. He could run and hide but they'd still be with him. He longed to run away, but he couldn't run from himself. So, how could he overcome the pain and regret and live again? He must have faith! He knew that without a doubt. Yet, it was so hard to put his beliefs into action.

Sam gave a little shudder, his breath coming slow and even. They lay there together, both suffering in their own different ways. But Jesse was Sam's father. He must set a good example for his son. To show him that he truly believed *Gott* rules over all. That no matter what trials came their way, they could overcome anything through faith and obedience to *Gott's* will. Surely the Lord hadn't abandoned them.

Or had He?

In the wee hours of the night, Sam finally slept. Jesse felt the boy's body soften, his little chest rising slowly with each breath. But there was no peace of mind for Jesse.

Ever so gently, he eased away from his son and stood looking down at the boy. Dried tears streaked Sam's pale cheeks. He looked so innocent. So pure and defenseless. And an overwhelming urge to protect him flooded Jesse with deep and abiding love. He was Sam's father and owed it to the boy to care for him. To help him any way he possibly could.

Sam shivered and Jesse reached to tug the covers higher over his child's slender shoulders. Turning, Jesse walked out of the room. The stairs creaked beneath his weight as he went to stoke the stove and warm up the house. Morning would be here soon. They'd get busy with their activities and it would ease the tension for a time…until nighttime fell and they once again were tortured by their painful memories.

He stared out the dark windows, seeing the faint golden light of sunrise. The mountains were beautiful here, reminding Jesse just how small and insignificant he really was. And yet, he knew *Gott* loved him. Surely He would care for him and Sam.

It was Church Sunday and he must soon awaken his son for morning chores. They would drive seven miles to Bishop Yoder's farm where they would listen to the Lord's word and worship *Gott*. That must never change. Jesse's beliefs had become his anchor in life. He could never abandon his faith. If he did, he knew Alice wouldn't approve. She was counting on him to teach Sam. To show their son how to be a good man of faith.

Becca Graber would undoubtedly be at church too.

Maybe Jesse should speak with her about Sam. Perhaps he should swallow his pride and ask the pretty schoolteacher for advice. Maybe she had some good ideas that might help Sam.

In the kitchen, Jesse sat on one of the hard, wooden chairs he'd made with his own two hands. Hours of working late into the night as he strived to create a warm and welcoming place for him and Sam to live. In the past, he had enjoyed such work. Especially when he showed his new creations to Alice. She would smile with approval and reward him with a gentle hug and kiss. Now, she wasn't here and he wondered why he even tried. What did he have to live for anymore?

Sam!

The boy's name came to his mind as if in a shout. He must forgive and forget and keep striving to better serve others. As a father, he owed that to his little boy. He owed it to Alice and to his *Gott* too. He must not quit. Not now, not ever. The Savior would want him to forgive and keep going. Surely Sam would start to talk again on his own. If they just left him alone, the boy would figure it out and speak again. Wouldn't he?

Feeling overwhelmed by his convictions, Jesse leaned forward and rested his elbows on his knees. He stared at the growing light of day until the sun became a golden ring of light and his eyes burned and his vision blurred. And then, as the grief washed over him in a fresh wave of pain, he bowed his head, cupped his face in his hands, and wept.

He was watching her again. Becca felt Jesse King's eyes on her even before she turned and looked at him. Sitting on the hard, backless bench, she tried to concentrate on what the minister was saying. It was Sunday morning, a bright, crisp day that was perfect for worship services. For several minutes, she focused on the preaching. Quoting Psalms 127, Jeremiah Beiler's voice was filled with emotion as he described children as a heritage from God who should be loved and cherished.

Looking up, Becca saw Jesse gazing intently at the minister. Jesse's forehead was furrowed in a slight frown, his eyes crinkled in thought. Hmm. Maybe he should remember that Sam should be valued instead of being brushed off as a bother.

At that moment, Jesse tilted his head and his eyes clashed, then locked with hers. She looked away, her face heating up with embarrassment. She'd encouraged him to let her help with Sam's speech problem and he'd refused. She'd do what she could for the boy during school hours but she couldn't force Jesse to listen to her. He had to take the next step. She just hoped that was soon before Sam was too old and set in his ways to start talking again.

"What's going on between you and Jesse King?" Naomi Fisher asked Becca later as they cleaned up after the noon meal.

Naomi was Becca's aunt and had helped her get this teaching position in Riverton. Knowing how Becca's heart had been broken by Vernon, Naomi had written her in January to ask if she might like to stay with her and work as the teacher until the school year ended in May. Longing for a chance to escape Vernon and Ruth's happy preparations for their marriage, Becca had jumped at the chance.

"What do you mean?" Becca asked.

Standing in the kitchen at the bishop's home, she

washed another plate and set it in the dish drain. Aunt Naomi promptly picked it up to dry with a long, white cloth.

"I saw you two looking at each other during the meetings. You are lovely and he is a handsome widower. I'm not surprised he might be interested in you," Naomi said.

Becca snorted. "Believe me, Jesse King is far from interested. I've simply offered to assist Sam with his speaking problem and the man refuses to be helped."

Though she spoke low so the numerous other women working around them wouldn't hear her words, Becca couldn't prevent a note of irritation from entering her voice.

"I'm sure he's still hurting," Naomi said. "You know he lost his wife and two young daughters in a house fire a year ago."

"*Ja*, I know all about it. But it's no excuse to ignore Sam's needs," Becca said.

"*Ach*, did you also know it was Sam who started the fire?"

Becca gasped and turned to stare at her aunt. "*Ne*, I didn't know that. Are you sure?"

Naomi shrugged and set the clean plate aside before picking up another one to dry. "Since I wasn't there, I'm not sure of anything. But that's what Sarah Yoder said."

Sarah was the bishop's wife and would be privy to such private information like that.

"I'm surprised Sarah would tell you something so personal. It sounds like gossip to me," Becca whispered low.

Naomi drew her shoulders back, her expression filled with dignity. "She wasn't gossiping at all, I can assure you. I accidentally overheard her talking to Bishop Yoder about it right after Jesse and his son moved here to Riverton. She didn't know I was there listening and I haven't spoken about it since. I have only told you because you're my niece and I think the information might help you to resolve Sam's problem. The poor child. Losing his *mamm* and sisters so young. No wonder the little lamb doesn't speak. And no wonder Jesse is so sullen all the time. I feel bad for him, having to carry such a horrible burden on his shoulders."

Yes, no wonder. But knowing that Sam had started the house fire changed everything and nothing. He still needed help. And soon. Was it possible that Jesse was angry with his son for starting the fire? Did Jesse hold a grudge against his own son? Oh, it was too cruel. No wonder Sam didn't speak. Knowing what he'd done, he must be wracked by guilt. And living with a father who blamed him for what happened must be more than Sam could bear. No doubt Jesse fought against his own guilt as well.

"Ahem, excuse me, ladies. I'm sorry to interrupt your work."

Becca looked up, surprised to see Jesse King standing in the open doorway to the kitchen. And for the umpteenth time that day, her face flamed hotter than a bonfire. Had he overheard her and Aunt Naomi talking about him? Did he know how curious she was?

The room went deathly quiet. Sarah Yoder stepped away from the gas-powered oven and nodded pleasantly. Since this was her home, she was their hostess and responsible to see that everyone was comfortable.

"*Hallo*, Jesse. What can we help you with?" she asked.

His gaze drifted past the sea of smiling faces until it landed on Becca.

"I was hoping to speak with Miss Graber for a moment," he said.

Someone gave a breathless laugh and Becca wished the floor would just open up and swallow her whole.

"It's about Sam," Jesse continued, as if sensing the other women's interest.

A pulse of energy shot up from Becca's toes. He wanted to talk to her about Sam. Maybe he was finally ready to make a plan with her to help the boy. Everyone knew she was the schoolteacher and that Sam didn't talk. Not even to his school friends. She was duty bound to help the child in any way possible. What could be more natural than for Jesse to want to confer with his son's teacher about the boy's problem? But Jesse's timing couldn't be worse. Becca hated the thought that everyone in her *Gmay* might think there was something romantic going on between them. Because there wasn't. No, not at all.

"Of course! I'd be happy to discuss Sam with you." Giving an efficient nod, she quickly dried her hands and set the towel aside.

As Becca made her way over to the door, Lizzie Stoltzfus and Abby Fisher, her cousin's wife, ducked their heads together to share a whispered comment. Even Julia Hostetler, who had been *Englisch* before her recent conversion and marriage into their faith, was grinning like a fool. Only old Marva Geingerich, who was almost ninety years old, was frowning with disapproval.

Had they all lost their minds? Becca had no romantic interest in Jesse King. None whatsoever. She hated the indifferent way he treated Sam. Even if he was handsome and tall as a church steeple, his brusque manner made it difficult for Becca to like him.

He lifted a hand for her to precede him as she stepped out into the sunshine. As she stood beneath the barren branches of a tall elm tree, the frosty wind sent a shiver through her that made her gasp and wish she'd grabbed her warm shawl on her way outside. Before she knew what was happening, Jesse had doffed his warm frock coat and swept it over her trembling shoulders. She instantly caught his scent, a warm clean smell of hay, horses and peppermint. He was gazing at her lavender dress and she looked down, wondering if she had spilled something on it.

"That's a nice color on you. I'm sorry to bring you out here on such a cold day. I'll try not to keep you very long," he said.

She stared up at him, blinking in stunned amazement. All rational thought skipped right out of her head and she didn't know what to say. Had he actually paid her a compliment? Maybe her ears had deceived her. "I, um, *danke*, but that really isn't necessary."

She forced herself to hand his coat back to him. Though she really was freezing, a glance at the house told her that Aunt Naomi and Sarah Yoder were both staring out the kitchen window at her. To make matters worse, they had most certainly watched as Jesse offered her his coat. No doubt it would be all over the *Gmay* by early evening that she and Jesse King were an item. And having been the focus of romantic gossip back in Ohio, that was the last thing Becca wanted here in Colorado.

Seeing the smiling women at the window, Jesse inclined his head and seemed to understand her dilemma. "I'm sorry if I've created trouble for you. That wasn't my intention. I only wanted to ask if you know what is wrong with Sam."

She folded her arms tightly as he put his coat back on. Licking her dry lips, she tried to concentrate on the subject at hand. "I'm not an expert but I believe he has what is called *selective mutism.*"

She briefly explained what she knew about the disorder and that she didn't think Sam had any choice in the matter.

"His anxiety is so strong that he is literally scared silent. He's not trying to be rude or mean or cause you problems. He couldn't speak even if he wanted to," she said.

Jesse frowned. "You think he's too frightened to talk?"

She nodded. "Exactly. I know it must be a sensitive subject but I believe something about his mother and sisters' deaths has created so much apprehension in Sam that he literally cannot talk anymore."

Jesse looked down at the ground, scuffing one toe of his black boot against a small rock. "I was afraid of that. When I was in the library yesterday, I came across a couple of books on this topic but I haven't yet had the opportunity to read much about it. I was planning to start reading the book you checked out for me later this evening."

So. Maybe he really did want to help his son after all.

"From what I understand about the disorder, such children usually talk at home, where they feel more comfortable," she said. "But at school or in other social situations where they feel uncomfortable or nervous, they are silent. And punishing the child or making him feel guilty for not speaking would only exacerbate the problem."

Jesse's forehead curved in a deep scowl. "But Sam doesn't speak at home either."

He sounded so forlorn that Becca didn't have the heart to point out that Sam obviously didn't feel comfortable inside the walls of his own house. She figured that was possibly Jesse's fault. The boy must fear his own father. And whether that was because Sam felt guilt over his mother and sisters' deaths or for some other reason, Becca couldn't say.

"If you're amenable, there are a few techniques we can try to help Sam." She then launched into a rapid description of what those methods were. Last night, she'd done a lot of reading on the topic and put a great deal of thought into how they both might assist Sam with his problem. She'd even written up a plan of action last night. Things each of them might do to help Sam and techniques to measure Sam's improvement. She was eager to share her ideas with Jesse in detail and hoped he wouldn't refuse.

He listened politely to her explanations but made no comment.

"That all sounds like a huge time commitment on both our parts," he said.

She nodded. "*Ja*, it will take a lot of time. But I think Sam is worth it."

He hesitated, looking skeptical. "I do too but I'll have to think about it. I want to make sure I'm doing the right things for my *sohn*."

"I understand but I'd like to get started as soon as possible. The longer we delay, the worse the situation might become. It would be ideal if Sam could stay an extra hour after school several days each week so I could work with him one-on-one," she said.

Jesse frowned. "Since I'm alone and have to pick up Sam from school, that might not be possible. I've got my hands full already. Couldn't you just send extra homework home with him? I can make sure he does it."

She shook her head, thinking Jesse didn't understand. "More homework won't help Sam talk. He needs some intense interaction with other people. He needs to feel comfortable around us so we can help him speak and we need to provide opportunities to teach him how to speak again."

Jesse stood there looking down at her, his eyes unblinking as he considered her ideas. She didn't interrupt, allowing him time to digest and mull it all over in his own mind.

"I understand what you're asking. Let me think about it. And *danke* for your help. I appreciate your efforts." Turning, he walked away, heading toward the barn where the other men were lounging and visiting after their noon meal. Bishop Yoder and *Dawdi* Zeke hailed him over.

And just like that, Jesse was gone. Becca longed to call him back or chase after him to make him agree to her proposal. But something held her back. She felt almost desperate to help Sam. As if an unknown force were pushing her forward and her future happiness depended on it. But Jesse would have to decide. And she resolved then to offer a prayer to *Gott* that Jesse made the right decision.

Chapter Four

Becca set the last plate from supper into the dish drain. Sinking her hands into the hot, soapy water, she rinsed out the dishcloth before wiping down the counters and kitchen table. Supper was finally finished. *Dawdi* Zeke and Jakob were out in the barn finishing the evening chores. It was Monday evening and her mind whirled with all the lesson plans she still needed to review before school in the morning. Maybe she could grade some papers during recess tomorrow. And then she needed to assign some readings for the scholars to memorize for the end-of-year program. So much to do.

"Have you spoken to Bishop Yoder about Caleb's behavior at school, yet?" Aunt Naomi picked up a glass to dry off with a dish towel.

Becca slid the butter dish inside the gas-powered fridge, giving an absentminded shake of her head. She had explained in detail the troubles she was having at school. "*Ne*, I'm not even sure he's the culprit. I have no proof, just an instinct that he's the instigator. I've already separated him and Enos Albrecht. When the two of them sat together, they seemed to egg each other on.

Besides, what *gut* would it do to tell their *eldre*? The bishop would just think I can't control the school."

Abby Fisher, Jakob's wife, stood across the room, cleaning and sorting the eggs Becca had helped her gather before dinner. Becca knew they would sell the eggs in town to help supplement their household income.

"It might help to tell them what's going on. Then they could speak with their sons," Abby said.

"*Ja*, the bishop wants the school to succeed," Naomi added. "Especially since Caroline was injured in that horrible buggy accident last month. Without a teacher, we feared we'd have to send our *kinder* to the *Englisch* schools. It's a blessing you were able to *komm* here so quickly. I'm sure Bishop Yoder would be mortified to know that one of his own *kinder* is causing so much trouble."

Becca understood very well why the Amish didn't want to send their children to the *Englisch* schools. She listened to her aunt's advice, thinking over what she said. In the short time she had lived in this home, she'd become quite close to these two women and she valued their opinions. But maybe she wasn't cut out to be a teacher. Though she enjoyed her profession, maybe she had made a mistake by coming here to Colorado. If she couldn't even control her school, she wouldn't be able to make teaching a lifelong career.

"I hope Reuben hasn't been participating in any shenanigans." Abby looked at Becca and paused, her forehead creased with concern.

"*Ne*, he's been *gut* as gold. In fact, he tried to stop the trouble last week when I pulled the toy snake out of my desk drawer," Becca said.

Naomi showed a relieved smile. "*Gut*! There was a time when Abby first came to live with us that I was mighty worried about his behavior."

"*Ja*, I remember when I first came to live here, he put cracker crumbs between my bedsheets and dirt in my shoes." Abby laughed at the reminder.

Becca gasped, hardly able to believe her cousin's sweet, polite ten-year-old son would do such a thing. "*Behiedes*? He actually did that?"

Abby nodded. "He certainly did."

"But why?"

Abby shrugged. "He felt threatened by me. He thought I was trying to take his *mudder's* place after she had died."

Becca could hardly imagine Reuben being so obnoxious. Now, Abby was Reuben's new stepmother and they seemed to love each other very much. Becca just hoped Caleb and Enos didn't try such mischief on her.

"What did you do to get Reuben to stop?" she asked.

A smile curved Abby's lips, as if she were remembering something good. "I put uplifting notes in his lunch pail every day for school. He hated it at first, because the notes were from me. But finally, I convinced him I wasn't trying to usurp his *mamm's* place and I just wanted to be his friend. It took time to convince Jakob as well."

"Jakob?" Becca had known her cousin was brokenhearted when his first wife died in childbirth but she hadn't known he'd been resistant to the idea of marrying Abby.

"*Ja*, he wanted nothing to do with me, at first."

Becca snorted. "I can hardly believe that. You're so

wundervoll. What man wouldn't want to marry you? Besides, he's obviously crazy in love with you now."

Leaning her hip against the counter, Abby paused in her chore, holding a white egg aloft as she glanced at Becca. "*Ach,* he didn't always love me. It was a very uncomfortable situation. Here I was, living in a strange place, thinking he had proposed marriage, only to discover that it had been his *vadder's* idea and Jakob knew nothing about it."

"Hmm. That would be difficult. I doubt uplifting notes will work on Caleb and Enos, though," Becca said.

"But a stern talk from their *vadders* might do the job." Naomi lifted her eyebrows in a severe expression to make her point.

"I'm not so sure. Caleb's older brother and sister have been getting after him for some of the tricks he pulls and I suspect they've already told the bishop what's going on. Yet, Caleb continues to misbehave. Tomorrow, we'll start practicing songs and readings for the end-of-year program. Maybe if I ask for their help, Caleb and Enos might become vested in the school's success. I might even ask Caleb to start reading with Sam King. Maybe if Caleb feels needed, he'll behave better."

Abby slid a carton of cleaned eggs into the refrigerator. "*Ja,* that might help. You are very wise. Is little Sam still not speaking?"

Becca released a pensive sigh. "*Ne,* and I'm quite worried about him. His *vadder* doesn't seem concerned at all. He said he thinks Sam will start speaking on his own when he's *gut* and ready."

"But you don't agree?" Naomi sat at the table and folded clean laundry from a basket resting on the floor.

"*Ne,* I don't." Becca spoke rather harshly, trying not

to feel angry at Jesse's neglect of his son. But it still rankled her that he seemed a bit insensitive to Sam's needs. "Jesse King is an odious, contrary man. I realize he's lost a lot and been hurt but he should set aside his own pain and put his *sohn's* needs first. I think Sam is suffering badly from the trauma of his *mudder* and *schweschdere's* deaths."

A thud and then the sound of the front door opening came from the living room. Becca figured the men must have finished their evening chores.

"*Ach*, the poor dear," Abby cooed in a sympathetic tone. "And his poor *vadder* too. What a horrible thing for both of them to go through. I know how hard it was for Reuben and Ruby to lose their *mamm*. I don't think they'll ever get over the shock. And neither will Jakob. Sam is blessed to have you to comfort him."

Becca didn't agree. She didn't know what to do for the little boy. How she wished she were more experienced and knew more about special needs like Sam's. But her eighth-grade education didn't provide much insight on such things. The boy was obviously traumatized. Perhaps Jesse was too. And right now, she felt as though she were the blind leading the blind.

"*Ach*, what that little boy needs is a *mudder*. And Jesse needs a *frau*. It would do them both a world of *gut* if Jesse were to remarry," Naomi said.

Maybe so but Becca wasn't in the running for either role. Not after the way Vernon had broken her heart. She couldn't even think about marriage now. Not without feeling nauseous and trembly all over.

"I've heard Jesse has already made a huge difference at that run-down farm he purchased. Jakob drives by there almost every day and said he can see improvements already. And you must have noticed he's quite a handsome *mann*," Abby said.

Of course Becca had noticed. She'd have to be dead or blind not to. But that didn't matter. Not to her. Vernon had been good-looking too, but he'd turned out to be disingenuous. She'd rather marry an earnest, hardworking man who loved the Lord as much as he loved her than be shackled to a handsome, shallow man who didn't really cherish her.

"I'm not interested. I'm simply his *sohn's* teacher and nothing more," she insisted.

She slid into a chair and reached to help fold the socks. As she did so, she felt Naomi's gaze resting on her like a ten-ton sledge. She didn't look up, hoping the older woman didn't notice her flaming cheeks.

"Becca?"

All three women looked up in unison. Jakob stood in the doorway, still wearing his heavy winter coat and black felt hat. He'd obviously just come in from the barn.

"There's someone here to see you," he said.

She tilted her head, thinking it quite late for an evening caller. "Who is it?"

Jakob lowered his head, but kept his gaze pinned on her. "Jesse King."

Becca went very still. Her heart skipped a beat, then sped into triple time. What on earth was Jesse doing here at this late hour?

Jesse waited patiently for Becca to appear. Standing just inside the closed front door, he held his hat between his hands and gazed at the clock on the wall. He was grateful to get his son out of the cold night air.

Sam fidgeted nervously beside him, his eyes wide and filled with apprehension.

This was a nice, spacious living room, with a huge rag rug covering the wooden floor, a plain but comfy-looking sofa, two soft chairs, a simple but serviceable coffee table, and a rocking chair. A set of brown curtains covered the dark, cold windows. The walls were painted white, clean but simple. A black woodburning stove sat near the central wall, emanating enough heat to warm the entire house. It felt nice and cozy in this home. The way he wished his house could be. With time, he hoped he could make a comfortable place for him and Sam to live again. But they'd always be lonely.

Dawdi Zeke beckoned to Sam, enticing the boy to sit on the couch beside him. The elderly man held out a piece of peppermint candy. Sam took it into his hand but didn't say thank you.

A subtle movement across the room caused Jesse to lift his head. Becca Graber stood there, wiping her hands on her apron. Jakob stood behind her with his wife and mother. Jesse could see the curiosity in their eyes. As a new widower, he was highly aware of his marriage eligibility. In fact, Bishop Yoder had just reminded him at church that they had several attractive young women in the *Gmay* who needed husbands. Becca was one of them. But Jesse wasn't interested. He knew as an Amish man that it was his duty to remarry and bring more children into the world. To work and live and raise a good *familye* who loved *Gott*. But Jesse didn't want to marry again. He couldn't even think about replacing Alice. Not when his love for her was still so strong.

Naomi Fisher eyed him like a hawk eyed a field

mouse. He knew they were all wondering what he was doing here. It was already dark outside and he should be home, putting Sam to bed. In a glance, Jesse took in Becca's flushed cheeks, startling blue eyes and flustered expression. Tendrils of golden hair had escaped her *kapp*. She looked beautiful and a warning tingle slid down the column of his spine. All his senses ratcheted into high alert and his common sense told him to leave right now.

Becca stepped over to one of the soft chairs and sat down before smoothing her apron over her knees. "Mr. King, what can I do for you?"

Here it was. The big question.

Jakob and Abby still hovered near the open doorway with *Dawdi* Zeke still on the couch, and Jesse was suddenly at a loss for words. They could hear everything. Maybe he shouldn't have come here. Maybe he should have waited to speak with Becca until he picked Sam up from school tomorrow afternoon. But he feared by then he would have lost his courage.

He cleared his throat. "Miss Graber, I'm sorry for the interruption. I was hoping I could speak with you for just a few minutes about Sam. In private, please."

Okay, he'd gotten that much out. But his words caused another stir as Jakob and the other two women sought to move away from the doorway.

"I'll see if Reuben and Ruby are ready for bed yet." Abby climbed the stairs, her skirts swishing as she went.

"And I better go read them a bedtime story," Jakob said, following after his wife.

Dawdi Zeke came to his feet with a bit of difficulty and took Sam's hand.

"How about if you and I go see if there's any apple

pie left over from supper?" The elderly man spoke to the boy as he hobbled toward the kitchen.

Sam went with the elderly man. He didn't speak but his eyes sparkled and he nodded eagerly. Jesse wasn't surprised. With Alice gone, they rarely enjoyed anything sweet at home. A slice of pie would be a real treat for the child. Even Jesse's mouth watered at the thought.

Naomi welcomed the boy into her kitchen with a cheery voice. "*Hallo*, Samuel. There's plenty of pie to eat. Have you had your supper yet?"

Sam nodded but Jesse knew his son could eat again. The cold beans and burnt corn bread Jesse had prepared earlier hadn't done much to appease either of their appetites. Their stomachs were full but the meal had left a lot to be desired.

"*Ach*, and how about if I send an apple pie home with you and your *vadder* to enjoy tomorrow? You can eat it at your leisure and have some left over for the next day too," Naomi said.

Jesse almost smiled at that but didn't want to betray his eagerness. At this point, an apple pie seemed like a feast. This house smelled of pine needles and a delicious supper and his stomach rumbled in spite of having already eaten.

"Won't you sit down?" Becca invited with a lift of her hand.

He sat opposite her on the sofa, perched there as he set his hat on the coffee table. She folded her hands primly in her lap, her blue eyes unblinking as she gazed at him expectantly.

"*Ach*, so what did you want to speak with me about?" Her voice sounded calm and soothing, not at all perturbed by his unexpected visit.

Here it was. He didn't know what to say. He didn't move or breathe. Afraid to upset her. Afraid she'd say no. After all, he'd been rather rude to her in the past. Maybe he'd already burned his bridges with this woman. Maybe her offer to help him with Sam was gone.

"Ahem, I... I've been thinking about what you've suggested, with Sam. I mean, I've been reading the book you checked out for me and realize his problem isn't going away anytime soon."

He paused, taking a deep breath as he tried to gather his thoughts. She inclined her head but waited patiently, her gaze never leaving his face.

"I don't want Sam to grow up and not be able to speak," he continued. "I want him to have a *gut* future. I'm at my wits' end and don't know what to do to help him. Please. Will you work with him?"

There. He'd gotten his request out in one long breath. He hated to beg but that's what he'd do if it meant Sam could talk and be normal again.

"I would love to help," she said immediately.

It took a moment for his mind to digest what she'd said. And when he did, her words put him instantly at ease.

"You would?" He could hardly believe it. He was beyond relieved.

"*Ja*, you already know I'm not an expert in this area, so I can't make any promises. But I'll do the best I can to help Sam," she said.

He released a pensive sigh, only just realizing that he'd been holding his breath. A huge weight seemed to fall off his shoulders. Finally. Finally he could stop fighting it and get some help.

"*Danke*. I'm so grateful," he said.

"So I can understand what happened, can you give me a little background on Sam's situation?" she asked.

Memories flooded Jesse's mind. He didn't want to talk about this but knew Becca needed to know a few details if she were to help Sam.

"I... I was a certified firefighter where we lived in Pennsylvania," he said in an aching whisper, the memories making him shake like a newborn colt. "I was called out on another house fire and wasn't there when my own home caught fire. When I got home in the early morning hours, I tried to save my *familye* but I was too late." He looked down and saw the scars on his hands and arms. They were still there, reminding him of his failure. "I found Sam up in the hayloft, curled in a fetal position. When I asked him what happened, he became hysterical. All he would say was that he was sorry and it was his fault. Two days later, we buried my *frau* and *dechder*. Sam hasn't spoken a word since the funeral."

Becca winced. "I'm so very sorry for your loss."

Her words made no difference but her soft, compassionate voice seemed to ease the ache just a bit. Even though it had been a year, the tale still rattled Jesse's nerves. He'd lost almost everything that horrible day. Now, all he had left was Sam. And he knew, no matter what, he had to help his little boy. Alice would expect nothing less.

Becca stood abruptly. "Wait here. I'll be right back."

The wooden steps creaked as she went up the stairs to the second story. She returned moments later carrying a booklet and several pieces of paper, which she handed to him.

"This is a copy of an intervention plan I've already

drawn up for Sam," she said. "Just a few simple steps on how we can offer positive reinforcement, some stimulus fading techniques to desensitize him when he's around other people, ways to help him build social skills, and tactics so he won't feel as anxious. If you'll read through these materials and try to incorporate them at home, I think we can help him overcome this problem. I'll do the same at school, only much more since he'll be with his classmates during that time."

Jesse glanced at the plan of action, surprised at how detailed it was. It was quite thorough and easy to follow with step-by-step instructions dealing with a variety of scenarios. For the first time in a year, a lance of optimism speared his chest with hope. He wasn't surprised to see that she'd assigned him to read with Sam each night. No matter how busy he was right now, he had no excuses. If nothing else, spending more time with Sam might increase his bond with the boy. And after what they'd been through, they both needed time together more than anything.

"*Ja*, I will do these things. I'll read to him each night," he promised.

Her shoulders relaxed and he realized she'd been tensed, expecting him to refuse again.

"That's *wundervoll*," she exclaimed, her smile so bright that he had to swallow. "And I'd like to suggest one more thing that I hope will help all of us."

He quirked one eyebrow and waited. It wasn't until she spoke again that he realized he was holding his breath.

"I think Sam needs extra tutoring, to help with his school studies. Since you live only a short way up the road, I propose that I bring Sam home from school every Monday, Wednesday and Friday afternoon. Then I can tutor him for an extra hour or so. And the added benefit is that you won't have to pick him up on those days, which should alleviate your workload too. Since today is Monday, I'd like to start tutoring him tomorrow, even though it's Tuesday. Does that sound all right?"

Jesse just stared, his mind struggling to absorb what she'd suggested. It was true that the Fisher farm wasn't far away from his place. In the darkest part of the night, he could even see their lights gleaming across his fields. They were his neighbors, though he hadn't developed a very close friendship with them yet. He just hadn't had the time for the niceties. Maybe later in the summer, after his fields were planted, he could do something about that.

"*Ja*, that would work fine," he said, suddenly willing to agree to anything she wanted.

Actually, her proposal would be an unexpected blessing. Living so far outside of town provided the quiet and solitude he desired but it also meant he had to take Sam to school early in the mornings and fetch him home in the afternoons. Some days, that posed a great hardship, depending on what he was working on. He did it because he believed an education was so important for Sam and because he loved his son. But it hadn't been easy.

"*Fie*. We'll start with the tutoring tomorrow and go from there." She smiled and came to her feet, signaling they were finished.

He stood slowly. As she stepped over to the kitchen and invited him in for a huge slice of pie, he felt like he was moving in a fog. Naomi and *Dawdi* Zeke welcomed him. They laughed and chatted as though he were a member of their *familye*. Jesse didn't say much but nodded and smiled in return. It felt so mundane and normal and he appreciated their kindness more than he could say. His gaze kept roaming over to Becca as she offered Sam a chilled glass of milk. The child smiled and chewed with relish. And that's when something dawned on Jesse. He hadn't seen his son look this happy since before the house fire. Already, Becca had made a huge difference in Sam's life.

By the time Jesse loaded his sleepy son into their buggy for the short drive home, he couldn't help thinking that his *familye* used to be fun like this. They used to laugh and talk and eat pie together around the kitchen table. Oh, how he missed them all. How he missed the love and companionship they used to share.

How he missed Alice.

He had Becca to thank for today. She was so dynamic and outspoken, but also kind and generous. Because she was Sam's teacher, she seemed to think she was entitled to make demands on Jesse and his time. The most irksome part was that she was right. Sam needed help. His father's help.

Becca was pushy, insistent and giving. She was so different from his gentle, quiet, submissive Alice. Jesse just hoped Becca's plan worked and Sam would soon start talking again. And as he drove them home through the cold night air, all of a sudden the world seemed to be filled with amazing possibilities.

Chapter Five

The following morning, Sam didn't show up for school. They'd had another bad snowstorm in the night, so Becca thought perhaps Jesse couldn't get his horse and buggy through the tall drifts that covered the dirt road leading from his farm. Since she lived just one mile away from his place, she knew the plows had been out early that morning to clear the county roads so the school buses with the *Englisch* kids could get to school safely. And that benefited the Amish too. But each farm had a dirt road that extended quite a way down and no one plowed that for them. Maybe tonight, she'd suggest to Jakob that he take his horses and sleigh over to Jesse's place to help clear his driveway and road.

Two hours into the school day, she was standing in front of the chalkboard, helping the fourth-graders work through some particularly difficult arithmetic problems. The front door suddenly blasted open with a gust of chilly air. Becca whirled around and saw little Sam standing there with his father. Both of them were bundled up in heavy black coats, boots, knit caps, gloves and scarfs. While Jesse closed the door, the boy hurried over to the coatracks where he doffed his winter wear and hung it up. A quick glance at the other first-graders told him what subject they were working on as he slid into his seat and took out his penmanship book. And that's when Becca saw his red eyes and tearstained face. The boy had obviously been crying. But why? What was the matter?

"I'm sorry we're late. It couldn't be helped." Jesse lifted a hand as he spoke in *Deitsch*.

Under normal circumstances, Becca would have just smiled and welcomed Jesse and Sam to school. But the fact that Sam had been crying upset her. Setting the chalk aside, she walked over to Jesse and indicated she'd like him to accompany her outside where they could speak in private.

"Continue with your studies, please," she called to the scholars before shutting the door against intrusion.

Standing on the front step, she faced Jesse, her emotions a riot of unease. "What has happened? Why is Sam so late?"

It was only when he responded that she realized she had also spoken in *Deitsch*. His and Sam's sudden appearance had flustered her more than she liked to admit.

Jesse shrugged, not meeting her gaze. "Sam had a bad morning. He is all right now."

"Are you sure? He looks distressed." She spoke in *Englisch* this time, trying to remain professional.

"*Ja*, he is fine now."

Hmm. His comment led her to believe it wasn't the heavy drifts of snow that had caused Sam to cry. So, what had happened?

"Are you sure you're up to bringing him home this afternoon after school? We got nine inches out at our place and I don't want you stranded on the road some-where," Jesse said.

He acted like everything was completely normal, which confused her even more. Little six-year-old boys didn't cry for no reason. Maybe she could find out what was the matter from Sam, although that might prove difficult since the boy didn't talk.

"*Ja*, the sky is clear and the snow is melting now," she said. "We shouldn't have any more storms for several days. I should be able to bring Sam home and tutor him this afternoon without any problems."

"*Gut*, I'll see you then. I'll watch for you and *komm* looking for you if you're late arriving at my place."

His words gave her a bit of comfort. It was nice to know someone was looking out for her in case she had trouble with her horse and buggy.

Jesse turned and walked down the steps, his long legs moving fast as he stepped around muddy areas where the snow had melted into puddles.

Rubbing her arms against the frigid air, Becca didn't call him back or question him further. She had no right to interfere.

She returned to the classroom and discovered that the students hadn't made much progress without her help. Lenore Schwartz, an eighth-grader, had just stepped in to offer assistance. With Becca's arrival, Lenore handed over the piece of chalk and returned to her desk.

"Thank you, Lenore," Becca called after the girl in a pleasant voice.

"You're *willkomm*." The girl nodded and smiled shyly.

Becca could tell some of the scholars were becom-ing more relaxed around her. After all, this was only her sixth day of teaching these kids. She was delighted to know they were starting to feel comfortable enough to step in and help the younger children.

"Let's see, where are we?" Pressing a finger to her lips, Becca stepped up to the chalkboard and studied the problem once more.

She glanced at Susan Hostetler, one of the fourth-graders who was working this particular problem. Becca pointed at a specific area of the addition. "I think you're getting hung up right here."

"*Ach*, I told you so. You're adding it wrong." Caleb Yoder spoke with impatience.

Since Caleb was her only fifth-grader, she had brought him in to work with the fourth-graders. He brushed past Susan, picked up a piece of chalk and started to work her problem. Becca intervened, quickly erasing what he had written on the board.

"Caleb, this is Susan's problem to work out. Please wait patiently for your turn," she said.

The other children frowned with disapproval at Caleb's rude behavior and he stepped back with a huff. Becca was glad. Maybe peer pressure would help keep Caleb in line.

Becca faced Susan again. "Did you remember to carry the nine?"

For several moments, Susan stared at the chalkboard, her forehead knitted in a deep frown of concentration. Then, the light clicked on inside her brain and she gasped in comprehension. "*Ach*, it's right here!"

The girl quickly worked the problem, wrote the answer below, then turned to face Becca with an expectant smile. "Is it right this time? Is it?"

Becca nodded, showing a wide smile of approval. "You are absolutely correct. Well done!"

"Yay!" the girl cried, her face wide with a happy smile.

A laugh broke from Becca's throat. She loved this part of teaching. When she saw the light of knowledge glimmer in one of her student's eyes, it made her happy too. Yesterday, she'd doubted herself so much. But maybe she could do this after all. Once again, a part of her couldn't help wishing she could marry and have a *familye* of her own. Since Vernon had broken her heart, it wasn't to be. After the way he'd treated her, she didn't think she could trust another man ever again. And moping about her shattered dreams wouldn't do her any good. She had better get on with her life and make the best of it. But successes like this brought her a great deal of satisfaction and joy.

"Very well done," she praised Susan again, then glanced at Caleb. "I think you're a bit too advanced for these problems. You'll need a more difficult fraction to add."

She could tell her words pleased him. Praise usually brought on *Hochmut*, the pride of the world, so it wasn't encouraged among the Amish. But Becca thought a small compliment might help Caleb in this situation. While he watched her quizzically, she quickly wrote out a more strenuous problem with multiple fractions. Then, she handed her piece of chalk to him and stepped back to give him room to work.

He pressed his tongue to his upper lip while he studied the equation. Within moments, he had solved the problem with very little hesitation. He was definitely a bright scholar. Maybe that was the reason he kept getting into trouble. He was bored.

Well, she would just have to give him more work to do.

"Yay!" the other children called, quick to forgive him for being discourteous and quick to offer encouragement.

Becca laid a hand on Caleb's shoulder and met his eyes. "Very well done, Caleb. In fact, I think you are advanced enough that you should start helping one of the younger children with their arithmetic. How would you like to become Sam's math partner?"

Caleb glanced at the little boy, who sat quietly studying at his desk. A frown curved Caleb's mouth downward and Becca feared he might refuse.

"You know he doesn't speak, but you're such a *gut* student that I know you can explain things to him." Becca whispered the words for Caleb's ears alone. After all, she didn't want to hurt Sam's feelings. "You're quite a bit older and Sam really looks up to you. I'm sure he'd appreciate your help. And I'd love to tell your *vadder* that you're one of our school tutors."

A flicker of delight blazed in Caleb's eyes. He liked that. A lot.

"But you mustn't do Sam's work for him," she cautioned, still speaking softly so the other kids wouldn't overhear. "Just help show him where he might be getting the problems wrong and let him figure things out himself. Then we'll tell everyone what a *gut* tutor he has."

That did the trick. Caleb nodded and immediately went over to sit close to Sam and help with his simple addition. Caleb sat up straight, his movements filled with confidence. And Becca knew she'd done a good thing. Caleb was very bright and getting too bored, which led to him causing trouble in the school. But elevating him to tutor would help him focus more on helping Sam. It would help him concentrate on helping someone else instead of getting into trouble. Caleb would now be Sam's protector instead of his tormentor.

Feeling good about her day of teaching, Becca returned to her work with the other scholars and the morning whizzed by way too fast. She felt happy inside, knowing she'd just resolved a huge problem with Caleb. It made her glad she was a teacher. Glad she had come here to Colorado.

"Teacher Becca?"

She looked up and saw Karen Yoder holding her hand high in the air.

"Yes, Karen?" she said.

Karen indicated the clock on the wall. "It's lunchtime, teacher. I thought you might be too busy to notice."

Glancing at the clock, Becca gasped and realized her mistake. It was already eleven thirty. Where had the morning gone?

"Thank you, Karen. Scholars, please return to your desks and stand while we say our prayer of thanks," she said.

The children at the chalkboard returned to their seats and all the students stood while they recited in unison. When they finished, the scholars each gathered their lunch pails and congregated in several huddles to eat.

"When you're finished with your lunch, you're welcome to go outside and build a snowman. Or if it's too cold and you prefer to stay inside, feel free to get out the game boards and play quietly together," Becca told them.

The kids nodded, speaking in muted voices, an occasional laugh piercing the air. None of them went outside today. They stayed inside and played games instead.

Becca sat at her desk, putting the finishing touches on the end-of-year program while she took bites of her ham sandwich. And that's when she looked up and saw something amazing. Instead of teasing the younger boys, Caleb had invited little Sam and Andy over to join him and the older boys in a game of Life on the Farm. Sam didn't speak but he participated silently and smiled when he did something right. The other children encouraged him, acting the way she expected them to.

Becca smiled to herself, realizing maybe she could be a good teacher after all. Last week, she'd felt as though she were a failure. That she never should have come to Colorado. But what she had done with Caleb Yoder had been a big achievement. Maybe she could make it as a teacher after all.

Now, if she could just figure out how to help Sam speak again, she would be truly happy. This afternoon, she would drive the little boy home and offer him some tutoring. She'd be sure to spend a little extra time bouncing ideas off Jesse as to how to help his son as well. She prayed that he wouldn't resist and would take her advice well. And maybe during their conversation, she could find out what had caused Sam to cry that morning. She just hoped Jesse hadn't been cruel to his son. She liked Jesse. She really did. She just wished he was more sensitive to his son's needs.

By four o'clock that afternoon, Becca and Sam hadn't arrived at the house and Jesse was ready to go find them. He stumbled on his way out of the back shed and headed toward the barn. Even though it was still early, the sky was overcast with a cluster of gray clouds. Maybe the roads had iced up already. It was certainly cold enough. He didn't know how good a driver Becca was and started to worry.

He led Jimmy, his road horse, out of the barn. Taking a deep inhale of fresh air, he tried to clear his muddled mind. A blaze of panic almost overtook him. The horrible feeling of being out of control and losing everything that was good in life. And he couldn't do a single thing to stop it from happening. Maybe Becca hadn't been paying attention and went off the road. Maybe she and Sam were lying hurt somewhere in a ditch...

The jingle of a harness brought his attention and he looked up. Becca's horse and buggy pulled into the graveled yard. Jesse saw her and his son sitting on the front seat, both of them bundled up against the frigid air. Becca held the leather lead lines with her gloved hands, seeming alert and attentive as she drove with confidence.

"*Danke*, Lord. *Danke* for bringing them home safe." Jesse whispered the prayer of gratitude beneath his breath.

They were here. He could stop worrying. At least until Becca had to drive to her farm in an hour or so.

"*Hallo!*" she called as she hopped out of the buggy.

She reached back to help Sam down. The boy rested his little hands on her shoulders without hesitation. And that's when Jesse noticed his son seemed to trust his teacher quite a bit.

"Were you going somewhere?" she asked, looking at his horse as they walked over to greet him. Her blue eyes were bright and alive, her cheeks and nose pink from the chilled temperatures. He could see each of her exhales like a puff of smoke on the frosty air. And looped over one arm, she carried a rather large basket covered by a clean cloth. Probably her school books for tutoring Sam.

He nodded, leaning against Jimmy's front shoulder. For some reason, he felt extra tired today, though he'd never admit it to Becca. "*Ja*, I was getting ready to go and find you. Now that you're here, I'll put your horse in the barn until you're ready to leave."

Without being asked, Sam helped his father. Becca stood near the wide double doors, watching silently as they stabled her horse and offered it some water.

"It's barely four o'clock," she said. "I don't know why you were getting ready to *komm* and find us. School gets out at three thirty and I had to make sure all the scholars were picked up by their *eldre* and secure the building before I could leave..."

He turned to face her and her eyes widened and she gasped. "Jesse! What happened to you?"

Feeling confused, he reached up and touched his forehead where he discovered a giant bump forming there.

"It's nothing. I was working to repair one of the walls in the back shed and took a fall off the ladder a little while ago." He reached for the halter to lead Jimmy back inside the warm barn too.

Becca and Sam followed after him. The boy didn't speak but took hold of his father's elbow, his face creased with concern. Jesse could tell Sam was worried about him.

"*Geht es dir gut?*" Becca asked.

"*Ja*, I'm all right," he reassured them both. "The fall

just knocked the wind out of me. I didn't realize I'd hit my head until just now."

He released Jimmy back into his stall and shut the door. No wonder he had a mild headache and had been disoriented a few minutes earlier. But now, he could feel his mind clearing and realized he'd been stunned by the fall.

"Let's go inside the house. It's too cold out here," Becca said.

She still looked anxious and for some crazy reason that touched Jesse's heart like nothing else could. It had been a long time since someone had fretted and cared about him.

Even though he still had cows to milk and chickens to feed, he didn't argue with her. He wanted something warm to drink and then he'd finish his evening chores.

They went inside the back door, the warmth of the potbellied stove engulfing them. Though this house and the surrounding corrals and outbuildings needed tons of repairs, at least the old stove worked well as long as he kept it supplied with fuel.

Becca set her basket on the table and doffed her gloves and heavy shawl. She helped Sam do the same, tossing his hat and coat carelessly on a chair. While Becca went to the kitchen cupboards, Jesse placed more wood on the fire. When he set the kettle on the stove to heat up, he glanced over and saw Becca retrieving a clean dishcloth from a drawer. Thankfully, she didn't say a word about the sink filled with dirty dishes. He planned to wash them later tonight but knew his home suffered from his lack of tidiness. Alice had always kept their place immaculate and in good order. But with all the work he had to do just to get ready for spring planting, he couldn't seem to keep up with everything.

He didn't question Becca when she went outside to fill the dishcloth with small chunks of ice. By the time she'd returned, he had sat down to rest a moment. Without a word, she promptly placed the cold cloth over his forehead. He flinched and she moved more gently, her fingertips warm against his skin.

"Hold this against your head for a few minutes. It'll help the swelling go down," she said.

"I don't need this," he said.

"*Ja*, you do," she insisted. "I'm wondering if I should take you to see Eli Stoltzfus. He can tell if you need to go to the hospital in town."

Jesse had met Eli and knew the man was a certified paramedic who worked for the small hospital in Riverton. Since Jesse was a firefighter, he wasn't surprised to find an Amish paramedic here. He knew they never drove any automotive vehicles, but the Amish had quickly discovered the benefits of having EMTs, paramedics and firefighters among them.

"I don't need to see Eli. It's just a little bump on the head and I feel fine," he said.

Her forehead crinkled slightly but she didn't argue as she bustled over to the table and began emptying the contents of the basket she'd brought. Watching her, he couldn't help thinking she had a way of taking over his home every time she arrived. And yet, he didn't mind. Not really. Because she seemed to bring lots of comfort and order with her. But he was surprised when she removed a casserole dish, a loaf of homemade bread and a cherry pie from her basket.

His mouth watered at the sight of so much good

food. His hunger alone told him that his head was okay. "What are those for?"

She didn't look up as she slid the casserole into the gas-powered oven and turned it on. It looked like some kind of pasta, cheese and hamburger mixture that smelled delicious. Simple but filling food that made his stomach rumble. Sam had homed in on the pie, climbing up on a chair so he could gaze longingly at the golden crust and plump red berries that had oozed out of the lattice top when it was baked.

"This is for your supper," she said. "It was easy to keep the food chilled until we got here and I figured you were busy and might appreciate a night off from cooking."

He laughed out loud. He couldn't help himself. "Is this your polite way of letting me know I'm a lousy cook?"

She laughed too, the sound high and sweet, her eyes sparkling with pleasure. "*Ach*, I don't mean to offend but you must admit that you really are a poor cook."

He nodded without argument, still smiling at her sense of humor. "I'm willing to concede your point and will admit I have come to dread meal preparation. I think Sam dreads it too."

Her smile stayed firmly in place as she removed several books from the bottom of the basket. "And these are for my tutoring session with Sam."

She handed the boy one book, which he took readily. A feeling of deep and abiding gratitude for her thoughtfulness rested over Jesse like a warm blanket. And that's when he realized something important. He had laughed just a few moments ago. A loud, full-bodied laugh that came from deep inside. It was the first since Alice and his little girls had died. And that made Jesse pause in startled wonder. He felt suddenly unfaithful to their memory. Disloyal for feeling happy when they were gone.

He stood abruptly and tossed the dishrag onto the cupboard. "This is fine now. I've got chores to do."

Placing his black felt hat on his head, he closed the door firmly behind him and hurried to the barn. After tossing hay to the animals, he fed the chickens and milked the cow. The work gave him time to gather his thoughts. To remember who he was and what he was doing here.

Becca was efficient, bossy and wonderful but she wasn't Alice. And he was not going to let her take over his life or his thoughts. In his heart, he was still a married man who was faithful to his wife. And he wouldn't allow himself to be taken in by Becca's competent ways.

Thirty minutes later, he returned to the kitchen, carrying a bucket of frothy white milk. As he set it on the table, he could hear Becca in the living room, reading to Sam. He stepped over to the doorway and peeked into the room without revealing his presence. They both sat huddled together in the new rocking chair he had finished making last night. Little by little, he was getting things done but he was impatient to paint the ugly, scarred walls inside his home. However, that would have to wait. There were more pressing issues he needed to tend to right now or they wouldn't have a livelihood. Issues such as getting the corrals and sheds repaired so he could buy livestock for their farm.

He listened silently as Becca read Sam a story about a cat named Elmo and a dog named Patches. The feline played a lot of tricks on the dog and got away with all sorts of antics. Finally, Becca finished the story with a laugh.

"I really like Elmo. He's so funny. He's always sneaking up on Patches," she said.

Sam nodded in agreement.

"But who do you like the best? Elmo or Patches?" Becca asked.

A slight movement from Sam told Jesse that his son had pointed at his preference.

"*Ach*, pointing at the picture will never do. Can you say his name out loud for me?" Becca asked, her voice calm and inviting.

There was a long, quiet pause. Becca didn't intrude. She gave Sam plenty of time to think. And then, the softest whisper wafted across the room. So quiet that Jesse almost didn't hear.

"Patches."

Jesse blinked. Had he heard right? Had Sam actually said the dog's name out loud?

"That's very *gut*," Becca said. "But why do you like Patches the best?"

Every nerve in Jesse's body went on high alert. He leaned forward slightly, eager to hear his son's response. Would Sam speak again? Could he do it?

"Dog," Sam whispered low.

Okay, not a complete sentence, but Jesse understood only too well. Before Alice had died, Sam had asked him numerous times if they could get a dog. They already had several barn cats who kept the mice population down but Sam wanted a puppy of his very own. Jesse hadn't gotten around to getting the boy one before tragedy had struck and then they'd moved here to Colorado. Maybe it was time…

"Very *gut*," Becca said, closing the book with a slight snap. "You're doing so well, Sam. I'm very pleased with you."

She leaned her head down and kissed the boy's forehead. When they stood, Jesse pulled back into the kitchen with a quick jerk. He didn't want to be caught eavesdropping, yet he felt mesmerized by the two of them. He could listen to them all day.

Hurrying over to the kitchen sink, he noticed that all the dishes had been washed and put away. He stared at the clean countertops, stunned down to the tips of his worn work boots.

"We're all done for this evening." Becca spoke from behind and he turned.

She stood in the doorway, holding Sam's hand. The boy smiled shyly but didn't speak.

"How did he do tonight?" Jesse asked, clearing his throat.

"*Wundervoll*. He even spoke twice," she said.

"*Ja*, I heard. That's great news."

Jesse smiled at his son, trying not to overreact so much that it startled Sam and shut him down. Jesse had enough common sense not to push the boy until he was ready. But it was an amazing, wonderful start. And he had Becca to thank for all of it.

Chapter Six

"**I** see you've finished making more chairs for the table. You're a *gut* carpenter." Becca glanced around the kitchen in Jesse's home and couldn't help admiring his simple handiwork.

There were now four wooden chairs surrounding the long table, which had enough room to seat eight people. That wasn't surprising. Most Amish families had an average of seven or eight children. But since Jesse's wife had died, Becca wondered why he had made such a large table. Maybe he hoped to remarry and have more children. She wasn't sure. She figured he'd lost all his furniture in the house fire and it would take time to rebuild. Already, she'd seen enough of his house to know the walls needed painting and the cold wooden floors needed covering.

"Ahem, supper is ready. Would you like to join us in our meal?" Jesse asked.

His voice sounded a bit stilted, as though he wasn't used to having a woman in his home who wasn't his wife.

"I would like that very much."

She rolled up her sleeves and reached inside the cupboard for some plates so she could set the table. As she did so, she thought it odd that she already knew where he kept the utensils. Having washed his dishes, she knew quite a bit about his kitchen, including the fact that his cupboards were now filled with a variety of canned goods.

"I see you've got plenty of food in the house." Wearing two mitts on her hands, she lifted the casserole out of the oven and set it in the middle of the table. Steam rose from the hot dish and filled the air with a yummy aroma.

He chuckled as he sliced the loaf of homemade bread. "*Ja*, I don't want Sam to go without his meals just because I can't cook."

They sat together at the table and bowed their heads. No one spoke and Becca simply recited the Lord's Prayer in her mind. She also asked *Gott* to help Sam continue to make progress in his speaking and to help Jesse be safe while he worked on his farm.

After a few moments, Jesse released a low sigh and they dug into the delicious food. Sam ate ravenously and Becca realized it had been a long time since he and his father had enjoyed a home-cooked meal that wasn't burnt. Maybe she could do something about that from time to time, just until Jesse got back on his feet with his farm chores.

"What was the name again of the little dog in the story Becca was reading to you?" Jesse asked.

He was looking at Sam expectantly. Obviously, he hoped the boy would respond. But he didn't. Sam glanced hesitantly at his father, then stared down at his plate. He didn't say a single word but set his fork on his plate, as though he'd lost his appetite.

The silence continued and Becca realized the mute boy had returned. To break the stilted moment, she reached across the table and squeezed Sam's chilled hand.

"It's all right," she said. Then, she looked at Jesse. "The dog's name was Patches. We had fun reading about him and Elmo."

Jesse's gaze met hers and she could see the disappointment in his eyes. Sam had spoken for her but not for his father. And that must sting Jesse pretty hard.

They finished their meal in silence and Becca quickly washed the remaining dishes. She was startled when both Sam and Jesse helped her clear the meal away.

"It's getting late. You go on up and get ready for bed. I'll be up soon to read you a story," Jesse told his son.

A glint of eagerness sparked in Sam's eyes but he merely nodded and did as asked. When they were alone, Jesse reached for a clean dish towel and started drying the dishes.

"You're *gut* with him," Jesse said.

Becca sank her hands deep into the hot, sudsy water as she scrubbed a particularly stubborn fork. "It's easy to be helpful with Sam. He's such a sweet, innocent little boy."

"I... I want to thank you for what you did tonight. I know it wasn't much and he didn't speak during dinner but just hearing his voice again was amazing," Jesse said.

She nodded. "I know. I couldn't believe it when he actually spoke. In all honesty, I didn't expect him to do it so soon and it was all I could do not to jump up and yell. It took everything in me to remain calm and act natural."

"Me too. He's comfortable around you. It's obvious you don't make him nervous." Jesse didn't look at her as he dried a spoon and placed it in a drawer.

"*Ja*, I think you're right. And that's a *gut* thing," she agreed.

"But I do. I make him too nervous to talk."

Jesse stood perfectly still. He lifted his head and looked at her, his eyes filled with a bit of misery. Becca didn't know what to say. She realized in that moment just how far apart Jesse and Sam really were. And the fact that Jesse knew it too made her feel a great deal of compassion for him. The house fire had taken more than just his wife and two daughters. In a way, it had stolen Sam from him too.

"I'm sorry, Jesse. I... I didn't mean to do anything wrong or create a problem for you," she said.

He shook his head. "*Ne*, it isn't your fault, Becca. It's mine."

She went very still as he told her about the night he'd come home to find his house on fire. Sam had cried and kept telling him it was his fault.

"The day I buried my wife and *dechder*, I was filled with such grief." He spoke in an aching whisper that caused goose bumps to cover her arms and neck. "I pushed Sam away. He tried to comfort me and I couldn't stand to even look at him. I think he knew what I was feeling inside. He'd started the fire and I blamed him for killing my *familye*. Now, he suffers from nightmares. He doesn't say anything but I know he relives the trauma of that night over and over again. We both do."

Jesse braced his hands on the countertop and hung

his head. Before she could stop herself, she reached out and touched his arm.

"I'm so sorry for your loss, Jesse. So deeply sorry," she said.

He lifted his head and she saw the anguish and sorrow in his dark eyes. For just a moment, he looked bereft. She'd seen that same look in Jakob's eyes when she'd attended the funeral of his first wife after she'd died in childbirth. Nothing Becca could do or say could console him.

"That's why he was late for school this morning. He'd had a bad nightmare and it took a long time for me to calm him down," Jesse said.

Ah, so now she knew. He hadn't been cruel to the boy. Sam had simply had a nightmare and been crying. Jesse had tried to comfort the boy. He wasn't an abusive father. Not from what she could see. He was just a grieving father and husband who was trying to help his troubled son. And knowing this brought Becca a great deal of respect for Jesse as well as a ton of relief. The fact that he had confided in her softened her heart.

Jesse swallowed hard and took a deep breath before glancing out the window. "It's dark already and you should be home where you'll be safe. It's time for you to go."

He didn't wait for her approval before he reached for her heavy, black shawl, scarf and warm traveling bonnet and handed them to her. He watched her silently as she put them on. Then, he walked her outside where he harnessed her horse to her buggy.

"I can see the lights of your farm late at night," he said.

"*Ja*, Jakob will leave a kerosene lamp burning for

me until I arrive home safely. If it gets too late, he'll *komm* looking for me."

"I figured as much. The roads are very icy. I'll watch for the light. If it stays on, I'll know you're in trouble and will *komm* find you. If the light goes out, I'll know you've arrived home safe."

Since they didn't have cell phones, this system would work. She let him take her hand as he helped her climb into her buggy. "I'll turn off the light as soon as I arrive home."

He nodded and, taking the leather lead lines into her gloved hands, she slapped them lightly on her horse's rump. Even though it was only eight o'clock, it had been a long day and she was eager to get home. Because they got up at four in the morning, most Amish were in bed by this time. Perhaps she had stayed too long. She still had lesson plans to review for tomorrow. She would take the kerosene light to her room on the opposite side of her house, so Jesse wouldn't be able to see it from his farm and get worried about her. No doubt she'd be up late preparing for school in the morning.

Within minutes, her horse had pulled onto the main county road. In the moonlight, she could see the shimmer of black ice on the asphalt. She drove very slowly and, as her horse settled into an even rhythm, she hoped they wouldn't encounter any automotive vehicles before she reached the turnoff to her cousin's farm. It was dangerous to drive a horse and buggy in the dark.

She stayed stiff and alert and, when she reached her home safely, she breathed a sigh of relief. Almost everyone in the house was already in bed but Aunt Naomi greeted her wearing her warm flannel nightgown and carrying a bright kerosene lamp.

"I was getting worried about you," the woman said, peering at Becca to ensure she was all right.

"There was no need." Becca spoke softly so she wouldn't awaken the others. "I did some *gut* work with little Sam this night. He spoke for the first time, *Aent* Naomi. It was only a whisper, but he spoke twice."

"*Ach*, that's *wundervoll*. I'm so glad. Now, let's go to bed. Tomorrow will come soon enough."

"You go on. I'll be up in just a few minutes," Becca said.

Satisfied that her niece was home safe, Naomi handed her the kerosene lamp before disappearing up the dark stairs.

Becca carried the lamp over to the kitchen window facing Jesse's hay field. She turned the light up bright, hoping he would see it. Then, she turned it off, knowing he would get the message that she was home safe.

Moving silently through the darkness, she entered her bedroom and pulled a chair over to the window. She rested her cheek against the cool windowsill, thinking perhaps she could delay her schoolwork for one more day. Because honestly, she was too tired to do any more tonight.

Lying on the bed, she closed her eyes and tried to rest. But her mind was too active to sleep. She thought about all that had happened that evening. Sam had spoken and Jesse had revealed some deeply personal things to her. She knew without a doubt that he was still powerfully in love with his deceased wife. He was still grieving for her and their two daughters. And perhaps that was for the best. She was Sam's teacher and had helped him make substantial progress today. That was her job. It was the career she had chosen for herself. She didn't need anything else. So, why couldn't she stop wishing for more?

* * *

Jesse stood on his back porch and gazed into the dark. Far across the rocky fields, a small pinpoint of light could be seen, coming from the Fishers' farmhouse. No more than a faint glow that flickered among the dark, barren trees bordering their two property lines. And yet, it was so clear. Like a beacon lighting the way for a ship lost at sea. Just a pale glow but easy enough to see. Jesse knew it was way past the time when Becca and her *familye* should have gone to bed. And because the light persisted, he started to worry about her. What if her horse and buggy had gone off the frozen road? What if she was stranded in a snowbank and needed his help? Maybe she hadn't made it home yet. Maybe she was hurt.

He turned, prepared to wake up Sam so he could go looking for Becca. But the light went out abruptly and he released a pensive exhale. She was home safe. He knew her cousins wouldn't turn out the light until she was there. Jesse could finally go to bed and rest, though he knew he would find very little sleep. His mind was too filled with riotous thoughts. Memories of his past happiness and the burden of guilt for losing it all.

Entering his kitchen, he was careful not to let the screen door clap closed and wake up Sam. He doffed his boots, making his way through the dark house in his stockinged feet. He had a hole in the big toe of his right sock but didn't plan to darn it, or any of his other socks and shirts, anytime soon. Sewing had been Alice's task and he doubted he could do a decent job of it. Maybe he could hire one of the Amish women from church to do his mending. Until then, he'd just put up with the holes.

After building up the kindling in the potbellied stove, he walked up the creaking stairs and paused just before Sam's doorway to listen. No restless shifting or low cries came from the room. His son was fast asleep, seeming content for the night. And Jesse knew they had Becca to thank for that.

Grateful for all that had transpired this evening, he made his way to his own room where he sat on the mattress and removed his woolen socks. As he lay back on the cool covers, his mind was filled with wonder. *Gott* had truly blessed them this night. Sam had finally spoken for the first time in over a year. It wasn't much, just two little words that were said in a quiet whisper. But it was enough. Sam had talked. Finally.

Until they got to the dinner table.

Then, the child had looked at Jesse and clammed up tight as a fist. Jesse knew it was because Sam feared him. Because the boy felt guilty for what he had done. And yet, there was no anger in Jesse toward his son. No guile or recriminations. Not anymore. The boy was only a young child. What had happened hadn't been his fault. Not really. Jesse was the patriarch of his home. If the house fire had been anyone's fault, it was his.

He wanted Sam to be happy. To go on and live a joyful life filled with good works. When Jesse had watched Becca's buggy pull away from his home, he'd been touched by her kindness. She'd provided them with a tasty supper. She'd washed the dishes and brought order to his house. And laughter. For just a moment, he had wished she could stay. But she wasn't Alice. She wasn't his wife. And he felt disloyal for being drawn in by her winsome smiles and easy manner as she moved around his home.

After she'd left, he'd kept his word and read a bed-time story to Sam. It had been a surprisingly pleasant task. Jesse had read one of the books Becca had brought them. Acting out the voices of each character, he'd made Sam smile several times. He'd even tried Becca's tactic and asked the boy who was his favorite person in the story. But Sam hadn't said a word. He'd simply pointed at the mother in the story and Jesse's heart had filled with so much pain that he thought he'd cry right then and there in front of his son.

Sam missed Alice. So did Jesse. More than he could say. He loved her with all his heart, mind and strength. And he could not forget her. No, not ever.

Sam's words spoken to Becca that evening hadn't been much but, in his heart of hearts, Jesse had cheered loud and hard the moment he'd heard them. Finally. Finally, Sam had spoken again. And if he could do it twice, he could do it again. Surely the dam of silence had been broken open. The boy obviously felt comfortable and safe with Becca. But that didn't matter to Jesse. Because other than educating Sam, Jesse must not let the pretty schoolteacher impact his emotions or his life any more than that. No, sirree. Not one single bit.

Chapter Seven

By Saturday morning, the skies had cleared to an azure blue. Rainstorms had all but dissipated the snow across the countryside, leaving the earth saturated and smelling of musty, damp soil. As Becca drove the horse and buggy over to Jesse's farm, she didn't care a bit. It was still early and, though she was glad the day was clear and free of wind for this outing, she was too happy and excited to worry about the weather.

Aunt Naomi and her eight-year-old granddaughter, Ruby, sat beside Becca on the seat. On her lap, Naomi held her sixteen-month-old granddaughter, Chrissie. Jakob, his wife, Abby, and *Dawdi* Zeke rode in a horse-drawn wagon behind them, with ten-year-old Reuben in the back. A sense of exhilaration swarmed Becca's chest when she considered the surprise they were about to offer Jesse and Sam. The buggy and wagon were laden with a nice lunch, hand tools, buckets of off-white paint and brushes, three large rag rugs that Aunt Naomi didn't need anymore, and plain muslin cloth to make curtains for Jesse's windows.

Dressed in a black chambray shirt, Jesse was just

crossing from the barn to his house when they pulled into his graveled driveway. When he saw the long entourage, he stopped and stared with wide eyes and a crinkled forehead. At the noisy rattle of the harness and wagon, Sam came running from the chicken coop. Becca was startled to see a little black-and-white puppy bounding at the boy's heels. Like his father, Sam gaped in surprise at the buggy and wagon. But when he saw Becca, he grinned and ran straight toward her.

"Guder mariye." *Dawdi* Zeke waved a wrinkled hand in the air. Jakob hopped down off the wagon first, then reached up a supporting arm to help his wife and the elderly man down off the high seat.

"Guder daag," Jesse greeted them, a heavy dose of curiosity filling his eyes.

Becca had stepped out of the buggy and greeted Sam.

"Hallo! Do you have a new puppy?" she asked, eyeing the little furball who gave several shrill barks.

Sam nodded and picked up the mutt, snuggling it close beneath his chin.

"What have you named it?" she asked.

Sam looked down and scuffed his booted feet against the damp gravel. He glanced nervously at Naomi, who still sat in the buggy.

"Patches." Jesse spoke nearby, looking a bit embarrassed. "I suggested he name the dog after the story in his book, and he acknowledged that he liked that."

Becca smiled up at him. *"Ach*, so you got him a dog. I'm glad. I'm sure that pleased Sam."

It was a statement, not a question. And she couldn't have been happier. This gesture more than anything showed her what a kind, loving father Jesse really was inside. He'd been hurt and seemed all gruff and dis-approving but Becca was quickly learning otherwise.

She reached into the buggy to take the baby while Aunt Naomi and Ruby hopped down. As the men spoke together, her ears were tuned to every bit of conver-sation going on around her. A feeling of happiness hummed inside of her. Last night at supper, Aunt Naomi had suggested they have a work project today, to help Jesse and his son. And the entire *familye* had agreed it would be fun, as well as beneficial to the King *familye*. Becca had concurred.

When she turned around, she caught Jesse staring at her. Something in his eyes told her he was both irri-tated and glad to see them here. His gaze swept over her, taking in the domestic scene as she cuddled Chrissie close in her arms. Suddenly, Becca felt out of sorts and a rush of heat stained her face. She hoped he didn't think this was her idea and she was being forward. Though she'd been over to his farm three times this past week to tutor Sam, she didn't want Jesse to believe she was interested in him romantically. Because she wasn't. No, absolutely not.

Deciding to let the men take the lead, she bounced the baby on her hip and waited.

"What brings you here to my place so early on a Sat-urday morning?" Jesse asked Jakob and *Dawdi* Zeke.

Jakob stepped forward to explain, his smile wide, his tone filled with a pleasantness that none of them could deny. "You've been a member of our *Gmay* for over three months now. Though you've never asked any of us for help, we understand you need some repairs done around your place. We know you can do the work over time, but it's winter now and some of the chores should be done immediately. If you'll allow us to assist you, the women will paint the inside of your house while us men repair your leaky roof and broken fence posts. Then you'll be ready to buy the livestock you need. And later, the women have prepared a nice lunch for us all to enjoy. We're here at your disposal, so use us well."

Jesse frowned and Becca held her breath. He hesitated, looking at all of them. They waited. No one said a word. But it was obvious they were hoping he would agree. Finally, it was *Dawdi* Zeke who broke the silence.

"*Ach*, of course he'll use us. We're here to work and that's what we'll do." The elderly man hobbled over to the back of the wagon and lifted out a silver toolbox. Without waiting for an invitation, he shambled toward the house.

"Where's your ladder?" he called over his shoulder in a commanding voice.

That spurred everyone into action. The men and Reuben hurried after him while the women gathered up their paintbrushes. Sam stayed close beside Becca. He clicked his fingers and the puppy scampered after him. She was surprised to see that he'd trained the dog to follow him with just a snap of his fingers.

"Jakob, don't let your *dawdi* up on that roof," Aunt Naomi called to her son.

At the age of ninety-six, *Dawdi* Zeke was too old and frail to be climbing any ladders. Naomi looked so concerned that Jakob tugged on his grandfather's arm.

"*Dawdi*, I don't want you up on that roof. *Mamm* would skin me alive if you fell and got hurt," Jakob said.

Zeke simply laughed. "*Ach*, of course I'm not going up, though I've been on more roofs than you can shake a stick at. But those days are long gone now. I'll stay safely on the ground and hand you up the wood and shingles you'll need."

"*Gut.* That will really help us out. Then we won't have to climb down as often and you can supervise things on the ground," Jesse said.

He sounded so positive that Becca wondered if he'd just needed friendship to open him up to the man he really was inside…to smile and be happy again. Either way, it was quite nice of Jesse to look out for her grandfather. It told her that he was considerate and respectful of the old man.

Dawdi Zeke clapped a hand on Jesse's shoulder and nodded with approval. His gray eyes danced with a zest for life and that's when Jesse smiled wide. It was infectious. Everyone felt happy today. Becca knew work frolics were like that. They were always a lot of fun. An opportunity to serve others and accomplish some worthwhile tasks for someone else. Knowing they could visit while they worked and that a nice meal awaited them was all the reward they needed.

"*Komm* on, let's get to work," Naomi called to the women and girls.

Carrying the baby and a bucket of paint, Becca followed them inside the house. Sam scurried after her, the puppy clambering at his heels. The boy didn't speak but he held up a forbidding hand and made Patches stay outside. Becca could see why. The dog's paws were muddy and would dirty the floors. She was delighted to see that Sam had a new friend and was actively training the little pup.

Becca almost told Sam to join the men. After all, he should learn from the hands of his father what he should do. But then she thought better of it. Maybe the boy needed a little more time to grow more confident. Later, once he was speaking regularly again, then he could join Jesse and the other men.

Since she'd been here before, Becca showed Naomi and Abby what needed to be done. Ruby was given the chore of tending the baby and fetching things for them now and then. With her arms free, Becca was able to set to work, helping to clean the house thoroughly from stem to stern. Sam helped all he could, scrubbing, fetching and carrying.

The women painted the living room first, the kitchen second and then the bathroom. As they finished removing the plastic drop cloths from the wooden floors, Becca and Abby carried in the large rag rugs with Sam's help. The heavy braids weaved together were big but looked absolutely lovely in the middle of the living room floor. Becca admired the colorful pattern for just a moment, thinking how pleased Jesse would be to have something warm beneath his bare feet. Then, she turned away. *Hochmut* was the pride of the world and something the Amish shunned. She must not allow herself to dwell on such things.

Their afternoon work would see them finish painting the three bedrooms upstairs, while Naomi measured and hand-stitched some modest curtains for the bare windows.

Now, it was time for lunch. Becca's stomach growled loudly as she wondered how the morning had passed so quickly. She stepped into the kitchen to lay out their noon meal, still able to hear the other women's jolly voices coming from the living room.

"Many hands make light work," Aunt Naomi answered her unasked question. "Look at what we've accomplished already. Jesse and Sam will be much more comfortable in their house after this. Those poor dears. I can't imagine how awful it's been, living here without Sam's *mudder* to love and care for them. A home needs a woman's touch, and that's all. Too bad our Becca isn't interested in marrying the man."

From the open doorway, Becca saw Abby surveying the empty living room as she sat in a rocking chair with Chrissie. "*Ach*, it's still a very empty house but at least it's clean now. And Becca could have any man she wanted. She'd make a real catch for some *gut* Amish man."

"*Ja*, she would. The house is definitely much more cheerful now. Those filthy walls made me want to shudder. And it was time for Jesse to make friends. We're his neighbors and his brothers and sisters in the faith. It's time for him to be a part of our *Gmay*," Naomi said.

As she lifted the heavy basket that contained their lunch onto the table, Becca silently agreed. Friendship would go a long way to healing Jesse and Sam's broken hearts. As the boy's teacher, this was all Becca could offer and she hoped it helped.

She laid a fresh loaf of bread on the pristine counter, wondering if the men had made as much progress with their chores. She glanced up at the windowsill, analyzing her paint job with a critical eye.

Oh, no! She'd missed a spot. Not very much but it was noticeable if you looked up. She'd just fix it before she finalized lunch preparations. It wouldn't take more than a moment to run the paintbrush over the narrow area and no one would even know it was there.

Pulling the ladder over to the sink, she climbed up. Dipping her brush into a bucket, she concentrated on her task as the ladder wobbled slightly. She quickly ran the bristles over the trim surrounding the windowsill, then set the brush across the lip of the bucket. There! It was almost perfect.

She was just climbing down when she lost her footing. A moment of panic rushed up her throat and she clawed the air for something, anything to hold onto. It did no good and she felt herself falling!

"Ooff!" Jesse's breath left him in a sudden exhale as he caught Becca before she could fall off the ladder.

She clasped his neck with one arm, the side of her face smooshed beneath his chin. He held her there for several long seconds, giving her a moment to recover her footing. Her sweet, clean fragrance spiraled around him as she stepped on his toes. Thankfully he was wearing heavy boots.

"*Ach*, I'm so sorry!" she exclaimed, pulling back just a bit.

He still had his arms wrapped around her tiny waist. Looking down, he locked his gaze with hers. Her face was so close to his that he could feel her warm breath against his cheek. He saw the confusion in her startled blue eyes. Her pink lips rounded in a circle of surprise. He could feel her soft fingertips against the back of his neck.

"*Geht es dir gut?*" he asked, his voice low and soft.

"*Ja, ja*! I'm all right," she said rather breathlessly.

"Ahem!"

Someone cleared their throat and he looked up and saw Naomi and Abby standing in the doorway.

Becca quickly pulled free and moved over to the stove. She patted her *kapp*, thrusting stray curls of golden hair back into the head covering. She looked as flustered as he felt.

"*Danke* for catching me." She spoke without looking at him.

"Did you fall?" Naomi asked.

"*Ja*, I fell off the ladder," Becca quickly explained, seeming embarrassed that the women might think she'd done something inappropriate.

"*Ach*, it's a *gut* thing that Jesse was here to catch you." Abby spoke with a knowing smile.

Naomi walked to the sink where she began washing red apples. "*Ja*, it was a very *gut* thing."

If Jesse didn't know better, he would think the older woman's voice sounded a bit strangled, as if she were trying not to laugh.

Having recovered her composure, Becca busied herself with setting the long table. He was suddenly highly aware of her as a lovely, desirable woman. And that thought left him feeling nervous and out of sorts.

"Um, I'll tell the men we're just about ready to eat," he said, practically bounding out the back door.

Anything to escape. He had to get out of this room right now. Had to get away from Becca and her innocent, confused looks and her aunt's knowing glances.

"*Komm* eat," he called to the other men.

He waited for them to climb down off the roof before following them into the house. No way was he going to be alone with these women again. He needed the other men as a buffer zone.

After prayer, the men sat at the table while the women hovered around seeing that their plates were filled. Abby spread a blanket on the floor in the living room for the children to sit and enjoy a little picnic of sorts. Jesse regretted that he had only four chairs made. With just himself and Sam living in the house, he thought there was no need to make any more. But now, he realized he needed double the number of seats if he was to accommodate his new friends. And the thought of making more chairs made him feel happy inside. It gave him a purpose. Something to work toward.

"How is the work going on the roof?" Naomi asked as she laid another piece of fried chicken on Jakob's plate.

"*Gut*! We've finished the roof and it should weather any future storms," he replied.

"*Ja*, we should have plenty of time this afternoon to work on the barn and broken fence posts before it's time to leave." *Dawdi* Zeke popped an entire boiled egg into his mouth and chewed with relish.

"And you *weibsleit*? How has your work gone?" Jakob asked. He glanced around the room, seeing the fresh coat of paint on the walls.

"We have finished downstairs. This afternoon, we'll finish painting the bedrooms," Naomi said.

The group chatted about their work and inconsequential things. Jakob offered to sell one of his best milk cows to Jesse and discussed the Rocky Mountain Expo Select Sale to be held at the National Western Complex in Denver next month.

"Bishop Yoder and Harley Troyer are the auctioneers. You can get all the draft horses and mules you need," *Dawdi* Zeke said.

"*Ja*, and in April, they'll hold a draft horse and equipment auction in Brighton. Us men commission a small bus from town and hire an *Englischer* to drive us there. They've gotten to know us Amish and will haul the livestock here to Riverton in a trailer. You're *willkomm* to go with us and see if there's something worth buying for your farm," Jakob said.

Jesse nodded. This was just the info he needed to acquire some good livestock to work his place. He glanced at Sam, wondering what to do with the boy while he was gone.

"I'll watch him for you," Becca said.

He glanced up at her as she leaned over his shoulder to refill his glass with chilled milk from the well house. Funny how she always seemed to anticipate his needs and offer to help even before he asked. Though Jesse hadn't asked, he was grateful for all that Becca and her *familye* had done. For the first time in months, he felt like he had real friends. People he could count on for help.

"*Danke*, that would be great," he said, conscious of Naomi watching him with glowing eyes.

Oh, no! He knew that look. The look of an Amish mother who wanted to make a match for her daughter. Except that Becca was Naomi's niece.

Same difference.

He looked away, feeling like a silly schoolboy who was smitten by his first girl. And he wasn't. Smitten, that is. Not with Becca. No, sirree. Nor was he a silly schoolboy. He was a fully-grown married man and the father of three. Or at least he used to be. Now, he wasn't grounded anymore. He couldn't get a feel for who he was and what he should be doing. It was as if the pieces no longer fit together. Somehow, he'd lost his way. He'd been clinging to his faith, hoping he found his path through the darkness.

They finished their meal and everyone returned to

their tasks. Jesse was grateful to be back at his labors. Work was something he understood. A distraction that made him forget the pain. For a few short hours, he could pretend that everything was just fine. That Alice and the kids were back at the house and he'd see them all later that evening when he came in for supper. That he'd laugh, tickle and play with them like he used to do.

It was several hours later when Jesse returned to the house for some plastic cups and a jug of water. The men were thirsty and, as their host, he had hurried to accommodate them. He planned to slip in and out of the kitchen without being noticed. But Becca was there, sitting in a hardbacked chair as she fed baby Chrissie.

"Hallo." She greeted him with a soft smile.

He nodded, going directly to the cupboard where he knew the cups were kept. As he pulled the door open, he couldn't help noticing the tidiness of the room, not a dirty dish in sight. The air smelled of fresh paint and he caught a yummy whiff of something good cooking in the oven. When he glanced in that direction, Becca offered an explanation.

"It's your supper. We thought you might appreciate something to eat this evening after all of us have left," she said.

"You didn't need to do that. I've got lots of canned goods in the house and have gotten quite good at heating up soup for Sam's dinner."

"It was no trouble." She lifted a spoon to the baby's mouth. Like a little bird, Chrissie opened wide.

It seemed his guests had thought of everything, taking care of him and Sam like they would their own *familye*. He shouldn't be surprised. It was the Amish way. Alice had done the same on numerous occasions, taking meals in to another *familye*, tending their sick children, washing their dirty laundry, doing whatever she could to ease their load. And it made him love her and his faith even more. He cherished the way they looked after one another. If only Alice and the girls were still here, he could feel whole again. That was why he'd left Pennsylvania. To hide from the memories. But they'd followed him here. And he knew he had to figure out how to go on without them.

As he filled the jug with water from the kitchen tap, he glanced over at Becca. She'd propped little Chrissie on the table and had wrapped a dish towel around her neck so she wouldn't soil her dress as she ate. Keeping one hand on the child's leg so she wouldn't fall off the table, Becca spooned in something that looked like mashed potatoes.

"You seem so natural with *kinder*," he said.

Becca gave a sad little laugh. "I hope so, since I teach an entire school full of them. But you wouldn't have thought so during my first week here."

He chuckled, remembering how flustered she was that day he'd walked in on her class when it erupted into absolute chaos. "Everyone is bound to have a bad day now and then. Have you had any more snake incidents?"

She laughed. "*Ne*, thankfully."

He shut off the faucet and reached for the lid to the jug. As he screwed it on with several quick twists of his wrist, he asked a question that had been on his mind for quite some time.

"Instead of teaching, I would have thought you would be married by now and have *kinder* of your own."

She didn't respond right off and he looked at her. Her

eyebrows were creased with consternation and a flash of pain filled her eyes.

"*Ach*, I always wanted to marry and have *kinder* of my own but it didn't work out. I… I was engaged once," she said.

Oh. Maybe he shouldn't have asked. He instantly regretted his question. It was too private. Too personal.

"I'm sorry. I didn't mean to pry," he said, feeling like a heel.

She shook her head and fed the baby another bite of food. "*Ne*, it's all right. I'm better off, actually. I would never want to marry a man who didn't love me. And it would be even worse if he loved someone else."

Okay, his curiosity was piqued. Even though it wasn't his business, he couldn't leave without knowing more.

"What happened?" he asked.

He set the cups and water jug aside as he leaned his hip against the counter.

She shrugged and wiped a dribble of potato from the baby's chin. "Nothing, really. I'd known Vernon all my life. We went to school together and always planned to marry one day. Everyone expected it."

Jesse sensed the admission caused her some embarrassment, as if it was something to be ashamed of.

"Did you still love him?" Jesse asked.

"Perhaps. But it didn't matter. He'd discovered that he was in love with Ruth, another girl in our *Gmay*. It seemed they'd developed feelings for each other that went beyond friendship. I'd always wondered why he refused to set our wedding date. Now I know it was because he…he didn't want me anymore."

"I'm sorry," he said.

His heart ached for her. He could just imagine how

it must have hurt her, living in a *Gmay* with a boy that everyone thought loved her. And then the embarrassment and pain of finding out he preferred someone else. All her broken dreams must have been painful but also demoralizing. No wonder she had wanted to leave and go somewhere else to start over again. He'd done the same thing after Alice and their girls had died.

She met his gaze, her eyes filled with strength and courage. "Don't be sorry. It was a blessing. Vernon and I would have been unhappy together. We'd been *gut* friends all our lives but we'd grown apart. He thought I read too many books and was way too opinionated and I thought he was too domineering. We wouldn't have gotten on well together. And I love teaching. I decided to make that my profession. I love working with the *kinder*. It's a *gut* career choice for an unmarried Amish girl like me. I just wish I didn't have to return to Ohio at the end of the school year. Vernon and Ruth will be married next fall and I'd really rather not be there to watch it happen."

Ah, he understood now. He could read between the lines. She didn't want to watch the man she had loved for so long marry another girl and start a *familye* together. And being Amish, that must hurt Becca even more because she was still single. In fact, Becca was quite old to be unmarried. By Amish standards, she was an old maid. But now, it appeared that she had decided she wanted to spend her life teaching. It was a noble profession too and he was glad she'd found something fulfilling and worthwhile to do.

He tilted his head to the side. "Why do you have to leave here? Why not stay?"

She shrugged before lifting Chrissie down off the

table. The toddler waved her chubby arms and laughed. She was so sweet and innocent and she immediately reminded Jesse of his own two little girls.

"My teaching assignment will be finished when school lets out the first of May," Becca said. "By next fall, Caroline Schwartz will have recovered from her accident and can resume her teaching assignment. I can't live off my relatives without finding some kind of employment. And Riverton is too small a town to offer many jobs, let alone another teaching position in another Amish school. I'll have to leave to find work. The logical choice is to go home, so I have a place to live until I can find another position."

Hmm. For some odd reason, he didn't like the thought of her leaving. She'd been so good for Sam. She'd been good for him too.

"You could find a different teaching assignment here in Colorado," he suggested.

She gave a sad little laugh. "I'm afraid there aren't that many Amish settlements here, let alone vacant teaching positions for their schools. The only reason I got this assignment was because I have *familye* here and they knew me well enough to give the school board a recommendation for me."

"Perhaps you'll find another position somewhere in Ohio or Pennsylvania. Maybe you won't have to go home after all," he said.

Even as he suggested the idea, he knew it was unlikely. Unless they were in a real bind, the Amish preferred to hire someone they knew and trusted to teach their precious children. Each *Gmay* had their own *Ordnung*, the unwritten rules they followed within their unique community. Unless Becca married one of their men and agreed to abide by their *Ordnung*, she would be an outsider in another Amish community. They would never hire her to teach their kids.

"*Ach*, I better get back to work. We're almost finished painting Sam's bedroom and the *weibsleit* need my help." She stood and walked to the door.

"*Ja*, I best get back to work too."

He wished he could stay and ask her more questions about her life. He found her quite interesting and he respected her pioneering spirit and desire to have a career rather than marry. It couldn't have been easy for her to come here to a strange land to live and work. But it wouldn't be proper for him to keep talking to her right now. She was hurting, just like him. And he didn't want to remind her of that pain. Besides, the *mannsleit* were waiting for him to bring them water.

As he carried the cups and jug outside, he found it hard to believe that Vernon would cast Becca aside for someone else. Becca would make the perfect Amish wife. Besides being capable of cleaning and running a household, she was an excellent cook and was beautiful and knowledgeable. Fascinating to talk to. When he was with her, he could almost forget his broken heart.

Almost.

If the situation were different, he might be willing to ask Jakob if he could court her. But Jesse couldn't forget about Alice. His heart still ached for his sweet wife. In his mind, he was still married to her and he couldn't let her go.

He'd heard of some Amish widowers with children marrying a woman for convenience. He thought about approaching Becca and Jakob, to see if they might agree to such an arrangement. After all, he badly needed a wife and Sam needed a mother. Becca needed a permanent place to stay so she wouldn't have to return to Ohio. But no. A loveless marriage wouldn't be fair to Becca. Or him, for that matter. Both of them deserved so much more. Besides, she'd just said she wouldn't marry a man who didn't love her. And right now, he couldn't offer her what both of them really wanted and needed most of all. A home where they'd be loved and cherished. A real marriage in deed as well as in name. Even without asking Becca, he knew that neither of them would settle for anything less. Not now. Not ever. It was that simple.

Chapter Eight

On Thursday evening, another snowstorm settled across the valley and didn't move all night long. Becca awoke the following morning to find six inches of the white stuff covering the countryside. She got up early to prepare for her day, wondering if she should cancel school. After all, it would take a lot of effort for parents to drive their horses and buggies through the heavy drifts. Maybe it was best for the kids to stay home. But the bishop had told her they rarely canceled school because they had to meet the state attendance requirements each year. And the plows were good to get out early and clear the county roads.

"You sure you'll be all right driving to school alone?" Jakob asked her at the breakfast table.

She nodded, knowing he would make time to drive her if she felt uncertain about the task. "I'll be fine."

Her cousin smiled with approval. As children, he had teased her for being a tomboy. Athletic and full of life, she was always the girl who could do anything. But since those carefree days, she wasn't so sure anymore.

Vernon's rejection had hit her confidence rather hard. He'd broken her heart and destroyed her trust in men.

Bundled up in her scarf, gloves and black traveling bonnet, she left early and drove extra carefully. No doubt she'd have to shovel the sidewalks at the school. She wanted time to build up a fire in the old stove so the schoolhouse was warm and toasty for the scholars when they arrived.

As she turned off onto the snowy dirt road leading to Bishop Yoder's hay fields, she saw the school. A thin stream of gray smoke rose from the chimney and she gave a cry of pleasure. Someone was already here. Probably one of the school board members, taking care of the school and seeing that they had their needs met.

As she pulled into the main yard, she saw a lone man standing beside the front porch, shoveling snow off the walk paths. Even from this distance, she recognized the solid set of his broad shoulders and the tenacious tilt of his black felt hat.

Jesse King.

And little Sam was just carrying another armful of kindling into the schoolhouse.

Tugging on the lead lines, Becca stuck her tongue in her cheek and couldn't contain a quiet laugh. It was the snowiest day of the year and Jesse had finally gotten Sam to school on time.

"Hallo!" she called, stepping out of the buggy with a flurry of lavender skirts.

Jesse paused in his work and leaned an arm against the handle of his snow shovel. He tugged the brim of his hat away from his face in a completely male stance and gazed at her with no emotion on his face whatsoever. But his dark eyes were filled with life. His breath exhaled in small puffs, his cheeks gleaming red above his beard.

"Guder mariye," he said in a low voice.

She made her way through the snow, stamping her feet when she reached the cement walk path he had unburied. "What are you doing here so early?"

He glanced at the cleared walk paths, which were quickly melting now that he'd removed the snow. "I would think that is obvious. I'm shoveling snow."

She laughed. "I know that, silly. But I didn't expect to see you here so early. *Danke* for clearing away the snow and starting the fire."

Jesse shrugged, a slight frown tugging at his forehead. "It's the least I can do to repay you for all the meals and tutoring you've been giving us. Besides, it's the duty of the fathers of the scholars to look after the school, unless they make an exception and assign these chores to someone. Bishop Yoder and the other men have more *kinder* than me, so I thought it'd be easier for me to do the task today."

How thoughtful of him. Yes, it was true that the board members were to look after the school's needs. But Becca knew each father had a farm and *familye* to care for too. Sometimes, it was easy to neglect the school just a bit. And even though she knew it was expected, she couldn't help feeling happy that Jesse had come to her aid. He'd saved her from the arduous chore of shoveling snow and fetching wood. Not that she minded the work. It was just nice to have it done already. Jesse's efforts told her that he wasn't as callous and harsh as he pretended to be. No, he was a kind and generous man and she appreciated his work on her behalf.

She scooped up a handful of snow and smashed it into a round ball between her gloved hands. "The snow is heavy. There's lots of water in it."

He grinned at that and she stared, simply because it wasn't often that she saw this man looking happy.

"*Ja*, it'll fill our rivers and streams," he said.

Feeling a bit reckless, she tossed the snowball at him, hitting him squarely in the middle of the chest. She laughed, thinking he might throw a snowball back at her but he didn't. He merely looked down at the splotch of snow marring his heavy black coat and then back at her. Without a word, he brushed the snow away.

Feeling suddenly awkward, she glanced up at the gray sky and shivered at the cold. "I may let school out early today. *Dawdi* Zeke thinks another storm is on its way. I need to give the scholars their assignments for the end-of-year program but I don't want them stranded here all night."

She mentally calculated that they had plenty of water to drink and fuel to burn but she had very little food, except for what the scholars brought in their lunch pails. If she had to feed the children before their parents could break through the snow to retrieve them the following morning, they'd be mighty hungry.

He inclined his head. "That's wise. I'll plan to pick up Sam at noon. That should give each *familye* plenty of time to return home before the next storm hits."

"But what about Sam's tutoring this afternoon?" she asked.

"*Ne*, you shouldn't *komm* over today. You go home where it's safe. It won't hurt him to miss one session."

"All right. Let's hope the next storm bypasses us altogether. I've never seen so much snow in all my life. And

I'm sorry to say this but I'm rather tired of it now." She laughed, amazed at the colder weather here in Colorado.

He chuckled too and she couldn't help jerking in surprise at the sudden sound. He'd actually laughed! Maybe he hadn't been as disgusted by her throwing a snowball at him as she first thought.

"*Ja*, we definitely have lots of snow here. I had to lock Sam's dog, Patches, in the barn last night so he wouldn't wander off and get lost in the storm. Sam wanted to bring the pup inside to sleep with him but I said *ne*," he said, a wide smile curving his lips.

She stared at him in amazement, thinking how handsome he looked in that moment. "*Ach*, I knew you could do that."

He blinked, looking confused. "Do what?"

"Smile. It looks *gut* on you. You should do it more often."

He looked away, his expression dropping like stone. Oh, dear. Maybe she shouldn't have teased him. But she was starting to feel comfortable around this man. Maybe too comfortable. She was a grown woman and he was the father of one of her scholars. She shouldn't be flirting with him like a brainless schoolgirl.

"*Ja*, the snow here has been an adjustment. But we'll be glad to have the moisture this summer when we're watering our crops," he said, ignoring her comments altogether.

He glanced at her, looking suddenly anxious, as if he wanted to get away from her. And that's when she realized he could decide to be happy or sad. Yes, he'd faced something horrible in his life. But he could choose to be miserable and walk around with a glum face, or he could put it aside and smile. So could she. And it reminded her that, in spite of the hurt she'd suffered at the hands of Vernon, the Lord wanted her to go on and live her life. He wanted her to be happy. She was trying to do that, though it wasn't always easy. But she had the responsibility of teaching a school full of children. She must set a good example for them.

Filled with her thoughts, she turned and walked inside. Jesse leaned the shovel against the outer wall and followed her. She noticed he stomped off his boots and removed his hat at the door, then stepped inside. Sam was stacking the wood pan high with plenty of firewood to last throughout the day. The boy tossed a shy smile in her direction, then ducked his head. His father watched with approval as the boy did his work. Then, seeming assured that the school was in good condition for lessons, Jesse waved a hand.

"I'll be going now," he said.

"*Ja, danke* again. I really appreciate it," she called.

"You're *willkomm*," he said.

"See you later."

She walked with him to the door and peered outside at the chilly day. Gusts of wind were sweeping the snow into drifts along the road. As if on cue, two black buggies and horses appeared at the top of the county road. They turned off, heading toward the school. She'd kept her warm woolen shawl on so she could greet each parent, to let them know school would let out early today.

As she went out to meet them, she watched Jesse climb into his buggy and slap the leather leads gently against the horse's back. The animal lurched forward and the man waved a hand to the other families as he passed.

Thankfully, she wasn't tutoring Sam this evening.

She didn't mind, not at all. But she was getting to bed rather late each night. She was tired and falling behind on her lesson plans. But Sam was speaking regularly for her now. Just simple words spoken in a mega-soft whisper within the walls of his own home, but he did talk. And she knew deep in her heart that he was making headway.

If she wasn't mistaken, so was Jesse. She sensed he wasn't an overly gregarious man by nature but he was much friendlier now, with her and her *familye* members, as well as with other people in their *Gmay*. She'd noticed him at church meetings, talking more openly with the other men, though he rarely laughed and was still shy around the women. The transition was gradual but an amazing sight to behold and she was happy for it. Now, if she could just get Sam to start speaking at school, she would consider this year a great success.

Jesse clicked his tongue, urging his horse up a particularly slippery slope as his buggy reached the county road. He thought about Becca throwing a snowball at him. No one had ever called him silly and it had been a long time since he'd felt like smiling. But lately, the urge to laugh was coming a bit easier to him. When he was with Becca, he could almost forget the sadness in his heart. Almost.

Shaking his head, he mentally reminded himself that he had to pick up Sam early today. He mustn't be late or it could put Becca in jeopardy. He knew she couldn't leave the school until all the children were gone and he didn't want to make her late getting home that afternoon. Even the slightest delay could force her to be caught in the coming snowstorm.

Looking down at the front of his coat, he saw beads of water from where her snowball had struck him. He brushed them away, feeling confused by her actions. The last girl who had flirted with him had been his wife. And yet, he didn't think that was what Becca was doing. She was just having fun. She was so full of life. He'd noticed the bounce in her step and happy lilt in her voice whenever she came over to his house. She'd confided that she'd been engaged to be married and he would have been a fool not to notice the pain in her voice. She'd been deeply hurt. All her hopes and dreams for a *familye* of her own had been dashed to pieces. It was easy to think that she'd find someone else to marry one day. That she'd go on and be just fine. But once you were really and truly in love with someone, it wasn't always that easy to move on. He knew that firsthand. Besides, she'd said she had chosen a teaching career instead of a *familye*.

When he'd been inside the school, he'd noticed how tidy everything was. Becca had made the same difference in his own home, washing the dishes when she came to tutor Sam. It had spurred him to be a better housekeeper, so he didn't appear to be taking advantage of her generosity.

Most days, she brought them something for supper too. She always claimed her aunt Naomi had made the food but he suspected she had helped. And her generosity had touched his heart. He'd heard his son's whispered words as she worked with the boy in the living room. He'd noticed how Sam's countenance lit up when he knew Becca was coming over. And honestly, Jesse had to admit he liked her frequent visits. She was working hard and making a real difference in his son's life.

As he reached the turnoff to his farm, he glanced over and saw the log house that belonged to Becca's cousin, Jakob Fisher. So different from the sprawling, white frame houses he had lived in back in Pennsylvania.

Turning toward home, he thought maybe he should speak to Bishop Yoder about Becca. He should tell him and the other board members what a good job she was doing as their schoolteacher. Then, the board would give her a good reference when it came time for her to leave and find another teaching assignment at the end of the school year. He wanted Becca to find a permanent job that would make her happy. One that would provide her with a firm and stable income all her life.

As he pulled into his main yard and directed the horse toward the barn, he felt suddenly quite sad. While he knew that Becca had to leave in the spring, he didn't want her to go. And yet, there was nothing he could do to help her stay. Nothing at all.

Chapter Nine

Jesse stepped out of the barn and glanced over at the house. After two weeks of cold, the weather had shifted. The warmth of the sun had finally melted all the snow, though the ground was quite damp. Patches romped around close by his feet, which was odd. The dog usually followed Sam everywhere. Speaking of which, where was Sam? It was Saturday morning and the boy should be outside doing his morning tasks.

Jesse had just finished his chores and was ready to head out to the fields. When he saw the two buckets of pig slop still sitting where he'd left them on the back porch almost an hour earlier, he shook his head. Why hadn't Sam fed the pigs yet?

Heaving a sigh of exasperation, he walked over to the porch and retrieved the buckets before carrying them to the pigpen. The three swine saw him coming and rushed toward him. Patches gave several shrill barks as Jesse dumped the contents of the buckets into the trough. The pigs snorted and grunted, scarfing down the food like they were starving. They were definitely overdue for their breakfast.

While the pigs were occupied, Jesse stepped inside their pen and checked their water cistern. Patches whined and scratched at the gate, trying to follow him. But no way would Jesse let the little dog in with the ornery pigs.

The temperatures were still mighty cold. Although the sky was filled with leaden clouds, he didn't think it would snow again. But it sure might rain.

Hurrying so he could get some work done in the fields before the weather turned, he used a metal bar to break the thin layer of ice that had formed over top of the water trough so the animals could drink. As he set the bar aside, he glanced toward the chicken coop, wondering if Sam had fed the hens and finished gathering the eggs yet. Stepping outside of the pigpen, he pulled the gate closed until he heard it latch, then walked toward the house with Patches at his heels. It was Saturday and they weren't in a rush to get Sam to school but Jesse needed to get out to that field if he hoped to make any progress in clearing the overgrown brush before it rained. The previous owner of this farm had gotten old and had neglected the fields, which were now overgrown by weeds, shrubs and saplings. Spring was just around the corner and Jesse wanted to make the best use of his land.

"Sam! *Waar ben jij?*" he called to his son.

He gazed at the chicken coop, expecting the boy to come from there. When he heard the screen door clap closed behind him, he whirled around and found his son standing just in front of the back door to the house. Patches scampered toward the boy, jumping at his legs. Though Sam was fully dressed for the day, his feet were bare. The boy didn't speak as Jesse walked toward him.

"What are you doing inside the house? Are you ill?" Jesse asked, feeling confused.

The boy shook his head and that's when Jesse noticed he held a book in one hand. A bad feeling settled in Jesse's stomach. Without asking, he knew what had happened. Instead of doing his farm chores, Sam had been inside the house reading.

"Did you feed the chickens and gather the eggs yet? Did you feed the cows?" Jesse asked, hoping his son said *yes*. If so, all would be forgiven.

Sam's eyes widened and he hung his head in shame. Finally, the boy shook his head.

Jesse reached to take the book out of Sam's hand. It was a library book that Becca had given him. "You've been reading when there are chores to be done?"

Grave disappointment filled Jesse's chest. Sam hadn't done his morning chores. Not a single one. Instead, he'd been languishing inside the house. He hadn't even put on his shoes yet! As a parent, Jesse was outraged by his child's disobedience. Though he longed for a quiet heart and wanted to retain his composure, he knew he must be strict and clear in his expectations.

"Why have you not done your work yet?" Jesse asked, forcing himself to speak calmly.

Sam didn't answer but he shivered as a brisk wind blew from the east. The child stared at his bare toes, which were scrunched against the cold, wooden porch. Jesse knew his son loved to read more than anything else. But too much of anything was not good. And Sam had plenty of time to read. In addition to school and trips to the town library every two weeks, Jesse had been reading to the boy each night, regular as clockwork. Also, for the past two months, Becca had been coming here several afternoons each week to read and tutor the boy. The strategies seemed to work. Sam's demeanor was happier and there was a bounce in the boy's step that hadn't been there for a very long time. But now, the books were getting in the way of Sam's chores. And work must always come first on a farm. It was critical to their survival. As Sam's father, Jesse had an obligation to teach his son how to work hard. To teach the boy how to farm and raise livestock. Jesse couldn't just let this go.

"I'm very disappointed in you, *sohn*. You know what is expected of you. Did you start reading and lose track of time?" Jesse asked his son.

Sam nodded.

A wave of annoyance rose upward within Jesse's chest and he couldn't prevent a note of irritation from filling his voice. He didn't have time for such nonsense. Not if he was going to get the fields cleared for spring planting.

"If you don't do your chores, who will?" Jesse asked, his voice stern but not overly unkind. "Do you want our hens to stop laying eggs? And what about the cows? They need to eat too. Do you want them to stop giving milk? Then what will we eat? What will we have to sell so we can live?"

Jesse didn't really expect a response and he got none. But he hoped his questions would make Sam think. After all, the boy was still young and learning his place in the world. This was a teaching opportunity. A time to reiterate Jesse's expectations and let Sam understand that he needed the boy's help.

"Unless you are at school, you will do your farm chores first and read only in the evenings after all the work is finished for the day. Except on Sunday, we have no time for reading during daytime. Do you understand?"

Sam didn't look up but he nodded. The boy's back was ramrod straight, his shoulders tensed. Jesse sensed the child was upset by the situation but he offered no argument.

"*Gut*. Now, go and get your shoes and coat on. Then, finish your work. After that, come and join me in the south pasture so we can clear the field."

Expecting his son to obey, Jesse turned and headed toward the barn without a backward glance. Because he hadn't purchased any draft horses yet, he harnessed Blaze, his road horse, to the wagon and headed out to the field with his hand tools.

Using a sharp spade to dig around the roots of small trees and shrubs, he worked alone for almost two hours. Even though the day was quite cold, he wiped the sweat from his brow. He dug, hacked and pulled up a number of slender saplings and tossed them into the back of the wagon. He could turn them into wood chips for use around the farm. Marvin Schwartz had a gas-powered wood chipper he could use for a minimal fee.

Resting for a moment, Jesse leaned against the wooden handle of his tool and reached for the jug of water he'd placed in the back of the wagon. He looked toward the house, wondering where Sam was. Surely the boy was finished with his chores by now. He wouldn't dare go back inside the house to read some more. Would he?

Stowing the water jug behind the wagon seat, Jesse continued his work. He wasn't pleased to see thistles growing in the field and knew they'd be stubborn to get rid of. As an experienced farmer, he knew it would take two or three years to clear them out completely and even then, he'd still have to watch out for new seedlings. But over time, he'd weed them out entirely. A variety of other obnoxious grasses and thug plants would sprout up as well. But effective farming was a patient man's chore. And Jesse was an effective farmer. Within a few years, his farm would be tidy and in optimal working condition. He'd work hard and build a fine place for Sam to inherit one day.

Speaking of which, where was the boy? He looked toward the house again, wondering if he should tromp back to the barn to search for him. He'd never known his son to be so recalcitrant. What had gotten into him?

Setting his tools aside, Jesse stepped over the uneven ground and headed toward the house. It was long past lunchtime and he needed to take a break. Before they returned to the field, he'd fix him and Sam some sandwiches. While they ate, he'd explain the merits of hard work to his son and encourage the boy to do better. If he found Sam reading again, he'd have to punish him. It was his duty as an Amish father to correct poor behaviors. He'd reprimanded Sam once but the next time would require harsher action. And Jesse didn't look forward to that. No, not at all.

"Sam! Are you here?" he called when he stepped inside the kitchen door.

No answer. He shouted again but still no response.

Turning, he walked out to the chicken coop and then to the barn. A large plop of moisture fell from the sky and struck him on the cheek. Yes, it was definitely going to rain.

He yelled again and again, to get the boy's attention. But he couldn't find him. Patches was missing too. Now that was odd. Where had Sam and the puppy gone off to?

Again, Jesse searched every room of the house. He peered into every stall in the barn, the shed and chicken coop. Where was his son?

And then, a thought occurred to him. Sam hadn't spoken but Jesse knew he'd been upset by the scolding he'd given him that morning. Was it possible Sam had run away? And if so, where would the boy go?

Several heavy raindrops struck Jesse on the face and hand. Soon, the sky would open up its waterworks. And Sam would be caught out in this storm.

Jesse ran to the field, a surge of panic rushing through his veins. He unharnessed Blaze from the wagon and led the horse back to the barn where he hitched him up to the buggy. By the time Jesse steered the horse out of the farmyard, a light mist was falling steadily from the sky.

As he reached the county road, Jesse noticed the rain increased in intensity. Great, heavy drops of water smattered against the windshield of his buggy and he was grateful to be inside, away from the damp and the wind. But his son was out in this storm somewhere. Possibly frightened and cold.

Jesse wiped his brow, filled with trepidation. His six-year-old son was all alone. Hopefully, the boy had worn his hat and coat but it didn't matter. Not if the child got wet. If Sam was out in this frigid air for very long, he could easily become sick. And that thought terrorized Jesse. Because he'd already lost the rest of his *familye*. He couldn't lose Sam too.

Maybe the boy had walked over to the Fishers' farm.

Maybe he'd sought refuge with Becca. It wasn't far. That's where Jesse would check first. He hoped and prayed his son was inside her house, safe and warm. Because Jesse refused to contemplate anything less. He had to find his son. He had to find him right now!

Becca clicked her tongue and urged her cousin's horse onto the county road. Driving the buggy, she'd left the town library and was eager to get home. It was late afternoon and several heavy raindrops thumped against the windshield. It was just a matter of minutes before it started pouring cats and dogs. Though she hadn't wanted to go into town this Saturday, her trip had been fruitful. Sitting beside her on the cushioned seat was a terrific book on skits that would help augment the year-end school program. She'd also checked out several new books for Sam. Wouldn't he be surprised when she gave them to him on Monday morning at school? He'd read all the other books she'd given him at least twice already.

More raindrops spattered the window and she blinked, thinking her eyes deceived her. Was that Sam walking along the side of the road? He was all alone, his shoulders hunched against the drizzling rain, his head bowed low beneath his black felt hat. Definitely an Amish boy. She couldn't see his face clearly but knew Sam's body build and the way he walked.

Tugging on the lead lines, she pulled the horse over onto the shoulder of the road. The boy sidestepped the buggy and looked up in surprise. She saw that he was carrying Patches, his little black dog, in his arms. He was trying to shield the pup from the driving rain.

What on earth was he doing out here all alone on this busy road in the freezing rain?

She opened the door and called to him. "*Hallo*, Sam. Where are you going?"

He shrugged and blinked in the rain as he scuffed his booted foot against a rock. Patches squirmed in his arms and the boy tightened his hold. His cheeks were rosy from the cold air and he hunched his back against the lashing wind.

"Do you need a ride?" she asked.

He hesitated, then shook his head. But that didn't deter her. This boy was always quiet but she'd learned to read his mannerisms. He was cold and upset. From his red eyes, she could tell he'd been crying. And then, she noticed a little bag slung across his shoulder. A plethora of questions hammered her mind all at once. Was he running away? And why would he do that? Where was he going? Did Jesse know?

Regardless, a six-year-old boy was too young to be out in this rain all alone.

The deluge increased, beating against them like a drum. It gave her the incentive to force her hand.

"Sam, get in the buggy, please. You don't want Patches to catch a bad cold, do you?"

Her reasoning got through to the boy. Thankfully, he did as she asked. If she was reading his expression correctly, it was one of relief. And no wonder. When she opened the door wide and he stepped inside and sat on the seat, he was shivering and his teeth chattered. Patches wasn't in much better shape. The little dog gave a good shake to get the water off before curling next to her side.

"You're both frozen clear through." She reached for

the warm quilt her cousin kept stowed on the back seat. After draping it over Sam and Patches, she tucked the edges around them both before rubbing the boy's arms briskly.

"What are you doing so far from home in this storm?" she asked, not really expecting an answer.

He glanced up, his big, brown eyes filled with so much misery that she made a sad little sound in the back of her throat. Before she could stop herself, she pulled him close for a tight hug. After a moment, she released him and clicked to the horse to walk on.

"*Ach*, it can't be all that bad, can it? Did you run away from home?" she asked as she drove the horse through the driving rain.

The boy sat close beside her and she was half-surprised when he gave a slight nod. Oh, no! She hated the thought of Jesse and Sam having trouble between them.

"Did you have a disagreement with your *vadder*?" she asked.

He stared down at Patches and gave another nod.

She hesitated, wondering what she could say to make the situation easier.

"Your *vadder* loves you very much. You know that, don't you?" she asked.

He tossed her a doubtful glare and shook his head. Her heart gave a powerful squeeze. For some reason, it hurt her to think that Sam doubted his father's affection.

"Sometimes it isn't easy to honor our *eldre* but it's a commandment from *Gott*. Your *vadder* knows what's best for you and you must obey him in all things," she said.

Sam's forehead crinkled and he stared out the window, at the sheets of water blanketing the buggy. It wasn't long before they arrived at Jesse's farm but he wasn't there. Maybe he was out looking for Sam.

Becca stowed her horse and buggy inside the barn, then hurried to the house with Sam and Patches. While she got a towel to dry off the dog, she sent Sam upstairs to change out of his damp clothes. Then, she built up the fire in the stove. Since it was late afternoon, she took the liberty of fixing Sam something to eat. She found a pound of ground beef in the refrigerator and made a quick casserole. The boy wolfed down the hot food, which told her he hadn't eaten in a while. She also fed the puppy, satisfied when both of them were warm again.

An hour later, the rain let up and Jesse came home. The moment he stepped inside the kitchen, his gaze riveted on Sam. The boy still sat at the table, sipping a cup of hot chocolate. Patches lay on the floor beside the warm stove.

Without a word, Jesse knelt beside Sam and scooped the boy into his arms to hold him close for several long moments. This action alone told Becca he was beyond relieved to find the boy safe. It displayed Jesse's fear and love for his son more than anything else could. But then, Jesse drew back and clutched Sam's upper arms as he gazed into his eyes. Becca could see that Jesse was cold and angry. No doubt he'd been outside in the rain for quite a long time, looking for his son.

"I've been so worried about you. Where have you been?" Jesse asked, his eyes narrowed on the boy.

Sam stared at his hands folded in his lap, his cup of hot chocolate ignored.

"I found him and Patches walking alone along the side of the road. I was worried because they were out in the freezing rain, so I brought them home," Becca supplied.

Jesse gave a stiff nod. "*Danke* for bringing them home."

"You're *willkomm*." She spoke in a cheery voice, hoping to alleviate some of the tension in the air.

It didn't help. Jesse rounded on Sam again, his face tense with annoyance. He swept his black felt hat off his head and tossed it onto the table before wiping his damp face with an impatient hand. Like his son, his cheeks were pink from the cold and his heavy wool coat was soaked clear through.

"Do you know how worried I was when I found you missing? I had to leave my work and spent most of the afternoon searching for you. I don't have time to go traipsing all over the valley looking for you because you'd rather read your books than do your morning chores. It is not right for you to throw a temper tantrum and run away."

Standing in front of the sink, Becca held very still. Was that what this was all about? Sam had been reading instead of doing his work? Oh, dear. No wonder Jesse was upset. Any Amish father would feel the same way. A disobedient son who didn't do his chores put the entire *familye* at risk. Jesse would be derelict in his parental duties if he didn't reprimand the boy.

"Go to your room now and get ready for bed. I'll be up to collect your books in a few minutes. Except for school and bedtime, there will be no reading in this house for a week," Jesse said.

Something cold gripped Becca's heart. Would Jesse really ground the boy from reading for an entire week?

Sam nodded in obedience as he slid out of his chair

and left the room in a rush. Patches padded after him. When they were gone, Becca looked at Jesse, finding his expression grim and forbidding.

"Surely you won't keep the boy from reading, will you? He's been making such great progress. It's his one true enjoyment," she said in a quiet voice.

He looked at her as if he had forgotten she was there. "He's got to learn that work comes before pleasure. He's reading so much that it's interfering with his chores on the farm. He didn't do any of his tasks this morning. And when I chastised him for it, he threw a tantrum and ran away. I wasted an entire afternoon looking for him. He must learn to obey."

"I'm sorry that happened, Jesse. But I'm certain, if you reason with him, he'll understand and want to do better. He's just seeking your approval. He wants your love so much." She held out a pleading hand, her voice gentle and nonconfrontational.

Jesse snorted. "He'll win my approval by obeying what I say. I won't have him reading books instead of doing his chores again. The livestock must not suffer because of his dereliction."

She nodded. "*Ja*, I agree. But maybe if you weren't so grouchy with him all the time, he might be more willing to obey. It's entirely appropriate to reprove your child with sharpness but then if you'd show an increase in love toward him afterward, he might not consider you to be his enemy. As it is, he thinks you don't love him. And I'm sure that's not the message you want to send him."

Jesse shrugged out of his damp coat. His eyes narrowed, his lips pursing tight with disapproval. "Miss Graber, do you presume to tell me how to raise my *sohn*?"

She blinked. "*Ach*, of course not. But it seems you need some help right now. I just thought…"

"I don't need your advice on how to handle my boy," he cut her off.

She stared at him, completely aghast. Of all the nerve! Who did he think he was?

The answer came loud and sharp to her mind. He was Sam's father. She was simply the boy's teacher and didn't have a right to tell Jesse how to raise his own child.

"This isn't your business and I won't allow you to interfere." Jesse's voice was low but powerful, like the sound of rolling thunder off in the distance. His hands were clenched, his features tight.

Some inner guidance told her not to challenge him right now. But she didn't have to like it.

"All right. If that's the way you want it," she said.

Drawing herself up straight, she reached for her scarf and shawl, which lay over the back of one of the kitchen chairs. Without speaking, she jerked them on, wrapping up tight against the frigid wind outside. It had stopped raining but the ride home would undoubtedly be as chilly as it was inside this kitchen.

She walked to the door, longing to say something more. Wishing she dared plead with him to show some compassion toward his son. Sam seemed so lost right now. So did Jesse.

He didn't speak as she stepped out onto the back porch. A blast of chilly wind struck her in the face and she gasped. It slapped the screen door closed behind her. It reminded her of the glacial man standing inside, watching her go.

He didn't walk outside to see that she was safely in

her buggy and on her way. But as she pulled out of the yard, she saw him standing at the living room window, watching her with a severe expression on his face. If she hadn't seen his deep concern for Sam, she might think he hated the boy. That he hated the world.

She tried to calm her trembling hands and beating heart as she headed home. She told herself everything was all right. Sam was safe. Jesse was obviously upset but, in the morning, things would look differently. Jesse would calm down and so would Sam. Unfortunately, the problem wouldn't just resolve itself. Deep in her heart, she knew the issue wasn't going away anytime soon. It occurred to her that Jesse's trust in *Gott* was in tatters. He hadn't said so but she knew without asking. His faith had been greatly damaged. And though she longed to help him and Sam, she had no idea how to go about it. Other than to keep tutoring Sam and trying to show both of them compassion, she didn't have a clue. She just hoped it was enough.

Chapter Ten

Sam didn't show up for school Monday morning. A part of Becca wondered if it was because of the disagreement she'd had with Jesse when the child ran away. Another part of her thought it might be just because Jesse was so busy with work that he couldn't drive the boy here. She thought of offering to pick Sam up every morning on her way. After all, they lived only a mile apart. But she was already tutoring the boy three afternoons each week and barely keeping up with her own work as it was. It also occurred to her that Jesse needed that time alone with Sam each day, to be a father. What he did with the time was up to him. He could make it a quality chat with his boy or a silent, sullen trip.

Deciding not to make more out of Sam's absence than necessary, she taught her lessons as usual. As she worked with the fourth-graders and Caleb Yoder, she couldn't believe the difference in him. Since that second week when she'd started teaching here, he'd been so good and helpful. Maybe his older brother and sister had told on him and Bishop Yoder had corrected Caleb's poor behavior. Whatever it was, Becca was grateful.

Now, the school was quiet and orderly and she really thought she was making headway with the children.

That afternoon, she set aside Sam's work and waited until all the other children had left for the day. Then, she loaded her books into her buggy and drove over to Jesse's farm to tutor Sam as usual. The day was cool but the sky was clear and the sun was shining. That was a good sign that spring was on its way.

She parked beside Jesse's house and knocked on the front door. Glancing at the flowerbeds, she noticed the tulips and daffodils had poked their heads out of the soil. The last church service had focused on Easter and the Savior's resurrection, reminding her to carry hope within her heart. Another month and school would be out for the summer. But that thought caused a brief surge of panic to rise in Becca's throat. The last day of school was on May first. One more month and she would have to leave or find work elsewhere. But where would she go? She'd been sending job inquiries to numerous Amish communities across the nation and received not one positive response. Her common sense told her to doubt the future but then she reminded herself to have faith.

The door creaked open and Sam peered out at her with his big, dark eyes. When he saw her, he thrust open the door and threw himself at her in a tight hug.

"*Ach, hallo,* Sam! I missed you at school today. Are you ill?" she asked, determined to be positive and act like he'd never run away. It must be a bit embarrassing to him and his father and it would serve no purpose in bringing it up again. After all, it really wasn't her business.

He released her and stood in the living room, looking down at his stockinged feet as he shook his head. Except for shoes, he was fully dressed but his hair was rumpled and he had holes in his woolen socks where his little toes poked through. No doubt Jesse didn't have time to mend the socks for him. And once again, she was reminded with glaring clarity that this little boy badly needed a mother.

"Then why didn't you *komm* to school today?" she asked in a light tone.

He just shrugged and stepped back so she had room to come inside.

Becca set her bag on the floor, noticing a new sofa and coffee table perched in front of the wide window. They were drab brown and plain but appeared comfortable enough.

"These are nice," she said.

Sam didn't respond but she really didn't expect him to.

A Bible and some of Sam's books sat on top of the table. Gas lights had been installed in each corner of the room. The added illumination brightened the room and even seemed more cheerful inside. Gradually, Jesse was creating a pleasant home to live in. He was trying to pick up the pieces of his life.

So was she. But it wasn't easy. For any of them. And that's when she realized Jesse wasn't the only one who had trust issues. So did she. Vernon's betrayal had made her feel unacceptable, like she didn't belong anywhere. As if she wasn't worthy of love.

Her hands trembled slightly as she reached inside her bag and pulled out the assignments Sam had missed that day. She would catch him up on that first, then proceed to his reading and coax him to answer her questions out loud. If he got it all done this afternoon, she would mark him down as attending school today and his attendance wouldn't be marred by any absences. She wanted that for him so she could give him a special certificate at the end of the year, to help build his self-confidence.

"Let's start with our English, shall we?" she suggested.

She set a McGuffey reader on the coffee table and scooted over on the new sofa to give Sam room to join her. She was pleased when he read several sentences out loud to her, though he still spoke in a soft whisper she could barely hear. But it was great progress when she considered where they'd started a couple of months earlier.

They had just finished their phonics and were starting on penmanship when she heard the back door open and close.

"What are you doing here?"

She looked up. Jesse stood in the kitchen doorway. His hair was slightly damp around his face and neck and she thought he must have washed up in the barn. The dust on his broadfall pants and shirt attested that he'd worked hard that day. He lifted a hand to brace against the doorjamb, looking genuinely surprised to see her here. Did he think she was so shallow that she'd stay away simply because they'd disagreed on the best way to handle Sam's running away? If so, Jesse didn't know her very well.

"I came to tutor Sam, of course," she said, feeling a bit offended by his question.

He glanced at the books, his eyes crinkled in confusion. "I… I didn't think you'd *komm* back after the argument we had."

He certainly was blunt, she'd give him that. He never seemed to hold anything back.

She snorted. "Of course I would. Sam needs help. I would never punish him because you're being so bull-headed."

She turned her attention back to Sam, thinking she shouldn't have said that. But maybe it was something Jesse needed to hear. Handing Sam a pencil, she kept her head bowed and focused on the child's work. He wrote several words on his big, ruled paper and she took every opportunity to praise him.

"Very *gut*. Your letters are so legible. You're getting better at writing every day," she said.

Sam showed a shy smile and wrote some more words. When she looked up again, Jesse was gone. She could hear him inside the kitchen, rattling pots around. No doubt he was scrounging up something for his and Sam's supper.

She thought of going to help. She knew Jesse wasn't much of a cook. But no. He was Sam's father. He needed to serve his son. It was his job to provide for the boy. And besides, he needed to learn that he couldn't treat people rudely. Not if he expected to have any friends. It was better to leave him alone and let him come to these realizations on his own. But a part of her dearly wished she could be his friend too.

"*Ach*, it looks like you've got everything under control here. Whatever you're cooking smells *gut*."

Jesse turned and found Becca standing in the kitchen doorway. She had already put on her heavy shawl, gloves and scarf…ready to leave. She sniffed the air and breathed a little sigh for emphasis. Her voice sounded jolly and she was smiling. He stared at her for several seconds, wishing she wasn't so cheerful all the time. It made it harder not to like her.

"Are you finished teaching Sam for the night?" he asked, turning back to the stove.

He had just finished frying several ground beef patties without burning them and planned to cover them with hot cream of mushroom soup. It was called poor man's steak and had been a staple from his childhood. A baked potato, string beans and canned pears would round out the meal. He even had whipped up some chocolate pudding for dessert. Sam would like that.

"*Ja*, Sam does better every day," she said. "He's made a tremendous amount of progress. I'm even hopeful he'll speak his part out loud for the end-of-year program. He's told me he wants to. I just hope he isn't too nervous when the time comes."

She stepped over to the stove and watched him whisk the mushroom gravy around in the meat drippings. He thought about inviting her to stay for supper but decided against it. For some reason, this woman made him feel nervous. He couldn't think clearly when she was standing so near. Besides, they were both single and it was getting late. She needed to go home. Right now.

Lifting the pan, he set it on a hot pad in the middle of the table. Alice would have poured it into a bowl with a ladle and made their meal as dignified as possible. But he didn't have time for such nonsense. After supper, he must return to the barn. His road horse had thrown a shoe so he couldn't take Sam to school that morning. He needed to use the animal out in the fields tomorrow, which meant the shoe must be replaced tonight. He really needed to buy some draft horses. Then he wouldn't have to use his road horse in the fields.

He reached for a dish towel to wipe his hands…a nervous gesture to give himself something to do. Again, he glanced at Becca, expecting her to leave. "Was there something else you needed?"

She shook her head, meeting his gaze. "*Ne*, I just wanted to apologize for the harsh words I said to you a couple of days ago. I fear I'm too bold at times and may have caused offense and that wasn't my intention."

"I'm sorry too." He spoke the words before he could think to stop himself. Their argument had been on his mind since it happened and he wanted to clear the air.

Her expression softened and she smiled. "*Danke*. I know you're doing your best with Sam and you were worried about him that day. Fear can cause us to say things we don't really mean. But you're doing a really *gut* job with him."

Her insight impressed him. It was as if she could see deep inside of him and knew exactly what he was thinking. The only other person to do that had been Alice.

"It's kind of difficult for me to admit when I'm wrong," he said. "I was raised by a rather stern *vadder*. He was always right even when he was wrong. He was a *gut* man but very stubborn. There was little laughter in my home when I was growing up. I've tried not to be that way. My wife taught me that apologies make us stronger. I didn't mean to come across as unfeeling toward my *sohn*."

He spoke the words slowly, surprised at how painful it was for him to make the admission. Although his father had taught him a strong work ethic and how to farm, most of the memories from his youth were not pleasant. And he wasn't sure why he was telling Becca this. She was way too easy to confide in. Too easy to be with. But he knew in his heart of hearts that he must apologize to her. He was trying so hard to start anew. For some reason, it was highly important to him not to have conflict with Sam's teacher. Mostly because she'd been good to him and Sam and they owed her a debt of gratitude. But he sensed there was another reason too. Something he didn't understand.

"*Ach*, just because the horse bucks you off doesn't mean you sell the horse," she said. "The Savior taught us to have a soft heart filled with humility. And when we are filled with His love, we are quick to forgive. But it can still be a hard thing to do. For all of us."

Hmm. Again, her insight surprised him. Just like Alice, it seemed that Becca was teaching him some rather difficult lessons. Her patient reminder of the Savior helped him realize he could learn a lot from this good woman.

"I've been meaning to ask, would you be willing to teach a fire safety class at school next week?" she asked suddenly.

Jesse stared at her, his mouth dropping open in surprise. Because of his past, he wasn't certain he felt up to the task. He couldn't do it. Could he?

"I… I'm not sure I'm the right person to do that," he said, trying not to sound insecure.

"Why not? You're a certified firefighter. It must have taken a lot of study and effort to master that skill. You must be very *gut* at it. And it's an interesting profession we can highlight for the *kinder*. You're a *gut* example of a *vadder* who has reached out to help his community."

He didn't know how to respond. He didn't feel like

a good father. How could he explain to this dedicated woman that he hadn't been able to fight fire ever since he'd lost his wife and daughters? Even now, he hated to add kindling to the stove in his own home. Every time he saw the flames, he thought about losing Alice and their girls.

"Do you feel reluctant because of how your *familye* died?" she asked, her voice achingly soft and gentle.

Wow! She really did lay it out in the open, no mincing words. And yet, hearing his own thoughts spoken out loud made his fears seem a little less threatening.

He ducked his head, a hard lump forming in his throat. He hated to show any weakness to this woman and fought to regain control. When he felt her hand on his arm, he looked into her eyes. She stood so close, her face creased with compassion.

"I know losing part of your *familye* must have been so difficult for you, Jesse. But for Sam's sake and also your own, you have to go on living. From what I've heard at church, you were *gut* at fighting fires. Who better to teach the scholars about fire safety? The people of our *Gmay* could really benefit from your skill too. I hope you'll think about it. You can let me know your decision tomorrow morning, when you bring Sam to school."

She turned and walked toward the back door, the heels of her practical black shoes tap-tapping against the wooden floor. He didn't turn to watch her leave but he heard the door close behind her.

Teach fire safety at school?

He couldn't do it. And yet, Becca's gentle encouragement made him feel like he could do anything. But surely not that. Then again, it had been over a year since the house fire. He used to love fighting fires. Used to love helping people save their homes and businesses. Until he'd lost his wife and daughters, he'd felt like he was doing something good for his community. That he was helping his Amish people save their houses and barns too. Maybe it was time to put aside his grief and take it up again. Maybe…

But what if he did something wrong? What if he panicked and made a mistake? He couldn't stand the thought of losing someone else on his watch. Especially someone he cared deeply about.

Becca thought he could do it. She seemed to really believe in him. She was counting on him. And it felt so good to be needed again. So good to have someone in his life that he could talk to about Sam and all that he had lost. Maybe he should think about it a little more.

Chapter Eleven

Becca arrived at school early the following morning. With no snow to shovel, she was able to get the classroom warmed up and set out her lesson plans before the scholars arrived. Then, she went outside to welcome each child. And when Jesse pulled into the schoolyard, she helped Sam hop out of the buggy and leaned in to greet the boy's father.

"*Guder mariye*, Jesse!" she called, purposefully trying to be pleasant.

"*Hallo*," he said, not returning her smile.

Sam hugged Becca, then ran off to meet Andy Yoder, who had just walked into the schoolyard with his brothers and sisters. Although Andy did most of the talking, Becca had seen Sam speaking a few words to the other boy on rare occasion. Andy was the same age as Sam and the two had become good friends. Just another subtle reminder that Sam was doing better and much happier at school.

Turning back to Jesse, she showed a smile of encouragement. "Have you thought more about teaching a fire safety class to the *kinder*?"

He gripped the leather lead lines and frowned, seeming a bit pensive. Maybe she shouldn't push him so hard. But the alternative was that she would have to teach the class and she thought it would be more effective coming from a firefighter.

"*Ja*, I will do it," he said.

"*Wundervoll!*" she exclaimed. "Will next Monday, first thing in the morning, work for you? Then you can leave right afterward and we won't take up too much of your day."

He nodded. "That will work but I'll need at least two hours to teach a proper safety class."

She blinked. "So much time?"

He nodded. "*Ja*, to do it correctly."

Hmm. Being Amish, she took fire for granted. After all, her people used it in their everyday life to heat their homes and cook their food. But she wanted to do this right. Maybe the schoolchildren had learned bad habits in building fires. Learning some safety techniques might make a difference for one of them at some time in their life. It might make a difference for her as well.

"*Allrecht*. You can have all the time you need," she said.

"I'll plan on two hours. But just one other thing. Don't start a fire in the stove that morning and I'll show the *kinder* the proper way to clean up a cold fire and how to prepare it for burning."

"*Ja*, I'll remember. And *danke!*"

She closed the door and stepped back. He tugged on the brim of his straw hat and gave her a slight smile before he slapped the leads against the horse's rump. And for some odd reason, his smile meant everything to her.

The buggy pulled away and she watched him go. A

sense of exhilaration filled her as she entered the school and taught lessons to the scholars. She felt inordinately happy today and didn't understand why. Maybe it was because the sun was shining, the tulips were peeking out from the chilled soil and Sam had a friend and was doing better in school. Caleb Yoder had taken the younger boy under his wing and was reading to him several times each day. Jesse had agreed to teach the fire safety class and had even smiled at her that morning. Not even the impending monthly school board meeting later that afternoon could diminish her spirits. The meeting was held on the first Tuesday of every month. Becca had already reminded the scholars and they were prepared for the visit.

The day passed quickly and she felt organized when Bishop Yoder, Mervin Schwartz and Darrin Albrecht came inside, a little bit early. They each removed their black felt hats as they entered the school. Their wives were with them, Mervin's wife holding their two-year-old daughter in her arms. A couple of other parents filtered in as well. They didn't interrupt the class as they quietly sat at the back of the room but the students were highly aware that they had guests.

Becca was leaning over Susan Hostetler, helping the girl sound out a particularly difficult word, when the door opened again. Glancing up, she saw Jesse King standing there, his gaze resting on her. And instantly, her face heated up like a road flare. She felt as if everyone in the room was watching her. What was Jesse doing here? Any of their people were invited to attend the school board meetings but he'd never participated before. And they'd just spoken that morning. So, what reason did he have to be here now?

He reached up and removed his straw hat, glancing around the room for a place to sit. Bishop Yoder motioned to him and he sauntered over to sit nearby, his legs overly long in the small desk.

Becca ducked her head further over Susan's reading book, hoping no one noticed her hot cheeks. She scolded herself, remembering to act professional. She had no idea why Jesse affected her like this. He was just the parent of one of her students. That was all. Nothing more.

Standing straight, she moved toward the front of the room, speaking loud enough for everyone to hear. "Scholars, we'd like to *willkomm* our visitors to our school. Will you please put away your studies now and stand at the front of the room?"

There was a slight rustling as the children did as she asked. As usual, they would sing a couple of songs for their guests, then go outside. Some of the children would go home to do their evening chores while others would play in the yard until their parents were ready to leave. They'd been rehearsing their songs and Becca had reminded them of the board meeting earlier that morning, so they were prepared.

She stood beside her desk, waiting for the scholars to line up with the oldest and tallest students in the back and the younger children in the front. They all looked so earnest, eager and innocent as they waited for her signal. And she loved each and every one of them. How she would miss them when the school year ended and she had to leave to find employment elsewhere.

Lifting her hand, she hummed a note to give them their starting key, then led them in two German songs. Their voices rang out in unison, sweet and melodious.

Out of her peripheral vision, she saw Jesse watching his son with unblinking eyes. The man's countenance was one of rapt attention and appreciation. In spite of his gruffness, she knew he loved the little boy very much.

The other parents in the room wore similar expressions. Like any caring parent, they adored their children. And a quiet pain settled within Becca's chest. Yes, she'd chosen the teaching profession. It was a career she hoped to embrace and excel at. One that would support her financially throughout her life. But teaching was also a labor of love. She took her responsibilities seriously, to mold her young scholars into upstanding Amish people. But a part of her ached with emptiness. All her life, she had hoped to marry a kind, loving man and hold her own children within her arms. Now, it seemed that would never happen. Because Vernon had broken her heart, she didn't dare trust another man again. And at times like this, she had trouble accepting that.

During church the previous Sunday, the sermon had been out of the Gospel of Matthew. Ask and it shall be given you, seek and ye shall find. It occurred to Becca that, if she wanted to remain in Riverton, she should ask the Lord and exercise faith that He could make it happen.

The last note of the song ended and Becca lowered her arm and smiled at her students. "*Danke*, scholars. You have done well today and are now dismissed from school. I'll see you tomorrow morning."

The children put on their coats and gathered up their bags and lunch pails before racing outside. Their laughter rang through the air as they closed the door behind them.

As if on cue, the school board members stood and

walked to the front of the room. With their long beards and black frock coats, the three fathers looked a bit intimidating. As was their habit, they sat facing Becca's desk.

Forcing herself to retain her composure, Becca picked up her notebook and pencil and waited for Bishop Yoder to conduct the meeting. She presented a list of supplies and they discussed a couple of discipline problems.

"I understand my son Caleb has been acting up in school," the bishop said.

Becca nodded. "*Ja*, he and Enos have caused a couple of disturbances in the past."

"They are not causing trouble now?"

"*Ne*, lately they have been *gut* as can be. In fact, I assigned both boys as reading and math partners with some of the younger scholars and they both seem to have taken this task quite seriously. I have had no more problems with either boy for some time now."

"*Gut*. I had heard there was a problem and waited for you to speak with me about it, but you never did," he said.

A moment of confusion filled her mind. Had she made a mistake by not talking to him about it sooner?

"I… I wanted to handle it myself, if possible. And it turns out that everything is fine now. The boys are being very well-behaved."

Hopefully, the board members were impressed enough with how she had handled the situation that they would write her a good teaching recommendation for a future position somewhere else.

"I am happy to hear this news. You are to be commended for how you have dealt with the problem," Bishop Yoder said.

Becca couldn't help feeling pleased by the bishop's praise. Not only did she highly respect this man but she also wanted to do a good job. She desired to help her students become better people.

The other two board members nodded their agreement and Bishop Yoder turned to face the rest of the parents in the room.

"Are there any other issues that need to be brought to our attention?" he asked.

No one spoke but Jesse stood, signaling he wished to make a comment.

"*Ja*, what is it?" Bishop Yoder asked in a kind tone.

"Ahem." Jesse cleared his throat and shifted his booted feet nervously. "I just wanted to say that Miss Graber has gone out of her way to provide extra tutoring for my Sam. She's done a *wundervoll* job working with him and he's even speaking a little bit now and then. I wanted the school board to know how grateful I am that you hired such a willing, capable teacher for our children."

A couple of the mothers in the room nodded their agreement. Becca stared, completely overwhelmed. She couldn't believe Jesse had gone out of his way to give her a good review. He seemed so harsh. So disapproving and downright difficult at times. And then he went and did something so kind and generous. And just in time too. There was only one month left before school let out for the summer. She was beyond grateful for what he'd done.

"*Danke*. It has been my pleasure to work with Sam and the other scholars. They're great kids and I care deeply for each one of them," she said, retaining her professional demeanor.

And she meant every word. She loved teaching. Loved serving these amazing children. She just wished she could stay in Riverton and teach them next year too. But Caroline Schwartz was out of the hospital and walking with the help of a walker. She'd possibly need the aid of a cane for the rest of her life but she was healing and would be back in the fall. There was no other position for Becca in this community. In order to support herself, she'd have to leave the area.

She'd have to leave Jesse and little Sam too. And though she didn't understand why, that thought made her feel so sad and forlorn that she wanted to cry.

The meeting ended soon after and Jesse slipped out the door before she could catch him to thank him privately for what he'd said. She watched him go, thinking maybe it was for the best. He was still hurting over the deaths of his wife and daughters. He had his hands full with Sam and making a go of his farm. He had no room in his life or his heart for an opinionated schoolteacher like Becca. And yet, she couldn't help wishing he did.

As promised, Jesse arrived early the following Monday to teach the fire safety class. He parked his buggy in the back and Sam helped him carry a couple of fire extinguishers into the schoolhouse. As they crossed the graveled yard, Jesse watched his little son race toward the front door, his arms filled with his lunch pail and a red extinguisher. The boy was smiling, eager to get inside and greet Becca. And Jesse couldn't help thinking how happy his son was lately. In fact, Jesse felt happier too. And though he didn't fully understand why, he sensed that it was partly due to Becca and her gentle influence in their lives.

"*Guder mariye*! I'm so glad you're here." She greeted them with her usual cheery disposition.

Jesse returned her smile. He couldn't help himself. She was depending on him and he wanted to do a good job for her.

"I've cleared the top of my desk, so you have a place to set your things during your presentation." She eyed the two red standard fire extinguishers he held.

"*Danke* but I won't need much room. This is for you. For the schoolhouse." He held one of the extinguishers out to her.

She took it and looked up into his eyes. He felt transfixed by her gaze.

"That's very kind of you," she said, her voice seeming to come from a haze.

He cleared his throat and moved away, trying to focus on the task at hand. Sam set the third fire extinguisher he'd been carrying on top of a desk, then picked up the wood bucket from beside the cold potbellied stove. He hurried outside to collect some firewood and kindling, just as Jesse had asked him to do before they'd arrived.

The students came in, doffing their jackets and placing their lunch pails on the shelf beneath the coatracks. They talked quietly together as they took their seats. Jesse stood silently at the side of the classroom and watched as Becca greeted each and every scholar. She asked them questions pertaining to their lives. One had a new baby sister at home and another one had found an injured starling they were caring for. It seemed she knew everything about these children's lives and took a genuine interest in them.

Sam returned with the wood bucket and set it beside the stove. Jesse was surprised when he waved to Caleb Yoder. The older boy smiled back before sliding into his seat.

Becca stood at the front of the room and folded her hands together as she lifted her chin higher in the air. The children quickly took their seats.

"Scholars, we have a special guest with us today. Mr. King is a certified firefighter from Pennsylvania. He has agreed to teach us some fire safety techniques. And I know you'll be extra polite and give him your undivided attention." With a satisfied nod, she stepped aside and sat at an empty desk near the front of the room.

Okay, Jesse was on. He cleared his throat and stood, gazing into each earnest face. They seemed so eager to learn. And he couldn't help thinking about the lesson he'd heard at church the day before. The minister had preached from the book of Matthew: Ask and it shall be given you, seek and you shall find. Jesse had been pondering the powerful message ever since. He'd been tempted to speak with Becca about the topic. It seemed he gravitated to her whenever she was near, yet something held him back. His love and loyalty for his wife. His own sense of guilt. Surely the message from the Gospel of Matthew was for other people, not for him. But then again, maybe he was wrong.

"*Danke* for inviting me here today," he said, trying to gather his courage. After all, it had been over a year since he'd had anything to do with the firefighting world and he wasn't sure he was ready for this experience. But no matter. He was here and would do his best.

"The first thing I want to teach you is how to ensure your stove and flue is clean." He stepped over to the cold potbellied stove and pointed at the filled wood bucket Sam had set there just minutes before.

"The wood bucket should never be this close to the stove. It should always be at least two or three arms' lengths away. That way, an errant spark from the stove won't strike the wood that's in the bucket and catch fire."

To emphasize his point, he moved the wood bucket several yards away, to the side of the classroom. Earlier, he had asked Sam to put the bucket right next to the stove so he could make this point. And he was pleased that his son had followed his instructions exactly. He glanced at his boy and found him watching intently. As a way of saying thank you, he smiled and winked at his son. Sam smiled back, looking pleased to have helped.

"Gather around me so you can see how to check the chimney flue to see if it needs cleaning." Jesse beckoned to the students and they instantly did as he asked.

Over the next thirty minutes, Jesse taught them the proper way to check the chimney flue for cleaning and showed them how to adjust the damper so they could control the amount of heat and smoke they got out of the fire.

"At this time of year, it's a bit warmer so you don't need as much heat from the fire. Back east, we used hard woods like oak and maple in our fires. Here in Colorado, we're burning Ponderosa Pine because it's plentiful in the area and easy to gather. But it's a soft wood that burns relatively fast. It's also a heavy soot builder, so the flue needs to be cleaned more frequently. I recommend four times per year," he explained.

The children listened intently to every word he said. When he remembered that first week when Becca had just started teaching here and he'd entered the school to find the students in absolute chaos, he was impressed by the order she had since established.

As the kids crowded close to see, he held up a book of matches. He was amazed that, without being asked, the older, taller students had put the younger, shorter children closest to him so they could see better. Sam stood nearby, watching his every move.

"When you start a fire inside your house or another building, you should never, ever use an accelerant such as kerosene or gasoline. It can explode out on you and burn you and the entire building. And do not play with matches. They aren't a toy and can burn your entire house down. Don't ever do it! I can't emphasize this enough," he said.

His words were a reminder of what his *familye* had gone through over a year earlier. A hard lump formed in his throat as he knelt before the stove to show the students how to clean out the ashes. When that was done, he discussed the proper way to start a fire and laid some wrinkled newspaper and kindling in the stove. His voice sounded calm and even as he talked but his hands were trembling. Looking up, he saw Becca watching him closely. Her forehead was furrowed and her eyes crinkled in a frown of concern.

Lifting the book of matches, he pulled one from the packet and scraped it across the coarse striking area. A little *whoosh* sounded as the match lit with fire. A commotion came from behind him and he turned, the match going out.

Sam stood there, his eyes wide with terror, his face

contorted in absolute anguish. He had backed up, knocking into two of the older kids. What was wrong with him?

"Sam?" Jesse called.

Had lighting a single match frightened his son? It shouldn't. But even Jesse felt a slight tremor in his arms and legs. Though he started all the fires at his house, he still disliked the chore. And then it dawned on him that Sam was never in the room with him when he started fires at home. Although the child brought in plenty of wood and kindling, he was always absent until the fire was going and the door to the stove was shut.

A small cry escaped Sam's throat. Without explanation, the boy whirled around and pushed through the wall of students. When he finally made his way out into the open area of the classroom, he raced toward the exit. Throwing the door open wide, he ran out into the schoolyard.

Jesse stood, his lesson on fire safety all but forgotten. He was about to run after his son but Becca held out a hand.

"I'll go after him. Please, continue your demonstration," she said.

He blinked in confusion as she hurried after his son. She closed the door behind her. Out of the wide windows surrounding the room, he saw a flash of her skirts as she ran behind the building.

A sniffle brought his attention back to the students. They stared at him in confusion, their eyes wide with worry.

"Is Sam gonna be *allrecht*, Mr. King?" little Andy Yoder asked.

Jesse showed a confident smile he didn't feel. "*Ja,*

he'll be fine. Don't worry. Now, let's continue with our lesson."

He put his thoughts on involuntary reflex, discussing the fire extinguishers he'd brought and how the children should aim them at the base of the flame. Then, he taught them how to recognize the exits of a building and escape a burning room in orderly fashion rather than panicking and trampling one another underfoot. He had them each get down low to the floor where they could breathe fresh air when smoke filled the room so they could crawl toward the exit. Then, he took them outside to teach them how to properly dispose of the ashes from their fires.

Out in the schoolyard, he looked around for some sign of Becca and Sam. He saw them some distance away, sitting on the banks of the creek that meandered past the bishop's property. Hearing his voice, they stood and Becca held Sam's hand as the two of them rejoined the group of students. Sam's eyes were red from crying and he wouldn't meet Jesse's eyes. Instead, the boy stared at the ground. An overwhelming urge to take his little boy into his arms and comfort him swept over Jesse. In the past, he would have resisted. But not now. Not today. Becca had taught Jesse to have more compassion. He didn't need to be as stern as his father had been with him.

Interrupting his lecture, he swept his son into his arms and hugged him tight, whispering in his ear for his hearing alone.

"It's going to be okay, *sohn*. I love you," Jesse said.

Hearing his words, Sam softened in his arms. Jesse set the boy back on his feet next to Becca. She nodded her approval as he returned to his lesson. His heart felt a bit lighter and he knew he'd done the right thing by showing some affection toward Sam. If nothing else, it showed the boy that he wasn't angry with him.

"If there's a fire in the schoolhouse, do you have an assigned place to gather outside so your teacher can count you and know that everyone got out safely?" he asked the group.

The children gazed at him with blank expressions.

"*Ne*, but we will assign a place right now," Becca said. "What about right here where we are standing in the middle of the play area?"

Jesse shook his head, a feeling of gratitude filling his heart. Though he pretended to act normal, he was beyond grateful to Becca for helping him with Sam.

"This isn't a *gut* place. It's too close to the schoolhouse. I suggest you meet over here, far away from any potentially burning structures." He walked over to the baseball diamond and stood on the home plate.

"*Ja*, I see what you mean. This is an open area, far away from any buildings, where we can easily be seen," Becca said.

"*Ach*, so where will you meet outside if the school is ever on fire?" he asked the students in a booming voice.

"Here!" they responded in unison.

"Very *gut*. Now, one last lesson and then I'll leave you for the day. I want to discuss the proper way to dispose of the ashes from your stove," he said.

As they walked behind the schoolhouse to a safe fire circle that had been set up specifically for this task, he showed them how to stir the ashes around with a bit of water but not bury them since that would bank the heat inside and keep the fire alive. He taught them how to feel carefully with the back of their hands to ensure no warmth came from the ashes. And only then could they be assured that there were no live coals that could spring to life and be carried by the wind to start a wildfire burning. And by the time he had finished the training, he was no longer shaking. Sam was smiling again too.

"Scholars, what do you say to Mr. King?" Becca asked the students when Jesse had finished his lecture.

They all smiled and responded together. "*Danke*, Mr. King."

He nodded, feeling relieved to have this chore finished. *"Gaern gscheh."*

"Scholars, please return to the classroom and prepare for reading time. I'm going to have a private word with Mr. King and will come inside in just a few minutes," she said.

A couple of snickers from the students accompanied her comment and she looked to see who it came from. But all the students looked completely innocent as they turned and walked back to the schoolhouse.

"*Danke* again for your very thorough lesson," she said.

She accompanied him to his horse and buggy. He felt drained of emotion for some reason and thought it must be because he'd faced a fear that had been haunting him for months now.

"Do you think Sam will be all right?" she asked. "He wouldn't tell me what was wrong."

"*Ja*, he'll be fine. I'll spend extra time with him this evening. I… I better let you get back to your school," he said. His emotions swirled around inside of him in a mass of confusion. He felt better but he also felt worse at the same time. He didn't need to ask Sam what was wrong to understand what the boy was feeling.

"*Ja*, I better get back." She stepped away, her lips and cheeks a pretty shade of pink.

"I'll see you later this afternoon when you come to tutor Sam." He spoke as he stepped into the buggy.

She didn't speak but merely waved. Then, she took off at a slight jog toward the schoolhouse.

He watched her go, thinking today was completely unexpected. When he'd arrived here this morning, he hadn't expected Sam's actions or his own response to the fire safety class. His feelings were a riot of unease. Becca probably thought he was crazy. He wished he could open his heart and let her in. But there was still one glaring problem. She wasn't Alice. And she never would be.

Chapter Twelve

The day of the box social arrived too soon. When Becca had first moved to Riverton, the school board had asked her to schedule the event as a fund-raiser so they could buy a teeter-totter and other playground equipment. It wasn't difficult. Just a few announcements made at church and some reminders sent home with the children. The bishop had agreed to let her borrow the benches and tables used by the congregation and the members of the *Gmay* provided the labor to set them up. She just hoped it was a success.

"It's a beautiful day for the social." Hannah Schwartz handed a roll of masking tape to Becca.

She glanced at the azure sky, grateful they wouldn't be rained out. "*Ja*, we couldn't ask for more."

She pulled off a piece of tape and spread it across the corner of the plastic tablecloth to hold it down so the wind wouldn't blow it off. Standing in the school-yard, she gazed at the other folding tables and chairs they had set up earlier that morning. It was Saturday afternoon and they were almost ready to begin. With the sun shining, they were sure to have a good turnout.

But she couldn't help feeling a bit melancholy. Even if they earned enough funds for the playground equipment today, she'd never get to see it. With just two weeks of school left, she'd soon be cleaning out the classroom and packing her things for her trip back home to Ohio. Hopefully, she'd have a glowing letter of recommendation in her purse. She must have faith that *Gott* had her best interests at heart and would guide her through life.

Deciding not to wallow in self-pity, she turned and picked up a stack of bread baskets. They also belonged to the *Gmay*. Since they held so many social events, the investment was well worth it.

Abby, Aunt Naomi, Sarah Yoder and Linda Hostetler were setting out vases of tulips and daffodils picked from their own yards as centerpieces for each table. Bishop Yoder and Darrin Albrecht were unloading a propane barbecue off the back of a wagon. Their teenaged sons helped lift the heavy weight. Since bidding was usually reserved for the adults and older teenagers, each *familye* had been instructed to bring side dishes and desserts to feed their children. More people were arriving, hurrying to lend a hand as they prepared for the fun occasion.

"How does the box table look?"

Becca turned and found Lizzie and Eli Stoltzfus standing behind her. The couple was newly married and Lizzie was just far enough along in her first pregnancy that she was glowing with happiness.

Eli pointed to the table they'd set up for displaying the boxed suppers. The women and some of the girls of the *Gmay* had each decorated a cardboard box with newspaper and tulips and filled it with a dinner for two. Except for the size of each box, they looked almost identical. Later, the men would bid on the boxes in anticipation of eating a meal with one of their womenfolk. Generally the boxes were kept anonymous, so the men wouldn't know whose they were bidding on. But sometimes, people dropped hints in order to rig the bidding so the single couples could eat together. At least, that was their hope.

For just a moment, Becca wished Jesse might buy her box. But she pushed that thought aside. His heart belonged to a dead woman and that was that.

A white cloth had been spread across the box table and Lizzie had pinned yellow and red tulips and daffodils along the edge to give it a special flair. They had already set the boxed dinners strategically on the table, to catch the eyes of the male bidders. Becca could see her own box sitting toward the back, decorated with sheets of newspaper and two red tulips affixed on top.

"*Ach*, the table looks beautiful!" Becca exclaimed.

"How about if we have the bidding on the boxes first? Then I can fire up the grill to cook for the *kinder* and other people who won't be bidding on a box." Bishop Yoder spoke from nearby.

"That sounds great. I'll leave that to you," Becca said.

Though she'd never seen him in action, she'd been told the bishop was a good auctioneer. And she was happy to coordinate everything and let him handle the business end of the occasion.

At that moment, Jesse and Sam's buggy pulled into the yard. Becca's senses went on high alert. She returned Sam's energetic wave but forced herself not to run over to greet them. She didn't want to look too forward. Not with almost everyone in the *Gmay* watching.

Children raced past and adults laughed together as everyone arrived in time for the bidding. Becca kept herself busy laying out stacks of paper plates, cups and napkins. She had no idea who would bid on her basket and hoped they liked fried chicken.

"Everyone! Gather round and we'll have a blessing on the food. Then, we'll start the bidding." Standing on a raised wooden platform, the bishop waved his arms and spoke in a booming voice to get everyone's attention.

The people stepped forward in anticipation. Some of the teenaged boys eyed the decorated boxes, bending their heads together and pointing as they speculated on who had made them. Glancing up, Becca saw Abby chatting with Jesse as she bounced little Chrissie on her hip.

Hmm. Abby wouldn't tell him which box belonged to her, would she? Both Abby and Aunt Naomi had been in the kitchen when Becca had packed and decorated her box, so they definitely knew which one was hers.

They bowed their heads and blessed the food. Then, the bishop called to the crowd.

"And we have our first box to bid on," he said.

Jeremiah Beiler picked up a rather plain cardboard box decorated with a single red-and-yellow parrot tulip. As he lifted the box for everyone to inspect, he sniffed the lid.

"Hmm, something smells good inside. Some meat loaf and apple pie, would be my guess," he said.

Dawdi Zeke bumped Dale Yoder with his shoulder and waggled his bushy gray eyebrows at the boy. "You should bid on it, *sohn*. It might belong to that pretty little Lenore you're so keen on."

The crowd laughed and Dale's face flamed bright red. Everyone knew he was crazy about Lenore Schwartz. In fact, they all expected the two to marry once they were old enough.

"That's not mine. I made ham sandwiches, macaroni salad and doughnuts. Mine's the one on the end with the three red tulips," Lenore said.

The group laughed harder. No doubt Lenore was petrified Dale might bid on the wrong box. Or worse yet, someone else might bid on her box and she'd have to eat supper with them.

"Who'll give me five dollars for this box? It smells real nice," Bishop Yoder called.

One of the fathers raised his hand.

Bishop Yoder pointed at the man and the bidding began. "I've got five dollars, who'll give me ten?"

Another hand went up. The bishop got into the groove of the auction, his voice firing off in rapid succession. And just like that, Becca realized this event had been a smart idea. Within two minutes, the first box had sold for thirty-five dollars.

Will Lapp won the box. As Minister Beiler took his money and held the box out to him, little twelve-year-old Emily Hostetler stepped forward to claim ownership. Since she was so young, Will's wife, Ruth, joined them. And once Ruth's box was sold to old *Dawdi* Zeke, the group made it a foursome so there would be no perceived impropriety as they ate together.

The bidding continued and Becca soon realized they would indeed have enough funds to purchase the teetertotter. She hoped they would make enough to also buy some new baseball equipment and bouncy balls for the playground. If they did really well, they might even be able to install a couple of swings. She couldn't be happier and counted the day as a great success.

"*Ach*, this box smells like fried chicken," Jeremiah called, sniffing the rim of the lid with relish.

Realizing the box belonged to her, Becca's face heated up in spite of her desire to remain incognito.

"Who'll give me ten dollars for this box?" Bishop Yoder called.

Ben Yoder, the bishop's shy nephew from Iowa, held up his hand. With a rather quiet, retiring nature, Ben was large for an Amish man. He stood at six feet four inches tall and weighed about a hundred and ninety pounds, all of it lean muscle. His shoulders were wide as a broom handle and his hands were huge and strong. A lot of rumors followed his name. Bishop Yoder called him Gentle Ben but Becca had heard he'd had trouble with fighting in Iowa and had even killed a man in self-defense, which was why he'd relocated here to Colorado. It seemed that many of their people were trying to escape a shadowed past. With so many members of their *Gmay* around, she was willing to eat supper with him but had no romantic inclinations toward him whatsoever.

"I've got ten dollars. Who will give me twenty?" Bishop Yoder shouted at the crowd.

Becca saw Jesse King lift his hand in the air. His expression was stoic, his eyes unblinking as he gazed steadily at the bishop. As if in slow motion, Becca watched as the bidding bounced back and forth between Jesse and Ben until, finally, Jesse won her box for a price even she could never have anticipated. Did he know that it was her box? Had Abby told him? Or was it just a coincidence? Becca had no idea.

She stared, her mouth dropping open in absolute surprise. On the one hand, she was delighted that Jesse would pay so much for her box. But on the other hand, she was mortified at the outlandish amount of money.

"Sold! To Jesse King for seventy-five dollars," the bishop cried.

A low murmur of awe swept over the crowd. Everyone recognized what a high price he'd paid. A subtle flicker of a smile curved Jesse's lips upward as he stepped over to receive his box. Becca didn't move. She didn't breathe. Her feet felt as if they'd been nailed to the ground. Finally, Aunt Naomi gave her a slight push forward and she took several steps.

A titter of chatter filled the air as everyone discussed this turn of events. No doubt the entire *Gmay* would be thinking she and Jesse were an item. That they were sweet on each other. And they weren't. But people wouldn't know that. Jesse wasn't interested in her. Or anyone else, for that matter. That thought brought an aching pain to Becca's heart. And that's the moment she realized she loved him. Heaven help her, she truly did. Somehow, during the past months she'd been working with Sam and Jesse, she'd fallen in love with both of them. Not just the love from serving other people, but a lasting feeling that made her want to be with them always. To take care of them and be a part of their life forever. Jesse might not think twice about her. Her box was filled with food that was quickly consumed and enjoyed but then forgotten. But for Becca, she couldn't think about anything but him.

"I guess I bought your supper." Jesse spoke low when Jeremiah handed him the box.

She looked at him, feeling trembly and confused by

her new realization. She stared up into his eyes, not knowing what to say. She only knew she loved this man and his little boy. Every time she was near him, she felt twitter-pated. And when they were parted, she could think of nothing but seeing him again. Her heart went out to him and Sam, for the pain and sadness they'd been through. She longed to make them happy. To see them both smile and hear their laughter again and again. Over time, the sting of Vernon's betrayal had eased and she realized she'd never really loved him. Not like what she felt for Jesse. Not the romantic love a woman should have for a man she wanted to marry. Now that she'd had some time away from Vernon to think clearly, she realized her love for her ex-fiancé was simply a habit built up over years of being good friends. But what she felt for Jesse was so much more. An overflowing desire to be with him and make good things happen in his life.

Yes, she loved Jesse King. And knowing he could never love her in return hurt most of all.

"*Ja*, you bought my supper. I hope it was worth it." She spoke the words in a whisper, forcing herself to look away. Because she knew, if she didn't, she would start to cry and she couldn't stand to have Jesse and the rest of the *Gmay* witness such shame.

Opening his wallet, Jesse counted out the bills and paid Darrin Albrecht, their deacon, the required amount. Becca stared as their work-roughened hands made the exchange. She still couldn't believe Jesse had paid such an exorbitant price for her simple supper.

Picking up a small blanket she'd brought, she followed Jesse as he led her off to a grassy mound beside the creek bed. They were just beyond the crowd and, though they had some privacy, anyone could see them if they stepped over the incline.

Sam didn't follow, but hung around the barbecue, waiting for a hamburger or hot dog, courtesy of the school board. He raced around the yard with little Andy Yoder, laughing and joyful as can be.

"He seems happy today," Becca said, jutting her chin toward the little boys.

"*Ja*, he's been much happier since you came into his life," Jesse said.

Becca shivered at his words, wishing she could remain in Sam's life. Wishing she could remain with Jesse too.

Holding her silence, she spread the blanket across the spring nubs of grass that were just beginning to grow along the creek bed and watched as Jesse sat down with her box.

"Did you know this was mine?" she asked, her mind whirling with wonder. If he did know, why did he buy hers and not someone else's?

"*Ja*, I must confess, I overheard your aunt Naomi talking to Abby about it."

So. Abby hadn't told on her but he had known and, if the high price was any indication, he'd made sure he bought it anyway.

She knelt on the blanket and lifted the lid of the box before setting the golden fried chicken, potato salad, fresh-baked rolls and peach cobbler within arm's reach. She watched as he picked up a drumstick and bit into the crisp, juicy meat.

"You paid way too much for this meal," she said.

He chewed thoughtfully before taking another bite and she watched him in silence.

"It was for a *gut* cause," he finally said.

She wasn't so sure. Seventy-five dollars was a huge amount of money to pay for a chicken supper. But there were so many questions she longed to ask him. So much she wanted to say. He had just paid a small fortune for her supper. Maybe he was interested in her after all.

"It seems that Sam isn't suffering any aftereffects from the fire safety class," Becca said.

Jesse looked at her, then studied his son. Sam stood near the creek bed with Andy and was holding a huge hamburger with both hands as he took a bite. The burger looked way too big for such a small boy and Jesse smiled at his eager efforts.

"*Ne*, he seems to have forgotten all about it, though I know that isn't true," Jesse said.

"When you picked up the book of matches and lit one, it was like a fire started inside him too. If I had known he might react that way, I would have excused him from the class," she said.

Jesse remembered how it impacted him as well. Until that day at school when he'd taught fire safety to the children, he'd believed he could never fight fire again. Now that it was over with, he realized he could. He just needed to be careful and vigilant at all times so another tragedy didn't strike his *familye* ever again.

He nodded, taking a spoonful of potato salad. The tang of the dressing was delicious and he wasn't surprised. Becca was an exceptional cook but he wasn't concentrating on his meal just now. "It probably did. You see, I caught Sam and Susanna, his younger sister, playing with matches. I really got after them and explained the dangers but it didn't seem to sink in. My house burned down a week later." The memory caused his voice to catch and he had to cough, blinking back the burn of tears.

She glanced down at the purplish scars covering his hands and forearms. They were ugly and a constant reminder of his failure. He flinched when she reached out and traced one scar with her fingertips.

"From what I can see, you did try to save them. You should wear these scars like a badge of courage," she said.

He blinked, his throat suddenly clogged with emotion. He coughed and took a quick sip of apple juice from a flask she had set nearby. He finally spoke softly, feeling as if his voice wasn't his own. "I… I tried but I was too late. I found Sam in the barn. All he would say was that it was his fault. I figured he must have been playing with matches again."

Becca cringed and he wished he'd never told her. This wasn't light conversation. They should be laughing and talking about simple, inconsequential things like the weather, the school and things going on in their community. Not the death of his *familye*.

She released a little sound of sympathy. "I'm so sorry, Jesse. But surely you understand you must forgive yourself and Sam for what happened. If you'll let it, the Atonement of Jesus Christ can wash away any pain you might feel over losing your *familye*. And Sam needs you now more than ever."

He agreed but forgiveness was easier said than done. In his heart, he knew what she said was true. And finally, because of her, he'd had the courage to pray and seek strength from the Lord. It was time, wasn't it? But forgive himself? He wasn't sure he could ever do that.

"It's taken me a long time to admit it, but it wasn't Sam's fault. He was only five at the time. Barely old enough to understand what he was doing," he said with a heavy sigh.

"Have you told Sam that?" she asked.

Jesse went very still, his mind frozen in thought. No, he hadn't. But maybe he should.

"Perhaps that's why Sam doesn't speak," she said. "Because he blames himself, just like you do. You know, your *vadder* was too stern with you but you don't have to be that way with Sam. You're not your *vadder*. You are your own man. A *gut* man of *Gott*."

He didn't know what to say. No, he wasn't his father. He could be different. He could be a better man. Couldn't he? But he sure didn't feel like a good man. Not in a very long time.

He looked at her, thinking he shouldn't have told her so many personal things. He'd laid his heart bare. As he gazed into her eyes, he felt locked there. Mesmerized by the deep blue of her beautiful eyes. And before he knew what was happening, he leaned close and kissed her. A soft, gentle caress that made him feel alive and happy for a brief moment in time.

She breathed his name on a sigh and lifted her hand to place it against his chest. Her palm felt warm and he wished they could stay like that forever. But the contact was like lightning and he jerked away.

"I... I'm sorry. I shouldn't have taken liberties. I apologize for my actions," he said.

She looked away, her cheeks filled with heightened color. "I'm sorry too. I know how much you love your wife."

He came to his feet, glancing around to discover if

anyone had seen his shameful actions. Thankfully, no one seemed to have noticed...except for Sam. The boy stood beside the creek a short distance away, his eyes wide with confusion. And suddenly, Jesse felt as if he and his son were the only two people there. For several long, pounding moments, Sam just looked at his father. And then, the child turned and ran to the back of the schoolhouse where Jesse couldn't see him anymore.

Oh, no! What had Jesse done? He felt the familiar weight of guilt settling inside his chest again. No doubt, he had upset Sam with his actions. After all, Becca wasn't the boy's mother. And he couldn't believe he'd been so disloyal to Alice. Why had he kissed Becca? She wasn't the love of his life. She wasn't his wife and never could be.

"I... I think I had better go and check on Sam. *Danke* for the delicious supper," he said, turning away.

Becca stopped him, coming to her feet as she handed him a pie tin of peach cobbler. He caught the sweet aroma of sugar and cinnamon. The oatmeal crust looked golden, bubbly and cooked to perfection.

"Here, take this with you. You paid a steep price and should have all of your meal. I hope you and Sam enjoy it," she said.

He took the plate, holding it with both hands. Feeling numb and empty inside. And as he walked away, he knew he had another huge problem on his hands. One that he'd never thought would trouble him again for as long as he lived.

He was in love with Becca Graber. In spite of fighting his own emotions, he knew it with every fiber of his being. She was like a breath of fresh air after being locked inside a cave for a year. And yet, he couldn't act on it. Never again. Because his devotion to Sam and Alice must come first. He couldn't betray his sweet wife's memory by loving someone else. Nor could he disappoint Sam, who was still missing his mother. Not after all that had happened. No doubt the boy saw this as a betrayal to his mother. Jesse felt the same way and was disgusted by his actions. He could never let down his guard with Becca again. No sir, not ever.

Chapter Thirteen

The following week, Becca returned to Jesse's house to tutor Sam as usual. Except this time, she felt more cautious than ever. Jesse had kissed her, or she had kissed him, she wasn't sure which. She was certain of one thing. It had been a mistake. Jesse still loved his wife and Becca had chosen a career in teaching. She wasn't about to be sidetracked. Vernon had played with her emotions often enough, holding her hand and declaring his love just days before he'd ended their engagement. It had all been a lie. He'd been leading her on for over a year because he didn't know how to break things off with her. And all that time, she'd allowed herself to believe he really cared. But after she'd learned the truth, she'd promised herself she'd never fall into that kind of trap again. She couldn't trust men to be honest with her. It was that simple.

On the ride to Jesse's farm, Sam didn't speak. He frowned and wouldn't meet her gaze. After witnessing his father kissing her and then running away, she feared he might not like her anymore. He'd been overly withdrawn at school all day and she thought he must be angry with her. And she couldn't blame him. No doubt he thought she was trying to usurp his mother's place. Because he didn't talk a lot, she dreaded asking him about it. Since she'd be leaving town soon, it didn't really matter but she'd rather part as friends.

"Are you ready for your lessons?" she asked as they climbed out of her buggy and she carried her book bag up the steps. She was trying to act normal.

He nodded and opened the door so she could come inside. The kitchen looked orderly, no dirty dishes in the sink. There was nothing cooking on the stove for supper but it was early yet.

"I wonder where your *vadder* is." She set her bag on a chair and removed her black traveling bonnet.

Sam pointed toward the barn. No doubt Jesse was still working. It was just as well. Maybe she could finish Sam's lessons and depart before Jesse came inside. Then they wouldn't have to speak. They could forget the kiss ever happened and go on with their lives as usual.

"*Ach*, let's get started then," she urged.

As she pulled out a chair, she eyed the boy surreptitiously. He didn't look at her as he placed his reading book, note paper and pencil on the table and promptly sat down to wait. Hmm. Was he avoiding her? Maybe he was more upset than she thought.

They went through their normal routine with one exception. Sam didn't speak to her in his usual soft whisper. Not even once. And when they finished their studies, she slid her own books into her bag and looked at Sam, thinking what she could say to ease the tension between them.

"Sam, I hope you're not upset with me. I'm so sorry if I've done anything to hurt your feelings. I know how much you love your *mudder*. And no one will ever take her place. She'll always be your *mudder*. I just want to be your friend," she said.

He peered at her with his big, round eyes before finally nodding. And though he didn't speak, she knew his body language well enough to believe he'd accepted her apology. But oh! How desperately she wished he would smile again. He looked so gloomy that she wanted to cheer him up.

"I'll tell you what. Before I leave, why don't we play a game of hide-and-seek just for fun? Would you like that?" She hoped he agreed. She'd seen him playing with Andy at recess and thought he enjoyed the game. In dealing with children, she'd learned that if she could make them smile, they seemed to trust her more willingly. And that was her goal now. To win back his trust.

"All right, do you want to count and be the seeker, or would you rather hide first?" she asked.

He covered his eyes with his hands to indicate he'd like to be the seeker.

"*Ach*, the kitchen table can be our home base. Close your eyes and count to one hundred. And no peeking." She laughed as he ducked his head over his arms. Because he didn't make any sound, she wasn't sure if he was counting but realized she had better get moving.

Hopping up from the table, she hurried into the living room and looked for a place to hide. She ended up crouching behind the sofa. Within moments, she heard him step over the threshold from the kitchen. She waited, holding her breath. When she thought he'd moved away from her, she bolted toward the kitchen… and ran smack-dab into Jesse's chest.

"Oh!" she cried, looking up into his startled gaze.

"What are you doing?" he asked, seeming just as surprised as she was.

Beyond him, she saw Sam standing in the kitchen doorway. His eyes were round with confusion.

"I… I was playing hide-and-seek with Sam. I thought you were him coming to catch me," Becca said.

She gazed at the damp hair that curled around Jesse's face. He'd removed his straw hat and held it in one hand. As was his normal routine, he must have washed out in the barn. To catch herself, she'd lifted a hand to clasp his upper arm and felt his solid bicep beneath her palm. She caught his scent, a mixture of clean hay and horses. And then, thinking how odd the situation must seem to Jesse, she burst out laughing.

"Ahem!"

In unison, they both turned and got another shock. Bishop Yoder stood just inside the front door. His bushy eyebrows were drawn together in a deep frown and his piercing gaze was pinned on them. Recovering her senses, Becca released Jesse's arm and stepped back fast, putting some distance between them. What must the bishop think, seeing them like this? She could only imagine. She blinked and felt her face flood with heat.

"I'm sorry to interrupt but I knocked twice. You didn't seem to hear me, so I came inside," the bishop said.

Jesse tossed his hat on the coffee table. Lifting a hand, he stepped over to greet the bishop.

"*Ja, komm* in. *Komm* in!" Jesse welcomed him with a smile but Becca could tell from his tensed shoulders that he was just as nervous as she was.

The bishop shut the front door and removed his black felt hat. He wore his frock coat, which indicated he was there on official church business. Becca couldn't help wondering what that was and she hoped it wasn't serious.

Looking straight at her, the bishop's eyes were unblinking as he asked her a pointed question. "Miss Graber, what are you doing here?"

She almost groaned out loud. Instead, she swallowed hard, knowing how this must look. Why did Bishop Yoder have to walk in on them just now? Why couldn't he have come earlier, when she was sitting primly at the kitchen table with Sam as they went over his studies? Why did he have to see her laughing and touching Jesse in a most improper way?

She opened her mouth to explain but no sound came out. She felt muddled and tongue-tied.

Jesse cleared his throat. "Miss Graber tutors Sam several afternoons each week, to help with his speaking problem."

Bishop Yoder's forehead crinkled as he thought this over. "I knew Miss Graber was tutoring Sam but I had no idea she was coming here to your home to do it. It isn't proper for a young, single woman to be coming here like this."

Oh, dear. The bishop didn't need to enlarge on the issue. Becca knew what he was thinking. She was the schoolteacher and must set a good example for the Amish children under her tutelage. When she'd started tutoring Sam, she hadn't thought that it might look bad for her to come here several afternoons each week. Even her *familye* members knew she was here and no one had ever suggested that it wasn't right. And everything would have probably been fine, except that the bishop had seen her behaving in a silly, unladylike manner. Not like the proper schoolteacher she was trying to portray.

"Becca has been nothing but proper while she's been here in my house. And Sam's schoolwork has greatly improved because of her efforts. She has been very generous with her time," Jesse said.

Oh, bless him for defending her. Becca was beyond grateful but feared it wouldn't help. Not this time. The bishop was a kind, nonjudgmental man but he was still the leader of their *Gmay*. The situation was bad enough that it could cause her to lose her teaching recommendation and she'd never be given another assignment again.

"I'm sorry, Bishop Yoder. I meant no harm. You see, I was playing hide-and-seek with Sam. I thought Jesse was him and I bumped into him and…" Her words trailed off. She was babbling and making no sense. What good would it do to try and explain? She knew how it looked and it wasn't good.

The silence was deafening as the bishop studied both her and Jesse for several long, torturous moments. The church elder's steely gray eyes were unblinking as he considered her. She waited with bated breath, not daring to say another word that might make matters worse.

"I trust this will never happen again," the bishop finally said.

Becca shook her head and quickly reassured him. "*Ne*, I won't come here alone again. In fact, Sam and I were finished for the night. School is almost out and… I was just leaving."

"*Gut*. Your lessons here are finished. You can tutor Sam at school from now on."

Though the bishop spoke gently, his words were an order, not a request.

She nodded and he watched as she hurried to the kitchen, gathered up her things and fled out the back door.

Jesse watched her go, his expression pensive. She knew how serious the situation was. It was no laughing matter. If the bishop thought there was any impropriety, both she and Jesse could find themselves shunned for any number of weeks deemed appropriate by the church elders.

As she hopped into her buggy and directed the horse down the lane, she glanced over and saw Sam standing on the back porch watching her. She lifted a hand to wave at him but he didn't respond. And as she drove home, three things troubled her mind. First, she worried that Sam hadn't fully forgiven her for seeming to usurp his mother's place. And it was beyond mortifying to her that the child might think she was making a play for his father. Because she wasn't. Not at all.

Second, she feared her teaching recommendation might now be in jeopardy. And she needed that to secure another position in the fall.

And third, she hoped she hadn't just created a huge problem for Jesse. After all, she was a young, unmarried woman and innocent to the world. But Jesse was a father and a widower and the bishop might hold him to a higher standard. She didn't want him to get into trouble because of her. Because she loved them, all she wanted was for him and Sam to be happy.

Maybe it was a good thing the school year was almost over and she'd be leaving town. It was for the best. Wasn't it? So, why did the thought of never seeing Jesse and Sam again make her feel even worse?

* * *

Except for Church Sunday and a few glimpses on the playground when he was dropping Sam off and picking him up from school, Jesse didn't see Becca again for two weeks. Two long weeks of worrying about her. He'd wrestled with the idea of going over to her cousin's farm to speak with her but knew that could only make matters worse. And what would he say to her? That he loved her but couldn't offer her any promises because of his devotion to his dead wife? Not to mention Sam, who was still missing his mother and sisters too.

And now, the end-of-year program was here. It was the last day of school. After today, Jesse wouldn't see Becca again. He'd been told that she was leaving in a couple of days. Returning to her *familye* in Ohio until she could find another teaching position.

Jesse parked his horse and buggy in the main schoolyard, then helped Sam hop down. Other parents were arriving with their kids and they greeted him. He waved, thinking how they had welcomed him and Sam into their community. The men had taken him with them to the livestock auctions and he now had four beautiful draft horses and another milk cow. They'd been kind to him and he felt almost relaxed around them now.

With his head down, Sam walked silently beside him as they entered the schoolhouse. While Sam went to sit at his desk, Jesse stood at the back of the room with the other parents. The bishop was there and gave him a friendly nod, not showing any sign that he was upset with him in the least. Becca stood beside her desk, rifling through some papers. Because he knew her well, the heightened color in her face told him she was slightly flustered. But to everyone else, she looked completely composed and in control.

She set the papers aside on her desk and stood up straight, her hands folded in front of her, a genuine smile on her face. "*Guder mariye*, scholars."

"*Guder mariye,*" the children responded in unison.

Becca looked at the parents. Her gaze clashed then locked with his. In that brief moment of time, he saw what he thought was a painful longing in her eyes. But then it was gone and he thought he must have imagined it.

"*Guder mariye*, parents," she said.

As a group, the adults in the room responded in kind, each one looking delighted to be here. After all, this was a culmination of an entire year of hard work and they were happy to see their children's progress.

"We are pleased to *willkomm* you to our school and hope you enjoy the program your *kinder* have prepared for you." She took a step. "*Ach*, without any further delays, we will get started. If the scholars will please *komm* forward."

In a rehearsed fashion, the children rose from their desks and walked to the front of the room where they stood in a V-shape with the youngest children to the front and the older children in the back. Turning to face them, Becca lifted her hands and hummed a note. Then, she led the students in a German song that Jesse recognized quite well from his own childhood.

As the last note rang out, little Timmy Hostetler stepped forward and recited a poem from memory. His voice sounded soft and shy, with no inflection. And when he finished, he stepped back into place and gave an audible sigh of relief.

The parents in the room smiled. They understood how hard their children had practiced this program and they couldn't help being pleased.

The scholars sang several more songs in both English and German. Dale Yoder, the eldest boy in the school, served as the *vorsinger* and set the pitch for each song before the other children joined in. All of the numbers were sung *a capella* and most were sung very slow, just like at church. The hymns were achingly beautiful, the scholars' faces sweet and earnest. And when they finished, there was no applause because they didn't believe in praise. But Jesse couldn't help reveling in Becca's success. She was a very good teacher and he couldn't help feeling proud of her accomplishment. She should feel good about what she'd done this year.

A few skits were shown by the scholars and most made the audience laugh. Tiny pieces of colored paper had been taped to the wooden floor so the children knew where to stand. But there were some moments of confusion when several of the students seemed to be standing in the wrong place. Becca glanced at the papers on the floor, frowned in bewilderment, then quickly redistributed the kids. It became obvious that the colored papers were not in the proper order.

One skit went quite badly when the scholars held up what appeared to be the wrong posters and their props had mysteriously disappeared. Becca quickly stepped in and sorted everything out, handing them new props to use, then stood back and tried not to look perplexed.

A snicker brought Jesse's attention to the side of the room and he saw Caleb Yoder whispering something to Enos Albrecht. Both boys chuckled, until Becca threw them a warning look. But Jesse couldn't help wondering if the two boys had hidden the props and changed the order of the posters on purpose, in an effort to cause mischief. Regardless, Becca was right on top of things, setting it all right. It spoke to her professionalism and how well she had planned and knew the entire program by heart. Jesse hoped Bishop Yoder and the other school board members had noticed all of this and took it into account when they wrote her recommendation.

When Sam stepped forward, Jesse's attention went on high alert. He'd been anticipating this day for months and eagerly waited with bated breath to hear his son speak out loud.

Sam stood at the front, showed a slightly insecure smile and took a deep breath. He glanced first at Becca, then looked directly at his father…and promptly burst into tears.

Before Becca could step forward to comfort the boy, he raced toward the front door. Pushing his way past the walls of bodies, he burrowed through them and fled.

Oh, no! Jesse's heart gave a giant leap of sympathy as he hurried after his son.

"Excuse me," he said when he bumped into Jakob Fisher and stepped on someone else's foot.

They parted the way and he didn't stop. He had to go after Sam. Just one thought pounded his brain. He must comfort his son and ensure the child was all right. At that moment, nothing else mattered in the world. Not his love for Becca, not anything. Because it was now obvious to Jesse that Sam was upset about his relationship with the pretty schoolteacher. No doubt Sam thought Jesse was trying to replace his mother in his life. And he wasn't. Jesse couldn't do that to Sam. Not after all that he had been through. Yes, Jesse loved Becca so very much. But he couldn't be with her. Not now. Probably never. It was futile to even try. Sam must come first in Jesse's life. He was the boy's father and had a duty to love and protect his child above all else. And for that reason alone, their *familye* unit could never include Becca. Jesse had to accept that now. Because fighting it would mean that Sam would eventually walk out of his life too. And he couldn't afford to lose any more of his *familye* members. Not even for Becca.

Becca watched in horror as Sam ran out of the schoolhouse with his father chasing after him. She couldn't believe this was happening. First, the colored papers on the floor had been changed, then the props had disappeared and the posters had been rearranged in the wrong order. Since she had checked them right before the program started, it didn't make sense. Until she heard Caleb and Enos's muffled laughter. And she had no doubt the two boys had created more mischief. But out of the corner of her eye, she saw Bishop Yoder gazing steadily at his young son and knew she wouldn't have to do anything about the situation. It was the last day of school and she was finished teaching here. She had no doubt the bishop would take care of his son without her interference. But now, she had another problem. Sam had run from the room in tears and her heart almost broke in two.

Though her heart was racing, she calmly stepped over to Lenore Schwartz, the eldest girl in the school, and gently squeezed her arm as she made her request.

"Keep things going. I'll be right back," she whispered.

Lenore nodded stoically and Becca knew she could

depend on her. After all, the girl had helped with most of the program and knew it by heart too.

Brushing past the gawking parents, Becca hurried outside to search for Sam and Jesse. She didn't know what she could do to help, but she had to try.

Out of her peripheral vision, she saw the flash of movement heading back toward the horse barn and followed quickly. One thought clogged her mind. The school board hadn't reprimanded her in any way or indicated they weren't pleased with her performance but she feared she wasn't going to get a good teacher recommendation now. Not after this. Coupled with the bishop finding her at Jesse's house when she was tutoring Sam, she figured the mistakes of the program might be the final nail in her coffin. And she dreaded returning to Ohio without any future employment options.

No! She mustn't think like that. She'd promised herself and the Lord that she would have faith. She was determined to put her trust in *Gott.*

"I… I'm sorry, *Daed.* It's all my fault."

She slowed, recognizing Sam's voice. The words were spoken quite loudly. Not in Sam's normally quiet, shy whisper. No, these were the words of a child filled with despair.

She glanced around the corner of the horse barn and saw Jesse sitting on a tree stump. His back was turned toward her as he pulled Sam onto his lap and held the boy close to his chest as he rocked him in his arms.

"Shh, don't be so upset. Everything's going to be all right now," Jesse said.

"I-I-I'm so sorry," Sam wailed over and over again.

Becca blinked in surprise. Sam had spoken to her several times in a pitiful whisper but he never spoke to his father. Not once since she'd known them. Now, it seemed as if the dam had finally shattered and the boy couldn't be quieted.

"It's all right. It's not your fault," Jesse soothed.

Becca realized they weren't talking about the school program at all. They were talking about the house fire. They were talking about guilt.

Pressing her spine against the rough timber of the barn wall, Becca clenched her eyes closed and didn't fight her own tears. She didn't want to interfere. Not now. She was too bold. Too outspoken for a proper Amish girl. That was one reason Vernon didn't want to marry her. As long as Jesse was being kind to Sam, she wanted to leave them alone. She'd said too much already. But she couldn't leave either. And so, she stayed where she was and listened to their mournful conversation.

"I... I didn't mean to kill *Mamm* and Mary and Susanna," Sam sniffled.

Jesse snorted. "You didn't kill them. You didn't."

"*Ja*, I did." The boy groaned and then he spoke in a frenzied rush, as if he were reliving what had happened all over again. "You were gone that night, fighting fire for someone else. I was the man of the house. It was my responsibility to make sure the chores were done and everyone was safe in bed. On my way out to the barn, I found Susanna playing with matches. I got after her and told her to put them away. She said she would and I went outside. I milked the cows all by myself and put the cans in the well house. But when I returned to the house, I saw smoke and flames through the kitchen window. I tried to run inside but it was too hot. I... I couldn't get to them. I heard *Mamm* upstairs screaming for Mary but she couldn't find her. Or Susanna either. And then, before I knew what was happening, the roof caved in. It was awful…"

Sam's words trailed off on a muffled sob. Becca pressed a hand to her mouth to stifle her own tears. In her mind's eye, she could imagine everything Sam had described. The horror of that night seemed all too real when she considered what Jesse and Sam had lost.

"*Ach*, listen to me, *sohn*." Jesse spoke gently, his voice firm. "The fire wasn't your fault. It wasn't. And losing your *mamm* and *schweschdere* wasn't your fault either. It was no one's fault. It was a terrible accident, that's all."

"But why did *Gott* let it happen?" Sam asked, his voice trembling.

"Because He gives us our free agency to act, even if it means there might be bad consequences. But that doesn't mean He doesn't love us. I want you to let it go now. I want you to be happy, not sad. It's time we both let it go," Jesse said.

"But… I miss Susanna and Mary," Sam sniffled, his words so pitiful that it broke Becca's heart.

"I know, *sohn*. I do too. So very much."

"And I miss *Mamm*. I wish she'd come back and we could be a *familye* again."

"I do too. More than anything else in the world. No one can ever replace her in our lives or in our hearts. We'll never love anyone the way we loved her," Jesse said.

Becca turned away, her heart wrenching. She couldn't listen to any more. She stumbled away, heading toward the school. She bit her bottom lip, ignoring the tears streaming down her cheeks. All of a sudden everything made perfect sense. No wonder Sam had run off when he'd seen Jesse kiss her. No wonder the boy seemed offish toward her that last day when she went over to his house to tutor him. And then, he had raced out of the school during the end-of-year program. Not only did he blame himself for his mother and sisters' deaths but he thought Becca was trying to take their place. She should have realized it early on but she'd been blinded by love.

Oh, how Sam must resent her. She was his teacher and had betrayed his trust. And Jesse too. He was loyal to his wife. He didn't want an opinionated schoolteacher like her to usurp his wife's place. Jesse didn't love her. His heart was too full of memories and devotion for his wife. He could never love Becca. Not in the same way. Not as a man should love the woman he was married to. And neither could Sam. Which meant they could never be together. Never be a true *familye*. It was foolish for her to think they could.

Realizing the awful truth, she stood outside the schoolhouse on the back porch and wiped the tears from her eyes. Jesse and Sam didn't need her anymore. If what she'd overheard was any indication, the two of them were on the road to healing and forgiving, both themselves and each other. It was a private moment between father and son and she was so happy for them. It appeared that they'd finally reconciled their anger and guilt. But it wouldn't make a difference for her.

She pushed several stray curls of hair back into her prayer *kapp* and smoothed her long skirts. This was the last day of school and she was still the teacher. She had a job to do and mustn't let her students down. She would go back inside, complete her assignments and present the certificates of achievement. And tomorrow, it would all be finished.

She didn't belong here anymore. Her teaching job was over with and it was time for her to return home to Ohio. And that was that.

Chapter Fourteen

Becca plucked a number of tacks out of the wall and set them aside before rolling up the various posters that had been hanging around the schoolroom. Wrapping a rubber band around each print to keep it from falling open, she stored them on a shelf in the back closet. She wanted to make sure Caroline Schwartz could find them in the fall when she came to set up the room for the new school year.

Becca picked up a bucket of sudsy water and carried it over to the windows. After wringing out a wash rag, she cleaned each windowsill and wiped down all the scholars' desks. She'd already swept and mopped the wooden floors, swept the ashes from the potbellied stove and cleaned the chalkboard until it gleamed silky black.

Laying her notebooks and pens inside a cardboard box, she checked her desk drawers one last time. She almost laughed when she found the rubber snake again. Someone had put it back in her drawer. Picking it up with two fingers, she threw it away, not wanting to leave it there to scare Caroline half to death when she returned at the end of August. Becca wanted to ensure she had all her things packed and ready to go. She was leaving early tomorrow morning, traveling by bus to Ohio. Anything she left behind would be lost to her.

Including Jesse and Sam.

Giving the expansive room one last look, she turned and froze. Jesse stood in the open doorway, wearing his black frock coat and vest, a white chambray shirt and his best pair of broadfall pants. He held his black felt hat in his hands, his clean hair combed and tidy.

"Hello," she said, startled by his presence. And all at once, a bubble of euphoria engulfed her, along with a feeling of bittersweet heartache. What was he doing here? She didn't think she'd ever see him again.

"Hallo," he returned, showing that slightly crooked smile of his. He moved further into the room, seeming tentative. As if he was a bit unsure of himself.

"You're dressed so nice today. Are you going somewhere special?" she asked, taking one step toward him.

"Ja." His answer sounded positive but not very committal.

She tilted her head in confusion. "Where are you going?"

His smile widened slightly, causing his dark eyes to sparkle. Oh, how she loved it when he smiled or laughed. It lit up her whole world.

"To see you," he said.

"Ach, did you need some more books for Sam? I'm afraid you'll have to go to the library and check them out yourself. You see, I'm leaving first thing in the morning and won't be able to do it any longer. I'm afraid that I…"

"Don't go."

He spoke low. So softly that she almost didn't catch his words. But she did hear. At least, she thought she did. Two little words that hung in the air between them, leaving her speechless.

"What…what did you say?" she finally asked, thinking her own wishes were causing her to hear things that weren't real.

He came to stand just before her. She stared up at him without blinking, feeling transfixed by his gaze.

"I said, don't go. Please stay," he reiterated.

Okay, so she wasn't hearing things. But what good would staying a few more days do them? It would only make the pain last longer.

She turned away, picking up a feather duster. To give herself something to do, she fluttered it across her already clean desktop. The movement gave her a badly needed distraction.

He gripped her upper arm gently, causing her to go very still. Slowly, he turned her to face him and she was forced to meet his eyes.

"I can't stay any longer, Jesse. I'm going home. I've got to find work. There's so much to be done. I've got to send out more applications and…" She rambled on, trying to convince herself that it was the right thing to do.

"I love you."

No, no! It couldn't be true. She couldn't believe him.

"Don't say things that aren't true," she snapped.

"But it is true. I mean it, Becca. I love you, so very much."

He tried to take her hand but she pulled away, refusing to listen. Vernon had said he loved her too and it had been a lie. Now, Jesse was doing the same thing.

Telling her what she wanted to hear before he broke her heart again.

She kept on chattering away, feeling nervous with him standing so close. "It's been wonderful working here. I've loved teaching Sam and the other children but I have to go now."

"Becca! Listen to me. I love you! And I mean it. Please, don't turn away from me." His voice sounded a bit anxious, as if he were afraid.

She whirled on him, her feelings a riot of unease. Oh, how she longed to believe him. But what if he were lying to her?

"You don't mean it. Not really," she said.

"I do mean it. Every word. I'm not some silly boy, Becca. I know my own mind. I love you. Would you mind not returning to Ohio at all?" he asked.

She swallowed, thinking she'd misunderstood him again, yet knowing her hearing was fine. "I… I'm afraid that isn't possible now. I heard you and Sam yesterday, out back by the horse barn. I know you two have reconciled and Sam is speaking again. That's so wonderful. But my work is done here. I have to go."

He showed a slight frown, his gaze never leaving hers. "Hmm. You heard my conversation with Sam? All of it?"

She nodded, feeling her face heating up. She didn't like to confess that she had eavesdropped on them. "I'm so happy for you both. I know Sam loves and misses his *mudder* very much. So do you."

And she was happy for them. So very happy that they'd reconciled. That they could be a loving father and son once more. But she didn't believe that love included her.

"You didn't listen to our entire conversation, did you?" he asked, watching her quietly.

"*Ne*, I thought it was too personal. Once I realized you had everything in control, I returned to the schoolhouse." She wasn't about to tell him that she'd cried too. That even without him telling her he loved her, her heart was breaking once more.

"Then you didn't hear Sam tell me that he loves you too. Nor did you hear me explain to him that it's time for us to move on with our lives and be happy again. Or that Sam wishes you could be his *mudder* now and I want you to be my wife," he said.

She stared, too stunned to speak for several pounding moments.

"You…you told Sam that?"

He nodded. "I certainly did."

"And Sam told you he loves me?"

Another nod. "He did."

It was too much. Oh, how she wanted to believe him. But that would require her to take a leap of faith. To trust him.

"But Sam ran away when he saw you kissing me at the box social. And then again during the school program." She felt shocked to the tips of her toes.

"*Ja*, he was still feeling guilty for the house fire. He didn't think he had a right to love you and be happy again. I told him that's not right. The fire wasn't his fault at all. I told him I love you too. I want us to be a *familye*." Jesse made the admission slowly, thoughtfully, as if he really meant it.

"I… I don't understand. Why would you say all those things?" She couldn't believe it. This was a joke. He was teasing her. Wasn't he?

"Because it's true. I love you, Becca. Please don't go. Don't break my heart. I want you to stay."

Don't break his heart? All this time, she'd been fearing he might hurt her, not the other way around. His plea made her want to love and keep him safe. To protect and cherish him the way she longed to be loved and treasured.

"But…but you love your wife. You don't love me. Not the way you loved your wife," she cried.

"My love for Alice was filled with a deep concern for her welfare, appreciation, respect and passion. That's exactly how I feel about you. I want to spend the rest of my life with you. I've fought my feelings for a long time but I can't fight them anymore. I love you, Becca. And if you'll have me, I'd like you to be my wife. I know it's what Alice would want for me too."

She gave a shuddering laugh of incredulity. This was happening so fast and she was having difficulty wrapping her mind around what he was saying. "Are you sure Sam feels this way too?"

"*Ja*, he loves you for being there for him. For helping us during a critical time in our lives. For never giving up on us."

She jerked when Jesse lifted his head and called to his son.

"Sam! Would you come in here, please?"

As if in a dream, Becca watched as Sam appeared in the doorway, holding his little straw hat in his hands. Like his father, he was wearing his Sunday best, his cheeks gleaming pink from a good scrubbing. It touched her deeply that the two of them had bathed and dressed in their finest clothes just to pay her a visit and…

They were proposing marriage to her! It finally sank

in to her muddled brain. They were really here, standing in front of her, asking her to marry them. Jesse wasn't lying to her. He was speaking the truth.

"Teacher Becca, *danke* for everything you've done for me and *Daed*." The boy spoke in a soft voice but it carried clear across the room. Not a whisper. No, not at all.

Hearing Sam talk out loud like this was almost more than Becca could take in. She went to him and knelt down.

"Oh, Sam! You're speaking again. It's so *wundervoll*." Before she could think to stop herself, she pulled him into her arms for a tight hug. Her emotions almost overwhelmed her and she realized tears ran down her cheeks.

Finally, she released the boy and he stepped back, smiling wide. She stood and faced Jesse, her thoughts zipping around in her head like fireflies.

"I can't believe all of this is true," she said.

"Believe it, Becca. It's all true." Jesse took Sam's hand and the two gazed at her with such adoration, so much expectation and love, that Becca felt like she was living a dream.

"Last night, Sam and I talked it over in depth," Jesse said. "I realized that, if I didn't tell you how we felt, you wouldn't know and might leave us forever. Until you came into our lives, I didn't realize how much *Gott* loves and cares for me and Sam. You've helped me realize that, no matter how difficult life's trials might be, the Lord is always there for us. I know that because He brought us you."

Jesse reached inside his hat and withdrew a white envelope, which he handed to her. It had her name scrawled across the front and she recognized the bishop's handwriting. Becca took it with trembling fingers but didn't open it.

"In case you're wondering, it's a very glowing letter of recommendation from the school board. Last night, after you left the school, I explained to the bishop and other board members how much you've done for Sam and me. Bishop Yoder has heard reports from other parents as well and was in agreement that you are one of the most loving, caring teachers he has ever met. You always go the extra mile. Nothing is too difficult for you. Not when it comes to your scholars."

She blinked. "You did that for me? The board really wrote me a *gut* letter?"

He dipped his head in acknowledgement. "*Ja,* but I'm hoping you won't use it. I'm hoping you'll be willing to make another career change to be a wife and *mudder* instead. I know how much you love teaching and I want your happiness more than anything else. But I'd rather you remain here in Colorado with Sam and me. I want you to be my wife and Sam's new *mudder.*"

"*Ja,* Becca. Please stay with us," Sam said, his voice loud and clear, as if it was gaining strength with every word he spoke.

"Oh, Jesse! Sam!" Tears of joy coursed freely down her cheeks. And just like that, the pain of Vernon's betrayal melted away into nothingness. Her heart was full of happiness, not pain. She knew deep inside that she could trust Jesse. That he truly loved and wanted her.

"I love you both so much," she said. "I never dared hope you could love me too. I thought… I thought I was unlovable and I didn't want to leave you but I didn't know what else to do."

Jesse stepped close and enfolded her in his arms. She clung to him, resting the palms of her hands against his solid chest. She fed off his strength, letting it fill her with such joy she could hardly hold it all. She didn't shy away when he kissed her deeply. In the background, she heard Sam's happy laughter.

Finally Jesse lifted his head and looked deep into her eyes. "You really love me too? Because I don't want to be hurt again either."

She heard the uncertainty in his voice and knew he'd feared her answer too. After all, it couldn't be easy to propose marriage when you don't know how the bride might feel about you.

As she gazed lovingly into his eyes, she reached up and cupped the side of his bearded face with her hand. "*Ja*, I love you, Jesse. So very much. You and Sam. I can hardly believe it's possible that he's overcome his silence almost overnight."

She glanced at the boy and saw his smiling face, his gleaming eyes. He looked so happy standing there, watching his father embrace her. He seemed so confident now. The complete opposite of the scared little boy she'd met all those months earlier when she'd first come here to teach school.

"Anything is possible with the Lord's help. You have healed our broken hearts. We have been so blessed," Jesse said.

"You are right. When we put our trust in *Gott*, anything is possible," Becca said, believing what she said. The Lord had truly worked wonders in their lives.

Jesse reached down and picked up Sam. Together, they shared a three-way hug, overjoyed by the day. They had each learned to put their faith in *Gott's* redeeming love and in each other. Becca felt an overwhelming trust in Jesse. She knew he truly loved her. That he was counting on her to love him in return. And together, she knew they would have a bright and happy future.

"You'll marry us, won't you, Becca?" Sam asked, resting his little hand on her shoulder. From the safety of his father's arms, he gazed down at her with expectation.

She wrapped her own arms around them both, squeezing tightly, determined to never let go. "Of course, I'll marry you. Just try and stop me."

"That's *gut*, because I've already spoken to the bishop about it and asked permission from your cousin Jakob and *Dawdi* Zeke too," Jesse said.

Her mouth dropped open in shock. "You have? When did you do all that?"

"I spoke to the bishop last night but I went over to your place early this morning, after you had left the house."

"Really? You're very sneaky. I had no idea."

He nodded. "I asked them all to keep it secret until I could speak with you," he said.

Becca laughed, filled with more happiness than she ever thought possible. "I'm so glad you did. Now we have something wonderful to look forward to."

"*Ja*, we do. Years and years of happiness."

She couldn't agree more. This was her heart's desire. To remain here in Colorado with Jesse, as his wife. To become Sam's mother and hopefully have more children as time went on. And as they walked out of the schoolhouse and locked the front door, Becca realized she wanted nothing more.

* * * * *

IF YOU ENJOYED THIS BOOK
WE THINK YOU WILL ALSO LOVE

LOVE INSPIRED
INSPIRATIONAL ROMANCE

Uplifting stories of faith, forgiveness and hope.

Fall in love with stories where faith helps
guide you through life's challenges, and discover
the promise of a new beginning.

6 NEW BOOKS AVAILABLE EVERY MONTH!

LIXSERIES2021

LOVE INSPIRED

INSPIRATIONAL ROMANCE

UPLIFTING STORIES OF FAITH, FORGIVENESS AND HOPE.

Join our social communities to connect with other readers who share your love!

Sign up for the Love Inspired newsletter at **LoveInspired.com** to be the first to find out about upcoming titles, special promotions and exclusive content.

CONNECT WITH US AT:

LISOCIAL2020

HARLEQUIN

Heartfelt or thrilling, passionate or uplifting—Harlequin is more than just happily-ever-after.

With twelve different series to choose from and new books available every month, you are sure to find stories that will move you, uplift you, inspire and delight you.